## A PIRATE'S PLEASURE

Brandy peeled off her chemise and drawers and stepped into the wooden tub, rosy with embarrassment from head to toe. She sank into the water up to her neck, relieved somewhat that her back was to Keir.

"You'll have to overcome this ridiculous reticence, brandy-eyes." His voice came to her from beside the tub. She stiffened, her lashes lifting until her eyes met his.

"Every man aboard this ship earns his keep. What will you do to earn yours?" he asked softly, one finger grazing her collarbone before dipping lower to trail down between her breasts.

Unexpected heat stabbed through her midsection, a heat that made the bathwater seem cool in comparison.

Then he was seated on the edge of the tub, one hand braced against the opposite rim, the other continuing its leisurely exploration. "Well?" he persisted. "What payment will you offer for your passage?"

She glanced up into his face, confusion in her eyes. His expression, however, was soft . . . as soft as she'd ever seen it. It made him look younger, more vulnerable, more human. And stunningly attractive.

*This* Keir she decided she could like . . . and, obviously, want . . .

# Linda Lang Bartell
# TENDER PIRATE

**ZEBRA BOOKS**
**KENSINGTON PUBLISHING CORP.**

ZEBRA BOOKS

are published by

Kensington Publishing Corp.
475 Park Avenue South
New York, NY 10016

First printing: January, 1992

Printed in the United States of America

*To the men and women of the United States Armed Forces who took part in Operation Desert Shield and Desert Storm . . . and to the memory of those who gave their lives in the service of their country and humanity*

## ACKNOWLEDGMENT

Many, many thanks to the following people:

CONSTANCE BURNHAM, of Havant, Hampshire, England, for kindly providing me with geographical information on the coastline of Devonshire and Somerset counties

SILVIA CLIMENT, for her help with the Spanish used in the story

DENNYS CRISTY, for several lengthy and informative conversations concerning his native Jamaica

KEITH CULVER, for answering my endless questions about sailing

ALISON NUNNEY, for the personal loan of books and maps of England

R.C. TOMAS, M.D., for answering my medical questions

And last but not least, DENNIS RODMAN of the Detroit Pistons, for being his graceful and good-natured self . . . and therefore the inspiration for the character Dionisio

*Southwest England — 1643*

A small vessel skimmed soundlessly toward the shore-line over the moonlight-dappled waters. Behind it loomed the silhouette of a ship anchored in the channel.

"Cap'n ain't gonna like this, I tell ye."

"We go only to look, my son. A man's life is at stake."

The sailor shook his head as he rowed the small boat through glassy, calm waters toward the shore. "Nobody cares a fig 'bout Pedro. And especially in the midst o' civil war." He jerked his chin over his shoulder to indicate the fire lighting the horizon behind him, its bright, glowing peaks leaping heavenward against the backdrop of an obsidian sky.

Father Tomas nodded his head. "We go where God calls us."

The sailor, Arthur Biggs by name, shook his head in the moonlight as he bent to the oars and muttered *sotto voce,* "God ain't a-callin' me nowhere." Then, in a louder voice, "If Cap'n Brewster tossed Pedro overboard, he ain't gonna take him back on again . . . Jesus!" he complained, "I can already taste the kiss o' the cat-o'-nine."

The priest squinted his eyes against the dark. "I will personally take responsibility for this," he assured Biggs in his heavily accented voice. *"El capitán* is sleeping the sleep of the dead." He frowned. "I do not understand how one man can consume so much rum, let alone sail a ship."

Biggs snorted. "Cap'n can drink more kill-devil 'n anyone I know, 'n he ain't sailin' no ship, Padre. 'Tis sittin' right out there . . . close enough to be commandeered by the devil knows who, what with the war goin' on. We won't set sail til Cap'n Brewster's good 'n ready."

The bottom of the tiny vessel scraped softly against sand. Biggs jumped out and dragged the boat further onto the beach, his well-muscled arms bulging beneath his tattered shirt. He glanced about uneasily before offering his hand to Father Tomas. "Be quick about it, Padre, afore we find ourselves . . ." He let his sentence trail off as he scanned the beach on both sides of them.

"Could the man have swum to shore and made for Bristol?"

"Pedro? He's more 'n likely shark food, Father, if ye know what I mean. He was as drunk as the cap'n."

*Pues bien,* let us look along the shore—"

Biggs grabbed Father Tomas's arm in a manaclelike hold as the latter moved to turn away. "Look!" he said in a hoarse whisper, and pulled the clergyman down behind the rowboat. In unison they peered around the bow of the vessel, the priest's head bobbing beneath Briggs's.

On a grassy knoll just above where the sand of the beach began, three figures bent to their task. Within moments, a small body went rolling awkwardly toward the surf, only to stop short of the water.

"Shouldn't we dispatch him and make it looked like he drowned?" a muffled voice asked as the miscreants followed the path made by their victim.

*"Dios mio,* is that a body?" asked Father Tomas beneath his breath, outrage making his voice quiver.

In answer Biggs poked him soundly in the ribs. "SShhh!" the sailor hissed softly but emphatically out of the side of his mouth.

"He's the heir, the only one to stand in your way now, Father," continued the muffled yet distinctly youthful voice.

"I'd leave him, Giles," added a second man. "He's as good as dead. Won't last the night. We've other things to do."

"Aye," came an answer from the first man, Giles. "We've a fire to put out. I can return at dawn to make certain he's dead."

For a moment the scene on the beach was plunged into darkness as the wind picked up and marauding clouds swept across the face of the moon. When the discussion resumed, however, the voices were clearer, carried on the rising wind.

"He never saw who hit him," said the second voice. "Better to take the slim chance that he will survive and be discovered rather than commit outright murder."

Giles nudged the still form at his feet with his boot. "Aye, and so it is. I want nothing to stand in the way of my rightful title of Earl of Somerset." He turned toward the youth and ruffled the boy's hair. "And my son after me, of course."

They swung away and disappeared over the top of the knoll as the moon momentarily broke free of the bank of clouds and bathed the beach in a faint light.

"*¡Gracias a Dios!* They never saw us."

Briggs slowly straightened, but did not move from where he was. "I don't like the looks o' this." He turned and put his shoulder to the prow of the boat. "Get in, Padre."

Father Tomas frowned, his dark eyes suddenly looking like two holes in his head beneath the glow from the heavens. His robes flapped in the quickening breeze as he raised an arm in dramatic command. " 'Tis our *duty* to minister to that unfortunate man," he said in his most chastising tones. "If Pedro is lost to us, then God has given us another soul to rescue."

"From the looks o' it, his soul's already gone," Briggs opined wryly and began to push the boat in earnest. "Get in, Father, while the gettin's good."

The priest's eyes narrowed. "Then I will remain here

alone, if I must." He shook a finger at the seaman, his accent getting heavier in his growing agitation. "It will be on *your* conscience if you leave us both here, Arthur Biggs."

Biggs dropped his head forward with a sigh of capitulation. "Why me?" he muttered, vexed, and turned to follow Father Tomas across the smooth, pale sand like a man going to the gallows.

Sir Aimery Spenser was livid.

"By the mass, how did *this* happen?" He slammed his fist against the wall, his tired, gaunt face now animated with umbrage. "What in the hell were *you* doing, Margaret Hill, while my daughter was out getting . . ." He couldn't finish his sentence.

The servant before him paled in the face of his fury. "She—she was with child before you left, m'lord."

His face turned an even darker red. "So now you would have me look the fool, too?" His eyes traveled to his daughter Catherine . . . Catherine, the picture of his late wife, his adored Juliana. The red-gold hair, the liquid amber eyes. But Catherine's eyes were those of a child who's mind had not developed apace with her body.

Sir Aimery's anger rekindled at the thought of a child bearing a child. He opened his mouth to speak, fresh condemnations hovering on the tip of his tongue, but the up-til-now silent Catherine began to speak.

"Please, Papa," she pleaded in her sweet, childlike voice. Her look brightened. "We can name the child Juliana after Mamma . . . if 'tis a girl. 'Twill be like having another doll . . ." She looked at Margaret. "And Margaret will help me care for it, won't you?"

"Another *doll?*" Spencer sputtered before Margaret could reply. He looked from Catherine to the servant, then shot out his arm and pointed a finger toward the door of the saloon. "You are dismissed, mistress. Gather your things and don't ever let me see you again this side of London!"

Margaret bobbed her head obediently, obviously casting about in her mind for something to say that would ease his anger, comfort her now distraught mistress in the face of Sir Aimery's decree, but words failed her. Only four years older than the seventeen-year-old Catherine, Margaret Hill was vastly more mature than her childlike mistress . . . mature enough to take upon herself completely the blame for Catherine's pregnancy.

"—no, no!" Catherine was crying. "Please, Papa, don't send Margaret away . . . Oh!" She sat down abruptly on the carpet-covered floor and hugged her swollen belly, tears streaming down her cheeks. "It hurts now, Papa, it hurts!"

"Who did this?" Sir Aimery raged at Margaret as he bent over his daughter.

Margaret raised her shoulders and lifted her hands, palm up, in denial. "I know not, m'lord," she mumbled, and, in spite of his dismissal, knelt beside Catherine.

"James . . . George . . . come quickly," Aimery called harshly as he lifted Catherine in his arms. The two servants came at a run, but he was already striding toward the door to the hall, his daughter in his embrace. "Get Maude . . . send her up to Catherine's bedchamber."

"How early is this child?" Sir Aimery asked Margaret after he'd set Catherine upon her bed and moved back to allow Maude and another woman to do their work.

Color flared in Margaret's face as she helped roll down the covers. "Two months, I think, m'lord."

"Well, you can thank yourself not only for allowing this to happen," Aimery charged, "but if the babe dies—which is likely—you can have that on your conscience, as well."

Tears formed in Margaret's eyes at his accusatory words. "I'm so sorry, m'lord," she whispered. "I—I didn't mean for—"

"Tell that to Catherine," he said and, turning his back to the scene, poured himself a drink from a decanter James had set on a table. He breathed deeply after downing the entire goblet of Rhenish. "And thank your stars

11

that the Royalists hold Bristol and the surrounding area, or your mistress would be having her babe in the forest someplace . . . or in gaol." His voice was suddenly tired, his shoulders sagging with the weight of not only England's troubles, but his own.

Catherine's pitiful wimpers pierced his heart unbearably. Because of a careless servant, his daughter was suffering — might even die. "And," he added, his back still to Margaret and the others, "if the child survives, you will take it with you when you leave, claiming my daughter's shame as your own for as long as you live. I'll have no lowborn man's bastard living beneath my roof."

# Part One

## Odyssey

*Claret is the liquor for boys; port for men; but he who aspires to be a hero must drink brandy.*

Samuel Johnson

# Chapter One

*London, 1664*

She was the very picture of innocence.

Keir St. Andrews drew up short at the sight of her. Her dark blond hair fell over her shoulders in disarming disarray, the August sunlight catching its strawberry highlights and accenting the striking hue. Her eyes, the color of which he could not discern from his position half-hidden behind several stacked crates, were wide and expressive and trained on two young boys standing before her. They were acting out some sort of play. A book lay open across her lap, the gentle breeze that eddied about the yard fluttering its pages with a soft, rustling sound. One slender hand rested on the head of a sleeping spaniel next to the stone step upon which she sat.

" '. . . 'tis all one, I will show myself a—a . . .' "

"Tyrant," the girl supplied in a voice as sweet as a singing brook.

The boy looked down at her, screwing his features into an expression of guarded impatience. "I ken the word, Brandy, but ye always blush when we come te this part."

"That's 'cause she's no loose wench," interjected a little girl seated on this Brandy's other side.

"Marry come up, Abra!" chided the girl called Brandy, her eyes widening in surprise beneath delicately raised

15

brows. "Such talk from you!" But the tone of her voice softened the words.

"Aw, git on with it, Tommy, will ye?" said the other lad, obviously impatient to continue the performance. And after a few more lines were recited, the reason was apparent.

" '. . . 'tis all one, I will show myself a tyrant; when I have fought with the men, I will be civil with the maids — I will cut off their heads,' " Tommy obliged, and then snickered behind his hand.

"The heads of the maids?" the other boy pronounced in stentorian strains.

" 'Aye, the heads of the maids, or their maidenheads. Take it in what sense thou wilt.' "

Abra looked up at Brandy. "You ain't blushin', Brandy," she observed soberly.

Brandy's laughter tripped merrily through the inn yard, and something deep within Keir stirred. The glow of youth and gaiety that lit her lovely face was unwelcomely captivating.

"We've practiced so much that I find naught to blush over now," she said, pulling Abra to her and planting a kiss upon the dark head.

*Get on with your business, fool,* whispered a mocking voice inside Keir.

"D'ye think we'll e'er be able to get to the part where I pull out my sword?" asked Tommy as he rolled his eyes heavenward.

" 'Tis 'Draw thy tool,' " corrected Abra innocently, "not yer sword."

The two boys guffawed at Abra's words and this time becoming color brushed Brandy's cheeks beneath her smile.

*"Romeo and Juliet?"* muttered a male voice in Keir's ear. "Is it the wench or the story that's caught yer attention, Cap'n?"

Keir's reverie was shattered as reality intruded. With a cynical twist of his lips, he answered softly, "Neither," and

16

turned and walked back toward the front entrance of the Hawk and Hound Inn.

The taproom was bright, cheery, and spotless. Keir noted the clean, whitewashed walls between oak beams and the shining implements that hung upon them, some broken, but all rust-free: bows and arrows, outdated swords and daggers, a few old lances from a bygone era. They added to the atmosphere, in spite of the time of day, and helped the Hawk and Hound make a statement all its own in Keir's mind. He felt oddly welcome, even though the room was almost empty of clientele.

He sat down at a table before a mullioned window facing the street, his mind suddenly on things far removed from the appeal of the Hawk and Hound taproom. His dark brows drew together in frowning concentration as he contemplated his future while awaiting an answer to his request for an audience with Charles Stuart, King of England.

The only proof he had of his connection to the St. Andrews of Somerset Chase, seat of the Earls of Somerset, was his own word and his father's signet ring. And now, if anything happened to the man he sent to Whitehall, the ring would be lost to him, as well.

His frown deepened. Mayhap I should have gone myself, he thought. Then his pride rose up within him. He'd be damned if he'd go crawling to Charles Stuart, king or no, to ask for permission to go after what was rightfully his.

Keir's hands fisted unconsciously at the thought of his uncle and his treachery. Giles St. Andrews, his late father's half-brother, was sixth Earl of Somerset now. Keir's mouth tightened and his look grew black. A muscle bunched along his jawline. His green eyes grew wintry as the north Atlantic.

"What will you have, my lord?" inquired a feminine voice from beside him.

Keir stiffened as he was pulled from his dark musings, and swiveled his head aside. The girl before him received the full force of his harsh countenance, and for a fleeting moment her bright smile wavered.

*Christ,* he thought, inexplicably irritated. *Mistress Innocence.*

His eyes locked with hers, and her gaze dropped self-consciously. But not before he noticed the beautiful amber-brown color of her eyes. Without thought he uttered the name of the wine they brought to mind. "Brandywyne," he said curtly, and, disgusted with the unexpected bent of his thoughts, he turned his head deliberately back toward the street.

He sensed rather than heard her move away and, oddly, it was as if a beckoning ray of sunlight withdrew behind a cloud, taking its benign warmth with it. He stubbornly kept his gaze on a hackney rolling past the inn, refusing to give in to the urge to follow her movements with his eyes.

"There ye are, Cap'n," called Peter Stubbs—better known as "Stubbs"—his quartermaster. Two more of the crew from the *Odyssey,* Jimmy and Oliver, tromped through the door and into the room behind him, forcing Keir to turn his gaze away from the window. He nodded and made room for Stubbs on the bench on his side of the trestle table. The other two slid in across from them.

"Anythin' worthwhile in here, Cap'n?" one of the men across from him asked with a meaningful leer.

"Aye, where's the bawds?" added his partner with an exaggerated wink at Keir.

A cup of brandywyne was slammed down before them with more force than necessary, making the two seamen across from Keir start. "If it's bawds ye want, then go to the Royal Saracen or Dagger Tavern," advised a tall, burly man. "The Hawk and Hound provides food, drink, and a clean room . . . naught else." The look on Jonathon Dalton's face left little doubt that he meant what he said.

Oliver's eyes narrowed. "What kind o' tavern ain't got women?" he demanded more loudly than necessary.

"Aye," said Jimmy. "What kind o' bloody—"

"Bring us three more drinks," Keir's voice cut in with the ring of authority. "And whatever you've got cooking in the kitchen. We came here for decent food and drink, not advice on where to find whores."

Stubbs made to get up in the singing silence that sizzled between the two men, proprietor and ship captain. "If we ain't welcome, we c'n go elsewhere . . ." he began. But Keir put a restraining hand on his arm and shook his head slightly, his hard green eyes never leaving Dalton's face. "We eat here," he said softly. "We're not about to scour half of London for a good meal after being at sea for the last three months."

The quartermaster stilled, and Dalton finally nodded his head. His gaze touched each man in turn, an implicit warning in his eyes, before he turned away.

" 'N send us a comely face, not another like yers," called Oliver.

The others laughed rowdily at this, but Keir merely took a long draught of his wine and stared into the cup, preoccupied once more.

"Ain't very friendly here," observed Stubbs. "Strange way to run a tavern." He shrugged and looked around curiously. "But, then, 'tis the middle o' the afternoon. Most women makin' a livin' on their back are still abed."

Another round of laughter rang through the taproom. A well-built youth emerged from behind the bar and served them ale.

"You don't look like a wench te me," commented Oliver, then snorted before he raised his drink to his lips. "I like that one better," he said and jerked his chin toward another table where Brandy was serving two well-dressed men.

Unthinkingly Keir's glance went to her. She was slim and of medium height, her movements smooth and sure. *Graceful,* came the thought, unbidden, as his eyes followed her every motion.

"A fetchin' piece, eh?" said Stubbs in Keir's ear, and

19

again the latter was roused from his absorbed contemplation of Brandy Dalton. "Too bad 'er employer don't like us," Stubbs continued, watching her himself. "Seems like she's the only one succeedin' in gettin' yer thoughts off yer reason fer bein' in England."

"And since when can you read my thoughts, Stubbs?" Keir inquired with a lift of an eyebrow. His eyes remained on Brandy, however, as she crossed the room, an errant shaft of sunlight striking the silken swath of her hair.

"Well, hell'll freeze over afore stone-face'll let her serve us," grumbled Jimmy. "If he's so damned touchy, we'll just look."

"Speak fer yerself," said Oliver.

Keir watched Brandy disappear into the kitchen and then looked at Oliver. "You heard what the inn-keeper said, Ollie. I don't want any altercations attributed to the men from the *Odyssey* . . . is that clear?"

"Aye," the sailor replied with a sigh, and held his tongue as the youth who'd served them earlier returned with a huge tray of pewter platters laden with food. He served them silently, his expression guarded.

When he was gone, Oliver complained churlishly, "The pretty wench is servin' *them*," his eyes narrowed at the two other well-dressed patrons who were obviously nobility. "Our gold ain't as good as theirs?"

Keir slapped the flat of his hand down on the oaken table. "So be it then, man," he gritted. "If you promise to shut up and behave yourself, I'll speak to the inn-keeper." He stood and Stubbs obligingly moved aside to allow him passage over the bench.

With a wink at the two across from him, the quartermaster said softly, "We're all gonna get our wish now, mates . . . cap'n included."


"I wonder if I might make a request, Master—" Keir paused expectantly, almost nose to nose with the inn-keeper.

"Dalton. Jonathon Dalton, at yer service." His eyes narrowed as he refused to give ground to the imposing man before him. "And what might that be?"

Jonathon Dalton was tall, almost as tall as Keir St. Andrews, and he was built like a bull. A blacksmith until three years ago, he normally needed only his son Simon to aid him in keeping rowdy seamen in line, except for holiday celebrations when he had to hire extra help. He was good natured, but virtually fearless as well.

He stared at the man before him expectantly, guessing what the request would be, and still reluctant to comply. Sailors were the worst. A rough and vulgar lot. And he normally refused to allow Brandy to serve them. He'd rather set her to cleaning the cinders from the great hearth in the kitchen than serving seamen.

Keir removed several silver pieces of eight from the pouch at his waist and pressed them into Jonathon's hand. "I would have the, er, young lady yonder," he indicated Brandy, "see to our needs until we leave."

"She's not—"

Keir held up a placating hand. "You have my word that my men will not touch her, nor insult her in any way." He noted the stubborn set of Dalton's jaw. "I take it she is your daughter?"

"That she is, and she's no whore."

*Every woman has her price, Master Dalton.* Aloud, Keir said, "No harm shall come to her, I give you my word."

"And just who are you?"

"Captain Keir St. Andrews of the *Odyssey,* just arrived from the New World."

Jonathon looked down at the money in his hand and Keir took advantage of his indecision and added a gold doubloon to the small cache. "Until we are prepared to leave . . . This should pay for any inconvenience our monopolizing the young lady may cause if we stay longer than, ah, expected."

"Papa, is aught amiss?" came a soft voice from beside them. Brandy looked down at the coins glinting in

21

Jonathon's hand, and then at the tall, cold-eyed man beside him. For the second time a light *frisson* passed over her at the icy, gem-green eyes. They were the color of semi-precious jade, and every bit as inanimate.

With an effort, Brandy pulled her gaze from the stranger's. "Papa?" she asked again.

"Brandy-girl, you will serve the men at Captain St. Andrews's table until they leave . . . *but,* if they do not act like—" he seemed reluctant to use the word, "—gentlemen . . . if they insult you in any way, you are to come to me. Ye ken, child?"

"Aye, Papa." The men seated at this Captain St. Andrews's table didn't bother her . . . rather it was the captain himself.

"You may begin by refilling my cup," Keir told her, his expression unreadable. With a last look at Jonathon, Brandy took Keir's cup from his outstretched hand and swung toward the bar.

"Well, I'll be damned!" swore Jimmy when Keir returned to their table. "Ye did it, Cap'n."

"And it cost me a pretty pile of coin," Keir answered. He frowned. "I gave my word to Dalton the innkeeper that there would be no taking advantage of the wench. Hands off, do you hear?"

Three heads bobbed in unison, then turned to watch Brandy bring Keir his wine. "There you are, Captain," she said with a hesitant smile. She looked at the others, all staring at her, awestruck, for none of them had seen her up close till now.

When in doubt, Brandy was in the habit of slipping on a sunny smile. It was as natural to her as breathing. So smile she did to hide her uncertainty before these rough men.

Oliver's jaw dropped until it was apparent that he felt Keir's eyes on him, rare amusement lighting them. "Keep that up and you'll not have to bring the food to your mouth," the captain observed. "You can scoop it off the plate with your bottom lip."

22

Oliver scowled at this, obviously embarrassed.

"May I fetch you anything else, good sirs?" Brandy asked with a lilting laugh.

"Another round," Stubbs said, coming to himself. "We've a sudden great thirst."

*They're not so wicked,* she thought with a mental sigh as she scanned their sheepishly smiling faces. But when she looked at Keir, he'd already transferred his attention to the view through the multipaned window. *A strange one, he,* she mused before turning away. He was dressed well, in what looked to Brandy, from her frequent dealings with the fops from Whitehall, like the latest French fashion . . . but there was nothing foppish about Keir St. Andrews. She shivered inwardly. He was pleasing to the eye, or so some might think, with tall, lithe form and formidable breadth of shoulders. His hair was probably a chestnut color, but the sun and salt spray had shot it through with hundreds of sun-gilt streaks, making it look more like a lion's tawny mane than a head of ordinary sable-colored hair. It was unusual in a very striking way.

Throwing covert glances at him as she served him and his men until well after the supper hour, she caught mostly his profile, for he sat sentinal at the window, as if he were watching for someone. But his profile alone was striking, with high forehead, strong chin, and aquiline nose. His lips were compressed much of the time, which made it hard to discern their shape. But on occasion when he would speak to one of the men, when he would allow his mouth to relax its grim setness, Brandy found his lips to be mobile and nicely chiseled.

Then his eyes would capture hers, and her thoughts would be sent scattering, a blush bathing her cheeks beneath his somber perusal. If eyes were the windows of the soul, she thought more than once while in his presence, he looked a man back from the fiery reaches of hell, for his were bereft of emotion.

In the kitchen, shortly after Brandy was assigned Captain St. Andrews's table, she caught her mother and father having words.

"How can you allow her to serve that riffraff?" Margaret Dalton insisted angrily. Wisps of fiery red hair, evidence of her Irish heritage, trailed out from beneath her white cotton cap.

"St. Andrews paid five times the coin we make in a sennight!" Jon defended himself.

"So you would sell your daughter for silver or gold?" she pressed, her hands on her hips, her chin thrust forward.

"Papa wouldn't sell no one!" Abra declared from where she was feeding scraps to Archie, the family's pet spaniel. " 'N especially not Brandy!"

"And you hush!" Margaret scolded as she pointed a finger at Abra for emphasis.

"The child has more faith in me than you have, Maggie," Jonathon said. "I told Brandy that at the first sign of insult or mistreatment she was to come to me."

Margaret was silent a moment. "But she's—"

"I'm all of eighteen, Mamma," Brandy said from behind them as she set down a tray of dirty dishes, "and you treat me as if I were a child . . . a royal child." She smiled a little and shook her head admonitorily. "No one can force me to do aught against my will . . . you and Simon would see to that, Papa. And I am no babe in the woods. I've heard and seen enough to know much of life, yet you would protect me more fiercely than Abra here."

Jonathon and Margaret exchanged a look that communicated much, although not to Brandy. "How will I ever meet a man and marry if I am kept locked away from life?"

"Surely not among those that frequent the Hawk and Hound," answered Margaret, moving away to check on the bread baking in the great brick oven.

"And why not?" Brandy pressed. "There are many decent men not connected with the king's court who mayhap would be willing to wed me . . ." She hesitated, feeling suddenly as if she were on the brink of extolling her own virtues. "Not that I wish to ever leave here," she added, "for my husband and I could, mayhap, work here and—"

Jonathon suddenly put an arm around her and squeezed her shoulders gently. "Of course we want you to wed, girl. And we wouldn't want to keep you or your husband here at the Hawk and Hound. You would have your own life to lead. 'Tis just that—"

"No one is good enough for you," Margaret declared firmly. "You deserve better than we could ever give you, yet those noblemen from court are so very decadent . . ."

"As though any of them would look at me twice," Brandy said as she gave Margaret a fond hug. "You all think too highly of me, and I cannot imagine why. I'm only a common maiden, with no desire for anything but an honest, hard-working man to love me one day."

"Braaaaan—dyyyyy!" came the simultanous call from several voices in the taproom.

Brandy stepped away from Margaret and turned.

"I think ye should lean out yer window, Brandy, and call for yer Romeo like Juliet did," Abra said.

All three adults looked over at the child calmly sitting beside Archie, a contemplative frown knitting her tiny brow.

Brandy was the first to react. "I shall consider it, sweeting," she said with a smile. "But I think Juliet already had her love before she called him from her balcony."

"Well, there's Tim Taylor," Abra persisted, and Margaret threw Jonathon a troubled look.

Brandy's gaze lowered briefly and silence reigned in the room for a moment. Then Simon poked his head in the doorway, a frown between his brows. He looked at Brandy and jerked his head towards the taproom . . . not, however, before erasing the disapproval that shone in his dark eyes.

"I know, Simon . . . I'm coming." Brandy adjusted her apron over her skirt and left the room just as another singsong "Braaaaan—dyyyyy!" filtered through the tap-

25

room to the kitchen. Abra skipped happily after her, with Archie at her heels.

"Stay out of the way, Abra," warned Margaret before the child disappeared through the door, then turned on her husband, her words but fierce. "How can you think to tell Juliana Spenser that we want her to wed? She's noble—at least on her mother's side—with bloodlines going back who knows how far? We've no right to encourage her to marry anyone—and especially the likes of Tim Taylor!"

"Tim's a fine lad—a young man now—and he's head o'er tail in love with Brandy. She's our daughter now, is she not?" Jonathon returned just as fiercely, his whisper just as angry. "Sir Aimery Spenser gave up any rights to her when he banished both you and his granddaughter from his home!"

"And what of Brandy? She is still genteel . . . the decision should be up to her."

"Then tell her!"

Margaret's face paled and her gaze slid away from his. Gladys, the head cook, stuggled to bring a huge hunk of meat into the kitchen just then, and as Jonathon moved to help her, she shook her head and plopped it onto the scarred, sand-scrubbed center table. "Don't trouble yerself, Master Dalton," she panted, her dumpling cheeks rosy with exertion. "I've only to bring in a few more smaller things, but I need te pay the vendor."

Jonathon handed her several coins from his purse, his gaze returning to his wife, who was removing the hot, fragrant loaves of bread from the oven. When Gladys disappeared out into the yard again, he went up to Margaret. "If ye won't tell the lass of 'er true parentage, then you've got to let her get on with 'er life like a normal young woman of our class, Maggie."

Margaret bit her lip, her eyes filling. "I don't know, Jon. I just don't know . . ."

He took the long-handled peel from her and put an arm about her, hugging her to him as he'd done with Brandy earlier. "Think on it, Maggie. But it has to be one way or the other . . . there's no in-betweens."

"Does your captain always sit and glare at the street when he comes into port?" Brandy asked Stubbs in a conspiratorial voice, a naughty gleam in her eyes.

Stubbs turned to Keir. "Aw, c'mon, Cap'n," he said. "Fergit Hodges . . . it could be days—even weeks—afore he returns from Whitehall."

Brandy was clearing what seemed to her like the hundredth round of tankards from the table, and couldn't resist the impish urge that demanded she coax Keir St. Andrews from his silent, steady contemplation of the darkening scene through the window. The three seamen were well into their cups now, yet their taciturn captain appeared every bit as sober and stern—and preoccupied—as he had since she'd begun serving their table.

"Cap'n's waitin' te see when he can get an audience wi' the king," Jimmy confided, slurring his words only slightly considering all the ale he'd consumed.

Brandy nodded, sensing the sailor was perhaps betraying a confidence before the man who said little yet commanded the obedience and deference of his men.

" 'Tis said it can even take months," Brandy offered in an effort to be helpful. She immediately regretted her words as Keir turned his attention to her. His features were as if carved from bedrock.

"And the entire civilized world knows how badly Charles Stuart needs funds. A man would have to be a fool to ignore the king's weakness." He smiled then, for the first time, and Brandy thought it was the coldest travesty of a smile she'd ever seen. "Every man—and woman—has his price. One has only to meet it."

The smile faded from her face in the wake of his words, and she suddenly had the strangest urge to be anywhere but where she was—to escape his presence now that his attention was fully on her.

27

"I grow weary of your attempts to lure my thoughts away from where they would dwell," he said as his gaze left Brandy's face and alighted on each man at the table for weighty moments. There was no mistaking the irritation in his voice. "I shall, however, attribute your behavior to the amount of ale you've consumed, gentlemen, and the need to find favor with a comely but overly inquisitive serving wench."

Brandy's cheeks flamed, but Keir was occupied with moving past Stubbs to quit the table. Then he was towering before her, his gaze flicking over her from head to toe with insulting brevity. "I am leaving the Hawk and Hound, mistress, for more peaceful surroundings, and therefore cannot be held accountable for the actions of my men in my absence." He bowed slightly, all elegance . . . and all detached disdain. "I would advise you to end your labors here, if you would protect your . . . sensibilities. I consider my payment for your attentions well-earned."

He sketched a bow again before placing his plumed cavalier's hat atop his head and turning to stride swiftly through the crowded room and out into the dusk.

"Because of your attempts to free my thoughts
away from where they would stay, penned up as his
in Bristol . . ." He said slightingly, his brow . . .
his . . . mockery of Tiara's . . . pull for the man . . .
saw . . . equally lapped . . . Crewon with his . . .

# Chapter Two

Keir absorbed the sounds of night around him. The
ship beneath his feet rocked gently, its seasoned timbers
creaking in the embrace of the gently lapping Thames.
Naked spars scored the crepuscular sky, swaying slightly
with the rhythm of the river . . . the ebb and flow of the
tides of the ocean that never failed to soothe him, to lull
him into a kind of contentment, albeit shallow and temporary.

A lighter glided by and the sound of low, laughing
voices drifted across the water to him. The wash of the
barge's wake disturbed the cadence of the *Odyssey's* rise
and fall upon the river's softly heaving bosom; the lapping
changed briefly to a rushing, intensifying the sensation of
rolling through a swell.

Keir raised one black-booted foot to the lower rung of
the rail and leaned an arm across his knee. He closed his
eyes and inhaled deeply. The familiar stench of the seaport
assailed him: fresh tar, salt and wet wood; various cargo,
from the pungent smell of tobacco to the heady scent of
spices; the stink of rotting garbage and decaying fish.

London, in all its bawdy magnificence . . . the majesty
of its soul, and the decadence of its underside.

Keir was home. Or was he? he mused bitterly as he tried
to envision living in England again. In London.

But it wasn't the great city before him, with its twinkling lights and imposing edifices silhouetted against the

29

Thames's banks, that called to him. No, he thought, as his lashes lifted and he guided his gaze into the dark distance to the west. What drew him like a lodestone was the memory of Somerset Chase, with its peaceful hills and woodlands, its scented orchards, its flower-strewn fields and giggling rills.

An unexpected pang of homesickness pierced his breast, so strong and poignant was the memory. Twenty years fell away suddenly, like unbuckled blinders slipping free, and he was back at Somerset Chase, sitting at his mother's knee with his younger sister, listening raptly to Shakespeare's beautiful, bawdy prose. He heard Elizabeth St. Andrews's soft voice in his mind and allowed the memory free rein until his head ached in accord with his heart.

Whatever had triggered such a remembrance after a score of years of scarred and scorching memories?

Fading fragments of levity drifted to him on the August breeze once again, and, like a flash of lightning webbing the sky above, it came to Keir that Brandy Dalton's voice reminded him of his mother's. The sweet, melodic strains of a tavern wench's speech reminded him of the musical sound of Elizabeth St. Andrews's. Soft and soothing, as beckoning as the chords of a harp, his father had once said.

Keir's fingers curled into a fist at his knee, his nails digging into the callused flesh of his palm. He'd repressed the memories for years, eventually realizing the futility of yearning for what was gone. And in their place had grown a soul-searing hatred, as his youth's heart was hardened and tempered by the brutal life of a sailor. When he'd turned twenty, having given up all hope for any of his family, Keir had begun to form a plan of revenge. He'd held the plan before him like a talisman, compelling him to continue the struggle to rise to the upper level of the hierarchy of savage and unscrupulous men among whom he'd grown to maturity.

His primary concern had been to stay alive while he patiently collected his share of the treasure from the galleons that trafficked the Spanish Main. He'd carefully hoarded his silver plate and pieces of eight, his gold doubloons, until he'd been able to restore a stranded and stripped vessel he and several trusted friends had discovered in a half-hidden cove on the southern coast of Hispaniola. He'd outfitted it, and collected his own crew. Then, under the French flag, he'd continued to stalk the virtually helpless Spanish galleons, ceding a percentage of the spoils to Louis of France. At last Keir was wealthy beyond anything his forebears could have imagined.

And then he waited. For the last few years he'd waited patiently for the restoration of Charles Stuart . . . something he'd had no doubt would eventually come to pass. His wealth had been acquired for one reason only: to regain his title and birthright. To wreak his revenge upon his uncle for his unspeakable crimes . . .

A cold, wet nose nudged his fisted hand, temporarily dispelling Keir's dark thoughts. The harsh cast of his features relaxed in the soft moonlight spilling across the smooth wooden deck as he uttered, "Dudley, you old rascal. 'Tis past your bedtime." His fingers relaxed and caressed the dog's head before scratching behind the long, floppy ears. "Hungry?"

The hound's tail beat against the rail at the word 'hungry,' and Keir's mouth softened into a smile. "Insatiable mongrel." He grabbed the folds of skin on the animal's neck and shook them gently. "Well, I've nothing to give you, so go find Jackie."

Dudley whined softly and Keir frowned with mock sternness at the animal, wagging a finger at his nose. "You dare to disobey the captain's orders? Why, I'll have you run the gauntlet for this, man." He squatted down and grabbed the hound's ears playfully. "Except every man on the ship but our Jackie would sport an aching back from bending over to reach your hide, you mangy miniature of a specimen."

Dudley's tongue whipped out and Keir adeptly dodged it. "Ah, ah, ah, we'll no have no kissing from one man to another. What kind of ship do you think I run, eh?"

"Oh, Duds, ye bloody nuisance . . ." exclaimed an exasperated voice that began in a baritone and then unexpectedly raised in pitch, telltale evidence of the whimsical throes of puberty. The youth stopped in his tracks when he recognized Keir fondling the hound. "C-c-c—cap'n," he stammered suddenly.

"Aye, Jackie. Duds was just out for his evening stroll and I waylaid him." An underlying gentleness softened his normally brusque tones. "Has he been fed?"

"Aye. But 'is belly's never full."

"Well, then fetch him a few more tidbits from the galley. Gonzalez is still carousing about London. He'll never know that you invaded his sacrosanct kitchen."

"Aye, Cap'n." He bobbed his head and whistled softly for the dog.

"And Jackie . . ."

The youth paused in his movements.

"See that there's plenty of ale in my cabin."

"No brandywyne, sir?"

"Nay. I've had quite enough of brandywyne," Keir answered tersely, and turned back to the rail in dismissal.

"Good night, Rob," Brandy said over her shoulder as she emerged from the stable.

A muffled "good night" sounded faintly behind her from within the building, above the lowing sounds of the two cows the Daltons owned and the wickering and stomping of the horses belonging to guests remaining the night at the Hawk and Hound.

Brandy paused near the pile of crates where Keir had covertly watched her earlier in the day. She stretched her arms toward the sky, back arched, head thrown back, hair trailing like a curling satin cloak past her shoulders almost to her waist. Her gaze sought the night sky as she yawned and then settled her hands on her hips, her head still raised to the caress of the breeze and the kiss of moonglow.

32

*What a beautiful night,* she thought, savoring the cool evening air for a few more moments.

She was exhausted from constantly waiting on Captain St. Andrews's table. She made a moue of annoyance with herself. *'Tis because you allow Mamma and Papa to spoil you so, Brandy Dalton,* she chided herself. Her brother Simon worked hard enough for three, and even Abra had her tasks. Two other serving girls, Babs and Mary, worked hard for their wages, as well, and the stableboy, Rob, also did more than enough to earn his keep.

But Jon and Margaret Dalton seemed content to have Brandy teach Abra and Simon to read from the books that they bought Brandy at every opportunity. Expensive, leather-bound tomes. Neither Margaret nor Jonathon Dalton could read more than a few words, but they had insisted that Brandy be tutored when she was small, and she'd not questioned it at the time. Yet as she grew older, even though she realized that the Daltons had every reason to use their eldest daughter to teach their other two children to read, they continued to treat Brandy as if she were made of priceless porcelain: light work, plenty of time for reading, gifts of books . . . As Brandy matured into a woman, she wondered if there was something wrong with her that neither parent would tell her, something that merited such preferential treatment.

Why, just this afternoon she'd been whiling away the time by engaging in playacting with Tommy Meldrin and Ian Green, two neighborhood urchins, while everyone else but Abra had been hard at work taking care of the afternoon clientele and preparing for the evening crowd. Struck by a sudden stab of guilt, Brandy had promptly closed the volume of Will Shakespeare's works and entered the taproom to wait upon the enigmatic Captain St. Andrews.

Until Jonathon had told her to do otherwise . . .

Invisible hands moved suddenly from behind her to shatter her reverie. A rag was shoved into her mouth. Before she could think to act, someone pulled a burlap sack

33

over her head and deftly fastened it around her neck with what felt like a rope. As she whipped her head about in an effort to free herself of the coarse, stifling hood, her cheek connected with something hard, and the result of the stunning contact made her reel.

"Easy, man. She's no use dead or maimed."

Her hands flailed out at her attackers, but were instantly caught and pinned behind her, then swiftly secured. Her ankles received the same treatment and, just when she felt herself lose her footing and sway to one side, strong hands caught her about the waist and tossed her over a man's back like a sack of feed, the bones of his shoulder digging into her soft abdomen and causing her to moan softly through her gag. Then, trussed like a sheep going to slaughter, she felt herself being carried off.

Brandy pummeled the back before her, her legs bending at the knee and jerking downward vigorously, like a beached fish flopping against the unrelenting sand. A solid slap on her bottom stung her into submission, and with the blood rushing to her head and her ears ringing from the blow to her cheek, she lay passively for awhile, trying to fathom who had abducted her . . . and why.

She soon discovered she hadn't a clue, and renewed her struggles in desperate frustration. The man beneath her staggered from her exertions.

"The bloody wench'll unman me the way she's kickin'!"

She received another smack to her backside, with an admonitory, "Keep still, drab, or we'll pitch ye into the Thames trussed as ye are!"

Tears of pain stung the back of her eyes. With an effort Brandy sought to ignore her physical abuse and concentrate on discovering clues as to where her kidnappers were taking her. The smell of the river, which was strong enough to permeate the musty burlap, came to her, and a sudden suspicion struck her. Before she could arrive at any more conclusions, however, her position suddenly shifted as her captor leaned into her weight to ascend an incline of some sort. Or a gangplank, she thought in dismay as his footsteps thudded against wood.

At the thought of boarding a ship—and especially a ship possibly captained by a grim, hard man with frigid green eyes, terror gripped Brandy.

*Better him than someone worse,* whispered reason. But reason was no match for terror, and she felt a wave of queasiness rush over her. In spite of his fine dress and his thin veneer of refinement, St. Andrews looked a man who took what he wanted and dared fate to intervene.

Warring emotions whirled through her head—outrage, anger, confusion, fright. But suddenly they were descending steps and someone's hand on her bottom, fingers splayed insultingly over her buttocks, held Brandy steady against her abductor's shoulder.

Ire boiled anew within her at this bold gesture. *How dare he—*

They came to an abrupt halt, putting Brandy's thoughts to flight as she was jolted still. A knock on a door echoed dully through the confined space around them.

"Hodges?" queried a muffled voice from the other side of the door. It was unrecognizable through the wood of the portal.

"Nay, 'tis Stubbs, Cap'n."

"The devil! Can't it wait until the morrow?"

Someone sniggered before Stubbs answered. "Don't think so, Cap'n."

There was a pause, and Brandy's heart sounded like a drumbeat beneath her ribs. Surely everyone could hear it . . .

"Come in then, and be quick about it."

Someone lifted the latch, and the man carrying Brandy moved forward, stooping slightly to accommodate the low door frame.

"Got a present fer ye, Cap'n," Ollie said, a grin slitting his round face from ear to ear.

All three men watched Keir as he narrowed his eyes at what were obviously the legs and backside of a female.

Keir frowned with irritation. "Give her to Jackie," he

said shortly. 'Tis time he learned what it is to have a wench."

Brandy could only squeak in protest through her gag.

"Nay, Cap'n," said the man holding her, "this one's special. Just fer you." And before Keir could object further, Stubbs unceremoniously dumped the bewildered Brandy onto the floor at his feet, jarring her already tender bottom as it hit the floor. Someone untied the rope about her neck, wrists and ankles, and removed the hood. The gag was jerked from between her teeth.

Keir found himself looking into familiar amber eyes, now narrowed and darkened to a cinnamon color with acute indignation. Fire-blond hair spilled past her shoulders and tumbled over her heaving breasts, drawing Keir's gaze.

"Well, well well," he said softly when his eyes met hers again. "Mistress Innocence." He looked up at his men. "You thought mayhap I needed more than drink at the Hawk and Hound?"

Stubbs grinned, revealing a missing bicuspid. "Thought the little lady might sweeten yer temper, Cap'n. Ye been sour as vinegar the last few weeks."

Keir opened his mouth to reply, but Brandy spoke first. "They—they *stole* me!" she accused. "You can't just—just steal a body and—"

"And why ever not, wench?" he countered softly. "Did you not bewitch my men with your swaying hips and jutting breasts? Your pouting lips and come-hither eyes?"

Brandy scrambled to her feet, flicking her hair out of her face and inadvertently exposing the darkening bruise on her cheek. Keir's gaze riveted to the blemish on her otherwise flawless face.

She massaged her chaffed wrists. "You'll find naught of 'come hither eyes' at the Hawk and Hound, Captain St. Andrews," she answered. " 'Tis a family owned and run alehouse and inn. The serving wenches—including myself—are not for hire!"

"Every wench in a tavern is fer hire, Brandy-girl . . . or

36

free if she fancies the fellow enough!" said Jimmy, and all three of the miscreants chortled at his words.

"As for the rest of my—my *anatomy*," she continued righteously, an enchanting roseate hue dancing across her high cheekbones, "I cannot help what God has given me. And I certainly do not flaunt myself to the likes of you . . . or anyone else."

"Ye have te keep her fer the night at least, Cap'n," said Jimmy slyly. "Wouldn't want te meet up with the boy or her hulkin' father until tempers have cooled." He shook his head, sending the knotted ends of his red silk head scarf fluttering behind him.

"What did you do to Simon?" Brandy demanded, her fists going to her hips as she rounded on Jimmy, the significance of her own predicament suddenly paling. "And my father?"

"The lad was the only one about. We gave 'im a love tap on the old pate." Ollie chuckled as Jimmy concluded, "He'll have one bloody headache in the morn."

Brandy's mouth fell open in disbelief before she realized how ridiculous she must look and snapped it shut. "You actually *struck* my brother?"

"Better'n takin' him with us . . . Cap'n don't like men—"

"Enough," Keir interrupted. "I'm not pleased with your behavior this night but," one corner of his handsome mouth lifted slightly, "I cannot in truth say that I regret the, ah, gift you've given me. A man occasionally needs diversion to take his mind from more weighty matters."

"But—"

"Now, if you will excuse us, mates?" he cut in when Brandy would have objected.

"Enjoy 'er, Cap'n," Ollie advised, "compliments o' the crew." And all three men trooped from the cabin, their laughter goading Brandy to recklessness. As the door closed behind them, she squared her shoulders and marched toward it, intending to let herself out with more dignity than she'd entered.

With the speed of a mountebank magician, Keir materialized between Brandy and the door, effectively blocking her escape. His eyes gleamed like emeralds in the muted light from the brass lamps mounted on gimbals on two walls, but they were still bereft of warmth.

"I'm rarely the recipient of gifts, brandy-eyes, and therefore I make certain that I accord each one the appreciation it deserves." He reached out to touch her tumbled hair. "And this one deserves much."

His voice was like deep-piled velvet, and Brandy instinctively retreated a step, more out of wariness than revulsion. The man reminded her of a picture she'd once seen of a sleek panther, crouched and ready to spring.

"Is it money you want?" she whispered, her earlier bravado fading beneath his unrelenting scrutiny. "My — my family will pay for my release, I'm certain, and —"

"I have more money than the Daltons will ever see in a lifetime."

She swallowed, begging her suddenly beleaguered brain to function. There had to be some way out of this. Surely it was a mistake . . . And then an unwelcome thought wormed its way into the confusion in her mind; a confusion vying for dominance over rationality.

"Your men were drunk, Captain St. Andrews," she began with outward calm, as if she were trying to reason with Abra, "and no doubt did not realize how serious a crime they were committing. Surely you, who left the Hawk and Hound quite sober, see the injustice of my abduction."

But even as she said the words, she realized her new tack was in vain. He remained motionless, negligently braced against the door, arms crossed over his chest. A lock of his streaked hair had escaped its queue and hung untidily over one temple.

The insidious suspicion strengthened, and Brandy threw a sidelong glance at the table beneath one of the lanterns. Several uncorked bottles stood beside a pewter tankard. They were all empty.

Her gaze sought the polished floor, her heart skittering around her chest. She wet her lips nervously before her eyes sought his in affirmation. He was no more sober than his men, although he seemed disinclined toward rowdiness. Thus far.

Dear God, what had Jonathon once told her? *Beware the quiet ones. If they withdraw into silence while drinkin', they're mean and unpredictable, Brandy-girl. 'Tis safer by far to be in the company of a man made boisterous from his ale or wine.*

As if reading her thoughts, Keir said, "I rarely get sotted in public. When the occasion calls for it I prefer to do it in the privacy of my own cabin." He pushed away from the door and moved toward her. Her eyes never leaving his, Brandy retreated further, searching for the words that would stop him.

Injecting an uncharacteristic disdain into her voice, she charged, "You cannot just kidnap someone from their home!"

He arched a dark brow in lazy affront. "I did no such thing."

"But—but your men did, and they are under your authority."

"Tsk, tsk, tsk, brandy-eyes, did you not hear what I said to you before leaving the inn? That I am not accountable for the actions of my men in my absence?"

His arm snaked out from nowhere to encircle her waist. He drew her close, the strength in his arm as great as that of Jonathan Dalton, former blacksmith.

"Please," she begged, "I'm no whore—"

His other hand came up to silence her protests before he replaced his fingers with his lips.

Brandy tried to draw away, despite the knowledge that her strength was as nothing against his. His lips worked over hers with devastating expertise, and the one time she would have opened her mouth in protest, Keir took wicked advantage and slid his tongue between her lips.

Her struggles increased at his bold move, for nothing

39

she'd done in her innocent experimenting with Timmy Taylor had prepared her for this. She felt the press of tears of frustration and fury, yet at the same time a fledging flare of some heretofore unknown sensation deep within her.

Incredibly, she felt herself still, responding to his kiss. Warm, wonderful feelings blossomed within her lower abdomen, and the faint taste of ale and his own essence were suddenly, unexpectedly heady. As she relaxed slightly, she leaned into him, answering his lean, hard body with the pliable softness of her own.

She tasted him, felt whipcord muscle and sinew through her clothing and beneath her questing fingers as her arms twined about his neck with a will of their own. He crushed her closer, his hold anything but tender now as he acknowledged his triumph over her with a low growl deep in his throat.

Then with a grunt, Keir suddenly pushed her away. Knees weak, Brandy sank to the bed behind her, the back of her hand to her lips, as she stared at him in wonder . . . and disappointment. His eyes were full of mockery, although as much for himself as for her. Yet she could not know that as his lips tilted upwards in a smug, and utterly humorless smile. She felt her face grow hot at the alien feelings still humming along her veins.

And he had pushed her away.

"You say you're not a whore?" He turned away and moved to the table of empty bottles. Picking up one from behind the others, he uncorked it, ignoring her studiously as he brought the rim of the vessel to his lips and drank deeply. He held it up to the lantern light and studied its contents most thoroughly. "Jackie knows how much I prefer brandywyne to aught else. He knows me better than I know myself, for I told him to bring me only ale. Yet, here sat a lone bottle of that most potent of wines, and it drew my appetite like magnet to metal." He swung toward Brandy. "Won't you join me, brandy-eyes? For not only do I believe that it would be appropriate to drink of the

40

stuff for which, I suspect, you were named, but also to toast a night of love."

He held the bottle out to her and Brandy's mouth compressed stubbornly. "What would you know of love?" she asked through stiff lips. "You who have no more decency than to take what you or your men desire, and damn those who stand in the way."

He crouched before her, the bottle dangling loosely beween his long, lean fingers. "Are you still so concerned about your brother, wench? Your family?" A spark of some indiscernable emotion flashed in his eyes and then was gone. "I am touched by your feelings for your relatives . . . if they are sincere, which I doubt."

"I care not what you believe, Captain. I only ask that you send a message to the Hawk and Hound assuring them that I am sa . . . alive."

He transferred the bottle to one hand and waved the other in negligent dismissal. "In due time, brandy-eyes. In due time." He offered her the bottle once more. "But first you must allow me to appreciate my gift in the manner it deserves."

She shook her head. "I'll strike no bargain with the likes of you . . . you *corsair.*"

He threw back his head in laughter for the first time since she'd met him, but it had a hollow sound to it and held little of merriment. "If that is the worst you can call me, I'll accept the title with pleasure," he said when he'd quieted. "Now drink before I pry open your lovely mouth and force you to drink . . . or choke."

She sat mute for a moment, debating the wisdom of crossing him. Yet she knew only too well how wine lowered a man's—or woman's—inhibitions. If her reaction to his kiss while perfectly lucid had been so natural and unrestrained, heaven knew but she would probably end up acting the part of the whore he'd named her.

"If I drink, will you send a message?" she hedged, loathing herself, but loving her family more.

"A compromise? But I thought that you'd have no part

41

of bargaining with me." He took another swig and held the bottle to her lips. "I will send a message attesting to your safety . . . but," he tipped the neck of the container until a drop of the amber-red wine dotted her trembling lower lip, "not to your whereabouts."

Brandy turned her head aside, the tip of her tongue automatically smoothing over her lip . . . an unconsciously sensual movement that was not missed by the man before her. The rim of the bottle brushed her bruised cheek. She was too preoccupied to heed it, but Keir's fingers tightened around the glass until his knuckles were bloodless. "Did Stubbs strike you?" he asked softly.

Her head slowly turned back toward him. Her eyes, distress-darkened and glistening, met his, half in surprise at his tone of voice and half in anger. "What care you about such a little thing if you cannot see the wrong in my abduction?"

His finger skirted the blue blot on her cheek with infinite gentleness, and Brandy was so surprised by his gesture that she didn't move, but only stared at him in bemusement.

"I would not have so precious a gift abused."

His eyes delved into hers with a mysterious and potent pull, and Brandy suddenly lost her tongue, spellbound by the beauty of his features as his green gaze softened to the warm color of fresh, spring foliage.

The *Odyssey* rocked ever so gently within its mooring lines and lulled them for a brief time. The water softly slapping the sides of the brigantine and the distant clang of a bell were the only sounds penetrating the cabin. A strange silence settled between them, dispelling the antagonism for a few, magic moments.

And then, as if suddenly regretting his moment of softness, Keir's eyes hardened, and the brief glimpse of emotion that had made him seem so much more human disappeared. "Answer my question," he said.

The corners of her mouth turned down. "Nay. I only turned my head beneath the hood and bumped something

42

or someone. Does that ease your conscience, Captain?"

"I have no conscience, brandy-eyes. Now drink." He handed her the bottle and straightened to his full height. "I prefer my women willing."

"I am not willing!" she returned heatedly. "I said I would drink only if you would send a message to the Hawk and Hound assuring my family that I am safe."

"No woman is safe with any man . . . and especially me."

Before she could reply, Keir turned and walked to the table. Taking a quill from an inkstand, he scrawled a few words across a sheet of paper and pulled a cord hanging from a small hole in the cabin ceiling. "My part of the compromise has been met," he told her. "And now what of yours?"

She glanced suspiciously at the folded missive in his hand and then to his face again. How could she know what he'd written? And how could she know that he truly meant to send it to the Hawk and Hound?

A single knock sounded on the door and someone asked through the panel, "Cap'n?"

At Keir's "Come in," a youth of about fourteen entered the room. His light brown hair was sleep-mussed, his shirt hanging half out of his breeches.

The first thing he saw was Brandy sitting on the bunk across from him. He halted his steps and stared at her as if she had two heads.

Keir handed the youth the note. "I want this delivered to the Hawk and Hound Inn staightaway."

"Aye, C-c-c-cap'n," the boy stammered, and blushed as bright a hue as Margaret Dalton's hair.

"Jackie, this is Mistress Dalton . . . better known as Brandy."

Jackie's head bobbed and the flush rose up to tint his ears.

Brandy's gaze lowered without so much as a brief nod. She felt ludicrous sitting on a man's bed, looking as if she'd been through a battle and holding a bottle of bran-

43

dywyne like some common slut. Humiliation rose in her cheeks and she clenched her fingers around the bottle as Keir had done earlier—only for a vastly different reason.

"See that 'tis done immediately," Keir said, "but no one is to know from whence the message comes, is that clear?"

Brandy heard Jackie's mumbled "aye," and then the door closed.

In the silence that ensued, Brandy struggled against the urge to throw the bottle at her antagonist. She wisely squelched it, however, and refused to meet his gaze.

Footsteps sounded on the plank floor until his boots came into her line of vision. "And now, sweetheart . . . drink."

# Chapter Three

Brandy raised the bottle to her lips and choked down a mouthful, her features contorting with the strength of the drink. Unused to drinking anything stronger than ale now and then, she coughed as the fiery liquid slid down her throat and hit her stomach.

"So you've never tasted brandywyne?" Keir asked her with a sardonic lift of one side of his mouth. "Or are you so consummate an actress?"

"You are vile," she said through set teeth, her eyes still watering.

"Is that worse than being a corsair, I wonder?" he asked with affected thoughtfulness. Then his eyes returned to hers with the speed of a striking eagle and he said, "Have another swig, wench. We'll see just how long you can feign your innocence." He reached out and lifted the bottom of the container, forcing the rim of it to her lips. "Again," he commanded.

She obeyed, her eyes flashing defiance briefly before she lowered her lashes. The second gulp wasn't as bad as the first, and a warm feeling spread from the pit of her stomach to her extremities.

"Will you be satisfied when you've taken my maidenhead and sent me back to the Hawk and Hound in shame?" she asked with unaccustomed bitterness.

" 'I will cut off their heads . . . or their maidenheads.' "

The corners of his mouth crested briefly and Brandy was once again reminded of the strangeness of his mirthless smiles.

"You make a mockery of the words," she said.

He sat down on the bed beside her. "I only use them to my advantage." He traced her profile with one finger, lingering over the fine, silken hair at her temple, then crossing the smooth expanse of her forehead before sliding down to rest upon the tip of her retroussé nose.

Brandy remained rigid, staring straight ahead, in spite of the effect of his warm breath upon her cheek as he explored her features with great thoroughness . . . and a surprisingly tender touch.

"Drink again, sweet Brandy, for the third time's the charm, they say."

Her cheeks had grown warm and, knowing that the wine would soon overwhelm her senses, thus making him the victor in this one-sided assault, she dipped her chin in defeat, ignoring his order. Her strawberry-gold hair fell over her shoulder in a shimmering satin shower, obscuring her features from his greedy gaze.

His fingers sifted slowly through the long, gossamer strands before he pushed the tresses back over her shoulder, restoring her profile to him.

She pulled her shoulder away suddenly, her gaze clashing with his. "I've had enough, Captain." She made to stand then, the wine giving her false bravado.

He grabbed her wrist, pulling her back down beside him. "Ah, ah, ah, Brandy-girl. One more pull and then you can put the bottle down," he murmured into her ear.

A curling heat stabbed her midsection at the feel of his breath sighing across the delicate flesh of her ear. She shivered in reaction and Keir pressed his advantage, flicking lightly the contours of the shell-like aperture with his tongue.

With a kind of desperate determination she brought the bottle up to her lips and drank one last time, thinking irrelevantly how beguiling the wine after that first draught. Small wonder some preferred it to ale.

"That's a good girl, now," he whispered in her ear and took the bottle from her. Raising it to his own lips, he drank deeply, the strong, smooth arch of his throat accented as he threw back his head.

Brandy stared in unwilling fascination at the proud cut of his chin, his adam's apple, the corded muscle . . .

"Do you like what you see?" he drawled, a new gleam in his eyes she'd not noticed before as he recaptured her gaze with his. Suddenly he was pushing her back on the bed, the bottle miraculously gone from his hands as he pinned her shoulders to the mattress. "Show me what other charms you possess, wench, besides a beguiling voice, bewitching eyes, and affected innocence. I've a great need for distraction this night."

"Why me?" she asked in an attempt to marshal her swiftly fleeing sanity. The effect of the brandywyne and the man looming over her were combining their power to successfully scale the ramparts of her reason. "Why, when you had the entire city of London, did you have to pick me for your . . . diversion?"

"I didn't pick you, Brandy-girl. Has the wine muddled your thoughts so much already? You were given to me."

He began unlacing her bodice, his warm fingers brushing the flesh beneath her chemise. Desire speared through her abdomen, settling low in her body. "Noooo . . ." she began, panic rising within her only to be diluted by the treacherous wine she'd consumed.

He cut her off with his mouth, his tongue delving into hers with lusty determination. As his tongue clashed with hers, Brandy felt herself arching toward him with a low moan that came of its own accord. Was that her voice? she dimly wondered as Keir's hands expertly slid her bodice to her waist before attacking the chemise covering her breasts.

His glowing green eyes bored into hers, mocking, tempting, daring, luring. She stared helplessly into their verdant depths, reminded of the fathomless sea she'd seen

47

once before moving to London. Beautiful, beckoning . . . and dangerous.

Then her breasts were bared and Keir lowered his head, his breath misting them for achingly long moments before he took one rosy crest into his mouth, suckling gently while his hand reached beneath her skirts.

Brandy gazed down at his head, his hair darker in the shadows of the bed. Dear God, what were they doing? one last echoing voice of reason demanded. Torn between desire and her sense of right and wrong, Brandy brought up one knee and tried to jam it into Keir's midsection.

The unexpectedness of the move and her lack of strength in the wake of a paralyzing languor acted in her favor. Although her knee stopped short of its mark, it connected with the more vulnerable area below and Keir grunted in pain, lifting his head from the pillow of her breasts.

"Leave off . . . you cannot do this!" she panted, pushing against his chest. "I'm no tavern jade that you can just—"

He released her suddenly and sat up, a dark frown replacing the more relaxed expression brought on by desire. "I ought to beat you for that little trick," he growled.

Brandy took advantage of his weight shift and turned to her side, her knees drawn up defensively, her eyes closed. "I owe you naught," she whispered, a tear threading its way over the bridge of her tip-tilted nose, with its light sprinkling of freckles, and down her other cheek. "You stole me like a piece of—jewelry. You can't just do that to another human being!"

The world seemed to tilt when she opened her eyes to look at him, and she lowered her lids immediately, squeezing them tight against the sudden, unexpected dizziness.

Keir stared down at her, watching another tear trickle from beneath the lush length of her sable lashes. It hovered precariously, a shimmering droplet of shame, and winked at him in seeming reprimand.

With a softly uttered imprecation, he rose, sweeping the

brandy bottle off the floor as he went and returning to sit before the table. He took another swig, acknowledging that he'd already had more than enough, and then pushed it aside.

He felt the beginnings of a headache, although not, he suspected, so much from his imbibing as from the tension that had held him in its grip since he'd sent Hodges to Whitehall. Christ, he thought acidly, he'd given his man enough money to grease the way to any monarch's ante-chamber . . . let alone one in dire need of funds. What was taking so damned long?

He closed his eyes and dropped his head into his hands, his fingers spread over his scalp. The flare of the lanterns whispered to him in the silence: *You'll never regain your title, sentimental fool . . . you'll never regain Somerset Chase . . .*

His fingers tightened their hold in a spasm of anger, and he felt his chest constrict with fear. Fear that the voice was right. That he would be forced to roam the seas, the *Odyssey* the only place he would know as home until he was buried beneath the waves that had taken him from England in the first place.

He pushed himself away from the table and began to pace the cabin, but his steps came to a halt on his first pass before the narrow bed. Brandy was curled up like a kitten, one hand outstretched over the edge of the bunk, the other tucked protectively beneath her chin. Her lashes still glistened from her tears, but her breathing was deep and even, a sign that she had succumbed to the effects of the wine.

A corner of his mouth twitched at the thought of the wench he'd been "given" falling asleep in his bed instead of easing his tension with her body. A corsair she'd called him, he thought as he crouched before her, carefully studying her features. An unexpected chuckle rose in his throat and he was forced to stifle it for fear of waking her and having her discover him gazing raptly at her face.

What manner woman was she? he wondered, having

read the innocence in her eyes from the first, yet also having dealt with other women who deliberately deceived men into believing they were naive only to increase their worth. It was one of the whore's many tricks, and some men bought it. Whether genuine or not, some men preferred the airs of innocence, savoring the experience of being the teacher as opposed to the student before the harlot's vast sexual experience in the art of pleasing her customer.

But not Keir. He had little time—and less use—for women and their wiles. He enjoyed them while they pleasured him, and then forgot them. He had more important things to concern him . . . Aye, he thought. He'd use this one until he'd taken his fill, and then he'd return her just a bit more used—seasoned, he liked to call it—to the Hawk and Hound.

That he would eventually need a genteel wife, he'd acknowledged long ago; a man could not beget heirs without a wife. But he would choose one who was healthy, fetching, and willing to go her way as he would go his. Keir had little doubt but that any woman who was part of the Restoration court would welcome the chance to bag a rich husband and have her diversions on the side, for love and fidelity were unfashionable.

That thought, however, left a bad taste in his mouth. His lips thinned with self-scorn, for somewhere, tucked into an all-but-forgotten niche within his heart, was the elusive echo of an unutterably foolish hope: that a woman might fall in love with him. And he would, perhaps, return that love . . .

The thud of footsteps on the deck above claimed his attention. His eyes still on Brandy's face, he turned his head slightly, listening for the sound of voices. But the silence of night remained, save for one man striding quickly across the deck and then down the ladder and toward the captain's cabin.

Hodges. It had to be. Jackie had sent a messenger and would have returned to his room long since. And Jackie had a much lighter step than Hodges.

Keir stood, turning his back to the sleeping girl . . . and waited.

Daylight poured in through the porthole across from the table, shining in Brandy's eyes. She brought her fists up to them and rubbed them in protest. Then she opened one lid and peered up at the source of the offending light.

In an instant she remembered where she was and came bolting upright on the bed. Captain St. Andrews's bed.

"Good morrow."

Brandy jerked her head toward the voice she recognized all too well, and was immediately aware of a dull, pounding ache in her cranium.

"You slept well, I trust?"

A kaleidoscope of thoughts burst through her brain. Did he . . . ? Had they . . . ? She touched her forehead and massaged her temples with outspread fingers, trying to remember. A frown drew her fine brows together.

"Nothing happened, if that is what you fear."

Brandy allowed her thoughts to focus fully on the man in whose bed she'd spent the night. Her eyes widened slightly at what she saw. He was dressed in a dove-gray satin doublet and breeches, trimmed with gold braid. The breeches were tied at the knee with gold ribbon above his spotless white hose and gray leather shoes with shining silver buckles.

Her gaze traveled back to his head where, free of its confining queue, his thick, waving hair fell loosely to just above his shoulders, that striking combination of gold over sable. When Brandy's gaze encountered his, she was greeted with what would have been on another man a lazy smile. In his case, it was only a curving of his lips.

With a graceful sweep of his green-plumed, gray cavalier's hat, he sketched her an elegant bow. "Do I look ready to face the king?" he asked when he'd straightened, his eyebrows lifted expectantly.

Anger rose in a hot surge within her. "Your heart is

51

blacker than any man I know if you can only think about your appearance when you've kept me against my will here and . . ." She trailed off, suddenly uncertain, wondering again what had happened after she'd drunk the brandy-wyne. "Did you . . ." she tried to think of the appropriate word, "*ravish* me last eve?" Becoming color shaded her cheeks.

"Do you feel *ravished?*"

She hesitated, attempting to ascertain if any damage had been done. She felt nothing amiss but a vague head-ache, a slight dryness of the mouth. Then, "You must let me go," she appealed, her anger vanishing in the face of a growing puzzlement. "If you don't need money . . . and you didn't take advantage of me, what can you possibly gain from holding me here?"

The changing expressions on her expressive face were so apparent, her puzzlement so obvious, that Keir could almost pity her, for such show of emotion could only reveal to others one's weaknesses.

*'Tis only a role,* a voice reminded him. *She's taking you in with the very trait you call weakness.*

Keir set his hat on his head. "That, sweetheart, is a good question." He motioned toward the chest at the foot of the bunk. "You can wear something of mine if you wish to change your clothing."

Her expression changed again, telling him exactly what she thought of his suggestion.

"Jackie will supply you with what you need to perform your ablutions. He has orders to bring you your morning draught and anything else you might require." He inclined his head and then swung toward the door.

"But—but you can't just keep me locked up in this room!" she cried, panic at the thought of spending hours on end in the cabin suddenly overwhelming all else. "There's naught to do . . . I surely shall go mad!"

Over his shoulder he said, "Make yourself at home, brandy-eyes. You may read from any of my books. Perhaps you can even persuade Jackie to entertain you with chess or a game of cards."

He let himself out and closed the door firmly behind him.

"But I can't abide chess," she exclaimed in frustration to the closed door. Only the sound of his footfalls ascending to the deck came to her in answer.

She rose and tried the door. It opened easily, almost unbalancing her. Looming before her and blocking her excape, however, was a huge man, sporting through one ear lobe what looked disconcertingly like a finger bone, and wearing a leering smile that revealed several gold teeth. A long, thick braid hung over one shoulder, stiffly tarred into submission.

"Were ye needin' somethin'?" he asked, crossing brawny arms over massive pectorals and causing the exotic yellow silk tunic he wore to ripple sinuously with the movement. "Lug c'n see te yer needs if Jackie can't."

Brandy could only shake her head at first, stunned into momentary silence. If she had ever encountered this man in a dark London street she would have feared for her life.

She slammed the door in his face . . . and repressed the childish urge to kick it for good measure.

"Where's my daughter, St. Andrews?"

Jonathon Dalton was standing at the lower end of the ramp connecting the *Odyssey* to the dock. His son was beside him, a white plaster over one temple.

"They been here since dawn, Cap'n," said Stubbs, straddle-stanced with a drawn cutlass in one hand.

"Your daughter? You mean the wench who served us yestereve?" Keir asked in mild surprise.

"You know damned well who I mean! I would wager the Hawk 'n Hound that she's on your ship, and we'll not leave until you release 'er."

"Curse me! but that's impossible. Why would I ever lay a finger on the girl if—"

"I didn't say you did," Jonathon said, the flush of tem-

53

per rising in his face. "I say your men knocked out Simon here and kidnapped Brandy last eve. And if you don't let her go, I'll come aboard and find 'er myself!"

Now it was Keir's turn to frown. "Take one step aboard this ship and I'll have you keelhauled. I know naught of the wench . . . and neither do my men."

"That's a bloody lie!" Simon charged, shaking his fist toward Keir and his quartermaster. "I've proof of your dirty work." He gestured to his temple. "They knocked me out and took my sister. And I know 'twas seamen because of their sorry way of speakin'."

Stubbs bristled visibly. "You got a complaint 'bout our speech, Master High 'n Mighty? An' are you callin' the Cap'n here a liar?" He advanced a threatening step down the ramp before Keir's restraining hand on his arm stopped him.

"Let 'im come, St. Andrews. And you come with him," invited Dalton, fists resting on his hips. " 'Tis time someone taught the likes of you and your drunken tars that you can't just take what you fancy."

Stubbs whipped his head around to look at his captain, *Are you gonna take that?* written across his features as clearly as if with quill and ink. But Keir only tightened his fingers warningly before he released his grip.

He advanced down the ramp alone, past the fuming Stubbs, and ignoring several other crew members who were lining the rail on both sides of the plank that bridged the river. He halted within an arm's length of Jonathon.

"I would advise you to look elsewhere for your daughter, Dalton," he said with quiet menace. "Mayhap she took a fancy to some gentleman and willingly left the happy sanctuary of your taproom."

"Why, you—" began Dalton, and jabbed his fisted hand toward Keir's face.

Keir blocked the blow with his arm, and for a charged moment they stood stalemated. "I wouldn't if I were you," Keir warned softly. "My men will be all over both of you in the blink of an eye at my command. And," he added, "they'll need little urging. If for naught else, do it for the sake of your son here."

Jonathon considered this briefly, his eyes glinting with suppressed wrath, before he disengaged his arm from Keir's. "And what of the sake of my daughter? What of Brandy?"

"She's not here."

Jonathon shook his head, the corners of his mouth curling downward. "Then I'll go to the king himself. You're in England now, not marauding upon the high seas. You cannot just abduct a woman like some plundering pirate."

"And I tell you I didn't."

Jonathon hawked and spat on the wharf at his feet. With slow deliberation he wiped his mouth with the back of his sleeve, eyeing Keir with a mixture of loathing, anger, and contempt. Then, without another word, he turned and strode away, Simon in his wake.

"Didn't realize she was 'is daughter until we got te yer cabin . . . but I'd keep the wench anyway just te get even with 'im," Stubbs muttered from just behind Keir.

Keir watched the two men, father and son, disappear among the toiling seaman and occasional civilians populating the riverfront. "That," he mused softly, "could be disastrous if, indeed, he appeals to Charles Stuart."

"Well then, ye just have to get there first and make yer offer to 'is majesty." Stubbs shook his head and spat on the ground at their feet. "Even so, don't see how a common innkeeper could have any more influence than a ship captain . . . an earl."

Keir swung his head to meet Stubbs's eyes. "That all remains to be seen, Peter . . . 'tis pure conjecture at the moment."

"Well, if 'is majesty don't recognize the unfairness of it all, then he don't deserve te be king."

Keir glanced down at the signet ring on his finger with its entwined onyx initials 'S' and 'A' against a gold background. "And if he doesn't accept my story, we may be

55

forced to pay reparation to Jonathon Dalton, depending on the king's sense of fair play."

Stubbs scratched his head and frowned. "Reparation? Fer a tavern wench? Damme! but 'tis unwarranted."

Keir's green eyes met those of his quartermaster, a rare gleam of humor flickering through them. "We've been too long away from civilization, *amigo*. Too long among the Indians and the greedy, bloody Spaniards . . . too accustomed to taking what we damned well pleased, as, perhaps, Dalton claimed." He shook his head, his eyes narrowed as he stared into the distance. "But I would see how Charles Stuart accepts me and my claim before forcing respectability upon any of my crew." He shot Stubbs a look askance, a corner of his mouth quirking in anticipation of the quartermaster's reaction.

But Stubbs missed his captain's look. "Respectability? Humph," he grunted, and spat again. "Privateering fer the king of England—or France, fer that matter—ain't no more respectable than piracy . . . just has the approval of a monarch is all."

"And the monarch's backing and protection. Don't forget that."

Stubbs grunted again to express his doubts before he turned back toward the ship. "Good luck to ye, Cap'n, but be careful, ye hear?" he warned gruffly over his shoulder. "I don't trust them blue bloods one bit."

Keir strode up to a hackney and asked the driver to take him to Whitehall.

"Goin' te see the king, are ye?" commented the driver, but said nothing more after opening the coach door for Keir and then closing it behind him.

Keir sat in brooding silence, dispassionately watching the sights of Restoration London pass by. Now that he had the king's attention, he suffered a different kind of apprehension . . . whether or not Charles would believe his tale of treachery and attempted murder, or tell him to go back to privateering in the Caribbean where he belonged.

But Keir couldn't envision Charles Stuart passing up the chance to obtain gold to help fill his constantly depleted coffers; nor could he picture Charles declining to cheat his French cousin and rival, who'd not treated Stuart with any great warmth or support during his exile, out of a source of revenue.

Keir sat back with a sigh, laying his head against the squabs. And, of course, if the king chose to take his side in his quest to regain all that should be his, he would have to find a wife.

In an attempt to hold at bay the dark doubts that plagued him in spite of his reasoning, Keir closed his eyes, forcing his thoughts to the noblewomen he'd met at Versailles. The females in the English court wouldn't be so very different from their French counterparts, for they imitated Louis's court in every way: elegantly combed and coiffed, elaborately gowned in every conceivable color and fabric; face-paint and patches, heavy perfume, and a studied affectedness to their every movement, their every word . . .

Unbidden there rose in his mind's eye the image of a young woman sitting in the sunlight on the back stoop of an inn, the wind rustling her hair and fanning the pages of the book in her lap. Her smile was as bright as sunshine, her laughter as sweet as the tinkling of bells, her shining copper-blond hair begged to be touched . . .

*You . . . you corsair!*

A smile softened his mouth. His clenched fingers relaxed as he gave himself up to memories of Brandy Dalton. The worst she could think to call him was a corsair. His lashes lifted, and an uncharacteristic warmth mellowed the harsh cast of his features, muted the cold green hue of his eyes. She'd not pleasured him physically, but her mere presence in his cabin had been miraculously diverting. What was it about her? he mused. Was she indeed as innocent as she appeared?

*If so, her father had every right to threaten you.*

He pushed the annoying thought away. Corsairs—or privateers—had no conscience.

*But what of an earl?*

"Royal Exchange!" called out the driver above the din in the streets around them, pulling Keir from his pleasant reverie. The coach stopped and the door was yanked open. A young woman was handed up the step and settled herself across from Keir with a flounce of her billowing skirts.

Kier slid across the seat to the far window, his face once again a study in imperturbability.

As he met the woman's glance, the coach lurched forward, sending her elaborate vizard sliding down her satin skirts to the coach floor.

"La!" she exclaimed, her folded ivory fan dangling from her wrist as she bent forward to pursue the bothersome bauble.

"Allow me," Keir offered politely, and leaned to retrieve it.

"Thank you," she said breathlessly, her fan opening instantly to hide her lower features while her great blue eyes studied Keir from over the implement.

He handed her the vizard. "Mistress—?"

"Lady Rosalyn Downing," she supplied with the faintest trace of hauteur.

"Of course, milady," he corrected, kicking himself mentally for such a stupid blunder. "My apologies."

He returned his gaze to the window, a scowl seaming his forehead. He'd allowed thoughts of Brandy Dalton to preoccupy him so thoroughly that he'd called a woman who was obviously well-born 'mistress.'

She must not have taken deep offense, however, for she inquired, "You are new to London, are you not, milord?"

He looked at her, taking advantage of his opportunity to correct her and even the score. *"Captain* St. Andrews, Lady Rosalyn."

"Oh." Disappointment dawned across her features,

58

lowered the pitch of her single-worded reply.

His eyes glittered coldly at her reaction, and he added perversely, "Had I said Earl of So-and-Such, would you be less disappointed?"

She plied her fan with more vigor in an obvious effort to cool cheeks pinkened beneath her rouge, appearing at a loss for words to counter his blunt query.

"Let us begin again," Keir offered, acknowledging with optimism that he would possibly be selecting a wife from among women such as her. Bluntness was not the way of a courtier . . . and especially in Charles Stuart's court. "Captain St. Andrews, of the *Odyssey*, recently docked from the Spanish Main."

She smiled then and pointedly glanced out of the window, in order, Keir suspected, to afford him a glimpse of her very fine profile. As he went to speak again, she cast him a look that conveyed her willingness to start afresh, her gaze traveling from his face down to his shoes and back again, assessing. With a new look of interest in her eyes as they met his again, she fluttered her fan flirtatiously and said in a sugared voice, "Aye, do let's begin again, Captain."

# *Chapter Four*

Brandy sat at the table — someone had cleared it of the bottles from the night before — chin in hand, tapping her fingertips against her lips thoughtfully. None of her previous experience had prepared her for the situation in which she found herself. Sheltered, cosseted, she'd spent the first fifteen years of her life in a country town with her parents and her brother Simon, and then later Abra. Jonathon Dalton had made a good living as a blacksmith, but had always talked longingly of owning and running his own tavern. With Margaret's help — for they'd done without many things to save money — he'd managed to accumulate enough to invest in an alehouse in London in partnership with his brother Ian.

Even then, Brandy mused, the Dalton's had managed to run a decent inn in the midst of bawdy Restoration London. The regular clientele quickly learned that the family-run Hawk and Hound was not the place to come for a quick tumble with the serving wenches, or a good, knock-down brawl. Newcomers were promptly brought into line by Jonathon if they were slow to catch on, and his intervention had always resulted either in cooperation or eviction from the premises . . .

Until yesterday.

A frown flitted across her vivid features. It was almost beyond her comprehension that men could be so bold, so base. Almost, but not quite. On the periphery of her mind Brandy was aware that such things could and did happen. She had just never thought to be the victim of such outrageous behavior. And not only did she worry about her family, in spite of the note Captain St. Andrews had supposedly sent to the Hawk and Hound, but she was really beginning to fear for her own welfare.

Last night was a bad dream, or so it had seemed, with the bizarre and unexpected turn of events, followed by the effects of the brandywyne; but with the light of day shining through the two windows on either side of the cabin, the reality of being held against her will was homing in.

A knock sounded on the door.

Brandy lifted her gaze from the table before her. "Come—" she began and then bit back the rest of her words. It wasn't her cabin, nor did she wish to see or speak to anyone but the captain . . . and only concerning her release. From the looks of the man guarding the door, it was obvious that the crew would be of no help. And, after all, she thought, *they* were the ones responsible for her abduction, for Captain St. Andrews's astonishment had appeared genuine.

"Mistress B-b-b-randy?" came a voice through the portal.

Jackie, she thought. The cabin boy.

Her naturally sweet nature momentarily quashed her annoyance as she remembered the stammering youth. How unkind to ignore him . . .

"M-m-mistress Brandy? C'n I c-c-come in?"

"Aye," she answered with reluctance. Let him see the captain's unmade bed, her own disheveled state—for she'd refused to touch anything that belonged to Captain St. Andrews—and come to what conclusions he might.

The latch moved and the door swung inward. Immediately the strangest looking dog Brandy had ever seen lumbered into the cabin. He made straight for her, his short, crooked forelegs working to carry his long body toward her.

"Duds, c-c-come back here," Jackie commanded from

61

close behind the hound, a tray balanced in his hands. His look was apologetic as it went from the hound to Brandy. A flush crept up his neck and cheeks.

Lug poked his head around the door just then and flashed his gold-toothed grin. "Ol' Dudley there knows a comely female when 'e sees one," he observed before jerking back his head as Jackie kicked the door closed with his foot.

Dudley sniffed Brandy's shoe and then, with a snuffle of canine rapture, laid his head with its long, drooping ears and multiple folds of skin upon Brandy's knee. Forlorn brown eyes met hers in mute appeal.

Automatically she reached out a hand to stroke the dog's head.

"Aw, don't p-p-ay no 'tention t-t-te Duds, there," Jackie said as he set the tray down on the table. "He's always l-l-lookin' te be petted."

"Marry come up, but I've never seen a hound like him," Brandy said, momentarily forgetting her situation as the animal-lover in her took over.

"G-g-gift from the French king," Jackie explained, obviously eager to speak of things other than Brandy's status as prisoner. "The cap'n says he's a b-basset hound . . . a cross between a b-b-bloodhound and the hounds of St. Hubert."

At the mention of Captain St. Andrews, Brandy's hand stilled. Her eyes met Jackie's. "Is your captain back yet?"

Jackie shook his head, sending his lank brown hair spilling over one eyebrow. He tucked it self-consciously behind one ear. "N-n-ay, mistress." He shrugged lamely. "I brought ye yer morning d-d-draught an' some victuals. Ye m-m-m-ust be hungry." He nodded toward the tray. "C'n I bring ye some clean water te wash in?"

Dudley's muzzle slipped fom her knee as Brandy shook her head and stood. "Thank you, but that won't be necessary, for with your help, I would like very much to go home."

Jackie's gaze went to the unmade bed and then roved the room, avoiding meeting hers.

" 'Tis not what you think," she said in a low voice, in spite of her earlier resolve to allow him to think what he would. "Nothing happened . . . and naught will if I have any say in it." She leveled her most solemn look at him. "Will you help me leave this ship?"

The youth's receding flush returned like the wash of a high tide, and his stuttering increased in his obvious agitation. "I c-c-can't help you," he said. "I have t-te follow the c-c-c-cap'n's orders." He nodded at the tray again, his gaze clinging to the mug of buttered ale like a drowning man to a piece of driftwood. "Ye m-m-must be hungry. Why d-d-don't ye eat some o' this an' I'll f-f-fetch ye some washin' water."

Brandy tossed her head in genuine irritation now, her eyes narrowing. "Surely you can't wish to be a party to this! Why, my father will go to the king himself if he must."

Jackie paled significantly, evidently ignorant of the unlikelihood of a tavern-keeper gaining the king's ear. Brandy was quick to press her advantage. "Papa is acquainted with King Charles," she bluffed, "and will waste no time in apprising him of Captain St. Andrews's crime."

"Cap'n St. Andrews ain't committed no crime, girlie," interjected a new voice.

Both Brandy and Jackie looked around to see Peter Stubbs step through the door. He shook a warning finger at Brandy. "Don't ye be tryin' te ply yer womanly wiles on Jackie here, wench. In the first place, Cap'n ain't guilty o' no crime. *We* took ye from the Hawk and Hound, an' not him. An' now that ye're aboard the Cap'n's vessel, he can do as he pleases with ye as ye're under *his* jurisdiction."

In the face of his unexpected attack, Brandy looked momentarily bewildered. Then inspiration struck. "We're not at sea, Master Stubbs," she retorted. "Captain St. Andrews is under the king's jurisdiction now, I believe." She had no idea whether she was right, but it was worth a try. Anything to gain her freedom.

Stubbs crossed one arm over his chest and thoughtfully stroked his chin with his other hand as he contemplated Brandy. "Now, don't we have a saucy one here, Jackie m'boy," he said softly. "Gettin' a bit rebellious, ain't she?" He pursed his lips and tipped his head. "Mayhap we should invite Lug in here te teach 'er some humility . . . what think ye?"

Brandy took a step backward in unthinking reaction to the name of the leviathan outside her door. The chair came up against the back of her knees and brought her up short. "That won't be necessary," she said, and hated herself for the coward she must appear.

"Then straighten out, missy, an' eat what Gonzalez made fer ye. An' make yerself presentable, 'cause the cap'n don't tolerate slovenliness."

This brought her head up sharply, and a glint of mutiny shone in her eyes, for the thought of being considered slovenly was, in her mind, little better than being thought a whore.

As the quartermaster swung toward the door, however, an idea silently suggested itself to Brandy. Yet she gave no indication of her thoughts, but rather made an effort to be kind to the awkward and obviously uncomfortable Jackie, the hope of her half-formed plan meeting with success giving her a false sense of magnanimity.

"I thank you for the fricassee of bacon and eggs and the buttered ale," she politely told the youth. "And I will do them justice." She seated herself at the table and pulled the tray toward her.

"If ye wish aught else, m-m-mistress," Jackie said, obviously relieved at her capitulation, "just pull the cord." He glanced at the rope hanging nearby.

Brandy nodded and gave him a bright smile before making a great show of tackling the fare before her.

Jackie quickly straightened the bed until there wasn't a crease on the bedclothes. When he withdrew, ordering

Dudley—who'd had his nose up in the air to catch a whiff of what was on the table—to follow him, Brandy ate her fill, deciding that she'd be foolish to refuse sustenance when she'd need her wits and, possibly, her strength as well before her ordeal was over.

So Captain St. Andrews didn't care for slovenliness, did he? her darker side considered as she ate. Well, they would see about that.

She studied the cabin like a general sizing up the enemy troops. The room was obviously designed to his taste—the taste of a meticulous man, she noticed, now that she took the time to examine her surroundings. The walls and floor were of oiled teak, polished to perfection. The chest at the foot of the bed was a dark wood ornamented with brass. Drawers anchored beneath the bed displayed shining brass pulls, and, now that she cared to notice, the bed itself was not so narrow considering it was in the cabin of a ship, where space was limited. Brass whale oil lamps were mounted in gimbals in two walls, and a fancy lantern hung over a japanned desk sporting graceful oriental figures. Two colorful Persian rugs decorated the floor, one before the bed, the other before the desk, which opened downward to form a writing table.

Scouting out her adversary's territory most thoroughly, Brandy opened the desk, ignoring the guilt that nagged her at invading the privacy of another's belongings. A heavy lead inkwell, pen, sticks of sealing wax and parchment were tucked inside. The desk also revealed two leather-covered notebooks, one obviously a captain's log and the other containing a block of wax—more easily erased and reused than paper.

One of several drawers revealed a neat stack of writing paper, another pen, and an adjustable pencil. The largest drawer contained navigating instruments, of which Brandy could identify only a few.

Carefully closing the desktop and drawers, she moved to kneel before the chest at the foot of the bed. Bottles of Madeira, Rhenish, brandywyne, and rum—or 'kill-devil' as she'd heard it called—were stored in one corner, along with rope, leather mittens, a pistol with lead shot and powder horn, and small bags of spices . . . one containing what smelled like garlic and pepper—an age-old remedy to treat a cold—and ginger root for seasickness. Bed linens and towels filled one half of the chest and wedged the other objects snugly against the wooden sides.

On a hunch, Brandy slid one hand beneath the stack of linens and found, to her delight, a silvered Venetian hand mirror. Ignoring the fact that it was a treasure in itself, she studied her reflection critically, noting with satisfaction that her hair was a tumbled mass of snarls.

She closed the lid of the trunk, keeping the mirror in hand, and quickly inspected the contents of the two drawers beneath the bed. Clothing and personal articles, like implements for shaving, scissors, a sewing kit complete with brass thimbles, buttons, hooks and eyes filled the first one; there were also several buckles, rings, a brooch, a carved ivory comb and boar-bristle brush. The lower drawer held what looked like more masculine apparel, but seemingly nothing else of interest, and Brandy didn't dig to the bottom as she had in the chest.

She closed the drawers and sat back on her heels, considering briefly that she could perhaps threaten her way off the ship with the pistol in one hand, the razor or scissors in the other. But the idea was absurd, even if she'd known how to load a pistol properly or shoot it with any accuracy. And, of course, she could never kill or injure a man unless her own life were in jeopardy. Just the thought of aiming a gun at Lug or Jackie made her knees weaken, her heart thud dully at the base of her throat.

That left only her original plan.

She stood and eyed the half-empty trencher of food on the table, then the hand-mirror still clutched in her fingers . . . and made her decision.


A page wiped Charles's brow with a tennis sheet, dabbing and mopping the royal countenance with great care and thoroughness. The monarch quickly nodded his dismissal of the servant and took the towel from him, walking from the indoor, wooden-floored tennis court to a nearby daybed. With remarkable grace and a studied indolence, he reclined his tall form upon the pallet, as he was often wont to do after his exertions, laying back his dark head and closing his eyes. His racquet slipped from long, elegant fingers to the floor.

"Odsfish, I feel a bit winded but wonderfully revived, Barbara!" he sighed, accepting a goblet of watered wine from her.

"Your Majesty does not usually play so late in the morn," replied the countess of Castlemaine, the king's reigning mistress.

"True, true," he said, lifting his lashes slightly to afford himself a covert view of her very beautiful bosom. " 'Tis much too hot this late. Faith, I believe I've lost at the least a pound or two."

"And no wonder, Your Majesty, you played so well this morn," she complimented him, her sultry eyes surveying his supine form from head to foot with a barely concealed hunger. "You've so splendid a body for sports . . . and excel at *everything* you do," she added in a husky whisper meant for Charles only.

"I beg your pardon, Majesty," interrupted a liveried servant from behind Barbara, "but Captain St. Andrews is here."

Charles raised his gaze fully. "Ahh, indeed. Send him in then, won't you, George?" He looked appealingly at Barbara, his dark eyes full of promise. "You will excuse us, madame? Until . . . later?"

With a toss of her titian curls, her eyes turning sulky, she curtsyed briefly to him. "Of course, Your Majesty," she said on an ungracious note.

Keir followed another servant past Barbara and toward the king, noting dispassionately her dark eyebrows raised in obvious interest as he passed her by. From the deep auburn of her hair, large violet eyes and famous pout, he surmised that this was the notorious Barbara Palmer, Countess of Castlemaine . . . the woman who had caused the queen such distress. And the king such pleasure.

"Forgive the intrusion, Your Majesty," Keir said as he stopped before the king and performed a deep and elegant bow.

Charles studied him through narrowed eyes. "Aye, St. Andrews. Sit." He motioned toward a chair that had been hurriedly brought forward by a hovering servant. "Would you care for some refreshment mayhap?"

Keir had no desire to sit, a pent-up anxiety making him as touchy as a powder magazine before an errant spark. Yet he obliged, willing to do anything Charles Stuart suggested in the hopes of tipping the scales in his favor.

He hated this sudden, strange willingness to fawn, but so very much depended upon this meeting. He felt his chest tighten with an unwelcome tension, a strange feeling, yet one that had become increasingly familiar since the *Odyssey* had neared English shores for the first time.

How would he approach Charles Stuart in a milieu where duplicity and subterfuge ruled? Where honesty and straightforwardness were viewed as boorish and unfashionable? Where intrigue and machinations came more naturally to the increasingly flamboyant and outrageous Restoration Court than perhaps even that of Louis XIV of France?

Keir took a deep breath, allowing it to start low in his belly and slowly climb up through his body, cleansing, calming, allowing him to rein in his rampant misgivings. He had not waited a score of years only to turn into a quivering, cringing mass of flesh when given his golden opportunity.

And Charles Stuart was reputed, among other things, to be fair.

"Thank you, nay. I — I come to you with no other words or trappings save the truth."

Charles raised a dark eyebrow and inclined his head. "A

refreshing breath of truth would be most welcome at the moment, Captain." Good humor flashed in his loam-dark eyes.

Keir's own widened slightly at this, relief skimming over him. "I have come to you as one man to another. As a man who, cast adrift against his will a score of years past, would present himself to another who knows well the desolation of exile, the anguish of being reft of his home—the home of his ancestors. And the exigency of regaining that which rightfully belongs to him."

The king's dark eyes were hidden from Keir for a moment as his lashes lowered and he stroked a spaniel pup who had managed to clamber up on the day-bed. Clearly he was reminded of his bleak years as Charles Lackland, forced to languish in an unwelcoming France and a lukewarm Holland after the execution of his father . . . and his own narrow escape after the battle of Worcester.

Keir struck while the iron seemed hot. "And I come to you as a subject to his king, to ask your help in righting a grievous wrong."

Charles's melancholy gaze met Keir's, the gleam of levity gone. Although the request was put in fairly humble terms, there was a steely determination in the cold, glass-green depths of Keir St. Andrews's eyes that the monarch did not miss. And there was also something elusively familiar about him. Speaking with unaccustomed bluntness, Charles asked, "Know you how many 'wrongs' I have been requested to set aright, Captain St. Andrews? There is no end to the requests for lands, titles, monies and the like to be restored unto faithful Royalists. Yet things have changed in the decade I spent away from my home, and 'tis no easy thing appeasing those who have asked for restitution."

He eased his long legs over the side of the pallet, sending the pup tumbling to the floor, where the royal hand softened its landing and then patted the tiny bottom. As Charles stood to his impressive six-foot-four inches, he bade Keir, "Come, walk with me, Captain. I sense in you a need for movement . . . as captain of a ship I suspect you are unused to sedentariness. We will have more privacy, as well," he added with a quirk of his lips.

Keir stood, noting the people suddenly milling about, reminding him of hungry sharks circling another's kill in an effort to gain a succulent scrap. "And Your Majesty has a reputation for being a man of action, as well," he said politely.

Charles silently observed that the compliment was not accompanied by the slightest curving of the lips, as was usual. Captain Keir St. Andrews and his somber intensity intrigued him . . . and so did his obvious wealth.

"Tell me how I can help you, Captain." The king's long legs briskly ate up the distance as they moved about the gardens and bowling green, before passing the tiltyard and cockpit. A bevy of servants collected and followed in their wake, as did the ever-present horde of yapping, frolicking spaniels with which Charles Stuart always surrounded himself.

If this was privacy, Keir wondered what number of courtiers, servants and dogs constituted a crowd. Still, he appreciated the king's effort, supposing himself privileged to have been granted an audience with the monarch. As long as they strode along ahead of the trailing melee, most of whom seemed hard-pressed to keep up with the king's athletic pace, no one could hear what they were saying.

"I am prepared to offer you fair payment—more than fair—for any support I may receive from you, Your Majesty. I am a wealthy man, having privateered for Louis of France for the last several years." He glanced over at Charles. "I am willing to grant you my sole allegiance on the high seas for as long as I continue my privateering. I need only a letter of marque from you . . . nothing more, for I have my own ship. Or I can offer you a flat sum here and now," he finished bluntly.

"You've done that well?"

"I have, Sire."

"And how long have you been at sea, Captain St. Andrews?"

"Twenty years."

Charles looked him full in the face for a moment, assessing, calculating. "And you think I can be bought?"

"Nay, Majesty. I only hope that you'll seize the chance to fatten the royal coffers."

"Ah, very clever of you, Captain." Amusement—and something much more subtle—brightened Charles's eyes once more. "You may also suspect that I cannot resist the opportunity to tweak my cousin Louis's nose? To poke a hole in that fat treasury of his in payment for the niggardly treatment I received in France?"

"Aye, Your Majesty. 'Tis a more than gentlemanly form of vengeance."

Charles wondered at Keir's reply, however, for the bleakness of the set of his features never softened. But Charles, the brilliant diplomat, allowed none of his musings to alter his expression or voice as he asked, "But you appear a slightly younger man than I, Captain. What made you go to sea at obviously so tender an age? Or did you run away, as some lads will do, perhaps yearning for adventure and riches?" Before Keir could answer, Charles glanced ahead, a faraway look in his eyes. "I love the sea myself . . . but will never leave England again to cross it."

" 'Twas no love of the sea, Majesty," Keir said softly. "I was . . . forced to join the crew of a slaver when I was but eight years old."

"Faith, what an end for a boy!" the king exclaimed, a troubled frown darkening his naturally saturnine features. "And a slaver, yet."

"A slaver that turned to piracy after a mutiny of its crew against a tyrannical captain. But I would rather not speak of it . . . if it pleases Your Majesty," Keir added almost as an afterthought. "I would have you know that I am very wealthy . . . and willing to give England the chance to profit by our harassment of Spain's treasure galleons."

Charles again took in the man by his side, noting the

71

fashionable clothing, the cultured speech, the pride and dignity that bespoke intelligence and . . . yes, nobility. "You are English then?"

"I am."

"Then why do you privateer for my cousin Louis?"

Keir's profile hardened, and Charles noted the clenching of his fingers at his side.

"I was robbed of my birthright . . . the title and properties belonging to my father before he was killed fighting for yours." The words sounded stilted to Keir, and far off, as if someone else were saying them . . . saying the words he'd longed to utter for a score of years. And one day to Charles Stuart, restored King of England.

They were drawing near the king's apartments, moving down corridors where liveried guards lined the walls and pages and servants bowed as they passed. Doors were opened and before Keir knew how it had happened, he was alone with Charles II of England.

The king peeled off his clinging shirt and shrugged into a crimson satin dressing gown, belting it at the waist over his breeches. When he looked up, his dark gaze bored into Keir's. "Now you may tell me what title your father held . . . and of the one responsible for your misfortune."

Keir pulled in a breath and let it out slowly. "My father was James St. Andrews, fifth Earl of Somerset. I am Keir St. Andrews, rightfully sixth Earl of Somerset."

Charles held Keir's eyes for a long, meaning-fraught moment. Then he walked to an inlaid cabinet and poured two goblets of Madeira. He handed one to Keir. "But Giles St. Andrews is sixth Earl of Somerset. Surely he . . . ?"

Keir's eyed darkened. "How can my father's half-brother be his successor when James St. Andrews's legal heir is yet alive and of sound mind?"

Charles gestured to a chair, but Keir shook his head, his agitation in the face of all his old demons making him restless. He paced the antechamber, struggling to contain the collected pent-up emotion of twenty years of waiting

72

and hoping and planning.

And the one thing that had the power to make him weak-kneed . . . fear of failure.

Charles studied him silently over the rim of his glass for a space of time. "You were believed lost at sea after your abduction, then."

Keir started to spin around, caught himself, and swung more slowly to face the king. "My uncle, Giles St. Andrews, left me for dead upon the beach the night we received the news of my father's death. Someone fired the manor house at Somerset Chase in the name of Parliament—undoubtedly my uncle's henchmen. I presumed my mother and sister were killed in that fire, but—"

"You are saying, Captain, that Giles St. Andrews was not only an anti-Royalist at one time, but a murderer as well?"

"Aye, Your Majesty. I was not abducted by any seamen, but rather discovered by two men from that moored slaver in the Bristol Channel, taken aboard and nursed back to health. Of course," he added, "I was forced to become a part of the crew . . . payment, the captain claimed, for the saving of my life."

Charles stared into his goblet for a time. "I remember your father . . . a fine man. And a good friend of my father." He looked up at Keir. "Truth to tell, I can see some resemblance to him in you." He compressed his lips and narrowed his eyes thoughtfully. "Yet is it enough to clap a man into gaol for less than honorable activities during civil war? When all of England was in turmoil and men changed sides with dishonorable ease whenever the wind shifted?"

"Some men." The words were clipped, acrid. "My uncle was guilty of attempted murder—and probably responsible for the deaths of my mother and sister. That would constitute the basest treachery, not merely 'less than honorable activities.' "

Charles shook his head, the dark, shoulder-length curls of his periwig sliding over his satin-covered shoulders.

"Giles St. Andrews has been a faithful Royalist since, at least, Oliver Cromwell's death. How can I arrange his fall from grace on the word of just one man? One man who cannot prove he is who he claims he is? Or can you?"

The words sounded harsh to Charles's ears, but in saying them he had struck the core of the matter. He had no proof save Keir St. Andrews's word that he was, indeed, legal son of the late earl of Somerset. If that was who he really was. He could even be possibly a by-blow, which would account for the resemblance, and would also make Giles St. Andrews the legal earl.

Charles stood and held out his hands in a gesture of appeal. "Can you prove you are Keir St. Andrews, lawful son of the late earl of Somerset?"

Keir's features were as carved from the chalk cliffs of Dover, two faint spots of color the only indication that he was flesh and blood; and his eyes, now transformed to some tempered substance like glass . . . icy, gemlike, and utterly inanimate. The ghost of a shudder seemed to pass through his tall frame, and his knuckles turned white from the strength with which he fisted his hands at his sides.

His mouth worked, as if something within him were reluctant to speak. Yet he said, low, and with a control that Charles guessed cost him much, "Nay, I cannot."

# Chapter Five

"I have my father's ring, which I suppose anyone could have stolen," Keir continued, essaying to gather the scattered remnants of his composure before the king could answer. "And perhaps I could find some surviving relative who could tell if a man grown was the same child of twenty years ago. But it seems to me that the proof of my uncle's sins is what you really need, Sire. For that would clear the way for justice to be done, restitution given." He looked away, still fighting for control. And everything he stood to gain . . . or lose. His rock-hard profile was all he could give Charles in those few moments. Rock-hard and etched in desolate, angry frustration. "I suspect, Majesty, that everything else would fall into place if you believed that Giles St. Andrews had done murder."

"And that you cannot prove?"

A low, harsh laugh escaped Keir. "Prove? Why, I would have to comb the entire Spanish Main to discover the wereabouts of the two men who found me on the beach that night . . . if they are yet alive."

Charles nodded as Keir's gaze was drawn back to his. "And they were witness to what happened?"

"Your Majesty?" queried a voice through the antechamber door.

"Aye, Progers. Give us but a moment more," Charles called out. The sounds of canine yipping and the low hum of human voices came to them through the closed door.

Keir knew, a sinking sensation sluicing through him, that his moments alone with the king were drawing to an end.

"I know not how much they saw," he answered, unable to keep the bitter defeat from his voice. "I only know that they found me, more dead than alive, and took me back to the ship."

Charles replaced his goblet on the cabinet and turned back to Keir, his expression very sober. "Then you must find them . . . nay, find the priest, for I would not lend any credence to the word of a common sailor. Find the priest and bring him to me, for without a reliable witness to attest to Giles's treachery, your uncle is guilty of naught but assuming his dead brother's title in the wake of your disappearance."

"And what of my mother and sister?"

Charles shook his head. "We have heard nothing of foul play concerning any of the Earl of Somerset's late relatives."

Keir lowered his gaze for fear of revealing not only his crushing disappointment, but also exactly how hopeless he thought the endeavor. And how very much the prospect of failure affected him.

Charles put a reassuring hand on Keir's shoulder, squeezing until Keir was forced to meet the royal regard. "I have forgiven many a man for fighting against the Royalist cause at some time in these past twenty years. And, in truth, I have heard the rustling of rumors regarding Giles St. Andrews's association with the Parliamentarians years back. Yet, though I have overlooked the implications of these incriminating innuendos, I would have no qualms about punishing your uncle in the face of evidence of murder and unlawful usurpation of another's rightful title and holdings. Do you understand, Captain?"

Keir nodded, holding the king's gaze, even as a depleting emptiness seemed to drain the vitality from him . . . obliterate his hopes and dreams.

Charles walked him to the door, guiding him with his arm in a fatherly fashion. "I need not be bribed with the promise of Spanish wealth if your cause is just and real . . . although," he added meaningfully but with a touch of lightness, "neither would I refuse any monies you might cede to me if you are serious about bearing our letter of marque."

"My offer still stands, Your Majesty," Keir forced himself to say in a natural voice.

"Good. Then I will have the document drawn up and sent to your ship, Captain, and meanwhile you are welcome to attend any activities at Whitehall until your departure. Perhaps you have some need of . . . courtly diversion before you embark upon your travels, ummm?" He smiled lazily. "We are having a ball this very eve to celebrate the first anniversary of my Catharine's arrival at Whitehall after our marriage. Will you join us?"

What could he say? Keir thought, reeling under the barrage of emotions blasting him. The last thing he wanted to do now was attend a court function in the face of this stunning turn of events.

*Anything to tip the scales,* his rational side whispered, *anything . . .*

"The St. Andrews are in the country just now," the king told him, "so there will be no chance of an unpleasant encounter. And you can depend upon my discretion in this matter."

Straight-faced, struggling to fight stiff lips and sluggish tongue, Keir managed to suck in a calming breath before inclining his head and answering with admirable composure, " 'Twould be my pleasure, Your Majesty."


"Cap'n?"

Keir was dragged from his dark ruminations by his quartermaster's voice. As he strode up the ramp to the ship, he focused his regard on Peter Stubbs and Andrew Tremaine, his first mate. "Christ," he swore under his breath. Stubbs seemed to be everywhere he looked, waiting like a mother hen anxious over a wayward chick. The man was getting soft in his dotage, Keir thought sourly.

"Is aught amiss?" Keir asked with trenchant impatience, his body as taut as a tightly strung bow.

Stubbs looked at Tremaine and then jerked his head toward a pyramid of lumber on the dock behind Keir. The latter glanced over his shoulder with an impatient flick of his eyes . . . and paused.

Jonathon Dalton's son stood watching the ship, not bothering to hide behind the refuge of the stacked cargo. His arms were crossed over his chest in an attitude of defiance. Animosity blazed in his eyes. His face was almost as pale as the plaster on his forehead.

Keir looked away from the angry youth and joined his men on the deck. "He can stand there until Armageddon for all the good 'twill do him," he said. "Prepare to set sail at dawn, Master Tremaine," he told his first mate, a slim, blond young man clad in open-necked shirt and breeches. "We leave for Dover and favorable winds. And, Master Stubbs," he added, his gaze cutting to the latter, "see to the rounding up of any crew not aboard."

"But what of the cargo?" Stubbs asked, bewildered.

"Have it unloaded straightaway . . . and sent to the king, compliments of Captain St. Andrews."

He strode on past them then, his steps stiff, his spine rigid.

"The king refused 'im, I warrant ye," Stubbs muttered to Tremaine. "We ain't 'Master' *anything* 'less he's roarin' drunk . . . or been crossed." He shook his head. "Fer the love o' God, we just put into port not twenty-four hours ago!"

Tremaine nodded, his lean, even features registering bemusement. " 'Tis the wench," he said with a sagacious nod of his head. He spat over the nearby rail and into the river. " 'Tis bad luck to have a landlubber aboard . . . and especially a woman."

Stubbs grimaced and stared at Keir's retreating back. Then, realizing the captain was heading toward the quarterdeck and his cabin, the quartermaster hurried to catch up with him. "Cap'n, about the wench . . ."

He trailed off as Keir stopped and spun toward him. "I don't care if the king himself comes a-searching for her. She stays here. If need be you'll hide her in the hold, do you understand?"

"She goes to sea with the *Odyssey?*" Stubbs asked, non-plussed.

Keir gave a short bark of laughter, devoid of any trace of humor. "And why not? My luck couldn't get much worse, I assure you." He swung away.

"But—"

Keir was already disappearing down the hatch.

Peter Stubbs turned away and walked briskly toward the lower deck, a frown between his eyes. Well, he had an almost impossible amount of work to accomplish between now and dawn on the morrow. The captain would just have to take care of things in his cabin himself.

Keir's eyes adjusted to the dim passageway to his quarters just in time to see Jackie hauling Dudley through the door of the captain's cabin. If he hadn't been in such a foul mood he would have seen the humor in the thin, lanky boy lugging the low-slung, heavy body of the hound, the latter cooperating not in the least.

"C'mon, ye stinkin' cur," Jackie muttered. "Afore the cap'n returns 'n sees ye like this."

"And just what state is 'this?' " Keir inquired.

Jackie jumped, startled, releasing the dog's collar. Dudley collapsed on the floor with a grunt, legs splayed out like an overgrown, elongated frog. "C-C-Cap'n," he stammered, the flush of his face visible even in the dimness.

"Well?"

"D-D-D-Dudley got f-f-foxed, Cap'n, sir."

Immediately a feminine giggle floated through the open door of Keir's cabin. Jackie dropped his gaze at the sound and bit his lip, but Keir saw nothing amusing in the situation.

"And just who accomplished that?" he asked softly.

" 'Twas an accident," Jackie mumbled, his voice full of misery.

Even as he spoke the words, Dudley's short legs moved beneath him, struggling for purchase on the floor. The sound of his nails scratching the wood echoed hollowly in the passageway, and the dog let out a soft wimper.

" 'e's got te pee, Cap'n," Jackie explained with a sheepish shrug. "And if I don't get 'im out o' here—"

"I believe it's too late."

Jackie squinted down at the tipsy canine. A puddle was spreading from beneath him, seeping in all directions with the gentle sway of the ship. The smell of warm urine wafted upwards in the sudden silence.

"Get him out of here and clean up this mess." Keir stepped over the dog and through the cabin door. With a swift motion he slammed the portal closed, only to stop short at the sight of Brandy.

But not the Brandy he'd left earlier in the day. Surprise flickered in his eyes, and then just as swiftly disappeared.

Her hair was a tangled, copper-gold cloud about her features . . . features that were smeared with dried food and smudges of what looked like dirt. Her smock was also stained, and she reeked of ale. She was sitting in the middle of the floor, a tray balanced upon her lap, eating her meal with her fingers and sucking the grease from them with great—and noisy—gusto.

"What the hell . . . ?" he began, and then stilled, a slow, seething anger boiling up within him like the gathering steam from a tightly covered cauldron, fueled by the frustration he'd been feeling since his interview with the king.

Brandy's eyes widened slightly at the sight of him, and then she gestured toward her tray with a chicken bone. "Will you join me, Cap'n?" she asked innocently, as if unaware of anything amiss. She gave him an impish smile that would have affected the hardest of men . . . under different circumstances.

Without answering her, Keir took in the untidy cabin, garments draping from the drawers beneath the rumpled bed, linens lying over the open chest, personal articles strewn about the floor and table. Then his eyes came to rest upon his desk. His nautical instruments protruded from yawning drawers, his log was opened and positioned perilously close to the edge of the opened desk.

The ship listed gently with the unloading of a substantial piece of cargo and the log slid toward the floor. Keir, ignoring Brandy's enthusiastic "oops!" as she righted her tilted tray, made a dive for his precious journal, catching it just before it hit the floor.

His eyes slitted dangerously as his gaze returned to her. She was washing down her meal with the bottle of ale she'd retrieved after some of its contents had splashed onto the tray. "What do you think you're doing?" he said in a voice weighted with menace.

Brandy gave him another gamine grin and waved the bone in the air expansively. "Why, I'm entertaining m'self, Cap'n," she slurred sweetly. "Surely you cannot mind my having a bit of fun, can you?"

His expression smoothed into comprehension as he realized that she was feeling the effects of the ale. Yet her appearance, to say nothing of the chaos in the cabin, was the last straw in a bundle that had long weighed heavily upon him.

He leaned over and gripped her upper arm, hauling her to her feet. The tray went clattering to the floor as he took her other arm and held her like a rag doll inches above the floor. His angry gaze bored into hers, and he saw the flickering of fear that passed through their clear amber depths.

But he was beyond caution now.

"I ought to bind you like the little bawd you are and throw you into the Thames. I don't find your tricks the least bit amusing." He shook her for emphasis, and Brandy's head wobbled as if it were attached by a thread.

"If you don't like my presence here, Cap'n *Corsair,* then

81

let me go!" She struggled for purchase, but her feet found none. "An' put me *down* . . . or I'll . . . I'll scream!" she threatened with righteous indignation.

The frigid green eyes held hers for a long, quivering moment. Brandy returned the look admirably, shored up by ale-induced bravado, in spite of the wisp of fear that feathered up her spine. He was so strong, she thought irrelevantly. She could feel the coiled tension in him, in the steady steel grip that kept her suspended in midair.

Then, without warning, he released his hold and she dropped to the floor, landing with a jolt that did much to dispel her pleasant euphoria.

"You'll go when I'm ready to release you," he told her coldly, "and not a moment before."

Brandy struggled to her feet, rubbing her abused bottom with one hand. Her eyes narrowed at him in outrage as her anger blotted out caution. She opened her mouth to speak, but he cut her off.

"I suppose you were responsible for misusing the hound. Do you enjoy torturing dumb animals when you cannot find a human subject for your childish games?"

Guilt flashed in her eyes, but then her chin lifted, her lovely mouth pressing into a tight line. " 'Twas an accident. Surely you are more versed in the art of abuse than I, Captain."

"My actions are not under question here, Mistress Dalton," he said, his voice flinty.

"They most certainly—"

Keir turned away from her and reached for the bell-pull. "You'll discover that I have an unquenchable thirst for vengeance. Perhaps next time you'll think twice before you rifle through my belongings and abuse my hospitality."

Disbelief temporarily immobilized her tongue. *Hospitality?* she thought in consternation.

At that moment Jackie entered the cabin after a perfunctory knock. His cheeks flamed at the sight of Brandy and his gaze sought the cluttered floor. "C-C-Cap'n?"

"You will bring me water and tub for bathing."

82

"Aye, Cap'n."

"And Jackie," Keir added, "you are to remain in your cubicle except for seeing to my needs until further notice . . . all privileges suspended."

"Aye, Cap'n," the lad responded, his face going from red to white. "Will 'at be all?" he asked, his eyes avoiding Brandy.

After he'd gone, Keir ordered Brandy to clean up the mess she'd made. "I want everything exactly as you found it. The longer you take to restore this cabin to its original state, the colder will be your bathwater."

Brandy's gaze clashed with his. "I don't want a bath. I want off this ship."

Keir's eyes narrowed. He ought to let her go, get rid of her. For all of her innocent-seeming allure, she'd brought him nothing but bad luck . . . if he chose to be superstitious.

Brandy suddenly wished she'd drunk more ale, for her fear of him was increasing in relation to the return of sobriety. She stood her ground, however, as a sudden thought struck her.

"Why are you punishing Jackie?" she asked, genuine distress creeping into her expression.

Keir unbuttoned his doublet and shrugged out of the gray satin frock. " 'Tis none of your affair."

She raised her chin stubbornly. Keir noticed it quivered ever so slightly. *Damn,* he thought, *she's going to protect the lad*.

"Jackie is responsible for this room," he found himself saying. The late afternoon sunlight spilling through one of the windows caught and reflected the gold flecks in his irises as he stepped closer to her. "I don't know yet how you did it . . . or mayhap I do. Mayhap this *is* your affair," he said, trailing off, his words fraught with meaning. He took a slow inventory of her, allowing his eyes to scan her with suggestive, insulting leisure.

Color flagged her cheeks as Brandy remained rooted to the floor, catching his implication.

83

"But no matter the reason," he continued, "he was instructed to contribute to your diversion, if he so chose . . . not the destruction of my quarters."

"Jackie was not responsible for . . . this." The last word stuck in her throat like a fish bone.

"Perhaps not, but then I don't understand how it happens that he allowed *you* to sack the place."

Brandy averted her gaze, embarrassed at how it must look to him . . . standing there in his court finery and looking so smug and confident. And self-righteous, as if he were the injured party and not her.

But her concern for the lad whom she'd wheedled and charmed into letting her have her way ate at her more than her anger at the man before her. She'd heard of the cruel punishment meted out to seamen, and suddenly her little prank seemed so very pointless . . . especially in light of the fact that obviously Captain St. Andrews still had no intention of releasing her.

"How long will you confine him?" she pressed, in spite of herself.

Keir watched the play of emotions on her vivid features and something within him leapt to life. Something that responded to her compassion, her vulnerability, even as his instincts told him he was a fool, as weak as she was.

He unbuckled his swordbelt and laid it aside before loosening the lace at his throat, his earlier anger and frustration curiously eased. "So now we come to the truth about Brandy Dalton . . . Mistress Innocence," he said, voice full of mockery. "The wench would strike a bargain." His features hardened, unexpected disappointment knifing through him.

*What did you expect, fool?* taunted his cynical side.

"Nay! I'll strike no bargain with the likes of you, Captain!" She swung away in an effort to escape his probing perusal, his potent green eyes, and went to kneel before the built-in drawers beneath the bed. What did she care if his cabin boy languished in the dim nether regions of the ship until this grim, harsh man commanded otherwise?

84

Had Jackie helped her make an escape? Hardly.

Keir laughed softly behind her, a hollow sound that raised gooseflesh on her neck. "What a pity, brandy-eyes, for as quartermaster, Stubbs is responsible for meting out punishment for minor offenses. You'll find me far more lenient than he. I can also on occasion be persuaded to strike bargains with comely wenches."

Her fingers encountered his razor and closed around it, desperation driving her to contemplate using it as a weapon. She ignored his last comment and said, "I find it hard to believe that anyone could be more brutal than you, Captain St. Andrews."

"What did you think to gain with your little tantrum, ummm?" he murmured in a voice that was oddly soft and husky. His knuckles lightly stroked the velvet flesh of her neck beneath the tangle of her hair.

A bitter taste filled Brandy's mouth, even as a frisson of excitement flitted through her at his caress. She automatically brought her shoulder up to meet the side of her neck in an attempt to escape those disturbing fingers. "Master Stubbs said that you abhorred slovenliness." With a stealth she would never have judged herself capable, Brandy eased the razor from the drawer and sat back on her heels to hide it among the folds of her skirt.

Another low, humorless chuckle greeted her ears. "You are either dull-witted, sweetheart, or incredibly naive to think no one would see through your charade."

"Cap'n!"

She heard Keir's footfalls as he moved to open the door. As Jackie and Lug brought a tub and several buckets of steaming water into the room, Brandy slid the lower drawer into place and straightened the contents of the upper. The two other men trooped out and Brandy closed it.

"And now the desk," Keir said from across the cabin.

Brandy rose to her feet a trifle unsteadily, a death grip on the unfolded razor. She turned, feeling as if she were underwater, her movements slow and clumsy. When she saw Keir, however, shock was added to the jumble of emotions that were bumping through her.

He stood naked before the tub, preparing to step into it. Fire crept up her cheeks as her eyes encountered the lean, powerful form of a man unused to inactivity. Her gaze alighted on the shadowed area at the apex of his thighs and his desire blossomed before her, chasing the blush up to her hairline and down her neck.

The razor felt like a heavy stone in her fist, her arm dead weight. Her feet were as if lashed to the floor, failing to carry her close enough to him to put into play her desperate idea.

"Having regrets about last night?"

Brandy swallowed and forced herself to step toward him. That self-assured voice, that knowing look, that preening male pride . . . She halted before him and, with a puppet-like movement, jerked her right hand from behind the fullness of her skirt.

"Move aside, Captain." She forced the words through stiff lips.

His expression registered only mild surprise. Was she that transparent? some detached part of her wondered.

"And if I don't?" He crossed his arms over his naked chest, his knees flexing slightly as the ship listed again. The shuffling, scraping sounds overhead had been increasing ever since he'd returned, but Brandy was more concerned with the man before her and her imminent release than the activity abovedecks.

"Move away from the door," she repeated.

"But if I do, you'll have to contend with my men," he informed her matter-of-factly. "Surely you don't expect to fight off my entire crew with naught but a razor?"

The weapon in question began trembling, to Brandy's chagrin, the tip vibrating like the quivering edge of a plucked saw.

"I suspect, brandy-eyes, that you've no more stomach for sticking a man than seeing one punished." He stepped toward her. "Here, let me demonstrate what I mean."

Oh, how she hated him in that moment! For proving her inability to do him bodily harm . . . for proving she was lily-livered, as he claimed.

The trembling tip of the razor stilled as the hard, sleek planes of his belly came up against it. "All you have to do is push," he murmured, his eyes riveted to hers.

Anger, fear, frustration . . . all faded as she felt herself being sucked into the green vortex of his eyes, bottomless and beckoning as the deepest seas. And just as cold.

His hand was suddenly over hers, peeling back her frozen fingers one by one. The razor clattered to the floor. " 'Twould seem that not only are you truly innocent for a common wench, Brandy Dalton, but soft as butter, as well. Small wonder you were so sheltered."

His other hand came up and cupped her chin. He tipped her face toward the light from the window and examined the bruise on her apricot-tinted cheek. An urge to place a gentle kiss upon the abused flesh gripped him suddenly and, for a fleeting space in time he was held immobile, the uncharacteristic urge warring with the sensible side of him . . . the side of his personality that had been forged from the brutal lessons of a score of years at sea.

A heavy thud from the deck above broke the spell, and Keir's hand fell away. "You will continue putting things to rights in here," he said with quiet authority into her flushed face. "You will then lay out my blue doublet and breeches, and clean shirt." A corner of his mouth tilted lazily. "You surely know where they are after rifling through my possessions."

She turned her head, the snarled swath of her hair shielding her features from him. But not the attitude of utter defeat in bowed head and sloped shoulders.

"I am returning to Whitehall early this eve, and you will not only make my quarters presentable, but yourself as well. Do you understand?"

She nodded, a tear tracing its way down the side of her nose to her upper lip. She caught it with the tip of her tongue, unwilling to allow him to see the full extent of her humiliation. How she hated herself in those miserable moments, for she was weak, just like he'd said. She hadn't the courage of a mouse, for she could have at least made her escape to the deck with a flick of that razor. *Sheltered, shielded, cosseted,* she thought darkly. Oh, why had her mother and father not thought to prepare her for the real world outside the Hawk and Hound? Why had they been content to encourage her to read the silly stuff of Shakespeare when there were hard lessons to be learned of life?

The sight of the razor lying upon the floor roused her from her silent suffering. As she bent to retrieve it she noticed out of the corner of her eye that Keir had seated himself in the tub. Faith, he hadn't even put the blade away, out of her reach . . .

She straightened and snapped it shut with a sharp click, the thought crossing her mind that she should have taken it to her own heart rather than allow herself to be kept a captive in this manner.

# Chapter Six

Evening's purple shadows lengthened until they enfolded the Hawk and Hound and its yard like a soft, comforting blanket. The noise from within the tavern was muted, surreal against the soothing, silent backdrop of the night. The yard was empty, the animals bedded within the stable for the night. Moonlight spilled over the byre, limning its partially open door, but all was quiet within.

Into that dusky and placid pool of calm strode Simon Dalton, his footsteps resounding through the yard as sharply as the splash of an unwelcome intruder in a glass-smooth pond.

He lunged through the partially open back door, flinging the portal back against the wall in his agitation.

"Simon!" Margaret Dalton started, then swung toward him; an astonished Gladys turned from a large kettle of dirty dishes and slapped the palm of one wet hand against her ample bosom in reaction.

"Faith!" the latter exclaimed, but Margaret checked at the angry, frustrated expression on her son's face.

"They're leavin' London!" Simon burst out. "I know a ship preparin' to set sail when I see one . . . and they're gettin' ready to do just that!"

The color drained from Margaret's face. "Leavin' London?" she whispered through bloodless lips. "With my Brandy on board?"

"Oh, mistress, nay!" breathed Gladys, her splayed fingers digging into her chest. "They cannot just . . . just sail off with our Brandy!" She flung out one plump arm dramatically, as if envisioning the ship in question disappearing round a bend in the Thames.

Abra came skipping into the room just then, with Archie trotting alongside her.

"Get your father, Abra," Margaret ordered the child. "Hurry!" She turned back to Simon as Abra wordlessly left the room again, her usual flood of questions obviously bit back in the face of her mother's expression and tone of voice.

"Did Father get to see the king?" Simon asked as he searched Margaret's face.

She shook her head. "Humph," she grunted in disgust. " 'Twould take every spare coin we've put aside and then some to gain an audience with him afore all those nobles queued up to kiss the royal arse . . . and there still would be no guarantee of the king's willingness to intercede—"

"What's going on here?" Jonathon demanded with a frown as he came in from the taproom, a tray crowded with empty cups and tankards balanced between his large, capable hands. He looked at Simon. "Did you see your sister?"

"Nay," Simon answered bitterly. "They've hidden 'er well. She's more than likely trussed and imprisoned in the hold, and that blackguard St. Andrews is off to Whitehall again."

Margaret poured her son a draught of ale with shaking hand and offered it to him.

"But there's worse to come," he told Jonathon after gulping a sustaining swig. "They're unloadin' cargo like the devil was at their heels. The crew is returning and provisions are bein' brought in as fast as they empty the hold."

"By God!" cried Jonathon as he slammed the tray down with a clatter. They're getting ready to sail?"

Margaret watched his normally placid features whiten with fury, then splotch with color. Alarm surged through her. "Easy, Jon," she soothed, putting one hand on his brawny forearm. "We don't know for sure that Brandy is on that ship."

But even as she looked into his eyes, her own misted with emotion, she knew that she didn't believe her own words. *He doesn't deserve this,* she thought. This good, kind man who'd taken her in with a bastard babe all those years ago, and now protected that child as fiercely as if she were his own . . .

"Where else would she be, Mother?" Simon asked. "You saw the way those varlets ogled Brandy the whole time they were here . . . You saw the way that pirate St. Andrews watched 'er every move and threw his gold at father like he was the king 'imself!"

"They can't jest up an' leave London wi'out their cap'n, c'n they?" Gladys asked, obviously so caught up in the moment that she forgot her place. "If 'n 'e's at Whitehall . . ." She trailed off, her face turning pink.

" 'Tis all right, Gladys," Margaret assured her. "We know how you love Brandy."

"Everybody loves Brandy," Abra said from the doorway where she'd crouched to hug Archie to her. Great tears slid down her cheeks. "They can't just steal 'er!"

"Come here, child," Margaret said softly, and Abra relinquished her grip on the spaniel to fling herself into her mother's outstretched arms. As Margaret lifted her, Abra wound her arms around her mother's neck and her short legs about her waist, pillowing her head against Margaret's shoulder as her tears continued to flow.

"I miss B-Brandy," she said through trembling lips.

"Of course you do, sweeting," Margaret soothed. "We'll find her and bring her back, don't you worry now." Her eyes sought Jonathon's over Abra's head.

"Well, surely they'll let 'er go afore they sail," said Simon as he replaced his empty cup on the great oak sideboard that dominated one wall of the kitchen.

"I should hope to God they would at least have the decency to do that," Jonathon agreed. "Soiled and deflowered as no doubt she will be," he added under his breath.

Simon flushed, and Margaret averted her eyes, rocking the weeping Abra. "No one need ever know," she murmured over the little girl's soft sobs. "Just so she's unharmed."

Jonathon nodded his agreement as Gladys discreetly turned back to the mound of dishes. "And what decent man could refuse a prize like Brandy because of somethin' that wasn't her fault?" Jonathon said in a threatening tone. "I always intended to provide her with a decent dowry so she could marry a good man." He plowed the fingers of both hands through his silvered, chestnut hair.

"Well I, for one, intend to be dockside at dawn," Simon declared. "They'll release 'er afore they leave or they'll have one more passenger aboard than they bargained for," he vowed.

"Nay, son," Jonathon corrected. "Two."

After Versailles, the hodgepodge of buildings that made up Whitehall Palace failed to impress Keir. A barge let him off at Whitehall Stairs and he followed the crowd toward the banqueting hall where the celebration was being held. As the Hall came into view, he acknowledged that this was the most beautiful edifice of the complex cluster of buildings, pure Roman classicism in style.

Yet he did little more than note briefly its rusticated masonry, tall square-paned windows and Ionic columns before he entered the tall double doors leading inside, his thoughts on his mission this eve. Even though Charles had assured him that the St. Andrews of Somerset Chase were presently in the country, Keir felt the tension slowly build within him, until by the time he arrived at the reception, he felt the beginnings of a now familiar ache creeping up the back of his neck and over his skull like a steel band.

He decided to remain on the periphery of the festivities as an unobtrusive observer. It just so happened that tables laden with refreshments skirted a section of one wall of the great room, thus affording Keir his pick of food and drink.

An orchestra played from the railed balcony that ran the length and width of the Hall, and at first Keir sipped a glass of brandy, pretending to study his surroundings as he waited for the spirits to soothe his jangling nerves, slow his thrumming heart. Unaccustomed to the unwelcome jumble of emotions that had played havoc with his temper since he'd landed upon English shores, Keir deliberately took his time in a most thorough assessment of, first, architect Inigo Jones's Banqueting Hall, and then the colorful courtiers who peopled it. Couples were already taking advantage of the semiseclusion of the windowed alcoves set at regular intervals in the two longer walls of the rectangular room. A bevy of court beauties and the gallants who escorted them laughed, drank, danced, and flirted outrageously.

The stifling scent of a host of perfumes combined with the aroma of food; the musky smell of sweating bodies beneath layers of elaborate clothing to remind him that he vastly preferred the rolling deck of the *Odyssey* with the fresh, tangy salt air blowing through his hair, caressing his face . . .

*Or the hills and woodlands, the orchards and fields of Somerset Chase,* a disturbing voice reminded him.

Sudden, poignant longing seized him, seeping through his body like an aphrodisiac . . . and to counter it, he drained the goblet of wine in his hand like a man dying of thirst.

"Why, Captain St. Andrews," gushed a feminine — and familiar — voice.

Keir looked into the bright blue eyes of Lady Rosalyn Downing, and he felt relief waft over him in a refreshing swell. He smiled, forcing his closed, distant expression to warm.

He took her offered hand and bowed over it, brushing the backs of her fingers with his lips. "How good to see you again, Lady Rosalyn," he murmured as he straightened. "Would you care for something to drink?" He gestured to a decanter of punch that rested on the table beside them.

Lady Rosalyn flipped open her fan and waved it with short, rapid strokes in an effort to cool her face. "Aye, thank you, Captain. 'Tis just what I need after a vigorous courante. La! but His Majesty has energy enough for three, even in this August heat." She made a moue with her painted lips. "Those with the slightest bit of sense are still in the countryside, away from the heat and threat of plague."

With a forced smile, Keir handed her a goblet of punch and changed the subject. "You look quite lovely tonight, Lady Rosalyn."

She canted her head up at him, her cascade of blond ringlets bouncing with the movement. She tapped his chest with her fan. "And you are the epitome of fashion," she countered. "Your costume is very *à la mode*." She scrutinized him with lazy boldness, her gaze taking in his silver-trimmed royal blue doublet and petticoat breeches. "Who is your tailor here in London?"

"This is my first time in England," he lied without a qualm. "I had this made in Paris."

Her widened eyes told him that she was impressed. Her fan slowed and she sipped her drink, eyeing him over the glass rim. "I would wager that you are a privateer."

She paused and one corner of Keir's mouth lifted in answer.

"And if you do not hail from England," she continued, "then you do not sail for the king."

"You are most astute, milady."

But Rosalyn obviously had not yet discovered enough to satisfy her curiosity.

"You've been to Paris . . . why, faith! but you must sail for Louis of France."

"Aye."

"Then you are not related to the St. Andrews of Somerset?"

Emotion clotted in his throat, and Keir straightened the bright white fall of lace peeking out from one sleeve to hide the look in his eyes that must surely belie his words. "St. Andrews of Somerset?" he repeated, regaining his composure and meeting her regard once again. "Not that I am aware. You see, I was born in Scotland and ran off to sea as a lad. My family was one of humble means, my father a fisherman." He shook his head. "Nay, I have no relations in England that I know of."

She nodded her head and pursed her lips thoughtfully, obviously not the least repentant about her rapid-fire questions. "Let me guess," she continued, allowing her fan to fall from its ribbon around her wrist and then fingering the creamy lace about her décolletage.

Keir's eyes automatically followed her slender fingers, as she'd obviously intended. She allowed the backs of them to graze the smooth flesh of her rounded breasts which protruded from her bodice in two provocative mounds. "You are come to offer your services to the king of England, as well as his French cousin?"

Keir's eyes narrowed a fraction, his mind working behind his facade of congeniality. Here not only was a shrewd and beautiful woman, but one whom he might consider as a wife, if she were unwed . . . and willing.

Yet somehow the thought soured even as it was formed, for Keir could just as easily envision her a permanent fixture at court, making overtures to newcomers even as her children remained hidden away in the country with a nursemaid.

Oh, yes! And while he grew old with his children surrounding him, but not a wife, lover, and helpmeet.

*Well, what did you expect, fool? If you want a noblewoman, you must accept that very real possibility.*

A *tableau vivant* unexpectedly flared within his mind with all the force and brilliance of a display of pyrotechnics. A young girl sitting on a stoop in the sunshine, contentedly stroking a sleeping spaniel. A young girl lovingly kissing a small dark head at her side . . . laughingly

95

consorting with the urchins of the neighborhood . . .

He pushed away the unwelcome memory with annoyance.

. "And where is my lady's husband?" Keir asked, ignoring Lady Rosalyn's last question. "For surely one as lovely as yourself is not without an escort?" he added to soften the bluntness of his question.

She smiled a seductive smile, her fingers traveling from her neckline to the string of sapphires about the slender stem of her throat. "Of course you wouldn't know," she said in a voice as husky as a purring feline. "But I am the only daughter of the Earl of Ashcroft." She leaned toward him conspiratorially, all but her nipples tantalizingly revealed in the pale glow of the huge candelabrum hanging overhead. "At the moment, I am considered the catch of the court, Captain St. Andrews."

She held out her empty punch goblet for him to refill. "Since you are new to London, I would be happy to make introductions."

Alarm shrilled like a clarion in his head. His thoughts tumbled over one another until he sternly told himself to bring them under control. He inclined his head in polite acknowledgment. "I would rather observe for now," he told her. "I tend to be of a . . . retiring nature, Lady Rosalyn, and disinclined to fling myself into the thick of things social."

Her expression turned to one of surprise, and then disbelief. "I'll warrant that you aren't the least bit so *disinclined* when you lead your boarding parties at sea, Captain."

His mouth quirked at her riposte. "My quartermaster is the first to board a prize, not I."

She shrugged and smiled at him from behind a very artfully employed fan. "Well then, at the least you can lead one dance for a lady, ummm?"

It hadn't been his intention to participate any more than nominally in this affair. Rather, he'd wished to watch and learn . . . perhaps to make his presence known to the king as a sign of good will, and then make his exit. When he was formally announced at Whitehall, it would be, God willing, as Keir St. Andrews, sixth Earl of Somerset. Certainly not as some obscure ship captain claiming to be an earl while Giles St. Andrews was firmly ensconced at Somerset Chase as well as in the minds of his English peers.

"I reget but I cannot tarry, milady. I sail before dawn."

"Surely you cannot refuse a lady's request?" She glanced aside and caught sight of the king making his way toward them, a head above everyone else. "And here is His Majesty himself, Captain. You must pay him your respects and then dance at least once with me or I shall never forgive you."

*What a brazen little wench she is,* Keir thought, deliberately tamping down the apprehension burgeoning through his chest. *She knows just how to get what she wants . . .* But then what else could he expect, he acknowledged with rue, from an earl's pampered daughter?

Keir drew in a sustaining breath and slowly blew it out. "Your Majesty," he greeted with a deep bow as Charles came up to him, wishing he'd ignored the desperate ambition that had sent him, unprepared, into the enemy's camp with nothing more than torturous, twenty year old memories.


The barge carried Keir toward the docks where the *Odyssey* was moored. The soft splash of the bargeman's pole dipping in and out of the water was somehow comforting to Keir, for over the years the sea had insidiously crept into his blood, even as he'd dreamed of and planned to return to his homeland one day for good.

*Damme! but you're the image of James St. Andrews, may he rest in peace!*

The Earl of Ashcroft, Rosalyn's father, had come up to talk to Charles and Lady Rosalyn as the king had engaged the reticent Keir in light conversation.

Chagrined at first in the wake of Ashcroft's words, Keir

realized almost immediately that here was the first glimmer of proof of his identity, if not his uncle's perfidy. His glance had met Charles' for a moment, but he had discerned no message within the dark depths of the royal regard.

"I hail from Scotland, your lordship," Keir had answered after a moment's hesitation. "And as I told the lady Rosalyn, I have no immediate kin in England that I'm aware of." What harm, he'd asked himself later, if Giles were to get wind of his appearance at Whitehall? Keir had revealed his Christian name to neither the earl nor his daughter, and he was quite certain that he could trust the king to keep it to himself. If his uncle did hear of it, let him fret and formulate all he wanted, for Keir intended to return with proof positive against any claim Giles might make . . . and at any cost.

Keir had made his exit not long afterwards, lingering only to pacify Rosalyn with two dances. He'd looked over the men and women of Charles Stuart's Restoration court with an assessing eye. But while he might have sought at least to familiarize himself with some of the faces, his presence was ultimately attributable to the king's suggestion that morning.

Rosalyn had cooperatively pointed out the Duke of Buckingham and several other confidants of the king. The Countess of Castlemaine, of course, he'd recognized immediately, yet the woman whom he'd partnered for a stately pavane and then a branle was obviously intrigued by the aura of mystery Keir knew would surround an entirely unknown face at court . . . and one on whom the king had bestowed the royal attentions. Lady Rosalyn had made her interest very clear and had asked when he would be returning to London.

"That I cannot say," Keir had told her truthfully. At her obvious disappointment, he'd assured her, "I do know that when I return 'twill be to stay . . ."

Keir roused himself from his musings, common sense telling him it was absurd to hope that a woman like Rosalyn Downing could be interested in the likes of him, even were he to regain his lost title. She was genteel through and through, while he'd literally been suckled by the seas and seasoned by the sailors who roamed them.

He paid the bargeman and stepped onto solid ground, up the stone steps and toward the wharves, his strides long and brisk. As he passed the spot where Simon Dalton had kept vigil during the daylight hours, Keir made a sudden, unexpected decision.

" 'Evenin', Cap'n," Ollie and another sailor greeted Keir in unison from their watch at the top of the ramp.

"Good evening," Keir answered. "Are we clear of cargo?"

"Aye, Cap'n," Stubbs answered from behind him.

Keir turned and looked into his quartermaster's shadowed face. "Provisioned as well?"

"Aye."

"Good. You may tell Tremaine that we weigh anchor before dawn . . . four o'clock, to be exact."

Stubbs followed Keir toward the quarterdeck. "Four of the clock? In the *dark?*"

Keir turned to his man. "Are you afraid of the dark, Peter?"

"What . . .? O' course not! But 'tis risky to guide a ship the size of the *Odyssey* out into the river without benefit of daylight."

Keir smiled grimly, the shadows sinisterly emphasizing its utter lack of humor. "There is little traffic on the Thames that early, and, of course, I'll be on deck to bolster your courage if need be."

Keir swung away and left a sputtering Stubbs standing below the ladder to the quarterdeck.


She was curled up in one corner of the cabin, asleep. With Dudley.

Dudley?

Keir closed the door behind him noiselessly and moved

99

with quiet steps toward the sleeping girl. The hound opened his eyes drowsily and threw a jaundiced glance at Keir as he paused before them, his shadow cast across girl and dog like a full-spread fishing net.

*How touching,* Keir thought, and abruptly turned away to prevent himself from staring at Brandy Dalton like an uninitiated youth anchored in adoration. The hound slept with Jackie, rarely in Keir's cabin, for the two were almost inseparable. As he undressed, Keir wondered just how she'd persuaded Jackie to give up his canine companion.

*You know perfectly well how she accomplished it. The wench could charm the breeches off a grown man. Surely persuading Jackie to part with Dudley for a night had been child's play to her.*

He glanced over at the sleeping pair once again. Dudley's eyes were closed once more, and he emitted a soft groan of contentment as he nestled his muzzle more deeply into the folds of Brandy's skirt. Evidently Dudley had held no grudge against his new friend for sharing her ale with him. Damme, the dog would be sitting at the board in the wardroom if someone didn't keep an eye on him.

*Sly devil,* Keir thought and leaned his head back against the wall behind the bed. His half-closed eyes moved from dog to girl, and he knew a sudden, alien urge to smile at the sight of the opportunistic hound. The temptation, however, was just as speedily squelched as Keir realized that Brandy Dalton obviously preferred sleeping on the hard floor with the dog to gracing Keir's own bed. He studied her most thoroughly while she slept on, her lips slightly parted, her upturned profile enchanting in the light from the single whale-oil lamp he'd left burning.

She'd cleaned her face and brushed her glorious hair, but she still wore her own stained clothing. Keir frowned. So she wouldn't wear anything of his. Well, that was just one more puzzling aspect about Brandy Dalton. One would think the wench would consider herself fortunate to have attracted the attentions of a rich, and — some would say—not unappealing ship captain. Most unwed—and many wed—lower class women would jump at the chance, Keir knew from experience. Nor, he suspected, would a tavern maid be averse to wearing a man's clothing, especially since Keir had heard that it was all the rage for young actresses in London to dress like youths to show off their charms to advantage.

So either Brandy Dalton cared nothing about her appearance, or was much too uppity for one of her class.

Keir immediately dismissed the first conclusion, for except for the mess she'd intentionally made earlier, there was nothing slovenly about her. As for her refusal to wear anything of his, it didn't seem out of character from what he knew of her. For a tavern girl, yes, but then again, she wasn't a common wench. Serving wenches were usually tough . . . many of them supplementing their meager income by taking customers to their beds. And they wouldn't be above using a knife—or a razor—if it meant protecting themselves.

But Brandy Dalton couldn't even hurt him with a keen-edged razor pressed against his belly.

His eyelids drooped even further, the gamut of emotions he'd run since this morning taking its toll. But he kept his slitted gaze on Brandy. Her people seemed decent and hardworking, yet surely they'd not gone into inn-keeping without teaching their daughter to fend for herself. Most inns passed from generation to generation, and although Jonathon Dalton and his wife may have insisted on keeping their daughter out of the hands of licentious customers, they had evidently neglected to teach her the rudiments of survival in a city tavern. And that was, in Keir's opinion, tantamount to leaving her extremely vulnerable, as his men had proven, for Jonathon Dalton and his son couldn't protect her every minute of the day.

Keir closed his eyes wearily. Thoughts of Jonathon Dalton reminded him that he was sailing early in the morn just to avoid trouble with the inn-keeper and his son. Simon Dalton wasn't stupid. If he had any intelligence at all, he would have recognized the preparations being made for the *Odyssey* to weigh anchor. And then told his father.

Keir would have bet half his wealth that Dalton and son—and possibly reinforcements—would show up at dawn to retrieve Brandy. Or die in the attempt. So just what was he trying to prove by keeping her on board while he sailed for the Spanish Main? With his crew certainly harboring resentment against not only a landlubber aboard, but a female . . . the presence of whom was considered even worse luck than wearing the color blue at sea?

"Well, mayhap your luck has run out anyway, St. Andrews," he murmured. "Mayhap you are chasing shadows, all your amassed wealth availing you naught in your futile quest to regain all that rightfully belongs to you."

He opened his eyes to look at Brandy one last time. "So what harm to take what pleasures are left to you . . . and with whom you wish?" he mused softly. "What harm to find physical surcease with one particular wench before returning her to England?"

*How can you be certain you will return her to her family alive, when you cannot be certain of your own safety on the high seas?*

He stretched out his long frame and ignored the voice. He would return to England, he vowed silently, and with Father Tomas. If the priest were alive, Keir would find him. And if he were dead . . .

His mind refused to contemplate the possibility.

At any rate, he would send a goodly sum of gold to the Hawk and Hound for the use of Jonathon Dalton's daughter. Beyond that, however, he hadn't the slightest inclination to take further action where the girl was concerned . . . or examine his motives.

# Chapter Seven

Brandy slowly opened her eyes, reluctant to leave the warm cocoon of the coverlet that had been thrown over her. Through the window across the cabin she could only discern a velvet blackness, indicating that it was still dark. The room, too, was shadowy except for one lamp burning on the wall above the table.

But something was different . . . the movement of the ship had pulled her from her slumber.

She sat up suddenly, her cramped, sore muscles making her actions awkward and bringing home the disconcerting fact that she was still a prisoner on board the *Odyssey*.

She flung the blanket aside, noticing in the process that Dudley was gone . . . and Captain St. Andrews's bed had been slept in. She stood with unaccustomed stiffness and almost immediately slumped down again as nausea spiraled upward from her stomach through her throat.

The ship was definitely moving, the creaking of its timbers coming to her now. Footsteps beat a faint tattoo on the deck overhead, yet, strangely, the sound of raised voices was missing.

Dear God above, they were moving out into the Thames!

Brandy surged to her feet again, ignoring everything but the need to get out of the cabin and onto the deck before it was too late. The door wouldn't budge, however, when she yanked at the latch.

"Lug!" she cried out in alarm. "Lug! Let me out!"

But there was no sound from the hall beyond the door. "Jackie!" she called this time, pounding her fist against the wood. "Jackie!"

Muted sounds from overhead reached her ears in answer, but no one came to her rescue. She swung back towards the middle of the cabin, her mind working frantically. Her gaze fell upon the desk and she lurched toward it, fighting the flutterings of queasiness in the pit of her stomach. Pulling down the desk front, she grabbed for the lead inkwell, forgetting that it was bolted down.

With a low cry of frustration, she jerked open the drawer holding several navigational instruments and snatched the first one she saw, a heavy brass sextant. Heaving it over her shoulder, Brandy took a deep breath before attempting to lob it toward the window beside the bed.

A grip of iron stopped her arm in mid-motion. Fingers squeezed until, with a cry of pain, Brandy slackened her hold on the instrument. Keir released her arm, and in a swift, well-executed movement rescued the precious sextant before it hit the floor.

"Just what in hell do you think you're doing?" he charged as he straightened and faced her.

"Trying to leave this ship, that's what!" Her eyes were brass-bright with fury. "How dare you try to leave London with me aboard as your prisoner?" She spun about and made for the window directly across the room. "Help!" she cried as she smashed her fist against the heavy glass.

A hairline crack zigzagged its way down the pane before Keir's arm wrapped tightly about her body, slamming her back against him and pinioning her while his other hand came crashing down over her mouth.

Pain took her breath away as he locked her outflung arm between their bodies. An involuntary moan sounded against the callused palm of his hand and tears blurred her vision.

Instantly his hold loosened enough to ease the pressure

104

on her twisted arm, but the hand over her mouth remained firm as he hissed into her ear, "Stop your hysterics this instant or I'll have you trussed and tossed into the hold . . . do you hear me?"

Brandy tried to shake her head negatively, a distorted growl of defiance issuing from her throat. "I assure you, wench, this cabin will seem like paradise compared to what you'll find belowdecks."

She stilled, her angry sounds ceasing in the face of his threat. She could only imagine the horrors of the hold of a ship.

Keir released her and spun her around, gripping her by the shoulders. The slow seepage of blood from her lower lip sent regret twisting through his chest, tangling around his heart and squeezing.

Her face was pale, the scarlet smear across her lip and purplish bruise on her cheek chastising him for his actions and those of his men more effectively than any words. For one mad moment he actually considered returning her to the docks . . . releasing her into the care of Jonathon Dalton and the rest of her family.

Brandy read the flicker of indecision in his eyes and sought to press the slight advantage. "Please?" she whispered into the hushed quiet of the cabin.

Her eyes appealed to him for her freedom in mute eloquence, the beautiful amber-brown color seeming to liquefy with emotion. "Must I beg you?" she added in a voice that reminded him of Elizabeth St. Andrews's with a shattering poignancy.

His fingers dug into her shoulders reflexively at the memory, longing sweeping through him like a powerful gale before he realized what was happening. She was appealing to his weaker side . . . a side that he'd ruthlessly repressed until he'd actually begun to believe that he'd succeeded in burying it forever. Burying it beneath a score of years of deprivation and danger at sea.

"We are bound for the Caribbee Islands," he told her when he'd found his voice. "I will release you

105

upon our return to England, you have my word."

Stunned, Brandy could only stare at him, slack-jawed. The words *Caribbee Islands* danced like taunting devils across her consciousness. The Caribbee Islands were halfway around the world . . .

"—can act in a civilized fashion and remain here with me, or you can continue your childish and destructive behavior to your heart's delight in the hold . . . for the duration of the voyage," Keir was saying. His words were clipped and unemotional, as if he were issuing a directive to a disobedient crew member.

He released her and moved to the washbasin.

"How can you tell me my behavior is uncivilized when you mean to just—just *hie* me off to the other side of the world!" she sputtered when she'd recovered her wits. " 'Tis . . . 'tis against all common decency!"

Keir wet the edge of a cloth in the basin, then went to dab her mouth. "I can do whatever I damned well please. I am master of this ship . . . and everyone on it. And 'decency' is the byword of weakness—most certainly not mine."

Brandy turned her head away from his gently marauding fingers. "Don't ever touch me again, Captain St. Andrews," she told him. "Not in friendship, not in anger. And never with intent to dishonor me." Her eyes met his, determination hardening hers to match the bleakness in his. "And of a certainty you are not *my* master. You cannot remain on guard every moment of every day, and I swear to you there will come a time when your back is turned."

He raised an eyebrow. "And then?"

"I shall either kill myself . . . or you."

A fraudulent smile curved his lips. "But we've already proven that you haven't the heart to do more than take advantage of a dumb animal, Mistress Dalton."

Mortification at the memory of her inability to do him bodily harm assaulted her and she clenched her fists at her sides in frustration. "Just because I'm not a man . . .

no plundering, pillaging pirate taking what I please—*doing* as I please, doesn't mean I haven't the courage to stand up for my convictions!"

Keir took hold of her evading chin with a firmness that made it impossible for Brandy to jerk away without appearing the recalcitrant child and losing what little dignity she had left to her. With an unexpectedly soft touch, he cleansed away the traces of blood. "Just what convictions are those?"

The condescending tone of his voice was irritating in the extreme, and she fought the urge to knock his hand away. He was toying with her, she realized, and decided that she wouldn't give him the satisfaction of further protestations or explanations of her beliefs. "You wouldn't understand," she told him, an uncharacteristic sullenness creeping into her voice. "You make a mockery of everything I say. What use to speak of things decent to a man like you when, by your own admission, you know naught of decency?"

"And you, in your righteous innocence, are a paragon of decency, no doubt." His hand fell away from her mouth, but not so his gaze. It rested briefly on her lips before delving into her eyes. Whatever she was, he acknowledged grudgingly, she was not the common tavern wench. The pain in her eyes at his insulting words was touchingly apparent in her expressive features. *Christ,* he thought, *she's as soft and vulnerable as an inexperienced child.*

For a moment, Keir knew regret. Was that why something deep within him would not let her go? Could she perhaps represent those traits that, of necessity, he'd learned to regard with disdain, yet at the same time drew him to her with all the allure of a missing piece of his life? A missing piece of his life that the child reft of his childhood secretly mourned?

He turned away and dropped the cloth into the basin, thoroughly disgusted with the bent of his thoughts. "I will send Jackie to you," he said over his shoulder. "And if there are any more scenes like the one I witnessed moments ago, you will force me to prove that I do not make idle threats." He swung toward her, leveling his cold, implacable gaze at her once more.

But Brandy refused to answer or meet his eyes. Turning her back to him, she stared stonily up at the window she'd struck, the fracture that forked down the glass seeming to represent the ever-widening rent in the fabric of her life.

"Cap'n?"

Keir swung away from the rail and the sight of the sky pearling with crepuscular light. "Aye, Peter?"

"There's . . . well, there's grumblings among the crew about havin' a woman on board."

Keir grimaced. "And, no doubt, Smythe is the ringleader."

Peter Stubbs shrugged. "Can't blame 'im. Every sailor needs somethin' te blame mishaps at sea for."

Keir lifted his face to the wind. "But not you, Peter," he said softly. "You know better."

Stubbs ran his fingers through his hair, a sigh escaping his lips only to be immediately swept away by the wind. "Damn it, Cap'n, but how d'you expect me to quell the makin's of a mutiny when they have every right to resent the wench's presence on shipboard?"

Keir's expression turned hard as he faced his quartermaster. "Every right? Hardly. And I've always stood behind you, Peter . . . as have my officers." He glanced out to sea again. "I've other matters on my mind at the moment."

Stubbs nodded and, reluctance slowing his movements, moved to swing away.

"Have you ever heard of a seaman by the name of Arthur Biggs?" Keir's words brought the quartermaster up short. "Or a Spanish Jesuit called Father Tomas?"

Stubbs turned back, his brows drawing together in a thoughtful frown. "Round the Main?"

"Aye."

"Seems like I might've heard o' the priest before, Cap'n, but them Catholic Spaniards have more clergymen than's decent, to my way o' thinkin'. There could be a score of 'em by that name anywhere on the Main."

"And so there could," Keir mused softly. "But I hope not."

Stubbs studied his captain's strong profile. "That why we left London so sudden?"

Keir nodded. "I must find the priest. I thought perhaps the sailor Biggs could tell me of the former's whereabouts if I found him first, but from what I recall of Arthur Biggs, he'd have been most anxious to disassociate himself from the pious Father Tomas."

Andrew Tremaine appeared from the shadows. As he approached them, Keir was suddenly aware of just how many other crew members were about. Mindful of the jealousy that could be engendered by too close and personal an association with the quartermaster who, though at the top of the hierarchy of the common sailors, was not an officer, Keir instructed Stubbs in a louder voice, "Bring the charts to my cabin. And, Tremaine, report to me there, as well, in ten minutes with Jackson, Reeves, and Foucher."

"She will remain in Master Tremaine's cabin until I tell you otherwise," Keir told Jackie, choosing to ignore Brandy and the questions with which he suspected he would be bombarded in typical female fashion.

While seeming to shuffle through several charts, Keir watched covertly as Jackie ushered her from the cabin. Although she'd performed her morning ablutions, her face was pale within the bright nimbus of her hair. She'd also refused to don clean clothing, obviously clinging stubbornly to the one thing that made her feel she had some type of control, no matter how minimal, over her situation.

Lips pressed together, her head tilted at a regal angle, Brandy followed Jackie from the cabin with as little notice of Keir as he'd deliberately taken of her. Yet, just before the door closed behind them, he caught the sudden, defeated slump of her shoulders.

Brandy entered the tiny cubicle that served as the first mate's sleeping room. Sudden panic surged through her, for not only was there room for little else but a single bed that folded up into the wall, but the room, unlike the captain's, lacked windows of any sort. A lone lantern held the gloom at bay and, in Brandy's mind, not very successfully.

Claustrophobia enveloped her like a smothering shroud at the thought of being locked in such a dark, confined space. She turned to Jackie, her eyes shaded with distress, and clutched at his arm. "Surely you won't leave me here?" she asked, the pitch of her voice raised unnaturally with apprehension.

The youth's gaze slid away from hers. "Aw, Mistress Brandy, I'm only followin' the cap'n's orders. He bade me—"

"You're angry with me, aren't you? For being responsible for your punishment . . ."

He shook his head, the loose ends of his brown hair flying with the force of the movement. "Nay."

"Aye, you are!" she told him in a panic-induced rush, her fingers unconsciously digging into his flesh. "If your quarters are anything like—like *this*—I wouldn't blame you . . . but I cannot abide closed in places—"

"Jackie!" Keir's voice came to them from the passageway.

"Aye, Cap'n!" Jackie called over his shoulder, and tried to pry Brandy's rigid fingers from his arm. "I *have* to g-g-go," he told her, the war between compassion and obedience apparent on his face. "D-d-don't think about it . . . 'twill not be long, I p-p-promise."

Brandy looked from his eyes down to his hand as his fingers worked over hers. Reason came rushing back. What must this boy think?

She released his arm and stepped away, hugging her waist with crossed arms and drawing in several deep breaths of the close cabin air. "Then go," she whispered, fighting the nausea that insidiously crept up from the pit of her stomach.

"I'm sorry, m-m-mistress," he mumbled before making a hurried exit. Brandy would have found his adolescent awkwardness as he stumbled through the door comical had she not been so preoccupied with her own frenetic feelings.

Only a few times in her life had she found herself overpowered by an irrational terror when in close quarters. Accepting her fear of confined spaces with typical equanimity, she'd deliberately forced herself to deal with the problem whenever it surfaced. Her determination had served her well, for after her early years, she'd convinced her parents that she'd outgrown her flaw.

And, to a large extent, she'd overcome much of it by sheer force of will. Until now. Until she'd been forced into a room little larger than a privy, and the combination of airless gloom and the soft sway of the ship as it rode the swells assaulted her like a two-fisted punch . . . one to her mind, and one to her middle.

The blood rushed to her head, searing her face and neck, and Brandy felt a scream clot in her throat. Her self-control dissolved like a dollop of butter in a mug of warm ale as an unbelievably powerful instinct to flee gripped her and propelled her across the cubicle in two strides. She attacked the door, her fingers clawing at the wooden panel. It wouldn't budge.

Then, just as suddenly as it had come, the heat drained from her head, leaving her cold and clammy.

She opened her mouth to cry out, but bitter bile rose to press against the back of her throat, sending her spinning around in search of a chamber pot. She spotted one beneath the bed and lurched toward it like a drunken sailor. Nearly unsetting it in her desperate grab, Brandy hugged the noisome vessel with welcoming arms . . . and heaved.

Keir watched his officers file into the room . . . First Mate Andrew Tremaine, Second Mate Will Jackson, Third Mates John Reeves and Geordie Ames, and Sailing Master Alain Foucher. Peter Stubbs brought up the rear, with Jackie slipping in just before the quartermaster closed the door.

Keir noted the easy confidence Peter affected in a roomful of officers. It was one of the things that had drawn Keir to him when they'd been shipmates on the Main for several years under another's command. Peter Stubbs knew his place, but he never allowed himself to be cowed by an officer . . . not even the pompous Frenchman, Foucher, one of Louis XIV's darlings.

"No doubt you wonder why we set sail so quickly after docking in London," Keir began. He motioned to Jackie, who immediately began uncorking several bottles of Madeira. "I will triple your wages—and those of every crew member—should we fail to intercept anything worthwhile between here and the Main this one last time. If we capture a galleon or two, I'll double every man's share of the plunder."

"And we fly the English flag now, *oui?*" commented Foucher as he accepted a tankard from Jackie.

"We do. If you like, I can let you off at Calais."

Foucher, a man in his mid-thirties and straight from a French naval academy when he'd been assigned duty on the *Odyssey* by his king, was standing beside one window. He wore his dark hair long, his shirt, waistcoat, and breeches spotless. He shrugged his shoulders in a gesture that was typically Gallic. *"Ce n'est pas nécessaire, Capitaine,"* he answered with a negligent pursing of his lips. "I will remain with you until we return."

"We *are* returning, are we not?" asked Tremaine with a lift of his fair brows. "You've not taken it into your head to start your own sugar cane plantation on one of the islands, have you?"

Keir's first mate was seated at Keir's desk, his slim legs stretched out before him, ankles crossed, obviously reveling in the greater-sized captain's quarters. The other three mates were sitting side-by-side on Keir's bunk, their position making the cabin seem cramped. Tremaine's posture and Foucher's negligent stance were deceiving, however. In spite of the good rapport Keir maintained with his officers, they were obedient to the letter, respecting him as a fair leader and a brilliant navigator, even if he was withdrawn and introspective much of the time. He ran a tight ship and had long ago earned the respect and admiration of just about every man aboard.

Now, as he leaned against the table, Keir eyed Andrew Tremaine over his tankard before he spoke. "If I can locate a certain priest and bring him back to England, I need never sail again save for pleasure." He paused, letting this sink in. "And if I cannot find him, I will never return to England." He looked down into his tankard, lazily swirling the contents with an easy flick of his wrist. "Perhaps I will, indeed, settle down in Jamaica or some such place and start my own plantation."

In the wake of his somber revelation, there was absolute silence in the room for long moments. Every man there knew that Keir St. Andrews had sailed the seas for most of his life. No one except Peter Stubbs knew anything significant about his background. Therefore, the decision to possibly settle down was obviously a shock.

Tremaine straightened in his chair. "Who is this priest?"

"Father Tomas, late of Spain. If he's still alive, and if he's not long since returned to Spain, he will have been on the Main for some twenty years."

Will Jackson, second mate, shook his head slowly, a thoughtful expression on his face. "The man could be hidden away in some mission in the jungles o' Panama or even further south . . . Cartagena . . . Maracaibo . . . 'Twould be like lookin' for a needle in a haystack."

*Isle de la Tortue,*" said Foucher.

"Aye, Tortuga . . . that's where I'd start," added the up-

113

til-now silent Stubbs. "Surely someone basing there would've heard o' this priest if he's still alive." His gaze met Keir's.

"Good. My thoughts exactly," Keir said. "I wanted verification from one of you, or any other thoughts you might have."

"Mansfield might know somethin'," Jackson mused. "Edward Mansfield."

"That battle-worn old marauder?" exclaimed Foucher.

"Aye," Jackson answered. "He's also the present leader o' the Brethren."

"But then the question is, where is he? The Brethren of the Coast have spread from Hispaniola to Jamaica," put in Tremaine.

"No way te find out but te go an' look, like the cap'n's doin'," Stubbs told them, his gaze going to Keir. "An' we have to pass right by Hispaniola to get te Jamaica." He shrugged. "We ain't sailed the Main the last few years te balk at a challenge."

Keir nodded in agreement. "Exactly."

A muffled thump sounded through the wall between the captain's cabin and Tremaine's. Keir glanced sharply at Jackie, who was sitting cross-legged in a corner. The youth immediately unfolded his gangly legs and made for the door.

" 'Tis to the advantage of every man aboard this ship to aid me in finding this priest as quickly as possible." Keir looked over at Stubbs. "See what you can find out from the crew . . . they come from all over the Main and mayhap one of them knows of this Spaniard. I'm offering a generous reward for any information concerning Father Tomas . . . or one Arthur Biggs."

The men nodded or mumbled their acknowledgment, then finished their drinks quickly in obvious anticipation of dismissal.

"And one more thing."

Five heads raised in unison.

"Stubbs tells me there is grumbling among the men concerning our, er, new passenger. I want any hint of it squelched." Keir's eyes locked with Peter's. "The wench was a gift from Master Stubbs, here, and two other crew members—Oliver and Jimmy. If there is any more talk of bad luck at sea, then you just remind them, Peter, that *you* three were responsible for bringing her aboard, and not I. I'm merely granting this *gift* the appreciation it merits . . . why should I cut my pleasure short? Therefore, I'll not tolerate complaints of any kind. Is that clear?"

*"You* brought the wench aboard?" Tremaine asked Stubbs incredulously.

The quartermaster gave him a sour look.

*"Eh bien,* you deserve your trouble," threw in Foucher, his lips twisting with disdain. "I hope you sleep well at night with your grumbling men."

Peter's eyes narrowed at the Frenchman's contemptuous sarcasm.

"Enough," Keir interjected. "She's aboard now, no matter who brought her, and I find myself disinclined to put her ashore."

"If they don't stage a mutiny, they'll be panting over her like hounds after a bitch in heat," warned Tremaine.

"Let me worry about that," Keir answered. "I'll have no talk of mutiny aboard the *Odyssey* and I'll maroon any man who even hints of it."

Ames and Reeves paled at the mention of marooning, a fate that even seasoned buccaneers of the Main regarded with horror. The condemned man was put ashore on a small and isolated cay with nothing but a flask of water and his weapons. It was almost invariably a death sentence, and a lonely and lingering one.

Keir set down his tankard and pushed himself away from the table, a sign that the parley was over. Stubbs let himself out and the others followed.

"Tortuga?" Tremaine asked as he passed Keir.

"Aye . . . Tortuga."

# Chapter Eight

Keir followed them into the passageway, wondering what was keeping Jackie.

The youth almost collided with Keir as he emerged from the first mate's quarters. "She's sick, Cap'n," Jackie told him, his expression grave.

"Sick?" Keir stepped into the tiny cubicle and squinted against the gloom. Brandy sat upon the floor, her head and upper body slumped over the edge of the narrow pallet, A chamber pot rested beside her, the sour smell emanating from it telling all. Dudley's muzzle rested against her folded leg, his forlorn gaze coming to rest on Keir with seeming canine condemnation.

"A bit of *mal de mer* will make her a seasoned sailor," Keir muttered to hide his concern.

"Or kill her."

Keir shot Jackie a look that, under normal circumstances, would have immediately quelled such uncharacteristic cheekiness. But the lad's eyes were on the unmoving girl.

Keir stepped forward. "Help me lift her."

"And she's afeard of confined spaces," Jackie added quietly, as if to himself. He stood rooted to the floor, mumbling, "I locked her in here—"

"I *told* you to put her in here," Keir said with annoyance. "Don't flog yourself for obeying an order, boy." With a roughness born of irritation Keir sought to draw Brandy up from the bed by one arm.

As he turned her, he caught the chalky hue of her face, and relaxed his grip. Dudley whined softly.

"Get him out of here," Keir ordered tersely. "Cursed hound thinks she's his dam."

Jackie grabbed the dog by his collar. "C'mon, Duds. Out with ye."

As the reluctant pair left the cabin, Keir bent to lift Brandy from the floor. Sweeping her up into his arms, he ducked under the doorway and then stepped through his own. He laid her on the bed with more care than he'd lifted her, and brought the washbasin over to the bed. With the wet cloth he sponged her face and neck, taking careful note of each feature as his hand passed over it.

The flawless flesh that had reminded him so vividly of the ripe apricots of the West Indies was pallid and clammy, and Keir found her stillness unnerving.

*Or kill her* . . . Jackie's words echoed chillingly in his mind.

In his selfishness, his preoccupation with his own problems, it had never occurred to Keir that the girl could become so seasick she wouldn't survive the voyage.

He frowned. It was one thing to use a wench for one's pleasure for a few months . . . it was completely another to be responsible for her death, however unintentionally.

Jackie's footsteps behind him roused Keir. "Bring a biscuit and some ginger root tea," he ordered over his shoulder.

Brandy's eyelashes trembled and lifted, their long, lush sweep unexpectedly reminding Keir of the fragile fluttering of a moth's wings. Her eyes were briefly unfocused, then disoriented, cinnamon-dark against the pallor of her skin. But as soon as she caught sight of Keir bent over her, recollection returned and a faint frown crossed her forehead.

She opened her mouth to speak, but another wave of nausea hit her and she turned her head aside to stare at the wall in silent misery.

"We'll get some tea and a biscuit into you, brandy-eyes,"

117

Keir said softly, "and then a walk up on deck. You'll feel better."

The soothing register of his voice was oddly comforting, sick and angry as she felt. He'd not spoken to her with such kindness before.

Against her will her eyes were drawn to his. She tried to wet her lips with the tip of her dry tongue, then raised a hand to protest his unexpected concern. "I — I'll not feel better until you return me to my home."

Home. What must it be like to have a home to which one could return? he wondered, sudden, unexpected longing tugging at his insides.

He caught her hand, outwardly ignoring her words, and examined her fingers. Blood had dried beneath several broken nails. He leveled a frowning gaze at her. "What happened to your hand?" He reached over and lifted the left one. It looked no better than the other.

"I'm no animal that you can keep caged like — like some keeper of a menagerie," she said bitterly.

"Less than a half hour's stay in the first mate's cabin and you felt like a caged animal?" But his frown betrayed the ironic tone of his words.

The very thought of that tiny, celllike room brought unwelcome sensations surging back to Brandy, and she felt the dreaded heat begin to engulf her. She glanced about the room, a wild look in her eyes, seeking relief. And there . . . yes, there it was. The morning sunlight pouring in through one window of the cabin, opening the room, brightening it . . . as reassuring as the presence of a loving friend.

She breathed deeply, relieved, and allowed her gaze to rest on that window, even though it hurt her eyes. It was infinitely preferable to enduring the censorious gaze of the man beside her. Yet she could never tell him of her weakness, for surely so harsh a man would use it to his advantage. She would be totally and utterly at his mercy if he knew he could induce her to do anything before the threat of close confinement.

Jackie entered with a small tray. He set it down beside

118

Keir, his eyes going to Brandy. He opened his mouth to speak, but then evidently thought better of it.

"Back to your quarters," Keir ordered. He turned to Brandy, ignoring the look on her face at his curt words to Jackie. "I suspect you suffer from a fear of closed spaces."

Her eyes met his. "Anyone would dislike being shut in such a closet."

Keir picked up a steaming mug that exuded a spicy fragrance. He sat beside her on the bed and lifted her head and shoulders. "Space is at a premium on board a ship." He raised the mug to her lips. "Drink."

Disagreeable memories tumbled into her mind, and Brandy turned her head, her lips stubbornly clamped together. "What devil's brew would you force on me now, Captain?" she asked stiffly. "Something stronger than brandywyne to bend me totally to your will?"

His lips brushed her ear, sending an unexpected shiver sliding over her like the chill of a premonition. "My name is Keir, brandy-eyes," he informed her in a hushed, husky murmur, "and 'tis ginger tea for seasickness. Now drink."

The last two-worded directive brooked no argument and, with a grimace of reluctance, Brandy took a sip of the hot liquid. She tried to pull from his embrace then . . . away from those probing green eyes that seemed to plumb the depths of her soul, but Keir only tightened his grip. "You must drink more than a swallowful," he said. She obligingly took another gulp, her eyes held by his. She winced as the scalding tea burned her mouth and throat, but she could only think to finish it as quickly as possible, for only then, she suspected, would he remove the disturbing presence of his arm from about her shoulders.

As if reading her thoughts he replaced the mug on the floor and then bolstered her up to a sitting position. Nausea threatened again as the *Odyssey* sliced through a swell, but he handed her a biscuit, saying, "Eat this. It will help the queer feeling in your belly. The tea will help, too, and you must drink it all."

Her stomach lurched at the thought of eating.

"If you eat it and drink your tea like a good girl I'll take you up on deck."

Her face lit up like a child just promised a sweetmeat, and Keir felt like a monster. While she forced down the biscuit, he sat and watched her, realizing how thoughtless he'd been to confine her to Tremaine's cabin. The evidence of her terror was on her fingertips . . . she hadn't had to utter a word. Such a fear was not uncommon, but certainly a man did not take up a life at sea if he suffered from the illness . . .

*She didn't choose her lot.*

Keir stubbornly chose to disregard that, but he couldn't ignore the fact that she was seasick. Death could easily result on a voyage of any duration if she couldn't keep down food and, more importantly, liquids.

*You can still take her back . . . or even let her off along the coast.*

He stood abruptly and swung away, moving to stand before the window closest to the bed. The churning Channel waters spread before him in a vast panorama of translucent blue-gray beneath the August sunlight. Seagulls dipped and soared against the deepening azure of the sky. But Keir was blind to the beauty before him. His features hardened unconsciously and his fingers curled into fists as he renewed his driving determination to regain what was rightfully his. He would make record time to the Caribbean, God willing. And even if He were not willing, by sheer dint of resolve Keir would conjure up the winds and weather needed for a swift voyage. The journey could take anywhere from five or six weeks to three months. His dependable *Odyssey* would not fail him. She would make it in less than two months. She had to, for every day that Keir was away from England was one more day Giles St. Andrews was unlawfully sixth Earl of Somerset, ensconced at Somerset Chase, spending James St. Andrews's fortune and bearing Keir's title.

And a swift return could not be accomplished by stopping for even an hour or so to let off a passenger.

Of what importance was one wench in a man's destiny? With a little luck and a lot of resolve a man could shape his future, Keir had to believe that, in spite of his past. And one did not go about forming his future by softening even the slightest. For anyone.

He turned toward her abruptly, his hands still tensed, his mien dark. Brandy caught the full force of his uncompromising intensity, and halfway to her feet she quickly changed her mind and resumed her seat on the bed, trepidation and uncertainty flaring within her.

What drove this man? she couldn't help but wonder. What devils goaded him until his expression, his whole demeanor changed like lightning from human to . . .

"Don't just sit there and stare at me like a cowed cur," he said tightly, then reached impatiently for her arm.

She took instant umbrage at his curt words. Ire briefly lit her eyes. Then she suppressed it. What good to anger him further? She was not clever with cutting words, she acknowledged. Nor was she any match for this hardened, worldly man with his lightning mood changes. Better to go along with him or heaven knew what punishment he would devise for her. Certainly he thought nothing of consigning Jackie to his quarters, which could be no better than those of Master Tremaine. If not for her debilitating weakness— and this unexpected seasickness—Brandy might have offered more resistance to his callous treatment of her. As it was, she was hampered by two very real physical entities. Nor was it likely that he would take her back to London until he was ready to do so.

And so, masking her frustration and the beginnings of homesickness, she followed him obediently from the cabin.


The stinging scent of salt water assailed her nostrils, and Brandy welcomed the balmy breeze as it caressed her skin and revitalized her. From their position on the quarterdeck she had a clear view of the entire ship all the way to the prow, eighty feet away.

Andrew Tremaine was at the wheel. He nodded at Keir, his gaze going briefly to Brandy, then returning out to sea.

Brandy braced herself against the polished wooden rail, closed her eyes and inhaled deeply. The sea air swept away the shadows of illness and, as she raised her face to the kiss of the sun, she felt the color return to her cheeks, the strength to her limbs. Her spirits unexpectedly soared, her status as captive fading in the face of the exhilaration of standing on the deck of a ship. She found the experience most heady.

Brandy opened her eyes, her face still tilted toward the sun, and yards of sun-bleached white canvas greeted her gaze. The brightness of the pristine sails was almost as blinding as that of the sun itself, but Brandy reveled in it for long, deliciously drawn-out moments, her eyes closing again with a sigh that was caught and whisked away by the wind.

Keir watched her hair whip about her face and shoulders, shining strands of fire-gold gossamer. He reached one hand to brush back several tendrils of the unbound tresses, the tender gesture betraying his ambivalent feelings toward Brandy Dalton.

Before he could withdraw his hand, she opened her eyes as his knuckles brushed lightly across her cheek. A tremor passed through her at the contact. She averted her gaze, and the glow in her cheeks vivified.

"Tell me about your ship, Captain," she said, breaking the spell.

Keir shrugged. " 'Tis like a thousand others."

Brandy looked at him askance. "Surely you are proud of your ship?"

Keir leaned one hip against the rail and crossed his arms over his chest. "Aye. But she is only a means to an end."

She frowned at his words, but he continued, acquiescing in the face of her apparent interest. God knew, it was better than arguing about the injustices done her.

"The *Odyssey* is a refurbished brigantine. She weighs roughly one hundred and fifty tons and presently carries a crew of seventy five men. She mounts ten cannon and is as fast and sturdy as they come."

"We are in the English Channel?"

"Aye, bound for the West Indies by way of the Canary Islands."

Mentioning their destination was a mistake. Keir watched as the animation that had lit her face faded. But he continued, "I hope to make the voyage in six weeks or less, attend to some matters in the Caribbee Islands, and return to England with all speed."

Brandy forced herself to watch the sailors about their work on the decks. Several climbed nimbly through the rigging. She marveled at their courage . . . and uninhibited freedom among the complicated network of cables and lines. Unbidden, the image of Jackie shut in a dim, tiny cupboard of a room came to her and Brandy turned to Keir. "If I . . . give my word to do as you ask in all things, will you release Jackie from his confinement?"

Her soft, wine-brown eyes were wide with unaffected appeal, her expression naively hopeful. Keir's gaze rested upon her parted lips . . . lips that lured a man to taste them and the sweet secrets beyond.

"All things?" he said softly, suggestively, for her ears alone. But before she could reply, he continued in a very different tone, "And what if Jackie's not learned his lesson?" His voice was gruff now, and he pulled his gaze away. "I'll have no disobedience aboard the *Odyssey*. Disobedience can mean death . . . for all."

"Oh, but . . ." her voice dropped, so much so that Keir had to return his gaze to her and bend his head to catch her words in the whip of the wind, " 'twas not Jackie's fault—the condition of your cabin, I mean, Captain." Color rose in her face. "I threatened to—to break the window and jump into the Thames when his back was turned if he didn't allow me to—"

"You've a penchant for breaking windows," he interrupted, his expression suddenly menacing. "One moment you cry 'innocent' and the next you persuade my cabin boy to allow you complete freedom with my belongings." He stepped closer to her and put a finger under her chin, lifting it toward him. Her cheeks were fiery now, guilt written

123

across every delicately-boned feature in her exquisite face. "Let me tell you something, Mistress Innocence." His voice lowered ominously. "There isn't a man aboard this vessel who wouldn't welcome a chance to take you to his hammock—or the deck if 'twas more convenient . . . Tremaine included. You are considered bad luck on board a ship—first as a landlubber, and second as a female. You'd best think twice about attempting to wheedle into the good graces of Jackie, or anyone else. I cannot guarantee your safety if you go against my wishes. Do you understand?" His grip tightened on the fragile bones of her chin, and she drew in a breath sharply in pain.

Instantly he dropped his hand. "Look at them," he directed, his voice still lowered so his first mate couldn't distinguish his words. He jerked his head toward the sailors swarming the lower decks. "They would just as soon throw you to the sharks as keep you aboard the *Odyssey* for the duration of the voyage. Barring that, they would jump at the chance to take your precious virtue. Why," he added for effect, " 'tis rumored that they're already grumbling about your presence."

The color left Brandy's face as he continued ruthlessly, "My advice is that you obey my orders to the letter. The voyage will be much easier on all of us if you cooperate."

Horrible visions of defilement—and worse—flashed before her, but she said with all the mettle she could muster, "I didn't ask to be aboard this vessel. Your *men* abducted me and brought me here, and *you,* Captain St. Andrews, kept me here against my will." She watched in unwilling fascination as his mouth tightened and his eyes narrowed in warning. She'd said enough, her sensible side told her, but some spiteful sprite prompted her to add with foolhardy candor, "If there is any ill luck aboard this ship, 'tis justice well-served."

"So you may believe. But remember, wench, any misfortune met during this voyage will be yours as well as that of myself and my crew."

The frightening truth of his words hit home, and Brandy

124

felt unease creep over her. She persisted, however. "Will you end Jackie's punishment, Captain?"

"Keir."

"We are not on familiar enough terms for me to address you so," she reminded him, an edge to her voice. She was reluctant to invite any kind of intimacy, be it even the use of his given name.

"I believe we've been intimate enough to put aside such formalities," he said. "You've seen me quite naked, and I . . . well, I've sampled enough of your charms to—"

"*Keir,* then!" she said through set teeth in an effort to silence him.

"That's better, brandy-eyes." He took her by the arm and guided her toward the ladder that descended to the officers' quarters. She kept her gaze lowered as they passed Tremaine, and Keir left her briefly to exchange a few words with his first mate. Then he was at her side once again, propelling her forward.

An alarm bell went off in her mind at the thought of returning belowdecks. She pulled back suddenly as they reached the hatch, panic making her dig in her heels.

Keir looked down at her and evinced a twinge of something akin to compassion at the very real fear in her face. "You can return abovedecks with me later," he told her in conciliatory tones. "You've need of a bath and a fresh change of clothing after your ordeal."

Brandy looked down at herself, her fear momentarily forgotten as she remembered that not only had she deliberately soiled her clothing the day before, but surely smelled like the chamber pot she'd clutched during her bout of seasickness.

She closed her eyes and nodded, gripping his arm and forcing herself to put a tentative foot on the first rung leading to the bowels of the ship.


Keir was absorbed in his logbook, his brow furrowed in concentration. His back was to Brandy and, uncertain at first, she looked over at him. The request for him to leave the cabin was on the tip of her tongue, but her courage deserted her.

She stood half undressed, eyeing the steaming tub of seawater longingly.

*Gemini!* she thought in sudden exasperation. *Don't act like a timid rabbit!*

She threw Keir a look through her lashes and unexpectedly found him watching her, the look on his face inscrutable. She almost wished his expression had been one of interest, for that she was accustomed to. But there was no Jonathon or Simon Dalton to interfere . . . to make certain the look of interest never went beyond just that.

And yet she remembered the first night aboard the *Odyssey*. If Keir St. Andrews had wanted her then, he could have easily taken her. In spite of her outraged objections.

"Are you going to stand there until we reach the Indies?" he asked, a sardonic tilt to his brows softening his expression only slightly.

Brandy dropped her chin, a host of emotions cascading through her. She was tired of blushing before this man, tired of acting the cowed cur, as he'd called her. The truth was, however, that she was at his mercy and they both knew it. All he had to do was threaten to lock her in Tremaine's cabin, or worse, and she would turn as malleable as warm clay in his hands. He'd even mentioned the hold . . . black, stinking, suffocating.

Terror crashed over her with all the devastation of a tidal wave.

Moved to action at the thought of confinement rather than anything else Keir St. Andrews could do to her, Brandy peeled off her chemise and drawers and stepped into the wooden tub, rosy with embarrassment from head to toe. She sank into the water up to her neck, relieved somewhat that her back was to Keir.

"You'll have to overcome this ridiculous reticence, brandy-eyes," his voice came to her from beside the tub. She stiffened, her lashes lifting until her eyes met his.

"Every man aboard this ship earns his keep. What will

126

you do to earn yours?" he asked softly, one finger grazing her collarbone before dipping lower to trail down between her breasts.

Unexpected heat stabbed through her midsection, a heat that made the bathwater seem cool in comparison. She remained unmoving, torn between wanting more and the urge to slap his hand away.

Then he was seated on the edge of the tub, one hand braced against the opposite rim, the other continuing its leisurely exploration. "Well?" he persisted. "What payment will you offer for your passage?" His finger touched a coral nipple and it hardened in a natural reaction.

Desire danced low in Brandy's belly, scattering the remnants of her defenses, the beginnings of a retort.

She glanced up into his face, confusion in her eyes. His expression, however, was soft . . . as soft as she'd ever seen it. It made him look younger, more vulnerable, more human. And stunningly attractive.

*This* Keir she decided she could like . . . aye, and, obviously, want.

*He's a rogue and a pirate. And you are a wanton fool.*

The warning beat at her conscience, but she continued to stare up at him, wicked and wonderful feelings wending through her. Her body responded to his every touch as if he were the maestro and she the medium.

"Nay," she murmured as a sap to her conscience, but to no avail. She could have said "aye" for all the good it did her as Keir bent his head to touch his lips to hers. His tongue teased the line where her lips met, then parted beneath his insistence. Engulfed by feelings of wondrous languor, her mouth opened in further invitation.

Keir's fingers combed through her hair and caressed her scalp before pinning her head against the back of the tub, and Brandy played the willing victim of his sensual assault. Her hand reached up to touch his where it balanced him against the tub, her fingers tentatively running over the solid strength of his. They continued with a will of their own up his taut and sinewy arm, then across his shoulder. They slipped into the V of his shirt at his throat . . .

A low groan sounded against her mouth, and she echoed his pleasure with the soft sound of her own as their kiss intensified.

"Cap'n?"

Brandy started like a cat deluged with cold water. Keir, however, pulled away more slowly, his eyes holding hers with all the force of an enchanter.

A knock sounded loudly. "Cap'n?"

"A moment," Keir answered, straightening as his gaze moved from her passion-flushed face to skim over her body. "You'll earn your passage soon, I suspect," he told her. "And then some." He pushed away from the tub, straightening his shirt, then returned to add something to his logbook. As he closed it and moved toward the door, Brandy kept her gaze upon the cloth she'd begun to soap with mechanical movements. Her pride smarted, however, for the ease with which he'd removed himself from their loveplay was insulting. She'd have given herself to him like any tavern slut had he pressed the issue, and he'd obviously been barely affected. Only his groan had betrayed him, while she . . .

*Oh, it doesn't bear thinking!* she told herself as another wave of humiliation swamped her. She forced her attention upon her bath as the door closed behind him, never suspecting Keir's reason for turning his back to her to toy with an already completed entry to his log.


"Your timing is rotten," Keir told Stubbs as they emerged onto the quarterdeck. No one but Stubbs or Tremaine would have dared interrupt him when they knew he was occupied with a woman . . . and then only if the matter was of utmost importance.

Peter grinned with comprehension. "Sorry, Cap'n. But I didn't think ye'd want te wait te hear what Gonzalez has to say."

"Gonzalez?"

"Aye."

Keir followed him across the length of the main deck to the forecastle, down the forehatch and into Gonzalez's sacred galley. The Spaniard was at work over his great cast iron stove, sweat running in rivulets down his wide face. He closed the door to the oven below it and straightened when the two other men entered the cluttered, smoky galley. His thick, dark hair was plastered to his head as he saluted Keir.

"Tell the cap'n what ye know 'bout the priest," Stubbs said.

The brawny cook ran a forearm across his sweat-soaked brow. "You look for a *padre, sí?* Padre Tomas?"

Keir nodded, tamping a flicker of hope.

"Padre Tomas de Almansa y Espinoza?"

A frown drew Keir's brows together. He hardly remembered what the man looked like, let alone his full name. "I knew him only as Father Tomas. That was twenty years ago. I was but a lad."

Gonzalez shrugged. "I knew a *cimarrón* in Jamaica a few years past . . . *sí,* before I come on with you. He spoke of this *padre,* of how he built a mission in the mountains for runaway Indians and *cimarrones.*"

Keir threw a look at Stubbs.

"Aye. The Cimaroons," the quartermaster repeated.

Cimaroons, from the Spanish *cimarrón* or 'wild,' were runaway African slaves imported to the West Indies by the Spanish for slave labor. After decimating the populations of native Arawak and Carib Indians, the Spanish resorted to the hardier Africans to work their farms and plantations, to carry their plunder from the jungles to waiting galleons.

"There undoubtedly are scores of Spanish priests and missionaries on the Main," Keir said. "And any number of them by the name of Tomas."

"Aye, but 'tis a start," Stubbs said.

"And so it is." Keir stared at Gonzalez, his expression carefully neutral. "Tell me again what this Cimaroon said to you . . ."

# Chapter Nine

"Ye want me t-t-te wash yer clothes?" Jackie asked her, flames leaping into his cheeks.

Brandy sat wrapped in a sheet on the sea chest, stubbornly refusing to don any of Keir's clothing. The very act would brand her his kept woman in the eyes of the officers and crew, she reasoned, no matter the state of her virtue; and that was unthinkable.

Also, the very thought of wearing anything of his sent shivers of excitement skittering around her insides. To wear *his* garments . . . garments that had hugged his flesh, draped his strong, supple frame . . .

Heaven help her, she was already enthralled by the man.

"Ye can't sit there wrapped in a sheet ferever," Jackie said, mild exasperation tingeing his words. His eyes, nevertheless, studiously avoided her white-shrouded form. Dudley lumbered past him and sniffed where the sheet touched the floor. "Ye can't get back into them dirty things, Mistress Brandy . . . can ye?" he finished uncertainly.

Brandy eyed the heap of soiled garments with a sigh. No, she certainly couldn't bear the thought of sour-smelling, soiled clothing touching her clean body.

Dudley swung toward the pile of her clothing and began snuffling rapturously among them.

Jackie smirked, then chuckled.

"What's so funny?" Brandy asked him, trying to retain a bit of her dignity.

"D-d-dogs love stinkin' things," he informed her. "The dirtier and smellier, the b-better."

Brandy stuck out her foot and gave the hound's hind end a shove. "Get out of there!" she exclaimed, embarrassment fueling her temper. "How long will it take? To wash my clothes, I mean."

" 'Bout two hours. One te wash, one te d-d-dry."

She considered her alternatives, which were not particularly appealing. Dudley settled his muzzle on her knee, his great brown eyes on her face in an obvious attempt to get back into her good graces.

"Very well, then." What was so bad about wearing a sheet for two hours? Worse could happen.

Jackie scooped up the clothing and turned to leave.

"Jackie?"

"Aye?"

"Did the captain lift your punishment?"

" 'E did. Else I wouldn't have c-come in here."

"Where exactly do you sleep?" she asked, curious as to the arrangements within the cramped officers' quarters.

"I sleep in the small galley across the way."

Her eyes widened in surprise. "The *Odyssey* has two galleys?"

"Aye." He brushed a hank of hair from his face with his free hand. "Gonzalez sometimes makes special dishes 'n the like fer the cap'n."

"I see."

He swung toward the door again, and sudden inspiration struck Brandy.

"Jackie?"

"Aye?"

"Can you read?"

He shook his head. "No, mistress. But the cap'n can. 'N all the officers an' Master Stubbs some, too." He shifted the bundle beneath his arm. "Cap'n said 'e'd teach me if I wanted."

She brightened at this revelation, instantly perceiving something to help pass the time that stretched endlessly before her. "Would you like me to teach you?"

His eyes lit with answering enthusiasm. "If the cap'n says 'tis all right . . ." He trailed off. "But ye have to ask 'im first."

Brandy scratched Dudley's head absently, her mind working. "I'll ask him then. I see no reason for him to object if he was going to teach you himself."

Jackie bobbed his head. He glanced down at the bundle of clothing under his arm. "I'll be returnin' these soon as they're dry." He paused awkwardly, then added. "Mistress Brandy, I'm real sorry yer here against yer will."

Tears sprang into her eyes at the reminder. And the thought of home and family. He left quickly, before she could answer, leaving behind Dudley . . . and a Brandy who was not only touched by his words, but also aware of the fact that he'd ceased his stuttering.

She didn't permit herself time to lapse into maudlin musings, however, as her eyes scanned the room searching for something to occupy her until Jackie returned with her clothing. Keir kept perhaps a score or more of books on a shelf with a wooden slat spanning their bindings to hold them secure. She could always read until Jackie returned.

She stood and moved across the cabin, the sheet — and Dudley — trailing behind her. She was diverted, however, by the sunlight spangling the waters to silver outside the window, and ended up looking longingly at the endless stretch of sea and sky. It was a beautiful day, as she'd acknowledged earlier abovedecks but, more importantly, the window and its view afforded her a life-sustaining buoyancy on the treacherous waters of her fears. Only at night, perhaps, when blackness pressed down upon the *Odyssey* and its crew, would she feel her confinement more keenly.

Brandy gazed for long moments at the panorama before her, the movement of the ship beneath her feet soothing now, triggering none of her earlier seasickness. The image of Keir St. Andrews rose before her, and would not be dismissed. Was he admiring the same seascape that she was, only from the deck? The thought made her admit to herself how powerfully she was drawn to him, even as the mental image of his stern-featured countenance produced a wealth of uncertainties within her and, undeniably, fear. A sweet, forgiving nature prevented her from hating anyone or holding a grudge. She'd already begun to accept her lot, clinging to the hope that Keir would keep his word and return her to her family on the return trip. There was no use in railing against something that one could not change, and as far as Brandy was concerned, her biggest problem was the preservation of her virtue.

In the expert hands of Keir St. Andrews, that commodity was in imminent jeopardy.

At the thought of his skill as a lover, at the emotions and reactions he elicited in her as easily as a sorcerer and his subject, bewilderment made her drag her gaze away from the window and toward the bookshelf in an attempt to divert her thoughts.

Her gaze crossed the open desk with its logbook sitting atop it . . . and paused. In his haste to leave the room, Keir had neglected to put it away and close the desk front.

It lay there, tempting as unclaimed treasure.

Brandy ran her hand over the rich leather binding, curiosity warring with ingrained habit. She supposed it contained calculations and notations concerning the course and progress of the ship. Nothing that could be of interest to her, and certainly nothing that would reveal anything more about Keir St. Andrews than his skill as a navigator.

She opened the heavy book and carefully turned to the last entry, ignoring her chastising conscience. To her surprise, it was more of a journal than she'd anticipated and, therefore, much more personal. And of much more interest. The last words he'd entered were written with the same bold calligraphy as the previous entry, but they were underscored so heavily that the ink had smeared: *I must find the priest at all cost.*

She stared at the words and pondered their meaning. Nothing in the lines above indicated the identity of this priest or the reason for the need to find him. The last sentence was a separate paragraph, standing out like a signal flag. Yet its significance eluded Brandy although, she mused, it certainly was in character with the driven man who commanded the *Odyssey*.

She went to close the log, but some vague impulse made her turn the page back to the beginning of that day's entry:

*. . . that the men are grumbling about the presence of a female on board. Orders to the officers and the quartermaster are to squelch any more such talk on my ship. Severe punishment will be exacted in any case of disobedience.*

Brandy shut the book with a snap, a frown furrowing her brow. Her left hand automatically tightened on the gathered sheet tucked into itself at her breastbone. So he hadn't been exaggerating when he'd told her earlier of the rumblings of discontent among his men.

It seemed that not only was she a prisoner for the duration of this voyage, but an unwelcome one among a crew of seventy-five . . . seventy-three if one discounted Jackie and Keir. And what good to her the cabin boy, who surely occupied one of the lowlier rungs of the ladder of the ship's hierarchy? Or the captain, who was at the pinnacle of that same system, yet was stalking her like a cat the canary?

Dudley, sitting patiently at her feet, yawned loudly, pulling her thoughts from their deepening abyss. Brandy crouched down beside him and hugged him, burying her face in his coat. "Even *you* are a male," she accused softly against his long, droopy ear. It twitched, tickling her chin.

She pulled away and looked into his soulful brown eyes, the shape of which gave him a perpetual look of empathy. "Well, you aren't Archie, but I suppose you'll do," she informed him gravely. "I shall need every friend I can win over."

Jackie returned and handed Brandy her clothing. "Cap'n said t-t-te hurry an' dress. 'Tis time t-te eat." He withdrew from the room and closed the door before Brandy could thank him.

She quickly shed her sheet and reached for her undergarments. They were stiff as planking. She shook out her chemise, but it only fanned the cabin air around like a sudden gust of wind. Her drawers fared no better. In bemusement Brandy donned both garments anyway in the wake of Jackie's message from Keir. Better to be fully clothed than caught clad only in bedclothes.

When Keir opened the cabin door, Brandy's face was rosy-hued with annoyance. He took one look at her salt-stiffened clothing and shook his head. "You refused my hospitality," he said, tipping his head toward the bunk drawers. What did you expect?"

"What did he *do* to these?" she asked darkly. "Did you deliberately devise this as another punishment for me?" She ran a finger beneath the stiff cloth of the neckline of her chemise in an effort to relieve the chafing of her tender flesh.

Something like regret flickered in his eyes and then was gone. "And are you comparing the donning of clean clothes to being shut in Tremaine's cabin?" he asked softly. "For if so, 'tis a poor show of gratitude for Jackie's efforts to teach you of cleanliness."

Her mouth started to fall open in disbelief before she collected her wits and snapped it shut. He thought her unclean?

As if reading her thoughts, he asked, "What did you expect me to think?" Irony infused his words. "You looked like a guttersnipe when I returned from Whitehall yesterday. And then this absurd refusal to part with your own garments . . ." He paused meaningfully as his gaze raked her from head to toe. "I'm surprised that you were even wearing shoes when my men brought you aboard. The first time I saw you sitting there in the sunshine, your hair falling about your shoulders, you were barefooted like the urchins that — "

He cut himself off in mid-sentence. He'd meant to put her in her place, tavern wench that she was, for her ingratitude. But not only had his own voice changed peculiarly with that vivid memory, but Brandy's expression had also altered. She

135

was watching him expectantly, her lips parted slightly . . . as if, he thought sourly, in anticipation of some idiotic declaration of affection. Some revelation of how very much a part of him that image had become . . . and how it had affected him, in spite of all his denials, more than he wanted or would ever admit.

"You watched us that morn?" she asked in some consternation. She frowned thoughtfully in the face of his silence while he struggled for the words that would rectify his blunder. Her delicate eyebrows lifted in sudden realization. "So that's why you recited the lines from *Romeo and Juliet* that first night."

Suddenly, Keir found the tables were turned, with him on the defensive. "What has that to do with your aversion to bathing and donning clean clothes?" he said harshly.

"Why, that makes you a spy. Someone who eavesdrops on others."

"I'm aware of the meaning of the word. And I wasn't eavesdropping."

"Then why didn't I see you?" She jabbed a finger at him, her earlier anger forgotten in the face of this newest revelation.

"You were too immersed in 'maidenheads' and 'tools,' as I remember." And he watched with a dark satisfaction as a slow blush suffused her features. "Tell me, brandy-eyes, do you enjoy hearing those bawdy lines . . . does it give you a vicarious thrill? Perhaps some private pleasure—"

"Nay!" she cried. "How can you think such vile things? Where did you ever learn to—to *sneak* up on people and *eavesdrop* on their affairs and then accuse them of even more—" she searched for the right word, *"sordid* behavior than your own? And you accuse me of being soiled!"

He closed the space between them in one long stride. "Which is the preferable, I wonder," he murmured as he took her by the shoulders and pulled her up against him until her face was inches below his. "Unclean thoughts or an unclean body?"

Brandy was instantly silent, seeing that she had pushed

him too far . . . the very thing she'd wished to avoid if she were to survive this voyage.

Or had she? Suddenly he wasn't angry but, rather, in one of his moods of seductive words and titillating touches. She lowered her gaze, in spite of his fingers gently imprisoning her chin and canting her face upward. Her eyes met the slight depression at the base of his throat where his shirt was carelessly opened. She concentrated on the smooth, tanned flesh, pinning her gaze upon the pulse that leapt within that bronzed hollow.

Keir gazed down at her, the scent of salt and soap, the fragrance of her still damp hair drifting up to him to steep his senses in the essence of Brandy Dalton. The dense thicket of her lashes hid her beautiful eyes from his searching gaze, but the freckle-sprinkled tip of her nose tempted him to drop a kiss upon it. And her mouth, angled toward his, beckoned with all the innocent allure of a shy new bride.

He lowered his lips to hers, his kiss unexpectedly tender.

Brandy jerked away as if singed. "Nay!" she protested, trying to pull free of his embrace. Another encounter like that in the tub and her virtue would go the way of a feather tossed into the wind.

He frowned, his brows drawing together like a dark thundercloud portending a storm. " 'Tis in your best interests to please me in all things." His arm tightened about her waist and he pulled her close once more.

Brandy grabbed at the first thought that came into her mind. "I need to use the chamber pot," she blurted as his mouth came to within a hair's breadth of hers. "Badly."

He drew back to look into her eyes, concern unexpectedly overriding his growing physical needs. "Are you ill?"

"Nay. But Jackie took the pot to empty it, and never returned it."

"No doubt because he was seeing to your clothing."

Her mouth tightened with impending mutiny and she jerked her head to the side to escape his unsettling scrutiny. The red mark on her neck where her chemise chafed caught Keir's eye. Irritation flared anew within him. Damn the wench! No matter what his actions, well-intentioned or no, she always managed to suffer some physical damage, like some raw recruit flung headlong into battle.

And for some odd reason every injury done to her, no matter how inconsequential, affected him in a way that was infinitely unwelcome. Every blemish dredged up a softness in him he'd thought buried forever. Hell, it wasn't his fault she wouldn't wear anything but her own clothing. He should have instructed Jackie to drag her bundle of garments behind the ship for an hour with *her* still in them. Then she'd have something to complain about.

Perverseness prodded him to say, "Then go to the head, like everyone else. Or through the rail into the sea."

She looked at him then, suspicion creeping into her expression. "And just where is this 'head'?"

"In the bow. Right beside the hawsepipe."

She lifted her chin. "I am unfamiliar with a 'hawsepipe.' "

He shrugged, tucking his thumbs into the waist of his breeches as he watched her discomfiture . . . and her valiant effort to make her own way in the face of his lack of cooperation. "Just ask one of the crew . . . any one of them will be happy to take you himself, you can be sure. Mayhap he will even offer to stand guard."

The words were mocking, careless. Even his stance suggested negligence, yet something in his eyes warned her.

"But you told me earlier never to leave the quarterdeck or mingle with the crew."

"That was before I realized what a little ingrate you really are. You're more trouble than a score of stowaways."

Her lower lip trembled as she willed herself not to cry in frustration. "Very well, Captain St. Andrews. I'll find this 'head' myself." *And if there is any justice in this world, I won't return, and your burden will be greatly relieved,* she added silently and turned toward the door. Dudley heaved himself to his feet to follow her.

"Leave the dog. Jackie would be devastated if anything happened to him."

Brandy nodded, her mind numb. That anyone could be so

indifferent—so studiedly heartless—defied her comprehension. "Sit, Dudley," she bade the dog softly, her eyes burning with unshed tears. "And stay." A lump filled her throat and threatened to choke her as the hound obeyed.

She pulled open the door, and suddenly Keir's arm shot out to block her passage. "Use Tremaine's," he ordered tersely.

She looked up at him through misery-misted eyes, uncomprehending.

"Use Tremaine's pot," he growled, and let his arm fall before he spun away.

After the hostility of their last exchange, Brandy quietly ate her midday meal, her attention carefully on her food instead of the man across from her. She was conscious of every move he made, however, and wondered miserably how she would ever get through the weeks and months it would take to get to the Indies and back. That it might take a very long time to find this priest—if that was Keir's reason for going to the Main—she refused to even consider.

After forcing herself to eat some of the mutton on her plate, she turned toward the window, assuming that Keir would be disinclined to take her on deck now.

Dudley poked his nose through the partially open cabin door, then shimmied through the narrow opening. Brandy noticed out of the corner of her eye that he made for Keir first. The latter reached down and lightly caressed the dog's head before he muttered, "Damned pest. Why aren't you with Jackie?"

The gesture, however, was not lost on Brandy, who loved animals. It only served to deepen the enigma surrounding Keir St. Andrews.

She had little time to ponder the question, however, as Dudley came to her when Keir neglected to offer him any tidbits from the table. Brandy stroked his warm, sleek head as he placed his muzzle upon her knee, then slipped him a piece of meat.

139

"Gonzalez wouldn't appreciate your giving him anything but scraps."

Brandy looked at him for the first time since they'd sat down to eat. "I'm not hungry."

His eyes were cold, his expression unyielding. "You'll be glad for what you can get should we find ourselves becalmed and running low on rations. In a few days, there'll be naught of fresh meat. Eat your biscuit, at least."

Brandy obediently complied, raising her eyes questioningly to Keir as she reached for the butter. "You're not a slave here. Anything on this table is yours for the taking."

She buttered one half of the biscuit, feeling self-conscious beneath his gaze. No, she wasn't a slave . . . she was less. A prisoner.

"Jackie tells me you've offered to teach him to read."

"Aye. With your permission." The answer was meek enough, but she couldn't quite keep the hint of sarcasm from her tone.

"You have it. It will help occupy your time." He sat back, folding his arms across his chest. "The tavern wench instructs the cabin boy . . ."

". . . while the corsair navigates the ship," the words bubbled to her lips before she could bite them back, "and tortures the captives."

"And the tavern wench's tongue sharpens apace with the number of hours she spends at sea. You should be an absolute shrew by the time we reach the Indies. I shudder to think," he added, "what you will sound like by the time I return you to the Hawk and Hound."

She despised the idea of sparring with him . . . with anyone, for that matter. Biting words and sharp retorts went against her nature. She remained stubbornly silent, trying to ignore his baiting and the feeling deep down that she would never see England again.

"And corsairs haunt the area around the Mediterranean, brandy-eyes. The pirates round the Main are called 'buccaneers.' "

She looked at him blankly, her thoughts awhirl, as he offered conversationally, "It comes from the Arawak word *buccan* — a grill of green wood on which meat is smoked over a slow fire."

She paid his explanation little heed, so desperately did she want to be free of him and his ship. "If I displease you so much, why don't you take me ashore . . . anywhere!"

"— and if you think you've already encountered torture, you've no idea what sweet tortures await you still."

She inwardly shuddered at the thought of confinement . . . the hold. Panic leapt to life. "I know I can find my way home if you'll only —"

" 'Tisn't likely, since we're too far south of England now," he lied, feeling suddenly the ogre in his refusal to set this fragile butterfly free.

*Fragile butterfly?* mocked a voice.

Keir pushed his chair away from the table and stood as Brandy absorbed this latest distressing news. "Join me abovedecks, if you wish . . . after you clean your plate." He snapped his fingers and Dudley left Brandy's knee to follow him from the cabin.


The breeze carried the tinkling of feminine laughter to Keir before scattering it out to sea. His hands tightened on the smooth, polished mahogany wheel, a scowl crossing his features. Once again that sound evoked memories that carried the sting of a shard of glass cutting into his heart.

And a tightening low in his gut.

He glanced covertly over to larboard, where Brandy and Jackie sat together in the late afternoon sun, ostensibly to begin Jackie's reading lessons. Between his decree of punishment for Jackie and his shabby treatment of Brandy, Keir's conscience had been resurrected by guilt. Jackie Greaves was unused to women. That he'd succumbed to Brandy Dalton's wiles the other morning was in large part the girl's fault. But Keir suspected that she'd suffered more than Jackie had . . . she was so very soft-hearted.

Then there was Keir's treatment of Brandy herself.

141

He'd had no idea of her terror of confined spaces or he'd never have consigned her to one of the tiny officer's quarters. Even his threat to throw her in the hold the other morn had been only a bluff. He doubted he could have locked any woman with the rats and bilge water and a dozen other horrors associated with the deepest recesses of the ship.

Worse yet, however, were his calculatedly cruel words to her earlier. There'd been no real reason for them except his unreasonable annoyance with her for her complaint concerning her newly washed clothing . . . surely not enough to treat her as he had.

Just why, after he'd decided to wisk her away to the Indies with him, had he behaved so wretchedly?

*You're not accustomed to falling victim to any female.*

He glanced their way again and watched as Brandy gently tied Dudley's long ears together and then laughed with glee at the doleful look the basset hound gave her. Jackie guffawed and slipped the loose knot free with his fingers. He said something to Brandy and she nodded her head and laughed again. She put her nose to Dudley's and spoke softly to him.

Boy and girl were only a few years apart, Keir suspected, even though he could only guess at Brandy's age. But the picture they made—Brandy, Jackie, and Dudley—transported him back to the Hawk and Hound that beautiful afternoon . . . was it only two days ago?

As the sun shone on her hair, giving it the sheen and hue of newly minted copper, Keir knew the strangest urge to touch it, to run his fingers through those long, silky strands. He suddenly envied Jackie.

*You know why you were unreasonable with her earlier . . . why you've been unreasonable with her from the beginning.*

Aye, he thought. Brandy Dalton was, indeed, like the fragile butterfly to which he'd unwillingly likened her. Every mark, every hurt she sustained, from her bruised cheek to her bloody, broken nails to the red ring that encircled her neck, only bolstered that conviction. He suspected that, in spite of his determination to believe otherwise, the girl was unused to rough treatment . . . obviously unbelievably sheltered. For what reason, he couldn't imagine. But whatever she was, she was not prepared for life and all its harshness, and her very fragility annoyed him because he'd learned to associate it with weakness. Weakness and, therefore, the inability to survive. And that angered and frustrated him.

It also brought out an alien protectiveness in him . . . and he didn't like it.

With a seaman's instincts, Keir sensed a change in the air and dragged his thoughts and his gaze away from the girl across the deck. The horizon had darkened almost imperceptibly and the faint smell of rain was borne on the breeze.

Foucher ascended the steps to the quarterdeck with the light agility of the small, wiry man. "We head into a storm, *mon capitaine,*" he said to Keir. "She comes right at us from the west."

"By dusk, if not sooner," Keir agreed. He retrieved his speaking trumpet from its place and raised it to his lips. His voice carried easily across the length of the *Odyssey,* calling the men to prepare for rough seas and stormy weather ahead.

"We can try to outrun her," Tremaine added from behind them. "Or turn toward France . . . we're directly across from Brest."

"Nay." Keir's features were set, his eyes on the southwest horizon. "Tell the crew not to shorten sail unless I give the word."

"But if we leave the main and fore set, they could blow out!" objected the Frenchman.

Keir was adamant. "The weather be damned. I won't be slowed by this storm."

# Chapter Ten

Keir's shadow fell across Brandy and her student. "I thought you were teaching Jackie to read. Obviously you prefer to torment the dog rather than make good your offer."

At the sound of Keir's voice, the 'tormented' hound heaved himself to his feet and immediately went to sit beside him.

Brandy looked up into Keir's shadowed face in surprise, her hand shading her eyes against the glare of the lowering sun on the water. "I—we started . . . see?" She held up the book that was lying in her lap. "But I told Jackie about Archie and we—"

"Archie."

"Aye, our spaniel at the inn."

Keir's stance didn't change, nor did his expression relent, from what Brandy could discern with the light behind him.

"Aw, Cap'n, 't-'t-'twas my fault," Jackie defended her. "I asked 'er if she had a dog since she got along so well with Duds here—"

"—and if she continues to refuse to provide the service for which she was brought aboard *and* also neglect to teach you to read, then perhaps she can help the gunner . . . Lug," he added with quiet emphasis, "clean the cannon . . . or Jimmy mend the sails. Or even Gonzalez in the fo'c's'le galley. Cookie can always use an extra hand."

"Fo'c's'le?" Brandy repeated uncomprehendingly.

"Forecastle," he enlightened her. "The front of the ship, where the crew's quarters are located."

Brandy hadn't seen the *Odyssey's* cook as yet, but Lug's very image sent all thought of anything save performing her task fleeing, and she hastily searched among the rustling pages of the book to regain her place.

"You will end this lesson by the next bell," Keir directed Jackie. "A storm's abrewing to the west and I want the wench and the hound below deck and out of the way."

"Aye, Cap'n," Jackie said.

As he strode away, Brandy cast him a look through her lashes and then turned to Jackie. "A storm?"

Jackie shrugged in imitation of his captain. " 'Tis nothin'. Our *Odyssey* can weather any storm with the cap'n at the helm." His eyes lit with obvious anticipation.

Brandy digested this for a few moments, then said, "Jackie, will you do something for me?"

A mixture of suspicion and an eagerness to please played across his face. " 'Pends on what it is," he said slowly. "Cap'n'll have me lashed if I disobey 'im again fer you, Mistress Brandy." His gaze fell to the book in her lap.

She touched his hand, a gesture that was very natural to her. He jumped, jerking away from the contact and glancing over at Foucher, who was manning the wheel. "Don't *touch* me!" he exhorted in a strangled voice. "Ye're Captain St. Andrews's woman! Ye want 'im te think I'm—I'm . . ." He was at a loss for words, but Brandy knew exactly what he meant.

"I'm not anybody's woman!" she told him indignantly. Then, her expression somber, she added in a lowered voice, "Would Captain St. Andrews ever have you whipped?"

"O' course! I'm a crew member, ain't I?" His chest expanded with pride. "Cap'n'd have Master Stubbs take the cat-o'-nine te me jest like any other man." His face lost

145

some of its color, however, as he mentioned the dreaded cat-o'-nine-tails.

Somehow Brandy doubted that Keir would ever order Jackie whipped. As stern as he was, she'd noted his gentleness with Dudley, and his way with the youth. Whether anyone else was aware of it or not, Jackie's stutter subsided whenever he spoke at length to Keir or herself. Surely the youth knew she was as harmless as Keir had named her, but then, too, the lad's behavior revealed something about the captain that the latter himself would undoubtedly deny.

"All I want is for you to teach me everything you know about this ship."

He stared at her a moment, as if he couldn't quite trust what he heard.

"Just a bit every day," she pressed. "No one even has to know."

"B-b-but why?" he asked, his stuttering giving away his confusion.

She smoothed her hand reverently over the open pages of the book in her lap, her expression thoughtful. "I'm tired of having everything explained to me as if I were a simpleton. I would know what the men mean when they speak of things concerning sailing and the sea." She looked at him appealingly. "What can it hurt?"

Jackie glanced at Foucher's back again, and then looked at Brandy. "All right, then. But ye mustn't make it obvious . . . as if I'm doin' aught but learnin' and you the teachin'."

She nodded eagerly. "And will you tell me what some of the foreign words mean?" Pure deviltry danced in her eyes.

His look turned to one of embarrrassment and he glanced away. "Sailors come from all o'er the world. Some speak Spanish, some French, some English, and others—"

"Oh, just a bit here and there," she explained. "Like Master Foucher is always saying 'merde' . . . or something

146

like that." She feigned a frown, suspecting that Jackie was still ignorant of the fact that anyone who lived in an inn would be acquainted with bits and pieces of the languages spoken by foreign visitors and salty sailors.

Jackie shot her a look bordering on pure horror. "Don't *say* that, Mistress Brandy!" he admonished. " 'T'ain't fer a lady's vocabulary."

"Well, I'm no highborn lady," she said with a laugh. "And I wish you'd just call me 'Brandy.' "

He nodded, a naughty grin suddenly spreading across his face. "All right then, but I'll not tell ye what Master Foucher's word means 'til ye give me my first lesson."

With a bright smile of victory, Brandy pointed to the first words of her favorite play. Jackie bent his head close to hers as she began to slowly recite, " 'Two households, both alike in dignity . . .' "


"She's bewitched 'im, I tell ye," Smythe muttered to Oliver Stinson. They were wolfing down their evening rations before going abovedecks to man the sheets in a sea that was already roughening. " 'E's already made a bad decision."

"Ye heard what Stubbs said," Oliver returned around a mouthful of hardtack. He washed it down with a swig of rum from his daily quarter pint. "Any hint o' complaint 'n ye'll be marooned,"

In the dim light of the wooden lantern hanging nearby, Roger Smythe regarded his shipmate with slitted eyes. "Ain't no way fer 'im te know 'less ye tell 'im now, is there?" In the face of Oliver's silence he added, "Yer soft on 'er too. Ye brought the bloody bitch aboard with Stubbs 'n' Jimmy."

" 'N' how was we supposed te know the cap'n'd keep 'er aboard?" Oliver bit into his beef, which was still fresh only one day out of London. " 'Sides, 'twas Stubbs's idea, not ours."

147

"Well, 'e's thick as thieves with the cap'n . . . always has been."

Oliver's mouth tightened. "Quartermaster's the second most important man aboard a ship 'n' you know it. Stubbs 'n the cap'n go back a long way . . . longer 'n' any of us."

A man across the way glanced over at them as he raised his dented tin mug to drink. "Whatcha doin' down here when ye could be abovedecks wi' the others?" Smythe sneered.

"Might ask the same thing o' you, mate," answered the other man. He returned his attention to the remainder of his meal in unconcerned dismissal of the other two.

Oliver made to stand in the cramped, low-ceilinged quarters. Roger Smythe's hand clamped on his arm made him pause. "If 'e ain't besotted," he hissed, "—ain't thinkin' like e's *loco,* then why ain't e' furlin' the fore 'n main? I'm one o' the blokes what's got te climb the riggin' 'n furl em in the middle 'o the blow if 'e has a change o' heart when we're bobbin' about like an apple in a wash-tub." He paused. " 'N if one of them sheets blows with me 'n the others in the riggin', we're gone," he snapped his fingers, "jest like *that.*"

Oliver pried the other man's fingers from his forearm. "The cap'n knows what e's doin, 'n it ain't yer place te question 'im 'less he's been unfair or mistreated ye. Now shut yer yap 'n no more o' this talk, ye hear?" And Oliver left Roger Smythe to finish his rations.

As Oliver passed the hole beside the hawsepipe, Jackie flattened himself against the wall in the shadows. He'd overheard enough to give the captain an earful, yet he was part of the crew and felt a certain loyalty to them. And he hated squealers. Even though he'd been forced to sleep separately from the crew—a merciless lot in the face of a perceived weakness like stuttering—Jackie still identified with the common seamen. As cabin boy, he was on a par with the lowest of them. He wanted to be accepted as one of them, and divulging what he'd just heard to Captain

148

St. Andrews would do nothing to further his cause. He also had no wish to be responsible for a crewman being lashed . . . or marooned.

On the other hand, his first loyalty was to the man he served. Also, the resentment of the cruelest and least tolerant of the crew that would have led to Jackie being the butt of endless jokes and pranks—to say nothing of the possible victim of sodomy—fueled his own ill will toward them. He knew the captain kept him apart from the rest of the men out of concern for Jackie's own well-being.

He frowned and chewed his bottom lip. As he slipped from the head and along the passageway to the ladder leading to the main deck, he pondered his dilemma.


Brandy couldn't help but notice the change in the movement of the ship. The increased rolling motion caused, first, a warmth to invade her face. Then she yawned, a prelude to the familiar queasiness.

She drew in a long, steadying breath and looked over at Keir. He was deep in consultation with Foucher and Tremaine over a chart spread before them on the table. Jackie was clearing one corner of the table of drinking mugs. Common sense told her not to interrupt, but her stomach was quietly beginning to rebel.

A knock on the cabin door sounded and drew her attention away from the immediate problem. Peter Stubbs poked his head through the door at Keir's bidding. All three men looked up.

"Lookout says it's comin' up mighty fast. Lots o' lightning an' pitch-black clouds." He shook his head. " 'Tis a big one." His eyes held Keir's for a long moment, full of meaning that Brandy could only guess was some kind of warning.

"My orders still stand," Keir said with a grim set to his features.

Thunder rumbled in the distance.

Stubbs withdrew with a nod and Keir turned to Brandy. "You are to remain in this cabin. Jackie is needed on deck, so he can't watch over you."

Brandy opened her mouth to retort and then thought better of it. Jackie carefully avoided meeting her gaze, but Foucher and Tremaine were watching her from behind Keir. It wouldn't do, she decided, to argue with him before his officers. Then, too, the look on his face warned her to silence.

"Watch the hound. He has a habit of getting into trouble at the most inopportune times. We have no need of further distractions on deck right now, so you'll remain here until we're clear of the storm. Do you understand?"

Brandy nodded, fighting the queasiness that fluttered in her stomach as the *Odyssey* dipped and them climbed with a slow, rocking movement . . . and the ire that burgeoned within her at his curt command consigning her to the cabin with the dog.

Keir turned and quit the room, his first mate and sailing master right behind him. With an apologetic look, Jackie nodded at Brandy and ordered Dudley, "Stay, Duds."

Brandy rose from the bunk and looked out the window. The water was a sea of swells, an opaque gray as far as the eye could see, reflecting the slate skies above. She concentrated on the play of darkening clouds that swept across the sky in everchanging patterns like smoke scudding before the wind. But still the nausea persisted. She would have given anything for a breath of that very wind that was churning the heavens above and the waters below.

Dudley's soft whine made her turn away from her post at the window. He stood at the door, sniffing the crack where the panel met the wall.

"Nay," Brandy said. She patted her thigh through her skirts. "Here, Duds," she coaxed, and he trotted in his ungainly way to her side. She bent to stroke his head and neck. "We must stay here, boy."

He whined again and moved back to the door, this time

scratching the wood with his front paw insistently. Did he need to relieve himself? she wondered in sudden dismay. She had no idea where he even did such a thing—nor did she have Keir's permission to let him out of the cabin.

"Nay!" she began in a firmer tone, hoping she was wrong. But when she opened her mouth, her gorge rose. She headed for the chamber pot, now conveniently sitting in the corner, and spewed forth the contents of her stomach.

Dear God, she thought as she raised her head and gulped in air, fighting for relief. Would she be forced to remain in this cabin for heaven knew how many hours, a passive victim of seasickness?

Dudley barked once and Brandy cast him a baleful look, her patience fading in direct proportion to the churning in her stomach. The door was undoubtedly secured from the outside, anyway, she thought darkly.

She leaned her head against the arm resting over the rim of the pot. Minutes passed and she lost track of time in her acute misery. She heaved several more times, but there was nothing left.

Dudley's cool, wet nose touched Brandy's cheek and roused her. He whined as she raised her gaze to meet his. "Have pity," she whispered, "upon the sick."

He swiped his tongue along her jaw in answer, and emitted a plaintive howl. The sound, so close to her ear, made her start and then wince. The words Jackie used playfully or in genuine irritation came to mind: *Bloody nuisance.*

" 'Tis exactly what you are," she accused in a ragged voice. "A bloody nuisance." She pushed herself up into a sitting position, essaying to ignore the increased pitching and rolling of the ship and the sound of many footsteps overhead. If only she could get a lungful of fresh air . . .

With an effort, Brandy rose to her feet and moved to

151

the door. Keir St. Andrews be damned, she thought in desperate defiance. If he'd dared to secure the door from the outside she'd . . . she'd—

She didn't have to invent a proper punishment for him as the latch gave way beneath her hand. She allowed it to open a few inches. Although she'd suspected that the hatch above the ladder was closed, the cool rush of air against her face told her otherwise. It was heavenly.

She stood there, half-leaning against the wall, sucking in the fresh air, relief seeping through her with every breath . . .

Until Dudley thrust his nose through the narrow opening.

The normally sedentary basset hound levered the door open wide enough to wriggle his body through it and out into the passageway. With a bark that sounded suspiciously triumphant he dashed toward the ladder leading abovedecks.

Alarm jarred Brandy out of her torpor. She flung open the door and scrambled after the dog. "Nay, Dudley!" she cried, lunging after him past the other cabin doors and making a mad grab for his tail as he took the steep wooden steps to the hatch with a speed she never dreamed he possessed.

He disappeared through the opened hatch like a shot, leaving Brandy with a few hairs in her clenched hand.

The roar of the wind assaulted her ears. She felt the prick of rain on her face as she poked her head over the top step like a mole from its burrow. She could only see Keir before her, fighting with the wheel, his body rigid with the struggle to control the *Odyssey* as she fought her way through the increasingly rough seas. The wind billowed the full sleeves of his white shirt, outlining bone and muscle taut with strain. Strands of hair had escaped his queue and whipped wildly about his head.

Brandy gripped the edge of the hatch, her eyes searching for Dudley as rain pelted the deck, stinging her eyes.

She tried to ignore the abysslike churning trough that sucked the ship downward. She closed her eyes, feeling her insides rise upward with the momentary weightlessness of the descent before the vessel miraculously rose up to the opposite side to scale the crest that loomed ahead like a mountain.

There was no sign of Dudley.

As the ship descended another trough, she scanned the deck again. The vessel began its next upward surge, and the angle of the bow afforded Brandy a view of the main deck, where men fought to maintain their footing on the water-slick boards. Some were in the process of lashing down one of the two smaller boats that appeared to have torn free of its lines. Others were clinging to masts or rigging. A few men were attempting to secure any movable objects that had torn loose and which were therefore in imminent danger of being swept overboard or posed a hazard to others.

Frozen in indecision, Brandy suddenly caught sight of Dudley as Keir shifted his stance. The hound was standing near the starboard rail, his stubby legs braced against the deck, his nose in the air, sipping the wind as if he were testing the breeze on a somnolent, sun-kissed day.

At the same time, Keir glanced sharply over his shoulder. His eyes met Brandy's. The tense look on his face turned demonic. "Get down!" he shouted above the shrieking elements.

Brandy was certain he'd seen Dudley . . . the dog was almost directly in front of him. Torn between the urge to obey Keir's order and the need to retrieve the dog, she took an uncertain step downward, indecision paralyzing her.

*Jackie would be devastated if anything happened to him . . .*

Keir's words pierced her conscious, leaving in their wake a stabbing guilt as she acknowledged that she'd failed both captain and cabin boy in her negligence.

153

Then Jackie appeared suddenly, leaping the steps to the quarterdeck before reaching for the rail to steady himself. He took one look at the dog and halted. He glanced at Keir, as if requesting permission. Brandy descended the ladder without another thought. She flew back to the cabin and threw open the trunk at the foot of the bed. Her fingers searched frantically among the articles for the rope she'd discovered earlier. She found it in the exact spot she remembered and fled the cabin.

When she reached the bottom of the ladder below the hatch, she tied the rope about her waist with shaking fingers, securing it with a bowline knot Simon had learned from one of the old tars who frequented the Hawk and Hound and then taught her.

Brandy scrambled up and out of the hatch, hazarding only a glance at Jackie, who was struggling to pull the recalcitrant Dudley away from the rail. In a double figure eight, she wound the other end of the rope about a belaying pin in the rail and swung toward Jackie and the dog.

A sheet of water washed over the deck in that moment, sweeping Brandy's feet out from under her. She slammed forward onto the boards, the air knocked from her lungs. As she raised her head, stunned, Keir was screaming something at her again. Fury and frustration were etched across every plane and hollow of his face. She couldn't hear him, and felt a perverse relief in the knowledge that he couldn't leave the helm to interfere.

The sight that greeted her eyes when she was able to focus on Jackie and Dudley, however, drove all thought of Keir from her mind.

Jackie had the dog by the collar, but was himself hanging over the side of the ship from the waist down. His other arm was wrapped around one of the rail supports as he struggled to clamber back onto the deck while anchoring the dog.

Instinct pushed Brandy to her knees. She crawled, hampered by her heavy wet skirts, toward Jackie. Reaching

154

out, she grabbed Dudley's collar with a desperate strength. The other hand she held out to Jackie. As the ship plunged downward once more, Jackie released the dog and latched onto Brandy's outstretched hand.

"Forget the hound!" Keir's shout penetrated her brain, but there was no way on earth she was going to take the blame for the animal's demise . . . unless it was to save Jackie.

As the youth managed to pull himself over and onto the deck, Brandy felt her energy begin to ebb. Panic had fired her determination, given her a temporary strength, but her earlier illness had left her weakened. Still, she maintained her death-grip on Dudley, who was now—in an obvious if belated attempt at self-preservation—trying to pull away from her and toward the hatch.

Lightning scored the sky as another wave threatened to send the ship listing, but Jackie had regained the deck.

"Back up!" he shouted hoarsely.

They were swamped again. This time Jackie held secure, but Dudley was flattened. He remained riveted to the wooden deck with his claws, however, and Brandy clung to him and the same rail support that anchored Jackie. Salt stung her nostrils. She opened her mouth to gulp in air and got a mouthful of brine instead. Coughing out salt water, she regained her knees in the aftermath of the last blast and, releasing the support, dragged both herself and Dudley back toward the open hatch.

She shoved the hound through the opening, more intent on getting him safely below than the manner in which he descended the gangway. He tumbled into the hatch as Jackie gained her side.

"Get in," he cried, bracing his legs in a bent knee stance against the crazy tilt of the ship.

Something made Brandy pause and look around at Keir. What she saw looming directly ahead of the ship turned her to stone where she knelt. A towering wave rose directly before the bow of the *Odyssey,* poised and hovering, a living wall of water about to crash down upon the fragile vessel and send them all into oblivion.

Andrew Tremaine's presence beside Keir somehow penetrated her benumbed mind. The tableau was burned into her brain as if with a branding iron . . . the two men struggling to control the storm-tossed ship while thunder shook the deck and silver fire pitchforked the stygian skies.

Jackie tried to push her toward the hatch, but she refused to budge. She couldn't flee to safety while Keir St. Andrews was about to perish.

*"Move!"* Jackie screamed in her ear, giving her a second, mighty shove.

But it was too late.

Sea water rolled over them, lifting Brandy like a piece of driftwood and heaving her backwards through the larboard rail. For a moment she was encased in a watery prison, suspended in time, falling into nothingness.

Then she was slammed against the side of the ship as the rope about her waist held fast. The force of the collision jarred the breath from her body, the solid hull meeting the side of her face and sending her teeth sinking deeply into her lower lip. She hung limply for what seemed an eternity . . . mindless, stunned. The water roiled beneath her, like the snarling, snapping jaws of a starving beast.

The rope slid from her waist to her armpits, jerking her painfully back to reality. Her feet hit something solid as the rope settled beneath her arms. Brandy instinctively clutched at that frail lifeline between the sea and the ship.

The water lashed at her, chilling her, soaking her anew and sucking at her sodden garments. She glanced down to discover she was resting on a projecting plank that ran several feet in each direction parallel with the *Odyssey*'s deck. She didn't know what it was called or why it was there, but its support helped restore some semblance of rationality.

She looked up at the rail. It seemed so very high above her. If she could only pull herself up to it and the relative safety of the deck . . .

The wind shrieked in her ears, taunting, laughing. Waves geysered upward to batter her, belittle her, a puny, insignificant mortal. She closed her eyes in defeat. There was no way she could ever summon the strength to pull herself upward . . .

"Brandy!"

The shout above the cacophony dimly penetrated her swamped senses. She was surely drowning, she thought dazedly, for now the swirling sea below was calling her name.

"Brandy . . . can you hear me?"

Or maybe it was God.

She roused herself enough to raise her head. Heaven, one part of her acknowledged, was infinitely preferable to what beckoned below.

But it was no heavenly countenance that greeted her gaze. It was the stern visage of Keir St. Andrews. Jackie was to one side of him and Peter Stubbs the other. All three men were flat on their stomachs, and Keir was hauling up the rope, hand over hand, that held Brandy. Stubbs reached to help him even as the ship dipped and bucked.

"Answer me!" Keir shouted at her. "Are you all right?"

Brandy clung to the rope, but didn't have the desire or the energy to answer him. He was so very angry, she thought with a bizarre sense of detachment. Always angry with her. Just by the look on his face, she knew he was going to make her life a living hell after all the commotion she'd caused.

In the confused jumble of her thoughts, she refused to even consider what he might do to her as punishment. Without realizing what she was doing, Brandy shook her head as her glaze clung to that of the man above her. *Nay!* she mouthed.

Keir's face, plastered with wet hair, streaming with water, miraculously changed, his expression actually softening to resemble concern.

No, her mind was playing tricks on her, Brandy thought as she was bounced against the side of the *Odyssey* on her slow ascent, fish bait on the end of a tenuous line. Keir St. Andrews would never be so concerned about her . . .

# Chapter Eleven

Keir took in the blood threading from Brandy's nose and lower lip. How else was she injured? he wondered with a growing sense of apprehension.

"She don't look good," Stubbs said in Keir's ear as together they strained to haul her over the hull and onto the deck.

The fear that clutched his gut made Keir tense. "I can see that," he said through clenched teeth, his words swallowed by the sounds of the storm.

"She's almost over," Jackie shouted as he clung to a rail support and watched Brandy's progress. All three men were secured to the deck with rope.

"Easy," Keir cautioned as he took hold of Brandy's wrists and drew her upward. He winced with every movement of the ship, for the battered girl he was pulling onto the deck looked as fragile as a porcelain figurine. And her face was very pale, accentuating the blood that still trickled from her nose and mouth. Her eyes were closed from exhaustion . . . or had she passed out?

He enfolded her in the haven of his arms and braced himself against another dive and surface of the ship. Miraculously, the motion seemed less violent now. Her eyes opened, and relief swelled within him. Her mouth worked, and he leaned his head down to hear her words.

"I want to — go home," she said on a ragged breath. Her

eyes closed immediately and her head lolled against his chest.

He knew a soul-sundering guilt.

There was no time to answer her, however, or ponder the effect of her words on him.

"Want me te send Adams?" Stubbs shouted from behind him.

Keir glanced over at Tremaine and one of the third mates as they shared the helm. In the abating storm they appeared to be holding their own.

"Not yet," Keir called back with a shake of his head. "Help me get her belowdecks," he added before turning away. He staggered beneath her sodden weight toward the hatch. Even though Brandy appeared unconscious and had possibly, as Keir thought she'd indicated, sustained more serious injuries than a cut lip and bloody nose, he couldn't stand the thought of another man, even the ship's surgeon, touching her. Besides, Stubbs had at one time filled in as surgeon when Keir's first had washed overboard in a storm and perished.

With Jackie's help, he undid the knot at her waist and handed her down to the quartermaster, who waited at the bottom of the gangway steps to receive her. Jackie untied their own lifelines. Keir sent him down next, then descended himself.

Peter Stubbs carefully set Brandy on Keir's bunk. "Don't appear anythin's broken, or she would've stirred when we moved 'er." Keir nodded, his eyes on Brandy. "Will ye be needin' me here fer anythin' more?"

Keir shook his head. "We still have a storm to deal with, however." He moved to sit beside Brandy.

"Sky's brightenin' te the west," Stubbs told him. "I think the worst's over."

"Good." Keir didn't look up. "For now, you can see how the rest of the men have fared."

After the quartermaster took his leave, Keir began unlacing Brandy's wet shift and bodice, his fingers moving

160

quickly but deftly. "Get me a blanket," he said over his shoulder.

Jackie complied. "She saved me 'n Duds," he murmured, his eyes suspiciously bright.

Keir looked up at him sharply. "She disobeyed my orders. She let the dog out and, evidently, felt obligated to retrieve him. Whether she'd appeared on deck or not, someone would have come to your aid."

Jackie flushed at the rebuke. "But you don't know that she let him out—"

"How else would he have made it to the deck, pray tell, Master Greaves," Keir asked with heavy sarcasm, "since he's not yet learned to walk through walls or closed doors?" He unfastened her skirt and began peeling it down her hips.

Jackie averted his gaze as Keir proceeded to strip down the unmoving girl, but his fists clenched at his side. "Mayhap she got sick," the youth continued in the face of Keir's anger. "Mayhap she needed a breath o' air . . . or mayhap the door swung open by itself. You know how Duds can streak like lightnin' through an opening when 'e wants out in a gale."

"Give me a wet cloth," Keir demanded, deliberately ignoring Jackie's boldness as he gingerly felt for broken bones. Her flesh was cold, and he swiftly bundled her into the blankets, his eyes searching her features for some sign of animation.

He brushed back her wet hair and gently sponged the blood from her face. Her nose didn't appear to be broken, but the deep cut in her lower lip would cause her acute discomfort until it mended, especially when she ate. Or laughed.

"—d'ye keep 'er here if ye hate 'er so?" Jackie was muttering, his gaze returning to Brandy once more. He sniffed and hastily ran an arm across his eyes.

Hate her? Had he been acting as if he hated her? Keir wondered. Then he recalled every cruel barb he'd hurled

161

at her, every taunt, every insult. Like grapeshot from a cannon, they rampaged through his memory with sudden, devastating impact.

*It isn't her fault that you may never regain your inheritance.*

Keir's lips compressed. Of course it wasn't . . . he knew that.

"—didn't ask te come aboard the *Odyssey,*" Jackie continued softly.

"*Will* you be still?" Keir gritted as he raised his eyes from Brandy's pale face and threw Jackie a leveling look. "I'll have you thrashed to hell and back if you don't control that tongue of yours!"

Jackie blanched, and Keir instantly regretted his words. The reason he had rescued Jackie from a shipful of cutthroats in the Caribbean a year ago was because the boy had been so badly abused that his face was hideously swollen, his back crisscrossed with old scars and fresh cuts. Scars and lacerations that reminded Keir too vividly of his own early years at sea . . .

"I—I didn't mean that," he muttered.

Brandy's lashes lifted. Her eyes met Keir's. "Did you not? You're so very callous," she accused softly. "Jackie loves and admires you . . . and you threaten him as if he were . . . some common criminal."

Again, guilt weighed uncomfortably upon his conscience. The conscience that supposedly didn't exist. "How do you feel?" he asked, ignoring her words.

"Tired and . . . cold."

"Any bones broken?"

"Nay. I think not."

"Mistress . . . Brandy," Jackie said, his eyes lighting as he moved forward.

Then his eyes met Keir's, and he halted in his tracks. Brandy glanced at Keir questioningly, then mustered a weak smile for Jackie. She held out her hand, and Jackie took it.

162

"You and the captain here and Master Stubbs saved my life—"

"Nay, Brandy," Jackie said with a shake of his head. "You saved Duds 'n me."

Keir silently stared at their clasped hands. He stood abruptly and motioned for Jackie to take his place. "By all means, do sit down, Master Greaves."

Jackie relinquished Brandy's hand as quickly as if he were holding a snake. "I'll g-g-get 'er some t-t-tea, Cap'n."

"Aye, you do that, and then tell Tremaine I'll be up shortly. I'll want a report on the weather and any damage sustained."

After the youth had gone, Brandy stared at the cabin wall across from her. "How is Dudley?" she asked after a few moments of silence.

Keir stood looking out at the setting sun on the choppy seas. "No doubt sporting at least one broken leg from the manner in which he was shoved down the hatch," he said over his shoulder. "I don't know who is more trouble . . . you or the dog."

Brandy closed her eyes against the image of his angry face. He was always angry with her. Why, then, wouldn't he let her go?

"I regret that I caused you so much trouble. I was terribly seasick, you see, and when I opened the cabin door for a whiff of fresh air, Dudley forced his way through it before I knew what he was about."

She turned her head to look up at him, but Keir remained staring stonily out the window. It hurt her lacerated lip to speak, and her body ached in a dozen places. But she felt obligated to continue. "I never intended to go on deck, but I had to get Dudley. He was my responsibility, and I failed you . . . and Jackie," she added quietly. "I'm sorry that I jeopardized the lives of three men in my efforts to put things to rights."

Something within Keir gave way in the face of her simple, honest confession. He suddenly felt as if his chest was

163

rending with the force of long-repressed emotions . . . emotions bubbling up within him after years of numbness; emotions seeping through seams long-strained and stretched by unwavering resistance.

This untried young woman had unintentionally freed the dog, and everyone on board knew of Dudley's habit of gaining the deck in the midst of any action, be it a storm or a battle. Everyone, that is, except Brandy. And now she was taking the blame for her own rescue, when her selfless actions toward Jackie and the damned dog constituted the real heroism.

He looked down at her, reluctant admiration dawning in his eyes, but she was fidgeting with the edge of one coverlet, her eyes hidden by downcast lids and long lashes. She may have been fragile, unable to harm anyone, no matter how deserving, but she was no coward when it came to saving another life.

Keir opened his mouth to speak, but the words wouldn't come. He wanted to tell her that if he hadn't stubbornly refused to shorten sail, the *Odyssey* would have made less headway, but they would have ridden out the gale with less difficulty. He'd risked his ship and his crew in his drive to make record time to the Caribbee Islands, and if his sails hadn't been blown out, it would be more than he deserved.

He'd also been indirectly responsible for the near loss of Brandy Dalton's life.

He turned toward her, battling the instinctive urge to retreat behind the wall of his indifference. The seeds of decency planted and nurtured more than a score of years before, however, unfurled within him and fought for recognition with a vengeance.

Brandy, sensing his eyes upon her, glanced up at him. She was caught by the intensity of his green gaze, no longer angry but, rather, clouded by hidden depths of pain. "Nay, brandy-eyes," he said softly, slowly, as if the words were pulled from him with the greatest of efforts. "The blame is mine."

The ship rocked more gently now, the waves slapping its sides. A dying sun shone through the window behind him, turning the lighter streaks in Keir's drying hair to the color of old gold. The silence enfolded them like a benison.

And then Jackie knocked and entered with a mug of steaming tea. Keir took it from him and, bracing his arm around Brandy's shoulders, he raised her enough to drink it. She winced, in spite of his gentleness with her, for her cut lip screamed in pain as the hot cup first made contact with it. "Easy now," he soothed her, hardly touching her lip in an effort to spare her further hurt.

"Master Stubbs said both the crew 'n the *Odyssey* weathered the storm unscathed," Jackie told Keir. " 'N Master Foucher said te tell ye that we're headin' into clear weather." He paused, then added, "He said ye've got the devil's own luck."

Keir nodded, his eyes never leaving Brandy's face, now tinted with delicate color beneath his unwavering perusal. "Good. You can see to the hound now. Get Adams to check him for broken bones."

Brandy's eyes went to Jackie, an apology on the tip of her tongue, but he didn't seem concerned. He grinned at her. "Aw, Duds's limpin' on one leg a bit, and a couple o' ribs seem te be sore, but he's none the worse fer 'is tumble. 'Sides, he's lucky he didn't end up in the sea."

After Jackie left, Keir remained seated on the edge of the bed, making certain that Brandy finished every drop of her tea. She was at a loss for words, and a feeling of awkwardness settled over her.

Several times some of the liquid dribbled down her chin, partly because her lip was swollen and numb, partly because self-consciousness made her clumsy, and partly because Keir was loath to push the vessel against her torn flesh.

"Would you like the surgeon to look at your mouth?" he asked.

Brandy looked up into his eyes, a question in hers.

"Adams could possibly stitch it once or twice, but I think 'twill heal nicely if you're careful. Adams is really the ship's carpenter, but also doubles as surgeon. I couldn't guarantee his expertise with so delicate an undertaking." Rare, but nonetheless real, levity brightened his deep-set eyes to clear, sparkling green.

"Nay," she answered, feeling that her protruding lip made her resemble some grotesque gargoyle gracing a cathedral. Then a memory struck her, and her eyes glowed with an answering merriment, even as her tender wound made her try to stifle her laughter. "And mayhap I can just put my injury to good use."

Keir tilted an eyebrow in expectation, making him look, Brandy thought, younger and incredibly appealing, in spite of his damp, disheveled clothing and half-undone queue. "And just how is that?"

"I can scoop up the food from my plate rather than dirtying a utensil."

He smiled. For the first time since she'd met him, Keir St. Andrews smiled with genuine good humor. And Brandy's heart ached at the beauty of it.

The silence settled comfortably around them, with only the footfalls on the deck above and the sound of the sea splashing against the hull intruding faintly.

"You're good for me, brandy-eyes . . . do you know that?" he asked quietly.

Her gaze dropped for a moment. "Nay, Captain—"

"Keir, then." She looked back at him. "You only need to free what is already within you, I suspect." She shook her head. "I don't know why you are so angry and unrelenting, but Jackie and Dudley . . . even some of your own crew, bring out the best in you. When you let them."

He laughed bitterly, breaking their brief interlude. "There is no 'best' in me. That was destroyed long ago."

The color was returning to her cheeks, and when he

took the empty cup from her hands, they were warm. "Are you comfortable?" he asked.

"Aye. But surely you have more important things to do abovedecks?"

"Ah. The wench cares not for my company."

Brandy shook her head. "Nay, but I am not an invalid to be kept abed and coddled."

"You've just been through more than any woman ought . . . and," he reminded her, his expression suspiciously sober, "you have no dry clothing."

Brandy's look turned wary. "What do you have that I could borrow?"

"Something much softer on the skin than you've ever experienced."

His words were low, a soft, seductive quality to them. An increasingly familiar sensation tickled her insides, deep down. "Is this apparel . . . decent?" she asked, suspicion shading her words.

A corner of his mouth quirked. "See for yourself." He pulled open one of the drawers beneath the bunk and withdrew a yellow silk tunic, small enough for a woman. Printed with small birds and exotic flowers in greens and blues and reds, it was both feminine and seductive . . . and oh, so soft as he let it spill into her lap with a sigh.

"But—but what do I wear beneath it?"

"Nothing . . . when you are in this cabin," he murmured.

She flashed him a bemused look, embarrassment dotting her cheekbones. "But you can wear an extra pair of Jackie's breeches while Jimmy fashions you some of your own from your skirt."

The name of the sailmaker conjured up his red silk head scarf, among other things, and Brandy's face fell at the thought of a rough seaman making her clothing . . . and breeches, yet. No decent woman wore breeches, unless she was a flamboyant actress in one of London's theaters. But then, this was no ordinary situation.

"Or you can wear sheets until Jackie dries your own garments on the morrow. I leave that up to you."

He turned and strode to the door. "I'll be back shortly. I suggest you try to sleep. The sun is setting and we're past the storm, if that will set you at ease."

And, his brusque manner and somber demeanor back in place, Keir left the cabin.

The *Odyssey* sustained little damage . . . no blown-out sails or anything equally catastrophic. The crew, as well, suffered only minor injuries here and there, no more than during any big blow. It seemed to Keir that Foucher was right. In this instance, at least, fortune had smiled on him. If they encountered good winds, they could make the Canaries as Keir had planned, with only the loss of a few hours at most.

After inspecting the ship and reestablishing their course, Keir left Tremaine at the helm and returned to the cabin. Hoping that Brandy was sleeping and that he wouldn't have to deal with the feelings she aroused in him while she was awake, he opened the door quietly. Dudley came limping toward him, one leg in a splint.

"So, Duds, you old tar," he greeted the dog, crouching down to scratch him behind the ears and then gently examined the splint on his front leg, "you weathered the storm with only one battle scar." His fingers probed the dog's ribs, then stilled as Dudley grunted softly in pain. "And here is further proof that disobedience doesn't pay . . . although I think you'll survive the voyage." He straightened and let the dog out the door, then looked over at Brandy.

*I want to go home.*

The words tiptoed softly through his mind, a dulcet but damaging echo, reminding him of his sin.

Sin?

*Aye. Sin. Such behavior isn't worthy of an earl.*

"I'm no earl," he muttered beneath his breath as he went to stand and look down at the sleeping girl.

*Oh, but you are.*

Brandy stirred and opened her eyes.

"How do you feel?" Keir asked, his voice tainted with the ambivalence of his reflections rather than the kindness he'd evinced with Dudley.

The lean lines of his face were in shadow, with the lanterns behind him. But there was no mistaking the familiar harshness of his voice. It acted to bring Brandy fully awake. She glanced at the window across from her. The window she'd cracked in her foolhardy attempt to convince Keir St. Andrews that she wanted her freedom. It was dark . . .

And she was in his bed.

She raised herself onto her elbows, a grimace of pain twisting her face as aching bone and muscle protested. "I'm a bit sore, but you may have your bed back."

Keir put a restraining hand on her shoulder, and she stilled. "I have no intention of sleeping in the same bed, if that is what you fear. You are in no condition to . . . ah, pleasure me while you are stiff and hurting."

Surprise skipped across her features. "Some men would say it mattered not."

His gaze held hers for what seemed like forever in the quiet cabin. "I'm not one of them."

The blanket had fallen away from her chest, exposing the silk tunic she'd donned after all. Shrugging into it must have caused her more than a little discomfort, he thought, carefully noting how it caressed her breasts, clinging and accenting in a most seductive way. Silk was preferred by many courtesans, he acknowledged at the tempting sight of her nipples gently tenting the fabric. But this young woman, he realized now, was an innocent. And that very fact made her infinitely more desirable to him. It was what had drawn him to her from the first, however reluctantly.

She lay back down, her gaze never leaving his face. He'd donned fresh shirt and breeches and brushed his hair back into its customary queue. The severity of the hairstyle only emphasized the beautiful and masculine lines of his features.

"And what know you of such men?" he asked softly, shattering her musings.

"I think not enough," she answered on a sigh. "Or I would not be here now."

Self-reproach rose within him and his look reclaimed its former bleakness. His irritation, however, was directed at himself and not her. He turned away. "Sleep now . . . I've other things to do besides—" He caught himself before the last words were out.

What he'd omitted, however, stung as much as anything he could have uttered. Yet Brandy was growing accustomed to his acerbic manner of speaking. She watched him sit down at his desk and pull out his log. He removed the top of the inkwell, dipped a quill into it, and began to write, ignoring her as if he'd forgotten she was even in the room.

Brandy turned gingerly to her side and gazed up at the whale oil lamp near his head. The flame leapt and lowered with the invisible currents of air that eddied about the room. She slept, feeling oddly secure in his presence after her ordeal, and dreamt of Keir St. Andrews with amusement animating his eyes and softening his mouth. She dreamt of that warm, soft mouth touching hers . . . teasing her, tempting her to greater heights of pleasure . . .

She awoke again. The lamps had burned low, and darkness and silence pressed in upon them. And still he sat over the logbook. Only this time his fingers were furrowed through his hair, his head resting in his hands. His shoulders were slumped forward, as if he carried an enormous weight upon them, and his eyes were closed, as if either in fatigue . . . or defeat. Or both.

It was an attitude she would never have associated with Keir St. Andrews. Arrogance, yes. Relentlessness, yes. Strength and driving determination, yes. But not this

170

very human vulnerability. Not this mien of defeat.

What was it that drove this man? she wondered, forgetting, in the wave of compassion that overrode her, her own outrage, her own sense of having been wronged. What could have the power to pull down to the depths of despair a man such as Keir St. Andrews?

Brandy lay there watching him . . . and wanted suddenly to go to him and offer comfort. Her physical pain, however, and, even more than that, her very real uncertainty, held her immobile. There was no telling how he would react to her concern. Oh, yes, she'd glimpsed a lighter side of him, a gentler side. But he was a man of deep and dark currents, of shifting moods, of sordid secrets perhaps better left buried.

Yet he was no common mariner, she would have wagered in a moment. There was about him an unconscious elegance, a tarnished patina of culture beneath his abrupt words and ways. There was also, Brandy suspected, much, much more to the captain of the *Odyssey* than was outwardly apparent.

Keir unexpectedly lifted his head from the cradle of his hands and drew in a deep breath. He let it out slowly, as if releasing pent-up feelings, unwanted emotions. His head came around swiftly then, and Brandy was caught in her silent contemplation. For the space of a heartbeat his look was open and unguarded.

She lowered her lashes in the face of the unexpected responses that naked look aroused deep inside her. With a female's intuition she sensed that he would want no part of sympathy or compassion . . . or that other mysterious but potent something that instinctively drew her to him with all the fascination of fire for an untried child.

"Are you hurting?"

His voice was gruff, impatient, but with an underlying concern that Brandy heard. She could only wonder at his unexpected consideration of her since her brush with death.

She met his eyes, her own look guileless. "Not as much, I think, as you." She automatically went to bite down upon her lower lip in the wake of her unwitting revelation. Pain shot through her lower jaw as the edge of her teeth touched her lip.

She closed her eyes and winced, tears burning the back of her nose.

"Your reward for your astuteness," he said, and rose to uncork a bottle of spirits setting on the table. He poured a goodly amount into a tankard and took a deep draught, his eyes closing as he let the potent liquid slide down his throat and settle in his stomach. He gestured to her. "Would you care for some?"

Brandy shook her head and then eyed the chamber pot in the corner.

Reading her need, he set down the tankard and walked over to the bunk. He reached to help her sit up; then, after she'd swung her feet gingerly over the side of the bed, braced her with a firm gentleness around her shoulders to help her stand. The feel of the cabin air on her bare legs was strange, but other sensations demanded her attention.

Brandy stood propped within the circle of his arm, every muscle and tendon yelping in outrage. "Let me bring it to you," he offered.

"Nay!" she protested with less bluster than she'd intended. "I can walk." She moved stiffly, wondering through her fog of discomfort how she would ever find the courage to use the pot with him supporting her.

The discomfort lessened as she moved across the cabin, and when she stood at last before the chamber pot, she raised bemused eyes to his.

He cast an appreciative glance at her limbs before saying only, "Do give me some credit." Irony edged his words. "I am not a complete blackguard." He moved to the door, throwing over his shoulder, "Knock on the wall when you've attended to your needs."

Using the pot was even more difficult than getting to it, but Brandy managed fairly well, if more slowly than was her wont. She knocked on the wall then, as instructed; not because she didn't think she could get back to the bed unaided, but because she feared to disobey him.

When she was settled comfortably, Keir made up a pallet on the floor with extra bedding Jackie had evidently brought while she was asleep. He blew out one of the two lamps, leaving the faint glow of the other to keep the cabin from being engulfed by the darkness.

Swiftly divesting himself of his shirt and boots, Keir settled himself on the floor. "Take your rest while you may, brandy-eyes," he told her softly. "We've a long journey ahead."

In the wake of his considerate treatment of her, of what she'd observed upon awakening earlier, Brandy fought the urge to ask him any number of questions that nagged her with an annoying persistence. In spite of everything, she decided, *that* would be overstepping her bounds.

She lay staring at the single burning lamp for a long time, sleep eluding her in the wake of her earlier nap. She thought about her family at the Hawk and Hound. She ruminated, too, about the *Odyssey's* destination and all that had happened to her in the last two days . . . was it only two days? And, of course, she relived her ordeal of only a few hours ago, all the while acutely conscious of the man sleeping on the floor little more than an arm's length away from her.

The lift and fall of the *Odyssey,* however, eventually lulled her. With the song of the waves in her ears like the soft crooning of a mother's lullabye, Brandy finally succumbed to sleep.

# Chapter Twelve

The *Odyssey* made good time once away from the channel, sailing southward and clearing Cape Finisterre, the promontory at the westernmost point of Spain. Off the coast of Portugal they picked up the northerly Portuguese trade winds, which would carry them to the Canary Islands. After a brief stop for fresh water, the ship would catch the northeast trade winds as it turned toward the Indies.

"As long as we stay well below the Tropic of Cancer, we can depend upon favorable winds to the Indies," Keir had told Brandy in the face of her curiosity. If she couldn't ask him about anything personal, she decided she might as well learn as much about sailing as possible to help keep her mind occupied.

"What if we stray north?" she asked him several days out of London. The wind tossed her hair about her shoulders and molded her tunic and new breeches to her lithe form, drawing Keir's eye as they stood on deck.

Keir was smoking a clay pipe, the wind-whisked curls of smoke dissipating as quickly as they appeared. He looked down at her, approval in his eyes as he acknowleged the intelligence indicated by her curiosity, her retention of everything he — or anyone else — told her. Again, he was struck by that elusive quality that mutely denied the relegation of Brandy Dalton to the status of ordinary tavern wench. "Between the twentieth and thirtieth parallels of latitude is an area of variable winds interspersed with calms," he answered, sparing her none of the nautical terminology. "These are known as the 'Horse Latitudes' because the confused seas, muggy heat, and the rolling and pitching of becalmed vessels prove fatal to horses and cattle."

Brandy looked up at him, worry puckering her brow at the thought of a return of her *mal de mer* as Foucher called it. "We have no cattle or horses, do we?"

Keir's lips curved with rare humor. "Nay, brandy-eyes, but we'll remain well below the twentieth parallel, nonetheless, for the fastest and most comfortable passage. We need the northeast trades."

Brandy spent her time giving Jackie his lessons, reading herself from Keir's collection of books, or abovedecks with Keir or Tremaine or Foucher. Even Peter Stubbs was won over by her sweet nature and spun long tales for her benefit, in spite of Keir's skeptical glances their way when he was at the helm.

"Guilt does strange things," Keir commented once, but only received a slant-eyed look from his quartermaster in reply and a muttered, "And don't we all know it."

Some of the crew softened toward Brandy, as well, once word got around that she'd risked her life to save Jackie and Dudley.

The formidable Lug didn't seem so threatening to her as the days passed, and he would wave to Brandy in response to her own impulsive gesture, an expression of her natural warmth and friendliness. "You can't just wave to the men," Keir told her. " 'Tis like waving a red flag at a bull—an invitation to—" he searched for the appropriate word, "intimacy," he finished bluntly.

But soon Oliver and Jimmy were acknowledging Brandy in like fashion when they spotted her on the quarterdeck, as were others, and Keir took Stubbs's word that, to his knowledge, there was no more talk of bad luck aboard the *Odyssey*. Gonzalez, who occasionally concocted something extra special for Keir in the minuscule galley across from Keir's cabin, took an instant liking to Brandy when she complimented him on his culinary skill. Even though Keir secretly wondered if she was deliberately wheedling her way into the cook's favor, he decided if the world-weary, hardened Spaniard took to her, then her place aboard the ship was fairly well assured.

Brandy occasionally dined in the small wardroom where the officers took their meals, but only when Keir deigned to do so. Yet the captain of the *Odyssey* discovered a disconcerting preference for eating his simple meals alone with the girl he'd kept aboard his ship from motives anything but honorable.

Possessing an insight into people that had been inbred from generations of leaders in the St. Andrews family—and further strengthened by his role as captain—Keir observed in Brandy a need to be with people. His discovery of this natural gregariousness, combined with his awareness of her fear of confined spaces, made him tend to include her in things whenever possible. Brandy Dalton was not the type to be isolated from others, or left idle. Insulated from much of life she'd obviously been, but not isolated. And it was to Keir's credit that he took note of this characteristic and, without endangering her or risking stirring his crew to mutiny, he allowed her her freedom on and below the quarterdeck.

Late one afternoon, two weeks out of London, Brandy was mending a bedsheet, imagining—and not for the first time—what it would be like to share that sheet with Keir St. Andrews.

Warmth kindled in her cheeks and she mentally admonished herself for such thoughts. Although she'd caught him watching her many times since their truce, he hadn't touched her once, nor had he spoken to her on anything but an impersonal level. She knew an odd disappointment that grew with every passing day. And, worse, Brandy found her own behavior even more disconcerting than his covert looks, for she couldn't seem to keep her eyes from straying to him . . . whether he was lithely climbing the rigging, or carving a powder horn with a marline needle. She'd already admitted to herself that he had much too much power over her when he put his mind to it . . . that very first night on board the *Odyssey* and the tub scene the next day were proof enough. And every night that she was safely ensconced in his bed while he slept on the floor, she was relieved.

Or was she?

If she was relieved, then why did she find herself thinking such thoughts about . . .

The faint but distinct sounds of music caught her attention. The flash of her needle stopped as she tipped her head alertly toward the deck.

Jackie knocked once and poked his head through the door before she could answer. "C'mon abovedecks, Brandy," he urged her, " 'n hear our band."

*Band?* she wondered as she dropped the sheet and followed him to the passageway and up the ladder. On the forecastle, men were gathering about three crewmen, one playing a drum, one a jew's-harp, and a third a hornpipe. Several men were already doing a jig to the lively tune that drifted over the deck. Others watched and clapped their hands.

"That's Adams, the c-c-carpenter," Jackie explained excitedly as he pointed to a short man vigorously cavorting about the forecastle. " 'E's the best dancer on board . . . look!" Adams grabbed Jimmy—Brandy recognized his fluttering red silk head scarf—and whirled him round amid the laughter and off-key singing of the others.

Jackie's face was alight with pleasures and Brandy's was as well. Her foot began to tap time, and she wished in the worst way that she could join the men. Andrew Tremaine was at the wheel, a grin on his face. Foucher watched with Gallic aloofness from where he leaned against the rail, his ankles crossed, his clothing immaculate as always. Only his dark hair ruffled in the breeze, something even he could not control, perfectionist though he was.

Brandy automatically searched for Keir, but he was neither on the quarterdeck nor across the main deck amidst the action. Peter Stubbs was there, however, his play-dancing with a mop renewing the gusts of hilarity among the men.

Soon he partnered Adams, and before long the mop was separated from its handle and placed upon the carpenter's head.

Men up in the rigging or involved in other tasks about the decks paused to watch the proceedings or to join in. Even Dudley frolicked about, hobbling awkwardly back and forth with his splint and every now and then pausing to poke his nose into the salt-laden breeze and bay. His howls only encouraged the horseplay.

Brandy laughed until her sides ached. Even Foucher gave in to a bout of merriment. Before long only Jackie, Foucher and Tremaine were left on the quarterdeck as the other officers joined the rest of the crew members.

"Why don't you join them?" Brandy asked Jackie.

The smile faded from his face. "I — I'm just the c-cabin boy," he told her. At her slight frown, he elucidated, "They don't want me there."

Brandy made a moue. "And how many of them started out as cabin boys?"

"Undoubtedly very few," Keir said from behind her. She turned to look up at him in surprise. "Go on, lad," Keir said to Jackie. "It's all right."

Jackie looked uncertain for a moment, then brightened. "Aye, Cap'n." He left the quarterdeck with eager steps. But as he approached the gathering, he slowed and remained on the periphery of the group.

"Why doesn't he join them?"

Keir stared across the deck, his hand shadowing his eyes, his gaze alert and sharp. "The boy stutters, and common sailors are an intolerant lot. 'Tis a sign of weakness, any impediment . . . something to be looked down upon."

"But 'tisn't fair. Jackie's —"

"Life isn't fair."

She opened her mouth to retort, but Keir's eyes slitted, his mouth tightening, and Brandy followed his gaze across the deck.

Someone had grabbed Jackie by the arm and slapped the mop on his head. The music picked up in tempo and the

178

same man pushed the youth into the dancing area with such force that he stumbled into several other bystanders. "Dance, Jackie boy . . . dance!" the troublemaker cried. Several of the others joined in half-heartedly, and then backed away at a sharp reprimand from Peter Stubbs.

The music faltered, then died away on a few scattered, discordant notes. Foucher pushed away from the rail. *"Sacrebleu!"* he swore. " 'Tis that *cochon* Smythe." He began to move toward the steps in high dudgeon.

"Leave them," Keir commanded softly.

Foucher halted just as Stubbs intervened across the way. The quartermaster exchanged a few words with Smythe, then turned to the musicians. They recommenced, but much of the initial enthusiasm had been dulled by the incident. Several men moved back to their tasks, and no one seemed inclined to renew the dancing.

Jackie returned aft, the spring gone from his steps, his expression defeated. Keir moved to put a hand on the youth's shoulder, then let it drop to his side as he saw Smythe standing brazenly behind the musicians and staring straight at him.

"Go below and take the hound before he loses his balance and pitches himself into the sea," Keir told the youth.

Brandy remained on deck for a time, but her enjoyment was spoiled by the incident. She watched Smythe for a time, resentment rising in her, but when he began watching her in return while Keir's attention was claimed by the second mate, she swung away and moved to the rail to gaze out to sea. The ocean spray misted her burning cheeks, cooling them, and her anger subsided as well. It wasn't her place to question or accuse. She was completely out of her element, no matter how much she might enjoy sailing and learning about life at sea.

The thought did nothing to lift her spirits. It only served to remind her that she was leaving England farther and farther behind, leaving her mother and father, Simon, and Abra. And on a ship of some seventy-odd seasoned mariners. Seventy-odd men. The only thing that stood between her and them, she suddenly realized, was Keir St. Andrews. And what did she know of him? Virtually nothing. If it ever came down to the captain of the *Odyssey* having to place himself between her and his crew, what guarantee did she have that he could ultimately control them? She had just had a glimpse of how easily things could get out of hand. Peter Stubbs had quelled the rowdiness, but what if more of the men had become involved? What if this miscreant Smythe had had more support from his fellow crewmen?

The band members ceased their playing, rousing Brandy from her disturbing thoughts, and the remaining crew began to disperse. Stubbs rang the ship's bell for second dogwatch, and she went belowdecks with a heart pressing against her ribs like a stone.

"I expect to hear 'land ho' shortly after dawn," Keir said to Foucher. "We've made good headway in spite of the storm off France."

*"Oui, Capitaine.* We will stop for water?"

Keir nodded. "And any fresh meat or other supplies Gonzalez may want . . . we left London so abruptly. Have him talk to Rollins."

The cabin door swung shut behind them and their words were muffled. Brandy knew Rollins was the boatswain, the man in charge of stores, but her uncharacteristic melancholia dulled her usual interest. Let them talk in the passageway, or up on deck, it didn't matter, because suddenly, reaching the Canary Islands took on a new aspect for her. Rather than a goal, as viewed by Keir and his crew, it now represented the final stop before they turned southwest for the last — and longest — leg of the journey.

She stood at the cabin window, watching the coruscating disk of the sun dip into the silvered sea. The western horizon glowed golden, slashed with alternating striations of teal, then paler gold, then lavender, then gold again, then a cobalt that stained the upper vault of the deepening twilight sky overhead with the vividness of a stained-glass window in a medieval cathedral.

It was breathtaking, she silently admitted, but that endless stretch of sea . . . She'd heard talk at the inn of men who'd gone mad from being at sea too long, a desert of salt water more dangerous than sand. She understood why Keir was taking valuable time to take on additional fresh water, for it was the most precious commodity aboard a ship.

How many more days would they be at sea? she wondered. And then they had to return . . . if and when their mission was accomplished.

She heard the soft creak of the door behind her and asked over her shoulder, "How far is it from the Canaries to our destination?"

"Jamaica."

"Jamaica, then. How far is it to Jamaica?"

Keir didn't like the sound of her voice. It was dull. Unanimated. And he suspected he knew the reason. She was young, unused to life at sea, and certainly homesick. "A bit farther than the first leg of the journey, but—"

"How much farther?"

He sighed softly, apprehensive of how the knowledge would affect her. "Roughly three thousand miles."

She turned slowly to face him. "Three thousand miles?" she repeated, her voice a whisper of sound. Her eyes were wide with disbelief, her face leeched of color.

"Brandy," he began, his voice unusually gentle, and took a step toward her.

That very gentleness was her undoing. "Why?" she asked him, the word edged with the beginnings of hysteria. "Why did you force me to remain here when you could have—"

"Could I have?" he asked less gently, his look turning bleak.

"Oh, aye . . . you could have forced me. I was no match for you! Then you would have been satisfied and, soiled or nay, I could have gone home."

Emotion rose in her throat, choking her. She felt the ache of tears behind her eyes . . . tears of frustration and fear of the unknown.

"You are not the kind of woman with whom a man can

satisfy himself physically . . . only to let her go."

He knew it now . . . he'd known it then, a fortnight ago, whether he'd acknowledged it or not. That was exactly why he'd allowed her to keep her precious virtue, but not her freedom.

Brandy, however, failed to hear the ultimate compliment behind his words. She only knew that he'd had the power to seduce her that first night—hadn't he proven just how malleable she was before his skill as a lover at least once since?—and hadn't used it to get what he wanted. Now, here she was, in the middle of nowhere, because he'd given in to some bizarre whim and left her virginity intact . . . only to render her the victim of an infinitely more heinous crime, that of indefinite captivity.

She crossed her arms about her waist and huddled where she stood in emotional anguish. "If I'd but known," she cried, "if I'd but known, I would have let you have your—"

He was before her then, taking her stiff body into his arms and pulling her close. "Hush now," he soothed, his cheek against her hair. He expected to feel awkward in his attempt to put her at ease, for soothing a woman was not his habit. But this was different. "I'll see that you are returned to England, you have my promise." The words just came, but Keir realized that he meant them.

Until she broke away from him and looked up into his eyes, bright, shining hope in hers.

She wrapped her fingers around his forearms, the first time she'd ever touched him of her own free will. "Let me off in Tenerife," she said, her voice breathless with desperate hope, her fingers clenching with unsuspected strength. "I'll do anything you wish," she rushed on, afraid he would refuse before he could hear her out. "Anything!"

Keir glanced down at the bloodless fingers gripping him, more to shield the alien uncertainty he knew would show in his eyes. He could feel her tremble, a delicate shudder that traveled up her arms and through her body until, as he dared to lift his gaze again, he saw that even her lips quivered almost imperceptibly. He felt himself lost, washed away like a fragment of flotsam in the liquid amber depths of her very fine eyes. The appeal in those bottomless orbs touched his heart in a way he hadn't been touched in twenty years.

God help him, he wanted her so very badly, but not so that he would be forced by some desperate bargain to let her go afterward. He wanted to take her, make her part of him, delve into her body . . . but also her heart, her mind, her soul. He wanted to recapture that innocence she represented. That innocence of which he'd been brutally robbed in the first weeks aboard Captain Samuel Brewster's slaver in his initiation into that sacred and sordid entity of *matelotage*.

" 'Tis not enough," he heard himself say in a voice that sounded hollow.

The hope in her eyes dimmed, then died, replaced first by incomprehension, then by outrage. And finally by the agony of acknowledged defeat. Brandy Dalton was no shrew, no hysterical termagant to rail at him, to hurl insults at him, to kick and scream and resort to destruction, unless she were panicked. She possessed a quiet strength, an inner courage, and it was all the more shattering to see her crushed beneath the pestle of his selfish whims and driving ambitions.

"Brandy," he murmured, a plea in the rich resonance of his voice. "Sweet, sweet Brandy . . ." His lips ghosted over hers with a tenderness that took her off guard . . . so lightly, so carefully, even though her mouth had all but healed nicely, as he'd predicted. The heart-wrenching catch in his voice was not lost upon her. In its wake she allowed his arms to settle about her shoulders, to pull her up against him with a firmness that denied refusal, yet with a reverence she couldn't know he'd accorded no other.

She came to him without resistance, spellbound by the softening in his magnificent eyes when he pulled away slightly to fuse his gaze with hers. She allowed him his way as he conjured up the first, tentative stirrings of desire since he'd worked his magic while she'd been held immobile in the watery prison of her bath what now seemed months ago.

One hand glided up and down the length of her spine over

the soft silk of her tunic while his mouth tasted the corners of hers. His tongue slicked across her lips, coaxing open her mouth and flicking the hard, pearled edge of her teeth before slipping through that last barrier to encounter hers.

Hot, liquid desire pulsed through her lower body as their tongues met and meshed, and she groaned softly, her hips moving against his in ancient, instinctual invitation. A delicious madness invaded her blood, pounding through her veins, singing through her limbs. All thought of escape, of homesickness, of the unknown ahead of her, disappeared before the seductive song of passion, and, acknowledging every feminine instinct that had drawn her to this man from the first, she acquiesced with a natural sensuality that delighted Keir.

His hand left her back and joined the other to cup her buttocks, then slide upwards to follow the curves and cays of her hips and waist, ribs and breasts. "Ah, so sweet, my brandy-eyes," he murmured against her mouth, their breaths mingling like the warm morning mists that rose from the sea. He drank of her sweetness, succored by her eagerness, infinitely glad that he'd not forced her that first night, for *this* was well worth the wait . . .

He put an arm behind her knees and whisked her up into his embrace without effort. Before she could catch her breath, Brandy found herself lying on the bed with Keir looming over her, a shadow to her sunlight. He loosened the cord holding her tunic closed and uttered a soft imprecation upon encountering the barrier of her chemise. With an impatience sprung from spiraling passion, he tugged down the straps, finally rending it at her waist and tossing it aside.

Her breasts were pale in the waning light from the window nearby, and he smoothed his thumbs over their peaks, causing Brandy's eyes to widen in wonder. She arched up toward him. He lowered his head. The ends of his hair that had been loosened by the sea breeze tickled her ribs and added to the heightened sensations streaking through her body. He took one nipple into his mouth, his teeth gently nipping it to life. A tugging feeling rippled through her abdomen.

Brandy's hands moved over his shoulders and upper arms, then eagerly sought the V at his neck. With shaking fingers she unfastened the hooks and eyes and smoothed the garment over his shoulders, eager to feel his flesh against hers. Keir raised his head and shrugged out of the shirt, first one arm and then the other.

He gathered her to him, breast to breast, as a cherished thing, holding her to his heart, its beating in perfect rhythm with her own. Through her breeches, Brandy felt his need — turgid, pulsing — and she whispered shyly, "Will you let me touch you as well?"

"Not yet, Brandywyne," he teased. With an unholy grin he trailed one hand down to the waist of her breeches, slipping his fingers beneath to stroke the silky flesh, lower, lower, until they hovered tantalizingly close to the downy entrance to the essence of her femininity.

He watched the surprise of supreme pleasure spread across her face, hesitation banished by rapture. Her eyes went dreamy with heavy lassitude, his own enjoyment enhanced by hers as his fingers crept lower to seek the moist, slick sheath that was ripe and ready for him.

Her eyes closed, her body establishing a natural rhythm against him.

It was then that he realized just how long it had been since he'd had a woman. In his intense preoccupation with his business with Charles Stuart, he'd undoubtedly been the only man — aside, possibly, from Jackie — aboard the *Odyssey* who'd neglected to ease his physical needs with a wench. Even that had been secondary, literally forgotten in the face of his crusade.

Keir's own desire rose to a roaring pitch as he simulated the act of joining with gentle and steady purpose, loath to hurt the woman beneath him by a rough entry of his own raging need.

A soft, sweet moan rose in Brandy's throat, her body arching convulsively against him. He felt her constrict about him in silken contractions that caused him to clamp his teeth over his bottom lip as he held himself in taut check.

As her world shattered into bright fragments of delight, Brandy opened her eyes, floating, untethered, in bliss. "Keir," she whispered on a ragged sigh. She pulled his head down to hers, her lips moving over his face, tasting, gently worshipping, as if she couldn't get enough of him.

"Little wanton," he murmured in her ear, nuzzling the velvety lobe.

"We shall see who's the wanton," she answered with newfound coyness, her features flushed with passion. She put her hand between their bodies to feather over the light layer of curling chest hair that whorled about his breast and abdomen. Keir allowed her better access by settling to her side, one leg resting across hers, and allowed her to explore with tentative fingers.

She massaged his paps, feeling them harden in response, before trailing her fingers downward to his taut belly. She skimmed over his navel, circling it teasingly before unfastening his codpiece with a boldness that would have made her blush if she hadn't been so caught up with the man, the moment, the powerful sensations and emotions he continued to elicit from her like the wonderfully wicked wizard he was.

Keir aided her fumbling fingers until his desire sprang free, and he guided her hand toward it.

Suddenly, just sensing the size and solidity of it brought doubt prickling through her. It showed fleetingly in her expression, and Keir kissed her mouth leisurely but thoroughly before saying, "Don't worry, sweet, 'tis not so fearsome as that."

In the wake of her hesitation, he recommenced his lovemaking with his hand, preparing the way for their ultimate union.

"You're so very wicked," she murmured, her body beginning to writhe beside his with a will of its own. "And I am, as well."

"I am wicked," he agreed in dulcet tones, "but you are lovely."

He'd never said such a thing to any woman, but from somewhere the words came, easily, naturally. He would

186

make her forget everything but him, he swore to himself. He'd bond her to him with such strength and need that she would go with him to the farthest corners of the world if need be until he'd gotten enough of her. In that moment, his mission to obtain his stolen birthright was pushed aside, his vow to take a noblewoman to wife forgotten as he imbibed the heady and healing draught of sweet innocence that was Brandy Dalton.

"Be mine, Brandy-eyes," he urged her, leaving off his stimulation to shimmy her breeches over her slim, curving hips before he divested himself completely of his own. When they were both nude, he put one arm beneath her shoulders and braced her against him, his mouth marauding hers with exacting thoroughness. "Be mine, love," he murmured again, his voice deeper, richer, huskier than she'd ever heard it.

He positioned himself at the moist apex of her thighs while he kept her occupied with his kisses, tempering his desperate desire with the knowledge that he would have to hurt her, and dreading the moment.

But Brandy smoothed her hands down the sleek musculature of his shoulders and back, then settled over his hips, gripping, tightening, automatically pulling him to her with a growing need.

Keir entered her with a graceful twist of his hips. She arched her neck in abandon, wanting, needing more. Keir complied, gently continuing to sheath himself until she stiffened slightly, her eyes opening to encounter his in surprise.

"It won't last, sweeting," he reassured her, and thrust past her maidenhead, the need to brand her as his own overwhelming. He paused then, resting within her, his gaze melding with hers. "I'll never hurt you again," he vowed: some secret part of him so very thankful that he was the one who was given the privilege of initiating her into womanhood.

The trust in her eyes clutched at his insides, and made him exquisitely gentle as he began a slow, seductive rhythm of rapture. She began to respond as the discomfort disappeared and gave way to a building pressure of expectation, of impending physical release that would not be denied.

Together they strove, their tempo building, the tension burgeoning, until they crested, weightless as sea foam atop a breaker. Time hung suspended for both an ephemeral and eternal moment before they crashed like the surf against the shore, their satiation rolling them along like an expending wave, finally dissipating to a watermark etching an empty beach, the only evidence of their shared bliss.

Keir gathered her close to him, his lips resting against her forehead, and held her wordlessly. The silence surrounded them, bonded them in the intimate aftermath. The air hung heavy with teak, warm whale oil, and the essence of male and female.

Brandy's thoughts chased one after the other, despite her sense of peace and her physical surcease. She wanted to reassure him that she was no wanton, but that would have been a lie. With this man, from the beginning, she'd been wanton, needing only his touch to bring new and wondrous sensations flooding though her like riptides.

In the tempest of his lovemaking, he'd made her forget everything else but him. What had happened to her scruples? Her initial determination to deny him? Surely she was undone. . . .

The rhythmic rise and fall of his chest, the even cadence of his breathing, told her that the object of her thoughts was sleeping. She pushed slightly away from him and carefully leaned her head upon the heel of her hand to study him while he slept. It was a new experience, studying Keir St. Andrews at her leisure, without the fear of getting caught like a silly chit with her first infatuation.

The harsh lines about his mouth and eyes were relaxed. He looked little older than herself, although she suspected he had almost half a score of years on her. That masculine beauty she'd noted and admired was even more apparent, more potent in repose. And the driven look was erased, the almost ever-present preoccupation eased.

At first, realization was slow in coming. It began as a niggling, nebulous suspicion, then suddenly bloomed like a scintillating shower of sparks until it consumed her with its tremendous implications. She was not undone, not ruined, for the blush of passion and powerful emotion that still radiated from within her left her warm and satisfied. And something else. Something infinitely more important.

Nay, she may have been bewitched in some way, but she was not mad.

She knew now that if Keir St. Andrews agreed to free her in the Canary Islands in the morn, she would not go. She would not allow herself to be separated from him now, for she had given herself to him, body and soul. She was more securely tethered to the *Odyssey* than if with ball and chain in the darkest hold.

For she loved him.

"I love him," she whispered to the shadows, savoring the sound and feel of the words on her lips. "I love Keir St. Andrews."

What did it matter, she thought after moments of newly discovered wonder, if he was a pirate or corsair or buccaneer? She was only a tavern-keeper's daughter, after all. They were more a match than she had any right to deny.

She settled back into the circle of Keir's relaxed embrace. A smile bowed the corners of her mouth, the taste of him still on her lips, as she thought how wonderful was the gift of love. Surely it was something, like that shared by her parents, to be treasured, nurtured. And hadn't Keir treated her as something precious in their lovemaking? Surely that meant that he loved her in return, although she would wager her only set of clothing that he would not easily admit it. Not now, at least.

He was a man driven by private devils, but she would help him banish those dark secrets. She would enfold him in the cocoon of her love, teach him to laugh, to love openly. The intoxication of her discovery gave her new strength, new hope, renewed joy.

Her eyelids drifted closed, the smile on her lips slackening

189

but not disappearing completely. Oh, aye . . . she had plans for Keir St. Andrews, no matter where he took her. She didn't doubt that he would keep his word about returning her to England, but in the interim she would remain at his side willingly and out of love.

And she would do anything to fortify and protect that precious, newfound love.

# Part Two

## Island of Springs

*". . . the most lovely that eyes have seen . . ."*

Andrés Bernáldez
Columbus's chronicler

# Chapter Thirteen

*18 October*

" 'The most lovely that eyes have seen . . .' " Keir quoted softly as he watched Brandy'e eyes widen in wonder.

She nodded in silent accord as the breathtaking sight of Jamaica materialized before her in the clearing morning mists.

The island rose from the sea in majestic splendor, its blue mountains wreathed in clouds as they jutted upward from the ocean floor in seeming attempt to touch the heavens above. The *Odyssey* sliced through the aquamarine waters, sails billowing, gliding toward the island like a child unerringly homing to its mother.

"*Xaymaca,* island of springs," Jackie added from beside her at the rail.

" 'Tis the Arawak Indian name," Keir explained.

"I've never seen the like," she said, awestruck, her eyes drinking it all in as fast as the images registered in her mind. 'Tis wondrous, your Jamaica. No wonder the Spaniards have colonized the Main and would monopolize it."

The corner of Keir's mouth pulled down at her last words. "Hardly for the beauty of the area, but rather for it's material wealth." Brandy looked up at his stern, strong profile. "They've decimated the Indian population in their bloody greed, destroying whole civilizations for gold and silver."

"Aye, but they don't control Jamaica," Andrew Tremaine

added. "English captured it in 1655 and put the small Spanish garrison to rout." With a sweep of his arm, he included the harbor ahead of them and its heavily fortified reef. " 'Tis one of the world's great natural harbors, and between yon reef and the fortifications, as you can see, 'tis all but impregnable."

"Aye," Jackie said, his eyes alight with excitement. He pointed toward the extreme western end of a ten or twelve mile-long sandy spit jutting out from the island and nearly enclosing the huge natural harbor. "And some say that Point Cagway—"

"Port Royal now, lad," corrected Tremaine.

"Port Royal then, is one o' the wickedest cities in the world . . . full o' troops from the harbor forts . . . an' old discharged Cromwellian soldiers . . . an' *buccaneers!*" he breathed, with a mixture of reverence and fear.

"You do well to fear them, Jackie," Keir said over his shoulder. "They're a brutal lot."

His gaze caught Brandy's fleetingly, a silent challenge in the narrowed green eyes beneath his lashes. But Brandy merely smiled, unwilling to be baited, and returned her attention to the island.

"So many mountains!" she exclaimed. "is the entire island mountainous like this?"

"There are lower ranges to the east," Tremaine informed her, "but at this end, the flat, sandy strip of coast skirts the ocean and then, almost immediately behind, the Blue Mountains begin. They are higher and more rugged."

As they approached Port Royal, Brandy watched the deep blue waters slowly change to olive-green. "Why does it change colors?" she asked, fascinated with the sea's shifting shades.

"Silt," Keir said. "The port's waters are silt-laden."

Brandy took this in without speaking, then glanced sideways at Keir. The softness about his face when they'd first sighted Jamaica was gone suddenly, replaced by a set look to his features, a familiar bleakness that had been banished much of the time since they'd first made love. With his arrival at his destination, his demeanor had once again reverted to the familiar sternness Brandy had come to associate with the Keir St. Andrews she'd encountered at the Hawk and Hound.

Keir swung, then, to Foucher at the helm. "King's Wharf."

The sailing master nodded. *"Oui, mon capitaine."*

Men swarmed up the rigging, shortening sail, but Brandy had grown accustomed to the sight and gave them little more than a glance. The island before her recaptured her attention, seeming like something from a fairy tale, a mystical kingdom in shades of cobalt, emerald, and alabaster. The rising sun warmed her back, sparkling upon the clear surface of the sea, the balmy breeze caressed her cheeks like a benediction as it brushed by whispering, *Xaymaca . . . Xaymaca. . . .*

She felt Keir's eyes on her and lifted her face to his. He touched her chin with a gentle finger. "Already under the spell, are you?" he asked, something infinitely tender passing through his eyes before his expression hardened. "Well, brandy-eyes," he continued, his soft words carrying the unmistakable ring of authority, "I regret to inform you that you cannot leave the ship. 'Tis for your own safety . . . naught else."

Her features changed dramatically from excitement to acute disappointment.

"I never said you could debark once we reached the island," he reminded her, his tone firm. "You heard what Jackie said. English troops are bad enough, but former Cromwellian soldiers turned cattle-hunters for lack of anything more honorable . . . Well I won't have you put in jeopardy because you yearn to touch your feet to terra firma." He lifted her chin to close her mouth as it started to open in protest. "And as for the *boucaniers,* they are the worst . . . the dregs of society." He cocked an eyebrow. "On a par with your pirates, anyone can tell you."

He turned before Brandy could answer. "Tremaine?"

"Aye."

"I want regular watches—no anchor watch—while I leave

195

the ship to seek out either the governor or Mansfield. In fact, I want no one to leave or board the *Odyssey* until I return. You can tell Stinson to fill in for Stubbs. And I want no trouble; if the crew cannot keep themselves occupied for a few more hours, they can scrub the decks. Is that clear?"

"Aye, Cap'n."

Keir turned to Jackie. "Fetch Peter, lad."

The quartermaster had been standing on the main deck, hands on his hips, his face lifted toward the mountains. Brandy watched as Jackie spoke to him. Stubbs said something to Oliver Stinson—Ollie, the quartermaster's mate—who was standing nearby, and then returned to the quarterdeck with Jackie.

The *Odyssey* docked as smoothly as a great, graceful seabird. Less than an hour after the ship was moored, Brandy watched as Keir, sword and pistol at his sides, left the vessel with Stubbs in tow. A fine frown drew her brows closer as she watched the men disappear among the crowd that swarmed the dock area.

"What does he seek here in Jamaica?" Brandy asked Jackie as they watched the two men disappear among the milling seamen crowding Lyttleton's Warf.

They were left alone at the rail, and Brandy had decided that now was as good a time as any to corner Jackie about Keir's voyage to the Indies.

Jackie looked away from the seeming chaos that was a typical thriving port, and cast a furtive glance behind them. "The cap'n'd have my hide if 'e knew I was tellin' you aught I'd heard of his past."

His troubled gaze met hers, his previous excitement extinguished like a fragile flame in an uexpected puff of wind. "I know little of 'is past, but 'twas, I warrant, naught any man should like to remember."

Brandy's brow darkened, her curiosity piqued.

"They say 'e's spent the last score o' years roamin' the main. Driven by some kind o' wish fer vengeance . . . revenge fer somethin' that happened te him when 'e was a lad." His voice was low, so low that Brandy had to strain to hear it. "That's all I know."

She looked to where Keir and Stubbs had been swallowed up by the multitude of humanity toiling among stacks of cargo. Ox carts and horse-drawn drays carried hogsheads, chests, and large bags to the wharves. Waiting ships, their bowsprits lined up and jutting over the cobblestone street like lances from bygone days, received the goods or were relieved of their loads. The sounds of groaning timber, creaking winches, bumping cargo, and shouting, cursing men met and mingled with the susurration of the sea and the somnolent ocean breeze.

"Something unpleasant indeed, if he's kept it a secret," Brandy mused aloud. "Something, mayhap, important enough to ask the king's help while in London?"

His gaze dropped beneath the intentness of hers. " 'T-t-tisn't my place to say," he hedged with the beginnings of a stutter. "Even if I knew."

Brandy was silent awhile, thinking over all that she knew, meager though the information was. In the weeks of their voyage, Keir had told her nothing of his reasons for journeying to the West Indies. And in truth, she'd not asked him, either. Only now, after having come to know him better, did she realize that he had been grimmer than she had ever seen him that first time at the Hawk and Hound. Harsh, preoccupied, and certainly irritatedly distracted. In fact, if she'd been asked to put a name to his mood, she would have said it was a controlled desperation.

Her eyes narrowed in thought, seeing not what was before her as the *Odyssey* sat docked in Port Royal, but rather the image of Keir after he had returned from Whitehall that first day she'd spent aboard the ship. She remembered waking up the following morning, seeing him in sartorial splendor, his attitude almost light-hearted, a sense of expectation about him . . . almost eagerness.

Then, of course, he'd been furious with her when he'd returned both that afternoon and again that next morning. Yet he'd had every right to take umbrage—from his point of view, of course — considering that she'd made a shambles of his cabin and then, later, had tried to smash the windows.

But the line in his log book (which she'd never touched again) about the priest kept returning to taunt her and then skip away, with maddening elusiveness. There was some mystery regarding Keir St. Andrews that roused her natural curiosity. Perhaps it was the ease with which he slipped into the role of courtier, of the aloof aristocrat — and Brandy had certainly seen enough of that breed in London to recognize blue blood when she saw it.

Aye, she thought. Keir St. Andrews was hiding something that, if revealed, would dispel the enigma surrounding him, at least in her eyes . . . that combination of harsh, embittered seaman, and gentle, loving protector; of a man consumed by single-minded purpose, yet educated and enamored by the prose of Will Shakespeare . . .

Jackie was called away while she remained alone at the rail, looking to all the world like a slim youth, with queue, breeches, and silk shirt, engrossed in the bustling activities of Port Royal. Seemingly absorbed, her preoccupation was with her thoughts about the man she loved, and not the smell and sound and movement about her.

Suddenly it came to her.

Her hands gripped the rail in that flash of revelation, for the key to the contradictions that made up Keir St. Andrews had to be in his background . . . his life before he went to sea, something no one seemed inclined to discuss. Most probably, she decided, because no one really knew.

What, she wondered, were his origins? For in discovering that, Brandy suspected everything would fall into places like the missing pieces of a puzzle. And that answer, she strongly suspected, lay here . . . somewhere on the island of Jamaica. Perhaps it had something to do with the priest mentioned in the log.

*'Tis none of your concern, nosy chit,* warned a voice.

Aye, she thought. It wasn't. Natural, healthy curiosity was one thing, but poking ones nose in another's affairs was entirely different. If and when Keir decided to tell her about himself, she would be ready and willing to listen. Until that time, if it were to come, however, she would keep her musings to herself. She loved him as he was, now . . . a product of his past, whatever it might have been.


"Where is that *fou* Smythe?" Foucher asked Jackie, disdain curling his upper lip, causing his meticulously kept mustache to tilt to a villainous angle.

"Don't know, Master Foucher," the lad replied, unease crawling over him at the thought of the man who'd made a spectacle of him not so long ago. He bent to the deck with a new burst of energy behind the brush and sand.

Foucher studied the youth for a moment, then crouched beside him and said more quietly, "I did not see him on deck, *mon brave*. Better to have him out in the open . . . *en plein air,* than hatching some plot belowdecks, *n'est-ce pas?*"

Jackie squinted up at him against the bright tropical sky, essaying to hide his dismay at the sailing master's obvious intent.

The youth's apprehension unwittingly crept into his expression, and suddenly Foucher shook his head, his lips pursing, and stood. "I'll send another. 'Tis Stinson's responsibility, anyway. Finish up here." And, in dismissal, he quickly waved the back of his hand toward the hatch Jackie was cleaning.

Without thinking Jackie jumped to his feet. "I'll fetch 'im, sir, if ye want 'im."

The Frenchman's dark eyebrows tented. "You are certain?"

"Aye." Jackie wiped his wet hands on his breeches, dreading the lessening of Keir St. Andrews's esteem more than an encounter with Roger Smythe in the bowels of the ship.

*"Eh bien.* Tell him he is to —" Foucher glanced about the ship and the men busily cleaning and oiling and resecuring, "oil the oarlocks on the pinnaces." He inclined his head toward the ship's two boats lashed in place in their cradle amidships.

"Aye, sir." Jackie quickly moved toward the fo'c's'cle. He scampered down the main hatch and turned toward the crew's quarters, his steps suddenly less sure in the gloom of the lantern-lit passageway.

Just past the head, he stopped in midstride.

"I say we sell 'er."

"Ye *loco?*" another man muttered harshly. "She's the cap'n's woman, fer Christ's sake!"

The first man hawked and spat loudly. "She's a tavern slut jest like any other, I tell ye. Nothin' more."

" 'Tis just that *you* want 'er fer yerself, Smythe, 'cause we ain't had aught of bad luck since the Canaries," came the answer.

Jackie summoned his wits from where they'd scattered, and flattened himself against a shielding bulkhead. His heart throbbed in his throat, for here, as once before, was talk of direct disobedience. And nefarious plotting against Keir St. Andrews.

*Make a warning noise,* reason told him, *then let them see you.*

But his feet were moored to the floor, his limbs leaden with fear.

*The longer you skulk, the better the chance they'll catch you listening.*

Sweat popped out in beads along his forehead and upper lip; his armpits were suddenly wet. But he couldn't move, let alone get a word out of his mouth without violent stammering . . . which would give him away immediately.

Tears of frustration pressed against the back of his eyes. No wonder they made such fun of him. He was craven as the rawest recruit.

"Jest wait 'til St. Andrews leaves tonight . . ."

"I don't want no part o' nothin!" the second man cut off Smythe. "I—"

"—didn't have te come all the way down here, boy," Oliver Stinson's voice proclaimed in stentorian strains. "Cookie ain't all that un-understandin' . . . no need te try 'n hide it." He bent over Jackie after giving the boy a quick jab to the

200

gut, just enough to cause him to double over in stunned surprise. "Last time we'll have Gonzalez try anythin' new on ye, though," the mate added with a chuckle as he guided Jackie around the bulkhead to the hawsepipe and its 'head.' He gave Smythe and his companion no more than a cursory look.

"Up on deck, ye laggards," he threw at them over his shoulder. "Bo's'n's got somethin' fer ye to do 'sides dreamin' 'bout drinkin' and wenchin'.'"


Keir and Stubbs strode along the cobblestoned street toward Fort James.

"Place ain't changed a bit," commented Stubbs as they dodged the path of several nasty-looking pirates swaggering toward them. Painted prostitutes were pinned by burly arms to their sides, and two timid-looking merchants went out of their way to avoid them.

"Unhealthy place, I tell ye," Stubbs continued under his breath, eyeing the approaching ruffians reprovingly. "No proper landin' places fer decent ships, not enough streets, no house lots—"

Keir grabbed his quartermaster's arm just in time, and pulled him aside to allow the buccaneers passage. "Sweet Christ, what are you mumbling about instead of attending where you're walking?" Keir's words held the flaying edge of reprimand.

"At least I ain't lost the taste fer a good brawl," Stubbs countered with a sudden, sardonic shift of his mouth. His eyes narrowed, his smile immediately disappearing as he glanced over his shoulder at the offending ruffians.

Keir caught the spark of anticipation that ignited in his gaze. "Then you'll never fit in anywhere but on a privateer . . . or worse, changing allegiances as easily as the shirt on your back."

They proceeded on toward Lyttleton's tavern across Thames Street and down from the wharf where the *Odyssey* was moored.

"I don't need distractions just now," Keir added, regretting his irritation with the man who was his best friend. His eyes scanned the street ahead, searching for a familiar face. "I've got a shipload of wench-starved sailors itching to drink themselves senseless . . . and a vital personal mission. I need naught of trouble."

Peter Stubbs grunted noncomittally, then asked, "Lyttleton's?"

Keir nodded.

In a town of some four hundred buildings—most of them timber—Lyttleton's tavern attracted no more notice than a dozen or more tippling houses, brothels, and victualing places. The dominating edifices—aside from the three forts standing sentinal over the sandy strip of jutting land—were warehouses. Three and four stories high, all had great windows through which could be hoisted huge bundles, bales, and bags of merchandise for dry and safe storage.

On the left, the gaping doors of one of several buildings comprising the king's warehouses spit from its cavernous interior a column of twelve ebony-black slaves bent almost double beneath the weight of the casks of molasses they carried upon their naked backs, their leader cursing them in English and French as he herded them across the street, dodging the traffic, to a waiting ship at King's Wharf.

A lumber-laden dray creaked past them, the red-faced merchant in charge shouting at a slave driving the team of horses to slow down before they lost the load.

Lyttleton's came into view on the left. It was a two-storied, half-timbered building with a red-tiled roof. Keir and Stubbs cut diagonally across the thoroughfare, pausing once to allow a particularly mean-looking buccaneer, with a hideous scar deforming the left side of his face, to pass them by. Every few steps the cutthroat jerked a trussed—and very physically abused—Spaniard on a lead rope behind him.

The Frenchman alternated between quaffing from an uncorked bottle, the bloodred wine dribbling down from the corners of his mouth, and singing lustily and off-key in his native language.

"Poor bastard," Stubbs muttered as they neared and then

passed the buccaneer's captive tripping along behind him, the bloody tatters of his shirt and waistcoat flapping in the breeze. The man's battered face was a study in hatred, his dark hair plastered to his head, his once-olive complexion now mottled in shades of dull red to bluish black.

Keir ignored the pair as he touched Stubbs' elbow, guiding him forward briskly. "Don't go soft on me now," he told him.

Before Stubbs could open his mouth to reply, a trio of men exploded like shot through the open door of the building, narrowly missing the two from the *Odyssey*. They landed in various undignified—and painful—positions: one on his buttocks, another cracking his knees on the cobblestones as he pitched forward before saving himself with his outstretched arms, and a third tumbling backward in a somersault that ended before it was completed, with his unbending neck and cranium acting as a brake.

Beneath his fingers, Keir felt his quartermaster's arm go rigid in reaction to the loud crack of skull meeting stone. "Steady now," he cautioned softly as they sidestepped the unfortunates strewn across the street. Approaching the door with caution, Keir made to set his foot to the threshhold. An angry voice roared from inside, "And let *that* be a lesson to you, ye slimy sea snakes."

Keir prudently backed away just as the man appeared in the door, fisted knuckles set on his hips, against which rested a cutlass and a brace of pistols. "No one calls me a runt!"

"Oh, Jesus," swore Stubbs, *sotto voce,* 'tis the devil 'imself . . . Henry Morgan."

In the sudden silence, the two men standing beside the door caught Morgan's attention. "Well, well, well . . . if 'tisn't Captain Keir St. Andrews of the *Odyssey,*" he said, his Welsh-accented voice carrying both a lilt and a lash.

Keir nodded. "None other." He inclined his head toward the three dazed men on the ground. "I thought Henry Morgan had better things to do than brawling."

"Such as?"

"Sacking sleeping Spanish towns 'round the Main."

The small, lean Welshman narrowed his dark eyes for a

moment, then erupted into hearty laughter. "Haven't changed a bit, have ye, St. Andrews?" He motioned for Keir and Peter to come inside. "I thought ye were back in England . . . for good."

Keir hesitated only briefly before following Morgan inside the noisy tavern. The aroma of beef and turtle soup came to him over other, less pleasing smells, and Keir's stomach growled.

"Thought ye wanted Governor Modyford or Mansfield," Stubbs hissed in Keir's ear with a furtive jerk on the latter's coat sleeve.

"Morgan's just as good as Mansfield," Keir said through the side of his mouth as Morgan turned and motioned for them to sit at a table. They joined four other buccaneers already seated.

"Another round on Henry Morgan!" Morgan cried out above the din to a youth struggling beneath an unwieldy tray of tankards. "And be quick about it!"

He turned to Keir, then. "Allow me to introduce my, er, partners . . ." He grinned, sending his moustache atilt. "On the morrow we leave for the Yucatan and then" — he lowered his voice, "on to Villahermosa."

"That's more like it, Morgan," said Keir.

"One word of it to anyone and the *Odyssey* is without a captain."

Their eyes locked, arrogance and imperturbability, and the noise around them seemed to fade. Peter sat rigidly, not a muscle moving.

Finally, Morgan spoke. "You always were a cold one, never revealing what was behind those icy eyes but when it suited you."

"I don't take kindly to threats . . . not even from Henry Morgan."

Morgan waved a hand in dismissal. "Sail with me!" he said abruptly, breaking the tension. "Caitiffs and cullions abound, but I've always a need for good men."

Keir allowed his expression to relax slightly. "I've had enough of violence."

Morgan shook his head against Keir's refusal. "But this trip will be child's play . . . treasure enough for all of us with a minimum of bloodshed." He leaned toward Keir expectantly, his loam-dark eyes magnetic in their wild intensity. "Ye know what they say . . . 'Sail with Morgan and come home rich.' "

"Thank you, Henry Morgan, but nay. I'm in search of more important quarry than Spanish doubloons," Keir said evenly. "You've met my quartermaster, Peter Stubbs?" he asked, steering the subject to safer waters.

"Once or twice."

"And who are your friends?"

The dark-complexioned Welshman leaned back, bracing one bent, stockinged knee against the table as he leaned back on the two rear legs of his chair. His attention shifted, and he eyed the other men around the board slowly, consideringly. "These first three, Cap'n, are fellow countrymen of yours . . . Morris, Freeman, and Jackman." He nodded toward the fourth. "And the Dutchman, Marteen."

"I wish you good sailing, and much luck."

Morgan nodded his acceptance and unhooked the lace at his throat with one hand. He stretched the freed flesh of his neck by swiveling his head first one way, then the other, jutting his lower jaw. "And how do you come to be in Jamaica? Rumor had it that you left the Main for England, never to return."

"So much for rumor."

The drinks arrived and the group lifted their tankards in a toast proposed by Keir. "To a successful venture, Henry, for you and your partners."

Men leaned forward and pewter clashed, spewing rum onto the heavy wooden table. They drank deeply.

"Have you come a-carryin' the king's writ sayin' we can't attack the Spanish, St. Andrews?" Morgan asked over the rim of his tankard. " 'Tis said 'is majesty is anxious for peace with Spain since his restoration."

Keir shrugged, setting down his mug and grazing a thumb around its edge thoughtfully. "He gave me no such impres-

205

sion when we spoke. Rather, I had the feeling that the anti-Spanish and probuccaneer elements in the government were on the ascendant. And now with Thomas Modyford of Barbados as the new governor of Jamaica . . ." His eyes sought Morgan's in the dimness of the tavern. "You surely know what Modyford thinks of buccaneering."

The Dutchman interjected, "The buccaneers will always be an arm of the colonies' military forces . . . only a fool would fail to see that."

"Aye," added Morgan, "the most Modyford has done is pen paltry missives to the surrounding Spanish colonies, informin' them of his, er, *new* policy." He slashed the air with his hand in a negative gesture. "Bah! A pen is as nothing before a sword. The Main is ours to roam!"

Tankards clinked again in agreement, Keir's and Stubbs's included. It wouldn't do at all to insult Henry Morgan, Keir knew. Renowned for his ferocity, Morgan was also known for his cunning . . . and his ability to bend men to his will. The diminutive Welshman, though formally unschooled, possessed an immense capacity for learning through bloody experience. And he had the guile as well as the courage to put anything to the test.

Keir had no wish to have that guile, that mettle, brought into play against him.

"Furthermore," Morgan added, one eyebrow lifting in challenge, "we've privateers' commissions bearing Wyndsor's signature."

Ignoring the subtly cast gauntlet, Keir did not question the validity of documents signed by the former governor of Jamaica, who had now been back in England for almost three years. "A most prudent move," Keir acknowledged.

"I am rarely without an authorizing document," Morgan said, a smile lazing across his lips. He sobered then, pressing, "Did you have a change of heart after you saw that the king couldn't hold to his policy of peace with the Spanish?"

A corner of Keir's lip quirked with sardonic humor. "Nay. I seek a man here on the island." He paused, selecting his words with care. "I'd thought Mansfield could help me."

Morgan leaned forward, slitting his dark eyes. "Mansfield's in Ocho Rios just now. You'll have to settle for me, St. Andrews . . . or one of my friends here." He gestured to the others sitting along the trestle table.

Keir felt Stubbs's eyes on him. Then, on the periphery of his vision, he saw Peter unconcernedly raise a tankard to his lips. "I seek a Spanish priest . . . a Father Tomas. I sailed to the Main with him as a lad many years ago, and would know if he is yet alive. I've heard that he may be in Jamaica."

Morgan's forehead furrowed. "Tomas?"

"Aye."

The buccaneer scratched his head, setting his periwig slightly askew, then righted it as accurately as if his image were reflected in a mirror.

"There's a priest in the mountains," offered the man named Morris. "But I don't recall 'is name. Runs a mission fer Cimaroons and Indians up there somewhere, so they say."

Silence followed the man's words, while the noise and movement of the taproom swirled about them. Keir felt his chest tighten until he could barely breathe for those short yet endless seconds.

Morgan swigged his drink, then wiped his mouth with his waistcoat sleeve. "Aye. Father Tomas *de* something *y* something," he told them. "He's the only Spanish priest left on Jamaica that I know of, and he's either a fool or a madman to remain here. Up in the Blue Mountains somewhere, I've heard, savin' and protectin' — so he believes — a few miserable Arawak and Carib . . . and bothersome Cimaroons." He stared pointedly at Keir. "Why in bloody hell would you want to see him after all these years? Gettin' sentimental, St. Andrews?"

"Mayhap."

Morgan snorted in disgust and drained his tankard. "More rum!" he commanded the serving boy with a thunk of pewter against the battered table.

"But you can count on one thing," Keir informed him steadily, his green eyes firing suddenly.

"And just what might that be?"

"If I find him . . . if he's the Father Tomas I knew, my reward will be bigger than aught you could ever bring out of the Gulf of Campeche."

# Chapter Fourteen

An hour later they left Lyttleton's. The sun was high in the deep blue Jamaican sky, blasting the two men with its heat and brightness as they emerged. The ocean breeze, however, was a refreshing change after the stuffy tavern. It drifted over them, sweeping away the smell of spirits, pipe smoke, and the rank odor of crowded, unbathed bodies.

"Every opportunist in Jamaica will be a-searchin' those mountains by the morrow," Peter Stubbs declared as he hurried to keep up with Keir's long-legged stride.

Keir grunted in disagreement. "No one in his right mind would go chasing after what everyone knows isn't there," he replied. "The only treasure on any of the Antilles is the climate." He paused, throwing Stubbs a quick, measured look through his lashes. "Perhaps a jaguar or two for the menageries of Europe—"

"Jaguars?" Peter was quick to rise to the bait, his eyebrows flattening in surprise. Then he glanced up at Keir's profile and caught the slightest quirk at the corner of his captain's mouth. "Hummph. Ain't any jaguars hereabouts. Only on the mainland . . ."

"We'll need a pair of donkeys, Peter. What do you think?"

"Donkeys?" Stubbs scratched his bald spot. "I know naught of the beasts. If I could, I'd just as soon sail the *Odyssey* into them mountains."

Keir nodded, his lips curving suspiciously. "I'll warrant you would, you old tar. But," he lifted his gaze toward the

209

not-so-distant mountains, eyes narrowing speculatively. "We need dependable pack animals for the most basic of supplies, for we've no idea exactly where in the mountains the mission is located." He paused, his mouth tightening. "Nor how long it will take to persuade the good padre—if 'tis he—to accompany us back to England."

Both men veered toward the docks to avoid a tipsy pirate who was spraying passersby with wine from a cracked cask.

"Ye mean we could be searchin' fer days."

The undisguised bewilderment in his quartermaster's voice made Keir actually smile. "Only if you choose to go with me. Were I you, I certainly wouldn't risk my hide going on a crack-brained search into the Blue Mountains on hearsay."

"Well, o' course I'd—"

A rumbling sound drowned him out and, with an instinct developed from years of surviving by their wits at sea, both men looked over their shoulders just in time to see the cask of wine spinning downhill behind them. And gaining fast.

*"Gimme back my Madeira!"* bellowed the enraged buccaneer from where he stood, knuckles on his hips, drink-flushed features dark with drunken ire. He swayed with the wind and then straightened to put a foot forward in pursuit. But Keir had no time to hear or see any more. The barrel came catapulting right at them, forcing them to jump backward and out of the way as it bounced crazily on the cobblestones.

Peter ran an arm across his forehead in obvious relief. Yet when he looked up again anger seamed his brow. "Surely 'tis more peaceful up in the mountains chasin' Spanish Jesuits than this lawless place."

"Surely," Keir agreed as he turned to continue toward the *Odyssey,* then changed his mind, sidestepping the traffic on Thames Street and pulling his quartermaster with him. Keir halted his steps at the distant sight of the ship's bowsprit with its familiar figurehead of a long-haired siren.

"She looks just like the lass," Peter said softly, following Keir's gaze. "And she's brought ye good luck."

Keir frowned slightly.

"The siren, I mean," Peter quickly amended. "Ye once told me that you'd conquered the sirens, like Odysseus, and would use this one to yer advantage . . . a warnin' to others who would stand in yer way."

"And it worked, Peter, did it not?" Keir answered, his eyes still on the siren. "Just like Odysseus, who finally returned to his beloved Ithaca after almost a score of years, I shall return to England to reclaim all that is mine. But now, my friend," he said in a low voice, "we must decide who else is to go with us."

Peter Stubbs was quiet for a moment. His gaze moved from the *Odyssey* to Keir's face. He noted the absorbed contemplation on his profile . . . not the stern and grave mien that the *Odyssey*'s captain had effected as a buffer between himself and the world for all the years Peter had known him, but, rather, in that transient moment, a softened, more human thoughtfulness, as if in reflection of something too precious. Something or someone with the power to penetrate that barrier and reach the gentler side of the man.

"Aye, but what will ye do with *her?*" Peter asked softly, guessing his thoughts. "What's to happen to *her* when ye return to England an earl?"'

A troubled frown chased across Keir's face, banishing the new look of hope that had thawed his expression in the last weeks. Then it was gone. He looked at his quartermaster, a humorless smirk twisting his mouth. "Since when did you ever care about any wench I employed for my own pleasures? And since when are you assuming that the priest up in yon mountains is the Father Tomas who saved my life?"

Peter tucked his thumbs in the top of his breeches and canted his head upward to meet Keir's gaze head-on. He squinted against the bright sunlight, sucking in a breath. "I believe you were the one who jest said you'd return to claim what was yours . . . like Odysseus." He lowered his voice. "Ye asked me once if I'd stick with ye through all this . . . if I'd give up the sea if it came te that . . . An' I said I would."

"I haven't forgotten."

211

Peter gestured toward the *Odyssey* in the distance. "Well, ye can't just toss the lass aside like a useless piece o' driftwood when all this good fortune falls into yer lap."

Keir's face hardened instantly. "Good fortune? Fall into my lap? Damme, but you've acquired a distorted view of things, Master Stubbs!" He leaned an elbow against a pyramid of casks, of a sudden appearing anything but anxious to move from the spot. His narrowed eyes spiked into Peter like shards of green glass.

Stubbs dropped his gaze for a moment, and then glanced back at Keir. " 'Tis just that she deserves better. She ain't like the cullions we been dealin' with over the last ten years . . ." He trailed off, feeling his inadequacy with words before the wit and intelligence of Keir St. Andrews, cast-off aristocrat, but blue-blooded all the same.

"Feeling guilty, Peter?"

Anger welled up within Peter then, anger born of guilt. "I bloody sure am," he hissed, tossing aside rank for one careless moment. "Ye made 'er fall in love with ye, and you'll cast 'er aside once we reach England, I'd wager everything I own!"

"Nay, Peter," Keir said with maddening calm. "I'll deposit her on the doorstep of the Hawk and Hound with enough gold to allow Jonathon Dalton to retire to the countryside, never needing to soil his hands with common labor again." He straightened then and made to leave, indicating the conversation were over. "And," he added, "no man with his eye on her considerable dowry will give a fig for her lost virtue." He brought his face close to Peter's for the final salvo. "I'll make certain her dowry is worth a hundred maidenheads, never fear, our noble Peter!"

He turned then, and began striding toward the ship without a backward glance.

Peter stared at his retreating back, a most disconcerting combination of emotions tumbling through him, not the least of which was anger . . . continuing anger. He rarely got angry with Keir St. Andrews, but he was angry now. He forced his feet to follow in Keir's footsteps, admitting to himself for the hundredth time that he deserved his own self-reproach, his smarting conscience, for abducting a young woman, no matter the reason. He'd acted no better than the lowest sort of riffraff, and the scene in the yard of the Hawk and Hound had returned to haunt him night after night, flaying him with stinging memories.

But if he deserved what he was getting, not so the girl. And Keir St. Andrews' subsequent actions had been even worse than his own . . . to keep her aboard the ship against her will, to employ his expertise with the wenches on her until she'd actually fallen in love with him! It was written on her face every minute of every day. A man didn't' have to read *Romeo and Juliet* to see it.

Peter snorted in self-disgust, half-wishing suddenly that the priest in the Blue Mountains would not prove to be the same Spaniard who'd found Keir twenty years earlier. Maybe then Keir St. Andrews, as a common seaman, would consider a tavern wench like Brandy Dalton good enough to wed properly . . .

Which, in Peter's mind at that moment, he didn't deserve.


"C-c-cap'n?"

Jackie's voice came to Keir from the shadows at the bottom of the hatch ladder, rescuing him from his dark thoughts.

"Aye, lad."

Jackie gripped Keir's arm, a gesture that whipped the captain's attention fully into focus, so unusual was it. Extreme agitation was communicated to Keir through the stutter, the gesture, and now the stiffness of the youth's fingers as they clung to Keir's forearm.

"I . . . I m-m-must speak t-t-te you alone." Jackie swiftly surveyed the passageway before pulling Keir into the wardroom and closing the door behind them.

A stream of sunlight spilled through the single window, pooling on the table and brightening the austere room. Jackie's expression was strained, and Keir said the first thing that came to his mind. "Brandy?"

Jackie nodded.

Keir grabbed the youth's shoulders and gave him a shake, his look turning bleak. "What of her? Where is she?"

Jackie shook his head, obviously guessing his captain's thoughts. "B-B-Brandy's unharmed, Cap'n, but I heard somethin' b-b-belowdecks that I th-th-think you should know about."

Keir's grip relaxed and he studied Jackie's face. "If you're going to tell me what I think you are, then you need not worry about anyone discovering that 'twas you who told me. I know what a spot you're in, lad."

As Keir watched Jackie's expression soften to one of relief, he thought, *Indeed I know how you're torn between the crew and me, lad. But what you can't know yet is that they'll never accept you now, even should you completely overcome the stutter. You are branded forever among this crew as weak — an aberration.*

Yes. If left on his own, Jackie would have to find a different ship to start afresh once he'd rid himself of his handicap. But Keir had other plans for him.

" 'Tis Smythe, Cap'n," Jackie said into the silence. "I overheard him planning to . . ." His gaze fell to the floor, fingers of color reaching up into his pale cheeks.

"Planning to what?" Keir pressed.

"P-p-planning t-t-e sell 'er."

Rage rose in Keir. *"Sell* her?"

Jackie's eyes grew wide in the face of Keir's instant anger. "Aye." His head bobbed and he gulped once, his Adam's apple doing a dance in his throat. "And 'tis not the f-f-first time 'e's t-t-tried te get another t-t-te scheme with 'im."

With difficulty, Keir managed to swallow some of his anger for Jackie's sake. "I'll take care of this." He put a hand on the youth's shoulder. "Don't worry about any of it now. The matter will be dealt with, and no one need know you saw or heard aught."

A knock sounded on the door.

"Cap'n?" Peter's voice came from behind them.

Jackie jumped at the sound, then concern crept into his eyes again. "You'll not allow 'em te sell Mistress Brandy, will

214

ye, Cap'n?"

"Of course not."

"Cap'n?"

"You're dismissed for now, Jackie. Say naught of this to anyone."

The youth nodded and reached for the door just as Stubbs was opening it.

"We're suddenly most impatient," Keir told the quartermaster as Jackie left the room. "I don't remember answering your knock."

"I heard Jackie's voice," Peter answered, ignoring Keir's gibe. "And I suspect I know what he told you."

Keir's expression tightened again. "And how might that be?"

Stubbs waved a hand in dismissal. "Only Stinson and myself know what the boy witnessed. Stinson is loyal, ye know that. In fact, Stinson himself was approached by Smythe before the storm off the Canaries."

Keir frowned. "And he said nothing to you?"

"He thought to play along and mayhap catch Smythe at further collusion afore he came to me. What Ollie Stinson and the lad heard are more than enough to incriminate 'im."

"And who was the other crewman involved? Or were there more than one?"

Stubbs shook his head. "Only Reid . . . and he wanted no part of it."

Keir tapped the table with his knuckles, his eyes narrowed. "Every captain makes a mistake in judgment now and again. Mine was Smythe." He stared into the middle distance, his mind working. "To involve Jackie or Reid, especially when the latter was unwilling to become involved, would only cause distrust and trouble. I'd as soon not have either of them labeled 'telltale' among the crew. God knows, 'tis hard enough for a man to hold his own in the fo'c's'le."

Stubbs grunted his agreement.

"Are you certain no one else is in on this scheme?"

Peter exhaled with a hiss of resignation. "As certain as I c'n be. There's no certainty of aught . . . ever. I say we rout out

215

the snake. Have 'im keelhauled as an example."

"Nay. Why ask for trouble? If we quietly let him go, no one will be the wiser. Since Brandy will remain aboard ship for the return voyage, I'd as lief keep the entire affair hushed. Why put any ideas into a man's head?"

Peter Stubbs shook his head. "Many of the men've taken a likin' to Mistress Brandy. Say she brought the *Odyssey* safely through that big blow."

"And what of those who say she was the cause of it?"

Stubbs shook his head again. "I've heard no such talk since she risked 'er neck to save Jackie 'n the hound."

Keir swung toward the single window, his gaze upon the activities on the wharf. "You'll pay Smythe his due and let him go . . . quietly. If I ever see his face anywhere near the *Odyssey* I'll personally run him through. You can tell him that." He faced his quartermaster. "I want him off my ship. The sooner, the better."

Stubbs nodded in acknowledgment. "I still think yer bein' too lenient with 'im . . . especially with 'im threatenin' Mistress Brandy."

Ire flared in Keir's eyes, then was gone as he effectively snuffed it out, only an arched brow revealing his annoyance. "I see now why you sought an audience with me alone. You wouldn't be quite so cheeky in the presence of my officers."

Peter flushed at the rebuke before Keir added in a more conciliatory tone, "But I appreciate your concern for Brandy, Peter, if not your opinion of my decision."

Stubbs sucked in a breath, determination written on his features. He stabbed a finger at Keir emphatically. "Well, whatever ye may say te me, Keir St. Andrews, the fact remains that now ye have te take 'er with ye into them mountains. You'd be a bloody fool, Cap'n *Sir,* te leave 'er aboard the ship with Smythe on the loose 'n nursin' a grudge."

The silence stretched between them as Keir silently acknowledged the very thing he'd been thinking. He thrust his thumbs into his breeches and turned his head toward the window again. "Aye, Peter. I'd be a bloody fool indeed to leave her behind now, no matter how trustworthy her guard aboard the *Odyssey*." He laughed harshly, humorlessly, his profile as unrelenting as ever. "By the Mass, what a coil I'm in!" he said, more to himself than to Peter. "What I don't need on a trek into the mountains of Jamaica is a female." He caught Stubbs with his cold gaze. "More the fools we, for allowing her to take on such importance."

Peter took note of the bleakness in Keir expression and, after years of association with Keir St. Andrews, seemed to sense the pain behind the shield of icy disdain.

"Obviously, I haven't your approval anymore of anything I do or say concerning Brandy Dalton." Keir paused, half-hoping Peter would say something. "I would remind you, Peter," he added softly, "that 'twas you who brought her to me in the first place.

"And so I did. But there ain't a day that goes by that I don't regret it." And, as Keir's gaze remained locked with that of his quartermaster, he read the message, loud and clear: *In spite of all yer amassed wealth, yer position as owner and captain of the* Odyssey *. . . in spite of yer blue blood, I'd never wish te changes places with ye . . . never.*

They set off in the early afternoon, a small cavalcade consisting of two pack animals, Keir, Peter Stubbs, Francisco (Cookie) Gonzalez, Jackie Greaves, Pierre Foucher . . . and Brandy.

Keir and Peter had chosen the men: Gonzalez for his physical strength and his fluent Spanish, Jackie for his nimbleness and because Keir was concerned about his safety, and Foucher for his insistence that he had been born and raised in the mountains of Provence. "No one can outclimb me," the Frenchman told Keir without batting an eyelash. "I am more at home in the mountains than at sea."

"But ye'll soil them fancy clothes," Stubbs had informed him, still obviously smarting over the Frenchman's disdainful words early on in the voyage regarding Stubbs's part in abducting Brandy.

When Keir would have interfered, Foucher held up his hands placatingly. "We will be equals when away from *Odys-*

*sey, n'est-ce pas?* Therefore 'tis in our best interests to put aside any differences, Monsieur Stubbs. Would you not agree?"

Anchor watch was established, with Andrew Tremaine in charge of the *Odyssey* in Keir's absence. Tremaine, Ollie Stinson (as quartermaster's mate), and the remaining officers were apprised of Smythe's dismissal.

Before they left the ship, Brandy and Jackie were the only ones who had no idea why they were leaving for the Blue Mountains. Brandy was very curious, but decided to hold her questions for the moment. Keir's behavior ever since they docked had reverted to cool aloofness toward her. The driven man had taken over once again and, in an effort to give him a wide berth, she asked no questions. She would go where he went, for surely she was safer with Keir St. Andrews in the mountains than in wild Port Royal with only a few crew members to protect her.

Yet, as they gathered on the noisy, busy dock before the *Odyssey,* Keir advised her and Jackie that he sought a Jesuit priest in the mountains by the name of Father Tomas. Only this Spaniard could identify Keir with any credibility before Charles II of England and, therefore, allow the return of an inheritance out of which he'd been cheated years ago.

That was all he told them, but for Brandy, it was enough. It explained many things, not the least of which was Keir's behavior since she'd met him. Undoubtedly he, like many Englishmen under Cromwell, had lost lands or estates or money. He no doubt was some dead squire's son, or mayhap even a baron who wished to reclaim what was his now that Charles Stuart had been restored to power. Small wonder this priest — obviously the one mentioned in the log book — was so important to Keir.

Keir scattered her musings as he lifted her to the back of one of the donkeys. "But I can walk," she protested with a laugh. "I'm not so fragile as that. Save your animal for supplies."

Keir squinted up at her against the blazing blue bowl of the Jamaican sky. She couldn't read his expression because his eyes were so narrowed, but his words and the tone of his voice were clear enough. "I'm taking you only because you wouldn't be safe aboard the *Odyssey*. In the interest of speed and safety you will obey my instructions to the letter. Do you hear? I will allow nothing—no even you—to endanger my chances of finding Father Tomas and returning with him to England."

"But why would a lad ride a donkey through Port Royal if he were perfectly capable of walking?" she asked, genuinely puzzled.

Keir produced a blood-stained wrap and proceeded to bandage her one knee. "Because he was wounded and couldn't walk as swiftly as we. Does that answer your question, Mistress Interrogator?"

His words stung. Brandy looked down at his fingers splayed over her breech-clad thigh and swallowed her hurt. She reached out tentatively to touch that beloved hand . . . a small gesture to reassure herself that what they'd shared for all those weeks aboard the *Odyssey* had meant something. She was rewarded with its instant withdrawal. She kept her gaze lowered, her cheeks hot.

"I would not have any lad touching me thus on a bustling wharf," he said harshly, for her ears alone, as a sop to her feelings. "The world doesn't need one more sodomite."

Of course. She'd forgotten for a few moments that she was supposed to be a boy. Surely it had been stupid to attempt to caress Keir St. Andrews' fingers as they'd rested momentarily on her thigh.

"Aye, Cap'n," she said in perfect imitation of Jackie.

He stared up at her for a moment, impatient with her feminine sensitivity. But she lifted her chin then, narrowing her eyes against the glare, and gazed about her with admirable composure.

"Once we clear the Port, I'll set you on your feet to get your land legs back. For now, enjoy the ride and say naught to anyone."

He moved away and Brandy immediately riveted her gaze to him. All the sights of Jamaica couldn't outshine Keir St.

Andrews in her mind. She would never tire of watching him, whether he was climbing the rigging of a ship or striding over terra firma. She instinctively knew he would sit a horse well, although she'd never ridden one herself . . . knew nothing about horses and equestrianism. Only the upper classes owned and rode them.

A vague sense of unease feathered through her at the thought, warning softly, stealthily. But she ignored the feeling. If it wasn't readily identifiable, it wasn't worth considering.

A smile bowed one corner of her mouth. There wasn't anything, in her mind, that Keir couldn't do, and do well. He was the man she loved, and he was simply the best man she'd ever known, except perhaps, she generously conceded, for her father.

But Jonathon Dalton was in London and Keir St. Andrews was here. Even the niggling homesickness at the thought of the Hawk and Hound was dwarfed by her feelings for Keir. She would go anywhere with him, be anything for him, do anything for him. To Brandy Dalton, it was as simple as that.

With her bright hair braided and hanging down her back like any other long-haired seaman, a kerchief atop her head, and a patch over one eye, Brandy squinted with a vengeance against the sunlight, screwing up her face to mask her delicate features, as Keir had instructed her.

In spite of the impediment of the patch, she gazed around her once the party began to move toward Thames Street. The donkey's bony back was not the most comfortable, especially with bundles slung before and behind Brandy, but the sights around her were too intriguing to dwell upon such minor discomforts.

They wended their way across the cobblestones and toward the opposite side of Port Royal. Brandy took in the sight and sounds and smells of the raucus town with a sense of wonder. Having lived in London for the past three years of her life, she'd grown accustomed to the noise and activity, but Port Royal was different.

It was disorganized and dissolute, she decided as they

220

dodged boisterous buccaneers and brazen prostitutes. The buccaneers were armed to the teeth, haphazardly seeing to the disposition of cane, slaves, wine, jewels, spices, silks and cattle. The prostitutes were of every race and color and dressed in brightly colored silks. Merchants hurried here and there, black slaves scuttling along in their wake, or they huddled together in consultation beneath what little shade the wooden buildings offered from the sun and heat.

Brandy would have dearly liked to ask Keir or Foucher or even Jackie any number of questions, but she was effectively silenced by her disguise. She was pinned to the donkey by her fear of being discovered as a respectable female in a city in which that commodity seemed to be in short supply.

*Are you respectable?* asked a voice, taking her aback suddenly at the thought. The sight of women who sold their bodies for a livelihood made her think briefly about her own position. As she rocked along atop the donkey, she tried to push aside the unwelcome voice . . . and the issues it would have raised had she been willing to heed it.

*'Tis only because Keir seeks a man of God . . . someone who surely will condemn your position as his . . .*

His what?

For the first time in weeks doubt assailed her.

*It doesn't matter,* she told herself under her breath. She closed her eyes and tightened her grip on the reins. *Love has no conditions . . . "Love does not insist on its own way; it is not irritable or resentful,"* she recited softly, and raised her eyes to the mountains before them as they swung to the left along the sandy beach and toward the main island.

*"Love bears all things, believes all things, hopes all things, endures all things."*

A benevolent calmness invaded her soul and dispelled her doubts.

## Chapter Fifteen

When they were east of Port Royal, Keir signaled the party to a halt. He walked up to Brandy and helped her down from her perch. Cocking a knuckle under her chin, he examined her face, turning it first one way, then the other. Without a word, he delved into one of the bags hanging from the donkey.

"May — may I walk now?" she asked, her feet feeling suddenly constricted within her shoes. She'd envied the barefooted slaves in Port Royal and saw now that Jackie was removing his shoes.

"Aye," Keir answered, then produced a wide-brimmed straw hat and plopped it onto her head over her scarf. He peeled away the patch and allowed it to hang on its string about her neck. "You cannot appreciate the view one-eyed," he said, his voice softening.

" 'Bout another six, seven miles, I'd say," said Stubbs from behind Keir.

Keir nodded, his eyes still on Brandy's face.

"Don't the sand feel wonderful, Brandy?" asked Jackie, his eyes aglow with excitement as he came striding up to her.

Brandy slipped out of her leather shoes. Her tender flesh met burning hot sand. "Ahhh!"

"You'll have to walk closer to the surf," Keir told her, and she nodded in agreement, her lids drifting closed for a moment as she instinctively burrowed her feet beneath the upper layer and encountered the cool, damp sand beneath.

"We shoulda brought Duds," Jackie said. "He'd o' loved roamin' about the beach."

*"Bien sûr,* answered Foucher from the side, the sea breeze ruffling his hair and making him look more like a corsair than a respectable sailing master. He gestured in typical Gallic fashion, revealing just what he thought of bringing along the dog. "The hound would have completed this domestic . . . gathering." His eyes briefly sought the heavens before he pointed toward the mountains. "He would have chased every gull and sandpiper from here to Ocho Rios . . . and just how would *le chien* have climbed those mountains, eh?"

"One would hope, better than he negotiates the decks in a storm," Keir said, unwilling merriment playing about his mouth as he watched Brandy open her eyes and break into sweet laughter at his comment.

"We'd better get goin'," Stubbs said as he shaded his eyes and glanced toward the sky.

*"Eh bien,* we do not know how far we must go. 'Tis better not to tarry," agreed Foucher.

The light in Jackie's eyes diminished, and Brandy watched as Keir placed a hand on the youth's shoulder. "There will be time to frolic later, lad," Keir promised him.

She heard the tenderness that tinted his voice for an instant, and acknowledged once again that Keir St. Andrews was a good man, in every sense of the word. Whether he would concede it or not.

They continued eastward along the pristine sand, the cries of the sea birds cartwheeling overhead mingling with the lulling *shush* of the waves in their ears. Spindle-legged sandpipers darted here and there, one in particular seeming to follow along in their wake for a good distance. He seemed to tire of the game, finally, and flew off.

Brandy ran about the beach with Jackie, like two children exploring a new world and discovering any number of fascinating things from shells to strangely shaped driftwood.

Brandy loved the sting of salt in her nose and on her tongue when she ran it over her lips, the kiss of the cool wind as it skimmed over her, fluttering her garments and wisps of her hair, and counteracting the heat of the sun that shimmered in waves before them. The sea was a sparkling aquamarine. Foam-crested breakers rolled lazily toward the beach. The cobalt sky was dotted with cottony clouds. Ahead of them, the island of Jamaica was a verdant green, its sentinel Blue Mountains pointing heavenward with white-tipped fingers that reached into veiling mists.

The sun was lowering as they left the miles-long sandspit behind and continued east along the island's shoreline for almost a mile. They stopped at a tiny settlement consisting of a small number of Spaniards and their black slaves who worked the sugarcane fields. Gonzalez translated for them, although most of the men from the *Odyssey* knew bits of the language by virtue of their being sailors.

At first the Spaniards were wary, for Spanish troops had been routed from the island in '55 when the English had captured Jamaica. The buccaneers from Port Royal were a threat as well, exhibiting a derision born of stalking and sacking Spanish ships and Spanish towns. But Gonzalez was told to assure the Spaniards that the men from the *Odyssey* sought only a priest said to be living up in the mountains.

"Ask them if they know aught of Father Tomas," Keir instructed him.

The answer was yes. The priest came down from his mission occasionally when his flock needed something from Port Royal or other settlements. But he was said to be stark, raving mad, and the settlers were leery of him.

"What better way to keep others away from his mission

224

# MORE PASSION AND ADVENTURE AWAIT... YOUR TRIP TO A BIG ADVENTUROUS WORLD BEGINS WHEN YOU ACCEPT YOUR FIRST 4 NOVELS ABSOLUTELY *FREE* (AN $18.00 VALUE)

Accept your Free gift and start to experience more of the passion and adventure you like in a historical romance novel. Each Zebra novel is filled with proud men, spirited women and tempestuous love that you'll remember long after you turn the last page.

Zebra Historical Romances are the finest novels of their kind. They are written by authors who really know how to weave tales of romance and adventure in the historical settings you love. You'll feel like you've actually gone back in time with the thrilling stories that each Zebra novel offers.

## GET YOUR FREE GIFT WITH THE START OF YOUR HOME SUBSCRIPTION

Our readers tell us that these books sell out very fast in book stores and often they miss the newest titles. So Zebra has made arrangements for you to receive the four newest novels published each month.

You'll be guaranteed that you'll never miss a title, and home delivery is so convenient. And to show you just how easy it is to get Zebra Historical Romances, we'll send you your first 4 books absolutely FREE! Our gift to you just for trying our home subscription service.

## BIG SAVINGS AND FREE HOME DELIVERY

Each month, you'll receive the four newest titles as soon as they are published. You'll probably receive them even before the bookstores do. What's more, you may preview these exciting novels free for 10 days. If you like them as much as we think you will, just pay the low preferred subscriber's price of just $3.75 each. *You'll save $3.00 each month off the publisher's price.* AND, your savings are even greater because there are never any shipping, handling or other hidden charges—FREE Home Delivery. Of course you can return any shipment within 10 days for full credit, no questions asked. There is no minimum number of books you must buy.

# 4 FREE BOOKS

## TO GET YOUR 4 FREE BOOKS WORTH $18.00 —MAIL IN THE FREE BOOK CERTIFICATE T O D A Y

Fill in the Free Book Certificate below, and we'll send your FREE BOOKS to you as soon as we receive it.

If the certificate is missing below, write to: Zebra Home Subscription Service, Inc., P.O. Box 5214, 120 Brighton Road, Clifton, New Jersey 07015-5214.

## FREE BOOK CERTIFICATE

### 4 FREE BOOKS

**ZEBRA HOME SUBSCRIPTION SERVICE, INC.**

**YES!** Please start my subscription to Zebra Historical Romances and send me my first 4 books absolutely FREE. I understand that each month I may preview four new Zebra Historical Romances free for 10 days. If I'm not satisfied with them, I may return the four books within 10 days and owe nothing. Otherwise, I will pay the low preferred subscriber's price of just $3.75 each; a total of $15.00, *a savings off the publisher's price of $3.00*. I may return any shipment and I may cancel this subscription at any time. There is no obligation to buy any shipment and there are no shipping, handling or other hidden charges. Regardless of what I decide, the four free books are mine to keep.

NAME

ADDRESS _____ APT

CITY _____ STATE _____ ZIP

( )
TELEPHONE

SIGNATURE _____ (if under 18, parent or guardian must sign)

Terms, offer and prices subject to change without notice. Subscription subject to acceptance by Zebra Books. Zebra Books reserves the right to reject any order or cancel any subscription.

GET
FOUR
FREE
BOOKS
(AN $18.00 VALUE)

ZEBRA HOME SUBSCRIPTION
SERVICE, INC.
P.O. Box 5214
120 BRIGHTON ROAD
CLIFTON, NEW JERSEY 07015-5214

if he's harboring runaway slaves," Keir commented, refusing to be disheartened by anything he heard. "Have they any idea where the mission is?" Keir asked.

Gonzalez spoke again to the men who'd approached them. One of them pointed northeast as he talked. Gonzalez turned to Keir. "The mission is said to be up on that mountain, but he advises that you wait until morning before continuing on. *Las montañas* are treacherous."

They set up camp on the beach, well back from the reach of the tide. As the sun set, Brandy began to glimpse another side of paradisical Jamaica. Ferocious sand flies attacked them and left bleeding welts. And, as if that weren't bad enough, swarms of mosquitoes required the men to build several green-wood fires to windward.

Brandy lay beside Keir, staring at the palm branches waving in the wind, thousands of bright stars against the deepening night sky winking at her through the swaying fronds. The sound from the trees was lulling, combined with the song of the ocean, and, exhausted, Brandy barely noticed when Keir stirred and then gently smoothed a cooling unguent over her chapped lips. He kissed her cheek and whispered, "Good night, Brandy-eyes," but she only smiled a little and burrowed into the light blanket thrown over the sand.

Her sleep was cut short, however, by low, unfamiliar sounds that intruded into her dreams. She sat up with a start, straining against the darkness outside the perimeter of the small fires to see what was causing the furtive noises.

"What is it?" Keir asked, and immediately sat up beside her. Stubbs, who had the first watch, was on his feet in an instant.

"Listen." She tilted her head toward the sound, which now seemed to come from all around them.

" 'Tis only scorpions 'n' land crabs comin' out fer their nighttime feedin'," the quartermaster said.

Brandy bolted to her feet, gripping a blanket to her.

*"Scorpions?"* she hissed in alarm. Suddenly everyone was awake and sitting up, squinting towards Peter and his torch as he stood beside Brandy.

"There's scorpions all over the Antilles, Mistress Brandy," Stubbs explained further when Keir remained silent, "but they won't hurt ye unless ye provoke 'em." He held the torch higher and swung away. "Look."

Sure enough, the beach was crawling with the spindly creatures skittering over the sand beneath the moonlight.

Brandy shivered, the gooseflesh raising on her skin, but determinedly clamped her teeth over her lower lip.

"Aw, Brandy, jest pull the blanket over yer head," consoled Jackie. "Crabs 'n a few scorpions are nothin' compared te snakes 'n' crocodiles—"

She jerked her head around to look at the youth, eyes wide.

"Or mayhap you'd like us to prepare you a special shelter for the night?" Keir cut in, as much to stop Jackie from his well-meant explanation as in genuine irritation.

But the sarcasm in his words was not lost upon Brandy. She dragged her gaze away from Jackie and hugged the blanket about her, her eyes on her bare toes. "Nay. Of course not." She suddenly felt ludicrous, standing there clutching the coverlet with five males looking at her expectantly.

The torchlight caught the strawberry gleam in an escaped hank of hair that partly shielded her face from Keir, and he suddenly regretted not only his harsh words, but the fact that he'd brought her halfway around the world on a whim. A selfish whim.

God knew what still lay before them.

Tenderness welled up within him, even as he sought to crush it. "Come back to the blanket," he said in a more conciliatory tone. "Captain St. Andrews will protect his lady from the sand monsters."

She couldn't be certain from his face, for his eyes were narrowed against the glare of the flambeau, but the huskiness of his voice acted as an instant elixir, soothing away her alarm. And, more importantly, the words 'his lady' registered in her mind like fuel to the fire of her confidence in his unvoiced feelings for her. Suddenly the demons of the darkness faded into insignificance, and her gaze clung to his, her mouth softening into that heart-stopping smile that had captivated him from the first.

"Of course," she said softly. "How silly of me." She turned the full force of her smile on Peter. The torch leaned drunkenly in the breeze before he caught himself and readjusted his grip, muttering a few words under his breath, his look suddenly sheepish.

As Stubbs swung away, Keir added, "We'll move closer to one of the fires. The creatures shun fire."

"Aye," Jackie put in, "but ye'll sweat like a pig."

At Keir's look, he bit his lower lip and flushed. Then, obviously struck by a thought, he brightened and offered, "But I warrant the sea breeze'll keep ye cool enough."

"Nay," Brandy answered, taking the initiative. "We can remain where we are." Ignoring the activity on the beach, she assumed her position beside Keir. "Sleep well," she said to him, and pulled the coverlet over her head as Jackie had advised her.

"I don't make a habit of sleeping with mummies," Keir told the bundle that was Brandy, a corner of his mouth lifting.

" 'Tis either sleeping with a mummy or sweltering by the fire," she said in a muffled voice.

He lay back down and draped an arm over an indentation in the blanket that looked temptingly like her waist . . . and stared into the darkness toward the mountains, all trace of levity slowly fading from his features.

The morning found Brandy sleeping alone. She awoke, the now familiar presence and warmth of Keir's body missing. With a swipe of her arm she whisked the blanket from over her head, only to discover a few alien aches

227

from sleeping on the hard mattress of the sand as she pushed herself to a sitting position. The world was cast in gold, but before she could decide why, she saw Gonzalez and Stubbs and Foucher collecting the remnants of the simple camp. Why had they allowed her to sleep so long? she wondered, her eyes automatically searching for Keir.

Jackie came running up to her. "Look, Brandy," he said, pointing to the beach between her bed and the ocean. "The monsters're gone." He grinned at her and she smiled back before allowing her eyes to scan the sandy strip. There was no sign of the creatures who had frightened her the night before.

"And so they are."

Then her gaze moved to the east . . . and paused. Brilliantly scintillating, the newborn sun sat serenely on the horizon, turning the water to silvered-copper as it spewed its orange-gold rays toward the heavens and spilled them into the sea. Palm trees lining the beach scythed the sky with their fronds as they dipped and swayed gracefully in the balmy breeze.

Brandy's breath came out on a ragged sigh at the beauty before her. Surely this was heaven . . . in spite of the crabs.

"Here," Jackie said as he put half a coconut in her hand. "Taste this."

"Jackie!"

The youth hearkened to Stubbs's call as Brandy gazed down questioningly at the coconut.

"Don't spill the milk," Keir warned from beside her. She looked up at him in bemusement, as much from the foreign fruit she held, as his sudden appearance. "I saw you admiring the sunrise. Had you slept much longer, you would have missed it."

"Then why didn't you wake me?"

Keir shook his head. "You'll need all your stamina in the hours ahead." He inclined his head toward the half coconut. "Try it," he urged.

She raised it to her lips obediently and was pleasantly surprised at the sweet flavor as she took a tentative sip. She drank the rest and then held it out to Keir.

He took it from her and sliced a piece of the white meat. "Taste it."

Again, she sampled hesitantly, then decided she liked its nutlike flavor. "What is it?" she asked.

"Coconut." He pointed to the palms along the beach. " 'Tis the fruit of the coco palm."

"It's delicious."

"I trust you slept well?" he asked, his manner changing suddenly.

"Aye." She smoothed her rumpled shirt and breeches with one hand, conscious of her untidiness.

Keir pointed toward the fringe of the beach, where grew the beginnings of the bush that nestled at the base of the mountains. "You may tend to your needs in privacy, and then get something to eat from Gonzalez. He roasted a few of those crabs."

Brandy made a face. "The coconut will do," she said.

"No it won't. We've a hard day ahead. You'll need all your strength and endurance to go up into the mountains afoot. I have no idea how long 'twill take, nor how high we must go, and I can't guarantee your safety on a donkey on narrow paths and trails. So put your shoes back on before we leave, and be certain to eat until you are full." He gave her a half smile before brushing his lips over hers. "We shall soon see what stern stuff Brandy Dalton is really made of."

Still munching her coconut, Brandy disappeared into the foliage at the top of the beach. As soon as she felt she was invisible to the others, she took care of her personal needs. A profusion of wildflowers in a rainbow of colors laced the verdant flora of the coastal area, although Brandy didn't recognize most of them. But the familiar fern was everywhere, in thick, lush stands. The memory of Jackie's mention of snakes and crocodiles, however, did

229

much to hasten her movements in spite of the beauty around her, as every strange sound held unknown danger.

She returned forthwith to what had been their shared bed upon the sand, and began folding the blankets. She loosened her hair and combed it through with one of a pair of tortoiseshell combs, complete with carved case in exquisite scrimshawlike design, then swiftly rebraided it. The combs and small case were the one thing she'd refused to leave behind on the *Odyssey*. They'd been a gift from Keir just before they'd reached the Indies, and Brandy treasured the set.

She placed everything in a sack, then carried it over to one of the donkeys. A quick trip to the edge of the water allowed her to wet her hands and begin to rinse her face.

"Aw, Brandy, I got us some fresh water fer drinkin' and washin'," Jackie said from behind her. "No need te use seawater now. Remember? 'Island of Springs.' There's water aplenty here." He set down a pail at her side. "Here . . . this one's just fer you."

Brandy gifted him with a smile of gratitude. "You're sweet, Jackie, to think of me."

" 'Twas the cap'n who told me to give ye your own," he admitted.

By the time Brandy was ready to eat, everyone else was ready to leave. Gonzalez gave her a small cache of food, through which she carefully sorted, afraid of encountering anything, now in the guise of food, that had crawled about the beach the night before. The strange yellow fruit Stubbs told her was a banana topped off her morning meal. It was filling and tasty, and Brandy delighted in trying the unfamiliar food.

Foucher led the small cavalcade, with Keir saying that he would go on ahead to scout out the terrain and warn them of any unforseen obstacles. Jackie followed Foucher, then came Brandy, the two donkeys, Gonzalez, and Stubbs bringing up the rear.

Brandy had sensed in Keir a growing restlessness and

230

preoccupation ever since they'd left the *Odyssey,* but as they penetrated the bush at the base of the Blue Mountains she soon forgot everything else but the myriad sights and sounds around her. Great plumes of bamboo, over sixty feet high, clustered here and there and waved like gargantuan feathers in the breeze. Many trees that were strange to Brandy, as well as familiar ones like maple and ash, were also a part of the bush.

Trees reminiscent of pines, but with long, feathery needles, prompted Brandy to ask Jackie what they were. He identified them as Caribbean pine, and they were everywhere, adding to a host of scents that perfumed the air. He also pointed out the vividly colored hibiscus, many as big as saucers, that spilled across the countryside together with pink and white and red, roselike oleander, poincianas and poinsettias.

As they began to climb, they came upon deep gorges scarring the mountains, with falls of water rushing over volcanic rock to cascade into pools and rivers below. The bush changed slowly to tropical rain forest that cloaked the mountainsides. It was lush and magnificent, a primeval paradise that held Brandy in awe. Brilliantly plumed parrots and parakeets flashed overhead, not to be outdone in color by streamertail and mango hummingbirds, threading with ease through the deep green foliage above them, while other creatures scattered through the undergrowth before the intruders. The air was thick with the fecund smell of the warm, humid forest.

Once, when Jackie pointed out a lizard lazing across a low-hanging bough, a ruffle of skin encircling its throat, an instinctive scream clotted in Brandy's throat as she also inadvertently picked out a well-camouflaged constrictor coiled about the bole of the same tree.

She clamped a hand over her mouth, her eyes wide, as much from an unwillingness to reveal her fear, as the fear itself. She shied away to the other side of the narrow path-

231

way, until she realized she was off the track, into a world that held more of the same.

"Careful, Mistress Brandy," warned Stubbs as Gonzalez took her arm and drew her back onto the path. "As fearful-lookin' as them snakes are, they're not as likely te harm ye as when ye step on 'em." He indicated the emerald and white snake that had sent her scuttling into the foliage. "He's no danger to ye from over there. Rather 'tis the ones ye can't see that can kill ye."

Gonzalez grunted as he guided her forward again. "*Venenoso* . . . poisonous."

Brandy glanced down at the lush-hued orchids and scarlet ginger lilies strewn throughout the undergrowth, half-expecting a serpent from this Garden of Eden to rear its ugly head from between the beautiful blossoms . . . to clamp its poisonous fangs into her flesh or coil its muscled body about her and squeeze . . .

The bright world around her suddenly darkened as her imagination took over for a few moments. Dear God, what was she doing here in this savage setting . . . the Hawk and Hound a mere remnant of remembrance?

Half an hour of uneventful trekking, however, except for the incessant humming and buzzing of insects all about them, soothed her fears and helped her get hold of herself. But it was the sight of Keir returning to consult with Foucher that truly heartened Brandy. They halted as he came toward them after speaking to the Frenchman.

"We have to ford a stream," he told them, his eyes sweeping over Brandy, a question in them.

"Don't see no problem in that," Stubbs said, " 'less it's deep."

Keir shook his head. " 'Tis shallow enough, but the current is strong now during the rainy season."

"We don't have te swim then?" Jackie asked, relief evident in his voice.

"You can't swim?" Brandy was genuinely surprised.

"Few sailors can," Keir told her.

"But—but 'tis illogical!"

"*I* can swim," Foucher announced.

Five pairs of eyes went to him.

"Whether 'tis logical or not," Keir said, ignoring the Frenchman's comment, "I didn't apprise you of the stream up ahead to begin a debate—on a rain forest path, no less—on the logic of a seaman's inability to swim." He gave Brandy a level look before continuing. "I just wanted to prepare you for what lies ahead."

"Well, let's get on with it, then," grumbled Stubbs just as thunder boomed in the distance. He glanced upward at the trees that canopied over them as thickly as canvas in some places. A red-and-green-and-yellow parrot screeched mockingly as it swept across his line of vision. "Can't even see the damned sky, but looks like we're gonna get a sample o' this rainy season . . . and the sooner we find the mission 'n' get on with the cap'n's business, the more te my likin'." He turned away and moved to reassume his place.

Keir followed his quartermaster's example and they moved ahead, with Keir leading now instead of Foucher. The sound of churning water came to Brandy, and increased in volume steadily as they progressed. So did the thunder.

By the time they'd reached the river, the heavens had opened and released a torrential rain. They stood looking at the narrow but unwelcoming stretch of rushing water while the rain soaked them through in moments.

Brandy stared at the tributary, feeling like a rat trapped in bilge water. There were other, less appealing sides to this paradise, she acknowledged with dwindling enthusiasm, for the only way she could envision fording the river was by way of rounded rocks, some of which were large enough to rise above the water, while others were half-submerged and, obviously, slippery.

Well, she could swim, although the water didn't look deeper than her waist, but the swiftness of the current, as

Keir had said, was anything but inviting.

Foucher crossed first, the leading reins of one of the donkeys in his right hand, his left held out for balance. Keir stood on the near bank, slapping the reluctant donkey on the flank as it splashed into the stream, braying in protest.

"We'll go last," Keir called to Brandy above the roar of the river and the rain. Brandy nodded and moved to stand nearer to him. Jackie followed in Foucher's wake, his trepidation evident on his blanched face.

"Steady, lad!" Keir shouted. "Keep your eyes on where you're stepping."

Jackie's foot slipped just then, and he toppled into the water, landing on all fours. As Keir had said, the water wasn't deep, and came only to the youth's chest as he knelt for a moment, seemingly paralyzed.

"Stay here," Keir told Brandy, and stepped into the water.

But just then, Gonzalez reached out and grabbed Keir's arm. "Look," he said into Keir's ear, his gaze riveted to a point a stone's throw downstream from the ford. *"Cocodrilo."*

"What in hell is it doing at this altitude?" Keir demanded, following Gonzalez's gaze. "Say naught. I doubt 'twill bother us now."

But Brandy caught the urgency in the Spaniard's voice, if not his words, and squinted against the rain sheeting from the skies to a place where the stream widened and the water was calmer. She made out what looked like a log, with protruding eyes, resting on the muddy bank.

*Crabs 'n a few scorpions are nothin' compared te snakes 'n crocodiles . . .*

Dear God, she thought, as she dragged her eyes from the reptile to Jackie.

"Get him up!" she shouted to Keir, her concern for Jackie momentarily overriding her alarm at the sight of the lizardlike creature. She moved automatically toward the water.

"Oh, no you don't," Keir said, the authority in his voice apparent through the symphony of the elements around them. "Get her back," he shouted to Gonzalez, and Brandy found herself halted in midstep.

By this time, however, Jackie had collected his courage and pushed himself to his feet, oblivious to the danger downstream. He nimbly stepped from stone to stone, obviously eager to get to the safety of the other bank, and Brandy let out her breath in relief.

"I'll keep an eye on the croc," Keir said to Gonzalez and Stubbs. "Can you manage the other donkey?" he asked the Spaniard.

"*Sí,*" Gonzalez replied as he grabbed the animal's reins.

"I'll bring up the rear, Peter. Follow Gonzalez and I'll put Brandy between us."

Brandy looked toward the crocodile again, but it remained unmoving, apparently uninterested in the activity of the humans crossing the stream.

"It's alone, I think," Keir said into her ear, "fortunately for us. But I doubt that it will fight so strong a current for its next meal."

Brandy nodded as Gonzalez coaxed the second donkey into the water. It bleated noisily as it splashed through the fast-flowing stream, with Stubbs smacking it from behind. Brandy glanced again at the crocodile. It raised its powerful tail once and desultorily slapped the mud, but it stayed where it was.

She wondered what crocodiles preferred . . . humans or donkeys.

"Don't think about it," Keir said to her, drawing her attention back to the matter at hand. "You're next. I'm right behind you."

She sucked in a breath, and swiped sopping tendrils of hair from her face before stepping onto the first small, water-worn stone. Trying not to think of the danger downstream, Brandy concentrated on keeping her footing. She looked up several times to see the others waiting across the way, shouting encouragement.

Two thirds of the way across, she lost her footing on a slick stone, and slipped into the churning water. She came up sputtering, and fought for purchase. Keir instantly grabbed the back of her shirt and hauled her to her feet. "We're almost across," he assured her, "just a little farther."

The sound of his voice, the touch of his hand, ungentle as it was, was reassuring, and she scrambled out of the water. As they neared the far bank, the rain stopped as suddenly as it had started. The sun broke through the clouds, lances of light penetrating the dense forest here and there.

"We made it!" Jackie exclaimed, the color beginning to return to his face. He and Stubbs reached out and grabbed Brandy's hands as she jumped from the last stone to the bank. Keir was right behind her.

"Are you hurt?" he asked her, a frown between his eyes.

She shook her head. "I could brave anything before the threat of *that*." She looked in the direction of the crocodile, suddenly giddy with relief that they'd all crossed safely. The overhanging foliage on this side of the tributary was heavy with rainwater and all but obscured her view.

Jackie, now safely out of reach of the creature, admitted, "Glad I didn't see it when I went down. I hate crocs."

" 'Tis over and done with," Keir said in answer. He scanned the group. "Everyone is hail? And the pack animals weathered the crossing as well?"

"Aye," Peter answered for everyone. He bent briefly to examine the foreleg of one of the nearest donkeys. "And let's hope that's the worst. I'll take a storm at sea any day."

" 'Twas no worse than the slippery deck of the *Odyssey* in a gale," Foucher said as Peter straightened. "What difference to be eaten by a crocodile or a hungry shark?" He looked over at Keir. *"N'est-ce pas, Capitaine?"*

But Keir's attention was suddenly not on Foucher . . . or anyone else in their group.

Brandy followed his narrowed gaze, as did the others.

"Sweet Jesus," Stubbs said softly.

There, beneath a shaft of sunlight spearing the trees, stood a tall, mahogany-skinned man. Clad only in a loincloth and another strip of material draped diagonally across his broad chest, he carried an ax tucked in the cord about his waist.

And a European musket pointed straight at them.

# Chapter Sixteen

The sound of rainwater dripping from sodden greenery was suddenly intensified, seemingly the only noise in the forest. Even the screeching of the bright-feathered birds and the ever-present hum of clouds of insects subsided in the brief hush that followed Peter Stubbs's exclamation.

*"Cimarrón,"* Gonzalez said into the stillness, breaking the momentary spell.

The stranger, standing still as a statue, edged the musket over a fraction until it was pointed directly at the Spaniard's chest.

"Easy now . . . you know they hate the Spanish," Keir said softly to Gonzalez. "Tell him we mean him no harm."

Gonzalez's mouth worked, but no sound emerged. Keir wondered if the Spaniard was thinking of the fate of captured Cimaroons . . . a host of tortures ranging from castration to being roasted alive.

"Don't fail us now, fer the love o' God," Stubbs exhorted.

A savage hiss of derision emanated from the Cimaroon in the face of Gonzalez's momentary struggle.

"Padre Tomas," Keir said in a calm, steady voice. *"Donde está el sacerdote? Somos amigos."*

The African answered in a mixture of Spanish and his native language.

"What's *that* supposed te mean?" Stubbs asked, irritation edging his words.

"S-something about *el cocodrilo*," Gonzalez said, finding his voice.

Keir glanced through his lashes at Brandy, but she remained still, an even tilt to her chin. If she was afraid, she was hiding it well.

"The cap'n asked 'im about the priest, not the croc," Stubbs insisted, his limited patience obviously wearing thin.

Galvanized by Peter's obvious annoyance with him, Gonzalez pulled his gaze from the Cimaroon long enough to frown at the *Odyssey*'s quartermaster. "Then *you* talk to him!"

"Enough of this!" Keir warned in a low, terse voice. "He'd as soon roast you and have you for dinner as parley with you . . . both of you. Tell him you've not come to take him away. We but seek Father Tomás."

Gonzalez did as he was bid. As they waited for the answer, the Cimaroon eyed each one of them impassively, the musket still cradled in one lean, powerful arm. He paused when he came to Brandy, and Keir tensed.

"Bet 'e ain't even got powder 'n shot in his little pouch," Stubbs mumbled. "That weapon's empty."

"Then why do you not move toward him," Foucher challenged under his breath, "and prove your theory?"

The Cimaroon finally left off his examination and spoke to Keir, ignoring Gonzalez.

"What did he say?" Keir asked, having caught only snatches of the Spanish. The name 'Tomás,' however, in spite of the African's heavy accent, triggered a powerful churning in Keir's chest.

"Padre Tomás has no friends among the Spanish since they hunt his children, *los cimarrones*," translated Gonzalez.

"Tell him I knew Father Tomás before he came to Jamaica. And we do *not* hunt or harm his 'children' . . . or anyone else." Keir's gaze went to the slender African standing before them, still awesomely bathed in sunlight like some dark deity of the forest. "Ask him if he will take

239

us to talk to Father Tomas—and tell him also that the priest will be unhappy if he discovers that his *amigo* from long ago was not shown the simple courtesy friendship deserves."

Gonzalez translated Keir's words and waited.

The hush that had seemed to settle over the area was slowly being dispelled by the creatures of the rain forest, yet the Cimaroon remained unmoving, as if oblivious to everything but the men before him and their request.

He blended well with the wilds, this runaway African slave, a forest creature himself, yet he possessed a dignity and obvious intelligence that were readily apparent to the group from the *Odyssey.*

Brandy studied him from beneath her lashes, noting the animal hide pouch that hung from a cord slung across his chest, oppositely diagonal to the sashlike strip of cloth. She envisioned any number of strange things within that pouch and shuddered inwardly as her imagination ran wild. She noted also what appeared to be an amulet about his neck on a leather thong, but could not make out its details. Folds of cloth fell, mantlelike, from his back almost to his knees. Perhaps he'd been a chieftain in his own native land at one time, or his father before him. Certainly he held himself with pride, and seemed completely at home and in control.

Outrage rose in Brandy, momentarily pushing aside her other emotions. What right did any man have to make another a slave? To drag him from his home and family and carry him across an entire ocean to live out the rest of his life in servitude?

The Cimaroon spoke finally, the sound of his voice startling not only Brandy, but Jackie as well. The youth had remained unmoving up to that point, slack-jawed with wonder and obvious apprehension ever since the man had appeared like some avenging apparition.

"He says he will take you to see Padre Tomas only if you leave your weapons here," Gonzalez said.

"But we have no weapons," Keir answered, his eyes going to the African as he carefully lifted his hands, palms forward, from his sides.

Gonzalez translated and the Cimaroon shook his musket at them, the unexpected action sending Jackie colliding with the donkey standing beside Brandy.

"Easy, lad," Stubbs warned the youth, his own face drained of color at the swift, threatening movement of the musket.

A torrent of half-Spanish, half-African burst forth from the dark-skinned man, a note of outrage ringing through the close, humid air.

"A machete and dagger can kill a man as easily as a musket," Gonzalez interpreted.

"We need 'em te cut food . . . 'n hack our way through—" Stubbs began.

Keir sent him a quelling look and the quartermaster fell silent, his lips a tight line of disapproval.

"Damn savage'll kill us soon as our backs are turned if we surrender our daggers," Stubbs added under his breath.

Brandy caught his words, and so did Keir. He chose to ignore them, however. "Tell him we'll surrender our blades to him until we are ready to return to Port Royal. Does that satisfy him?"

Gonzalez spoke to the Cimaroon once more, and the stranger nodded his head, then pointed to the ground at his feet.

"Peter, will you do the honors?" Keir asked. "And, I pray you, move slowly and openly."

With a grunt—and what could only have been interpreted as a hostile look thrown at the interloper—Peter went from man to man, then to the supply bags on the donkeys, and deposited the small collection of knives and two machetes at the Cimaroon's feet.

"Let's see 'im carry all *that* while 'e keeps 'is musket pointed at us," Stubbs challenged, crossing his arms in a gesture of defiance after he'd backed a safe distance away from the Cimaroon.

The African raised his head briefly and emitted a call that sounded exactly like the cry of one of the exotic birds that inhabited the rain forest. Instantly, two other Cimaroons materialized from the trees, approached the leader, and bent to divide the cache of weapons between them. Without a word or a sound, they turned and disappeared into the forest behind them.

"Ain't that just splendid," Peter grumbled sourly. "Mountain pirates."

Keir cut him another reproving look. "I'm certain your sweet temper did nothing to aid our cause." To Gonzalez, he said, "Tell him we've kept our part of the bargain, now we expect him to keep his."

Gonzalez spoke to the stranger again, and the African nodded slowly, consideringly, his eyes moving to Brandy.

Keir tensed inwardly.

The Cimaroon spoke sharply, causing Keir's fingers to fist in reaction at his sides.

"He says he wants—" Gonzalez's words faltered momentarily, "er, *Brandon* to approach him."

"Nay!" Keir spoke unthinkingly, then wished he'd held his tongue. Surely his reaction would rouse the man's suspicions. God knew what this stranger would do if he discovered a woman among them. "Tell him the lad is timid . . . afraid of his own shadow, and 'twould serve no purpose to single him out."

Brandy slanted Keir a look in the wake of his words, but as his eyes met hers, his expression warned her to silence.

Gonzalez repeated Keir's refusal to the African, and the latter answered with a shake of his head.

Gonzalez turned beet-red, obviously at a loss for words.

The Cimaroon pointed to Brandy with his free hand and spoke more emphatically. Keir caught the word *mujer* . . . woman.

"What is he saying, Gonzalez?" he demanded, mentally calculating his chances of reaching Brandy before she did anything foolhardy.

"He wishes to know . . . . why you dress your woman like a warrior."

"Tell him we have no woman with us."

Keir watched a delicate pink suffuse Brandy's cheeks, even as she bit down on her bottom lip for control. Her nose was lightly burned from the sun, the sprinkling of freckles across the delicate bridge made more prominent by the kiss of the sun. Christ, he thought, she'd never looked more feminine than against the backdrop of a Jamaican rain forest, surrounded by five men. Six, if you counted the savage who'd detected her femininity with such unnerving ease. He wondered, for the hundredth time, what he'd gotten her into by bringing her along.

The Cimaroon shook his head, even before Gonzalez could translate Keir's denial. Then, without warning the warrior threw back his head and laughed aloud. The sound reverberated through the rain forest, sending scores of birds scattering through the trees with a deafening roar of flapping wings.

Keir made to move toward Brandy, but the African uncannily followed his movement with the musket barrel, his laughter ceasing as abruptly as it had begun. He shook his head and commanded Keir in Spanish to halt.

The captain of the *Odyssey* froze midstride, torn between his fierce protectiveness toward Brandy Dalton, and his self-disgust. When had he ever allowed his emotions to interfere with his instincts in the last half score of years or so?

*When you allowed her to creep under your skin.*

Gonzalez cleared his throat awkwardly. "He says . . . your actions say you lie."

"By the Mass, what difference does it make?" Keir said through set teeth. "Is he going to take us to Father Tomas or not?"

"Not, I think, *Capitán,* until we do as he says."

A tense, expectant silence ensued before Keir caught Brandy's movement out of the corner of his eye. "Stay where you are!" he ordered sharply, swiveling his head aside and spearing her with his angry green gaze.

The Cimaroon laughed again and said something to Gonzalez. "He wishes for you to follow directly behind him, *Capitán*."

Keir nodded, and watched as the Cimaroon, obviously having decided not to push the issue any farther, motioned to them with the musket barrel to follow him.

As the warrior turned his back and began to stride up the path, Keir moved to take up his original position. "Stay close to Brandy," he said under his breath as he passed Jackie.

Gonzalez moved to resume his own place in front of Stubbs, the sweat glazing his face an obvious testament to his ordeal. "He means Señorita Brandy no harm, I think," he whispered loudly to Keir as they came abreast.

A frown drew Keir's brows together. "Then why did he insist on singling her out?"

The seasoned Francisco Gonzalez colored again as he answered, "It would have been an insult to your taste in women had he not," he informed Keir, "for he said that any *cimarrón* warrior worthy of his name can smell a female a league away."

They snaked up the mountainside, the thick, shimmering air of the rain forest thinning out as they ascended. The lush flora gave way to conifers and more rugged terrain. Boulder-strewn gorges with foaming waterfalls and swift-moving streams replaced the heavy foliage nearer the base of the mountains, and Brandy feared that if they were fortunate to escape drowning while crossing several more tributaries they encountered, they would surely lose at least one of their party to a fall over any number of precipices to jutting rock below.

Their guide—or, perhaps more aptly, their captor—appeared thoroughly at home, no matter how the surroundings changed, and often Brandy lost sight of the tall Cimaroon as he nimbly skirted obstacles on the path or disappeared around a sharp bend. She found herself less fearful of the African than she might have imagined. They could not be in any real danger, she reasoned, if the Cimaroon was from the mission they sought. Surely no priest, whatever nationality he might be, would advocate violence in any form. Rather, Brandy found herself admiring the statuesque warrior's ability to continue at a brisk, steady pace, as sure-footed and confident as a mountain goat, as graceful as a gazelle.

The air thinned and the temperature dropped. Brandy found herself not only growing winded, but also chilled in her not-quite-dry clothing. She told herself that she could endure the chill after the muggy heat of the rain forest, but laboring to draw breath while engaged in rigorous climbing was another thing entirely.

Her life at the Hawk and Hound, and later within the limited space of the *Odyssey,* were in no way preparatory for this kind of activity. She saw Keir looking back to catch a glimpse of her more than once, and she was touched by his obvious concern. She'd read the self-reproach in his expression earlier, and she knew instinctively that he regretted what he thought was his part in revealing that she was not a male. Yet what Keir obviously interpreted as his own weakness was a sign of the feelings he harbored for her, as surely as if he'd declared them with words.

She felt she could brave anything in the face of that unspoken proof of his affection . . . and her deep and abiding love for him. She would follow him anywhere he would lead her. His quest had now become hers.


The mission was situated on the other end of a defile. It was all but impregnable, nestled within a pocket of mammoth volcanic boulders from which it could be effectively defended against any unwelcome intruders who'd managed to discover and slip through the narrow rocky passageway.

The mission church dominated the center of the clearing. It was made of rough stone, with thatched roof, and a carved wooden cross sitting atop it. Two others graced the double wooden entrance doors. A dozen or so small huts made of either thatch or the rocks and boulders that abounded in the mountains formed a crude semicircle about the church.

Before Brandy could take in any more, the growing commotion caused by their arrival claimed her attention. She looked back at Keir, who was standing near the Cimaroon. The latter spoke to a small boy who stood nearby gawking at the strangers, his large brown eyes wide with a mixture of curiosity and fear.

The child went scrambling toward the church, glancing quickly back at them once, and the Cimaroon turned to Keir. "Padre Tomas," he said in his deep, heavily-accented voice, and pointed to where the child had disappeared.

By now, a small crowd had materialized around the group from the *Odyssey* and were babbling in low, excited tones and pointing toward the newcomers. Brandy drew several piercing stares as the sun shone upon the bright strawberry-gold braid of her long hair. Most of the residents were Cimaroons, she surmised by their skin color, but here and there a copper-skinned man, woman, or child stood out. Arawak, she thought, for surely those native Indians of the Antilles fortunate enough to have survived the rigors of slavery would flee to a mission such as this for protection against their harsh taskmasters, the Spaniards.

They were dressed in tattered breeches and shifts, many of the men bare-chested. The children were naked, and the younger ones clung to their mothers, peeking from behind a leg here and there, with wide, dark eyes.

Nobody within the party spoke, for the reaching of their destination suddenly took on a new aspect. What, exactly, did Keir intend to do now? How could a Spanish priest help him? And why would Keir wish his help after preying upon the Spanish for years? The curiosity and

246

sense of expectation were almost tangible, but Brandy's concern was for Keir.

Before turning her own gaze toward the crude building, she noted the tension in his stance as he stood rigidly, his eyes trained unwaveringly upon the church. A dark-robed figure stepped out into the sunlight from its shelter and looked toward them as the child pointed in their direction, one hand shielding his eyes. As the priest approached, the undertone of the onlookers died away to absolute silence.

"*¿Quienes son esta gente, Dionisio?*" the priest asked the Cimaroon who'd brought them to the mission.

As Dionisio began to speak, Keir interjected with quiet urgency, "*Por favor, Padre . . .*" His heart was rapping against his ribs like a ricocheting stone, the loud staccato beat thundering across his senses as he moved his mouth to form the words. "I am . . . *Soy— *" His words died off before he could finish, so powerful were the emotions churning within him.

He suddenly couldn't even remember how much English Father Tomas had understood or spoken years ago.

Keir's lips were stiff, his tongue paralyzed, his muscles turned to milk as memories came rushing back; for he couldn't overcome his astonishment at the fact that the man standing before him was indeed the priest who'd rescued him from certain death on an English beach twenty years ago. Aside from being thinner and harder looking, aside from a few added lines in his olive skin and some silver threaded through the still-thick shock of his dark hair, this was the same man.

As they stood face to face at last, Keir realized that he could never have forgotten the priest who saved his life, either in deed or in looks . . . the Jesuit who tended him as long as he dared before Captain Samuel Brewster decided to impress Keir as an eight year old lad, in spite of Father Tomas's vociferous protests.

The silence stretched as the priest studied Keir through shrewd dark eyes in the wake of Keir's desperate but incomplete interruption. Father Tomas looked

247

as sane as any man Keir knew.

One of the donkeys brayed and stomped a hoof; muffled coughs sounded here and there from the men from the *Odyssey;* the mountain wind whistled through the pines around the sheltered area of the mission.

Finally, beneath the stern stare of Foucher and the fiercely expectant expression of Peter Stubbs, Francisco Gonzalez straightened his shoulders and stepped forward. He cleared his throat. *"Somos del barco* Odyssey, *de Inglatera, Padre,"* he explained. He gestured to Keir. *"Este es nuestro capitán,* Keir St. Andrews."

Father Tomas briefly acknowledged Gonzalez. *"Comprendo inglés, mi hijo."* Then he said to Keir, "I know you from a long time ago, do I not? And that is why you came here . . . because of that acquaintance? Not, I pray to God, because you hunt men?" He glanced pointedly around the periphery of the settlement, his eyes alighting deliberately upon each man crouched on the encircling boulders with a musket trained upon the group from the *Odyssey.*

"Aye," Keir answered in a low, emotion-strained voice. "You saved my life on a beach off Bristol twenty years ago, Father." There was a tremor in his tone as he pronounced the word 'father,' for not only did it bring back stirring memories of his own lost sire, but also because, deep within his soul, he could never quite bring himself to believe that he would ever find the same priest and address him face to face.

The word also brought to mind that perhaps, even for a bitter, hardened man who'd cared little for things spiritual over the last score of years, there might have been some kind of divine intervention on his behalf this one time.

He suddenly found himself stranded upon an emotional seesaw, his feelings, his hopes and dreams, the course of his life itself, so very dependent upon this man's recollection and consequent cooperation.

He wanted to weep in frustration at his unexpected inability to take command of himself. Old seams were stretched to bursting once again beneath the pressure of feelings long-repressed by necessity.

Yet he did not dare . . . not now, when so very much was at stake, waiting for him to reach out to this man.

This man whose expression seemed to register nothing of recognition, only a frown . . .

Keir's heart sank to his stomach like a lump of lead. *Reach out to him . . . force him to remember what you suffered beneath his disbelieving eyes,* one part of him commanded. *Don't let him deny you!*

*Don't be a fool. You're an earl, not a buccaneer,* his nobler side countered.

To Keir's horror, he felt tears filling his eyes. Oh, God . . . before his men, before these strangers, before Brandy . . . Brandy . . . Brandy . . .

She was suddenly beside him, her hand slipping into his, her fingers forcing his clenched fist open and twining with his.

Unexpected strength flowed into him, shoring him up, restoring his resolve, allowing him to open his mouth and speak. "Do you not remember, Father Tomas?" he asked, his voice still not quite steady. "You and Arthur Biggs dragged me from the beach, half-dead, and took me back to the—"

Father Tomas's expression changed to disbelief. "Keir?" he whispered, as if the name had only just registered. He stepped forward when Keir nodded. Words deserted the captain of the *Odyssey* for another quivering moment before Father Tomas threw his arms about him, hugging him with undisguised affection as he mumbled, *"Gracias a dios . . . ¡Gracias a Dios!"*


Father Tomas's living quarters were every bit as humble as those of his flock. He lived in a stone-and-thatch hut, with only the meanest of belongings gracing the single-room dwelling: a small, hand-hewn table and stool, a pallet on the earthen floor, a single sea chest which, Brandy surmised, contained everything else he owned. A tiny altar of crudely carved wood with crucifix and bible were the only evidence of his calling.

As dusk fell, the small group from the *Odyssey* were safely ensconced beneath Father Tomas's benevolent aegis. After Dionisio had pointed out to the priest that the party from Port Royal included a woman, the Cimaroon had been told to shed his loincloth for breeches, and Brandy was accorded every courtesy, in spite of her apparel and the unusualness of her having accompanied the men from the *Odyssey* up into the Blue Mountains.

Father Tomas didn't question her presence, however, or her relationship with Keir, and for that Brandy was thankful to the older man.

As the sun set, the seven of them formed a tight, cross-legged circle on the floor of the hut, and several Cimaroons brought in bowls and platters of food. Brandy decided, as she ate of the luscious fruit, strange vegetables, fresh-roasted meat, and grilled fish that was passed around, that Father Tomas was no more than forty-five or so, with a keen intelligence and rare compassion that communicated itself through, not only his words, but his dark eyes and warm expression. All of them were obviously equals in Father Tomas's eyes as they partook of a late evening meal, whether captain or cabinboy, man or woman, priest or former slave.

He asked endless questions about the world outside of Jamaica, obviously hungry for news of Spain, even as he spoke fiercely against his fellow Spaniards. His English was surprisingly good, if a little hesitant now and then as he searched for the right word. "They do not quite know what to make of me in the settlements," he said in careful, halting English, his ability to express himself all the more admirable in light of his isolation from English-speaking men. Laughter shone in his dark eyes. "If by thinking that I am mad they stay away from my mission, so much the better. They already have much fear of Moses."

"Moses?" Gonzalez asked.

*Sí. El cocodrilo* that Dionisio and Miguel carried up from the marshes below. It is said that he is *el dragón* of the mountain."

Stubbs snorted. "Cap'n 'n me wondered what it was doin' so high up. The Cimaroon was jabberin' somethin' 'bout the croc when 'e first found us." He shook his head. "Thought 'e had bats in the belfry."

Even Keir roused himself from his musings to smile at that, and the tinkling of Brandy's laughter made Father Thomas's eyes crinkle as he grinned at her conspiratorially. "Dionisio feeds him faithfully, so he has no need to attack a man, but, I trust, you will not . . . divulge our secret?"

"Your secret is safe with us, Father," Keir said. "Moses is an effective deterrent . . . if he could be enticed from wallowing contentedly in the mud."

"Only, I fear, if his belly is empty," the priest answered, then said on a more sober note, "And if my countrymen make the mistake of hunting for escaped slaves on our mountain, they will be . . . how do you say? . . . *fortunate* to escape the spit of our muskets."

"But a man of God does not resort to violence, *n'est-ce pas?*" Foucher commented around a mouthful of succulent pineapple.

Father Tomas's expression turned grave. "I do not . . . condone the use of slaves. I came to the Caribbean on a slave ship . . ." He trailed off, glancing at Keir, but the latter's expression was unreadable in the flickering light and shadow from several torches set in wall brackets. "As did your *capitán.* The horrors of a slave ship are unspeakable: men and women chained hand and foot, stacked like cordwood in the black hold of the ship for five to ten weeks, only seeing the light of day when brought up on deck once a day to eat *judías.*" He spat out the last word. "Many did not live to reach their . . . destination." He stared into the middle distance, as if seeing images from the past. "They had to . . . survive seasickness and disease brought about by lack of any type of . . . sanitation and

251

adequate . . . nutrition. And if the ship went down, it became a . . . deathtrap."

The hiss and sputter of the torches was the only sound in the room in the wake of the clergyman's description of the infamous slavers and their hapless human cargo.

"You were on a slaver with Keir?" Brandy ventured to ask in the uncomfortable silence.

"*Sí*. I tried to convince Capitan Brewster to let Keir accompany me when we reached the Main, but he was an evil man. *Un diablo*. He . . . impressed an innocent *niño* into the crew of that devil's ship."

"Ye c'n smell a slaver five miles downwind," Jackie added softly, then shuddered.

Brandy glanced at Keir, as Peter cleared his throat uncomfortably and helped himself with unaccustomed energy to more roast pig. She could read little in Keir's harsh, shuttered expression, but the horror of the thought of Keir being kept aboard a slaver as a lad spread through her with long-reaching tentacles. Hadn't he said it had been twenty years ago? He couldn't have been more than eight years old . . . ten at the most.

Dear God, she thought, everything suddenly falling into place. To what kind of hell had Keir been sentenced as a child?

# Chapter Seventeen

"But, I do not wish to remind you of that," Father Tomas said, breaking the awkward lull in the conversation. "I am happy to see you as a healthy and prosperous man. *Capitán* of your own ship!" He smiled at Keir with fatherly pride. "And I thank you for the supplies you brought us . . . material for badly needed clothing, and—"

Keir didn't hear the rest, although his expression did not change. With a valiant effort he fought back the unwelcome memories that surged into his mind in the wake of the Jesuit's words, his eyes avoiding the clergyman's for a few moments as he struggled for control. When he finally spoke, his words cut ruthlessly across Father Tomas's acknowledgment. "I am more prosperous than you could ever dream, Father," he said quietly, studying his fingers as they smoothed the cloth of his breeches over one bent knee. "I can give you anything you need to benefit your work here. Anything at all."

"That is most . . . generous of you, *hijo mio,* but you owe me nothing."

Keir's fingers stilled and he raised his gaze to Father Tomas's face. "I owe you my life."

The priest shrugged and gave Keir a fond, paternal smile. "A man's life is everything, in this world, *sí,* but I did what any decent soul would have done under the circumstances."

"Arthur Biggs would have had it otherwise, as I remember." The memory came to Keir unexpectedly, a flash of pain shearing through him.

Father Tomas's face darkened with ire. "The man was a *cobarde*. A coward . . . a poor, selfish fool whose fear of his *capitán* was greater than his sense of right and wrong." He lifted a jug of wine brought up the mountain by one of Keir's hired donkeys, and held it high. "Shall we drink to your visit? God led me to you once, long ago. Now He has brought you to me as a sign that I do his will here in Jamaica."

The wine was passed around, and cups clinked.

"You say a man's life is everything," Keir continued after a few moments, his eyes still on the priest's face, "but I say 'tis nothing if he cannot be what he was meant to be."

Father Tomas paused in raising his cup to his lips and narrowed his eyes questioningly over the rim at Keir.

Peter suddenly wiped his hands on his breeches and stood. "Beg pardon, Padre, but of a sudden all that climbin's taken its toll." He looked pointedly at Gonzalez, then Foucher, then Jackie. His gaze avoided Brandy.

*"Mais oui,"* Foucher agreed, taking his cue and rising to his feet.

Gonzalez followed suit.

"But we haven't —" Jackie began.

"Cap'n has *private* business with the padre here," Stubbs cut him off.

Jackie jumped to his feet, his face flushing. "O' course."

Dionisio appeared in the doorway. Father Tomas spoke to him in Spanish. The Cimaroon nodded and moved to stand outside the door. "Dionisio will show you where you are to sleep," the Jesuit said. He glanced at Brandy, who looked at Keir and then made to stand.

"She will be safe? Absolutely safe?" Keir's tone was soft but steely as the others filed out, his eyes hard in the unrelenting planes of his face.

Father Tomas nodded. *"Ciertamente."*

Both men watched as Brandy left the hut.

"She is your woman, but not your wife?"

"Would any man take his wife on such a voyage?" Keir drew in a deep, steadying breath and slowly let it out before abruptly changing the subject when he addressed the older man. "I am afraid I must ask a favor of you, Father, even as I acknowledge your having saved my life . . . even as I acknowledge, perhaps, the unfairness of my request."

Father Tomas looked puzzled, then shook his head and smiled. "What request can be so unfair from one who I love as a son," he asked gently, "who has been miraculously restored to me by God, and brings me much needed supplies for my flock? You are like a breath of fresh air with your news of the outside world, your—"

"Father," Keir cut in without ceremony, the words bursting forth of their own volition now that his chance had finally come, "you must come to England with me and speak to the king."

The priest's look turned surprised, then puzzled. "Go to England with you?" he repeated in bewilderment.

"Aye." Keir leaned forward, his eyes boring into the Jesuit's. "I need your testimony as to what happened that night on the beach off Minehead a score of years ago. My entire inheritance is at stake . . . my entire life."

"But—"

"Do you not feel 'tis your responsibility since you were the one who sent me into slavery at sea for the next twenty years?"

Father's Tomas's face paled. *"Madre de Dios,* you just told me 'I owe you my life,' Keir St. Andrews! How can you say such a thing?"

But Keir was not about to give up. Not now. "Then you should have left me to die on that beach, Father, for what you thought was so noble an act not only forced me into Captain Samuel Brewster's heinous service, but reft me of my birthright . . . my country, my family; and my title, my holdings . . . those of my ancestors before me." He leaned even closer, his body rigid, his face a study in unrelenting intensity. "You sentenced me to twenty years of roaming the sea, of violence and death, of brutality and perversion, robbing an innocent eight year old of his childhood . . . his very decency! And only you can right that wrong. Only you can tell Charles Stuart of England what happened that night with any credibility, for my scheming uncle stepped in after doing his dirty work on the beach that long ago night and usurped my rightful place. Only you can convince the king that I am the real heir to my father's title, and not Giles St. Andrews. And I will do anything — *anything!* — if you will bear witness for me."

Father Tomas's eyes darkened with ire, his temper coming to the fore. "You know that I never meant to leave you on that slaver! *Dios!* how can you even imply it? But my place is here. Surely you know that if I leave these simple people behind, the Spaniards will hunt them down and torture them. I am committed to my work here . . . to *them.*"

"You owe it to me."

Father Tomas pounded his fist into his palm. "I owe you *nada!* I will not desert my mission . . . not even for you. You, who by your own admission, are a rich man. You, who have everything now, while these — " he gestured toward the door of the hut, "have only a — " he searched for the word, "tenuous hold on their freedom, their very lives, from God, through me."

"Everyone knows of the ability of the Cimaroon warriors to withstand the Spanish, Father," Keir said in mounting frustration. "There are settlements in the mountains of Hispaniola, the jungles of Panama, the brush of Cuba, and here in the limestone hills and the mountains of Jamaica. None of these have the benefit of your protection, yet they endure, they prosper . . . cultivating crops and trapping game. Their men run strictly disciplined societies, and in many cases raid the Spaniards in retaliation. I hardly think your flock would perish without you."

Father Tomas stood and began to pace the small earthen floor, his dark, tattered robes swirling about his ankles. "And who are you to say that I must give up my work for God here, eh? These people, too, have been torn from their

256

home and loved ones, but they, unlike you, Keir St. Andrews—" he paused and pointed a finger at Keir, "cannot return to their homeland. They must spend the rest of their lives here in these mountains, wondering when the Spanish will send enough men to capture them."

"That is illogical," Keir said, the wind going out of him as his head sank into his hands for a moment. "The English control Jamaica now. There are only a few Spaniards here and there in small settlements."

"And who will work the cane plantations for the *English,* eh? I am told that slavers arrive in Port Royal regularly. Surely the English are as, er, ignoble as my own countrymen in their methods of obtaining free labor."

"These, your people, are in little danger up here. Their warriors are most capable of defending the mission from this position. And I swear you will be safely returned to them."

Keir's assurances, however, obviously had no effect upon Father Tomas. As the silence stretched long between them, Keir slowly raised his head and met the priest's eyes. "I can have you taken by force," he said in a low voice.

Incredulity tracked across the Jesuit's brow. "You would stoop so low?"

" 'Twould not be the first time. I learned many things in the service of Samuel Brewster that would shock decent men like yourself."

There was a note of bleak self-scorn in Keir's husky voice. But there was also an iron will behind his words. "I noticed Dionisio's amulet. I warrant he believes it renders him immune to musketballs. Just how much progress have you really made in your quest to convert these pagan people?"

"And who are you to judge my progress . . . or lack of it?

"Dionisio! Miguel!" Father Tomas called, an urgent note in his voice. Instantly the two Cimaroons materialized at the door. "You forget one thing, Keir St. Andrews," he said. "You and your men are not only unarmed, but are vastly outnumbered here." He rapped out an order in Spanish, and Keir was taken by the elbows and hauled to his feet.

He put up no resistance, however, merely allowing a corner of his mouth to lift sardonically. "I had not meant for it to come to this."

"Indeed." The Spaniard narrowed his eyes at Keir. "And just how did a lovely *niña* like Señorita Brandy become involved with a . . . self-professed *pirata?*"

"Why, you just answered that yourself, Father. I'm a pirate . . . and I abducted her. What else would I have done?" he answered, bitterness curdling his words.

He shrugged out of the light hold of the two Cimaroons. "Would you kindly have them show me to my quarters for the night? To where, I hope, you've also taken Brandy?" he asked with an ironic lift of an eyebrow. "She's quite the fallen woman, now, after the long voyage from England. She will be awaiting me most anxiously."

After Keir was escorted from the hut, Father Tomas de Almansa y Espinoza stared at the open doorway for long moments. *"Dios mio . . . What have I done?"* he whispered.

*A never-ending stream of emaciated, ebony-skinned men, women, and children emerged from the dank, dark hold and were herded across the decks of the ship, arms across their eyes against sunlight scintillating on the water. The stench from the open hatches made Keir gag from his hiding place behind a large spool of spare cable. He fought against the reflexive action, knowing that he would reveal his presence if he made a sound.*

*Children wailed and men and women groaned and cried out in pain as sailors roughly prodded the stiff-legged humanity along toward the huge cauldron of beans—and any other leftovers from the galley—that served as their daily fare. Their chains dragged over the deck, eerie echoes of enslavement and degradation.*

*Keir felt the scalding, unwelcome tears of release rise behind his eyes, but he was not allowed to cry. He would be lashed if caught, for exhibiting such a weakness. He dashed a hand across his eyes as the building moisture blurred his vision, but too late. Tears tripped over his lower lashes and down his cheeks. He savagely swiped them away . . . .*

*"Weepin' like a wench, are ye?" Captain Samuel Brewster's unwelcome voice rasped in the boy's ear.*

*Keir froze.*

*"We can't 'ave our lads snivelin' now, c'n we?" he hissed in the boy's ear.*

*Keir shook his head, unleashing more tears, as terror immobilized his tongue.*

*"Mayhap a taste o' the cat'd set ye straight, eh?"*

*The bile rose in Keir's gorge at the thought of his back being cut to ribbons. Oh God, no! he begged silently. Please, not that . . .*

*Suddenly Brewster's big hand was over Keir's mouth, his other over the boy's crotch, fondling suggestively. "Or we c'n find somethin' else as punishment. Somethin' a bit more fun . . ." The pressure of his marauding fingers over the boy's genitals increased with sudden, cruel strength, and through the waves of pain, Keir felt foully violated. He instinctively began to struggle, against his common sense.*

*"Ye like it, don't ye," Brewster purred. "I c'n tell . . . ye pretend te struggle, but ye're just like a soiled virgin, pretendin' innocence all the while ye're pushin' against a man . . ."*

*Keir made a retching sound and Samuel Brewster laughed softly. "C'mon, boy," he ordered in a low voice as his enormous hands fell away. "Down te my cabin, pronto, as yer pompous padre friend'd say. And one word o' protest from ye, 'n it'll be fifty lashes, comprende?"*

*Keir nodded, then spun dizzily toward the ship's rail and heaved.*

He awoke with a low cry and sat up. His face was sheened with sweat, his entire body shaking.

"Keir!" Brandy reached out for him in the dark and encountered his icy hand. "What is it?"

Sweet Jesus. The old, familiar nightmare. It was back again . . . and she was there to witness it. He had to get away

259

from her. He couldn't let her see how weak he was. How soiled he really was. She'd never touch him again if she ever found out what had been done to him aboard that slaver.

Jesus Christ in heaven. Why hadn't he had the guts to fling himself over the rail and save his soul from eternal damnation . . .

He pushed her hand away from him and stood on unsteady limbs. "Leave me alone."

"But, Keir," her sweet voice came to him in the dimness, edged with distress.

For some reason it irritated him. Mistress Innocence really got herself mixed up with the lowest of the low.

*You're an earl.*

He ignored the unwelcome voice and swung toward the hut entrance on shaky legs, guided by a thousand stars that glittered like diamonds just in his line of vision, winking at him, beckoning him to open air and freedom from sleep, freedom from his old night terrors. And from the stifling concern of Brandy Dalton.

"Keir—"

He plunged through the door, barely noting that there had been no guards posted nearby. A cool breeze caressed his damp skin and he felt the prickle of gooseflesh. Blindly, he made for the periphery of the mission, slipping through a gap between two mammoth boulders, expecting to be stopped by one of Father Tomas's Cimaroons at any moment. Well, the only way they could stop him now, he thought grimly, was with a musket ball through his heart.

A slice of moon sailed the sky, a bright beacon in the blackness. The sound of rushing water came to him and he paused, listening. He followed the sound, suddenly shivering violently. Damn this mountain air, he thought, refusing to blame his chill on anything but the altitude and the wind. It sighed through the pines and then was slowly replaced by the ever-increasing roar of falling water. Sound and instinct pushed him onward, with the delicate glow from the night sky casting everything about him in silver-limned onyx silhouette.

Then, suddenly, he found himself standing in a clearing. There, across the way, was a waterfall, the source of the sound that had called to him. A rain-swollen stream plunged over the precipice high above him and spilled in shining silver sheets to a pool below. Keir moved toward the spangled pool, the liquid column of water showering into it, then geysering upward, fountainlike, before it fell back to its final resting place.

He moved forward, the siren song of moving water never failing to soothe him, steady him. Yet, as he skirted the pool to stand within a stone's throw of the falls, he knew a deep, dark ache that even this familiar balm could not completely ease: the knowledge that he would never regain Somerset Chase . . . that he could not, even in his blackest moments, bring himself to abduct the Jesuit who could, by a brief interview with Charles Stuart, restore all that Keir had lost.

He stumbled toward the cascading water, seeking surcease from the pain, the disappointment, the growing grip of unreleased grief that threatened his very sanity. A sharp stone sliced into his bare foot, forcing him to crouch down in reaction, nursing his hurt. He wished he had a thousand hurts like that in the tender arch of his foot, for only then could the emotional pain perhaps be overshadowed for a few blessed hours.

He sat there, staring at the faint line of blood as if it belonged to someone else. Violent tremors seized him again, and with them came the overpowering urge to cry. But he would not. He would not weep . . . he would not . . .

"Keir?"

Brandy's voice, barely discernable against the backdrop of the waterfall, came to him unexpectedly, a whisper on the wind. He stiffened, lifting his gaze from the mindless contemplation of his foot. His eyes stared into the middle distance before him, through the crystalline curtain of water and into nothingness. "Leave me be," he rasped.

Brandy knelt down beside him. In the moonlight, she

could see the stark, cold set of his profile. It only reinforced his words.

Compassion moved within her, for she knew from long and intimate association with him that he was hurting. Hurting so very much that she might not be able to reach him.

The thought gave her impetus. Had his dream upset him so, she wondered? Or was it his interview with Father Tomas? Or had one triggered the other?

No matter. She couldn't bear to see such suffering in the man she worshipped. She would get through to him.

She reached out a tentative hand to touch his bare shoulder.

"Don't touch me!" He jerked away as if burned.

She reached out again, ignoring his words. "Keir, Keir . . ." she soothed. "What's wrong?" He didn't pull away this time, but his muscles were rigid beneath her fingers and his skin felt cold, clammy.

"Go away. I don't want you here."

She lay her head where her hand had been. "But I belong here, my Keir, for I love you," she told him for the first time, her lips close to his ear so he would hear every word. "I'll not let anyone harm you. Not a dream, not Father Tomas. Not anyone, ever." Her arms went around his tense upper body, holding him with unexpected strength, while she pledged again, "I love you, my darling, no matter what. My love is stronger than all . . . that. Please don't shut me out."

His face turned slightly in her direction, his gaze on the smooth limestone at her knees. "No matter what?" Soft, astringent laughter rumbled up from deep within him. "You know naught of life, Brandy Dalton, except what you've seen on board the *Odyssey*. I have done things that would make you turn from me in disgust." He retreated into silence, then; into his nightmarish memories . . . a Pandora's box opened by Father Tomas's musings.

Brandy raised her head from his shoulder and put a palm to his cheek, turning his face until he was forced to look into her eyes. The only thing that would ever make her turn from him in disgust would be the act of murder. And she knew Keir St. Andrews might be many things, but he was not a murderer.

"No matter what," she repeated. "I cannot undo your past, no matter how I might wish it. But I can tell you from the heart that, as you are the product of the years behind you, so do I love that man. I care not what came before, only for the Keir St. Andrews with me now . . . that I may be allowed to love you freely and openly." She leaned her forehead against his, her arms pulling his body closer. "I love the man you are now; this I know as surely as there is a God in heaven."

She was wearing her silk tunic, and could feel him trembling against her breasts through the fine material. She could only love him . . . attempt to soothe him, for the moment at least, in the one way to which he never failed to respond. After all, hadn't he transformed her life by teaching her of the physical act and, therefore, unwittingly ensnaring her heart forever?

"Let me show you my love, Keir," she said, her lips meeting his.

He did not respond, but remained as he was, as still as if his very breath was caught in his throat. Her hands came up to cradle his jaw, to cant his head gently for better access as her lips slid lovingly across his. Her thumbs stroked the unblemished flesh of his neck, as he had done to her so many times before. "Keir, Keir," she murmured against his mouth, coaxing his lips apart, conjuring up the sweet magic that never failed to ignite between them. She lightly trailed her tongue across his lower lip before joining the warm adhesion of her half-parted mouth to his.

Her heart beat a cadence of joy, for he slowly began to respond, accepting her kiss now, his lips pressing against hers of his own free will, leaving her hands free to glide down his neck and across his shoulders. Up and down Brandy skimmed her palms against the unnaturally cool skin of his arms, seeking to transfer her own warmth to him, if not by her gentle chafing, then by sheer dint of will.

Moments moved by, and slowly, as their tongues met and melded, giving exquisite pleasure, Keir's arms encircled her own body. He buried his face in the V of her tunic, clinging to her in obvious desperation. She kissed the top of his head, then buried her face in his thick hair, reveling in the scent of him, the feel of him close to her, where he belonged.

She felt a *frisson* move through him, but his skin felt warmer now, and Brandy guessed that the tremor came from deep within him. She rocked him back and forth, gently, rhythmically, infinitely patient. " 'Tis all right, my love," she repeated over and over again, a loving litany of reassurance.

The crystal arc of the rushing water shrouded them in a splashing, silver bower, the other night sounds barely discernable beneath the steady surge of the laughing, spilling stream.

Brandy lay back, pulling Keir with her, holding him at her side, her face buried in the warm cay where his neck met one shoulder. She felt the kindling of desire flicker through her as the length of his body stretched out alongside hers, the silken fabric of the tunic providing a fragile barrier against the relaxed bulge of his masculinity.

She slid a hand down toward him, lightly caressing him . . .

He stiffened.

Brandy stilled, then drew her hand away. Innocent that she had been when first brought aboard the *Odyssey* , she'd learned much during the past seven weeks. And she suspected, in light of Keir's fierce protection of Jackie aboard the *Odyssey,* and his words to her about turning from him in disgust, that he had been an unwilling victim of sodomy on Captain Brewster's slaver . . . something that could affect even the most stalwart of men — or boys — for the rest of their lives.

He felt soiled, she guessed, and realized that unless she could reach him with her unconditional love, she would be powerless to help him overcome his feelings of guilt and blame and unworthiness. That tough exterior, that harsh facade, were his protection against the indecencies committed against him, and the armor against further hurt. She sensed that a man like Keir St. Andrews would never succumb to weakness — weakness as interpreted by him, by the harsh society of seamen in which he'd lived for the past twenty years. But only when he allowed himself to feel those emotions that he'd ruthlessly repressed, and grieve for his lost youth and innocence and, yes, his lost inheritance, would he begin to feel cleansed and start to heal.

Brandy had seen him delicately balanced upon the thin line of control when he'd momentarily been unable to address Father Tomas upon their arrival at the mission. From what she could tell during their weeks at sea, that was the closest he'd come to breaking down.

Young, gay, and full of life she may have been, but Brandy suspected the man she loved was only a hair's breadth from either releasing the floodgates of his long-repressed sorrows and anger, or . . .

The thought didn't bear considering, for he could easily be lost to her if the other, unnamed result ensued.

She couldn't know, however, that to the onus of Keir's inner suffering, had been added the knowledge that she, Brandy, would be hurt by the ultimate success of Keir's mission, even as uncertain as it was now. That, as she'd said the words *I'll not let anyone harm you,* she'd only contributed to his tremendous burden: for Keir couldn't save Brandy Dalton from the pain that would be dealt her in the wake of the discovery that Father Tomas could provide testimony that could help prove that Keir St. Andrews was an earl.

And there was no room for a tavern wench in the life of the sixth Earl of Somerset.

"Keir," she whispered against his hair. "Let me love you." She trailed her fingers across the muscled planes of his chest, threading them through the light covering of crisp, curling hairs that made whorling patterns about his breast. " 'Tis I, only Brandy." Her hand leisurely meandered downward, lovingly and gently marauding, toward the straight line of body hair that led to the essence of his masculinity.

Desire wended through Keir, in spite of himself, and his body reacted naturally with a will of its own.

"Look at me, my love," she bade him softly. "It's only Brandy. No one else. I'll never hurt you." Her fingers deftly unlaced his codpiece, as expertly as any woman accustomed to undressing a man. But for weeks she had been under the tutelage of a most capable teacher. Her new expertise was no source of shame for Brandy. She felt only a need to cleanse his mind, if for nothing more than these few moments, of all but her . . . and a love that was wholesome and sincere in every sense of the word. A love of which Keir St. Andrews, in her mind, was most deserving.

He crushed her to him with a sudden groan. "Brandy . . . ah, Brandy . . ." he cried softly, and let the tears spill over onto his cheeks, wetting those of the woman so close to him, as well.

# Chapter Eighteen

Brandy kissed away the tears that streaked down his cheeks as he murmured over and over again, "Brandy . . . Brandy . . . ah, my brandy-eyes . . ."

Her fingers worked their magic on the lower regions of his body, and Keir clutched her with increasing fervor, the first grip of desperation turning slowly to one of a healthy man in a state of arousal.

"Help me, Brandy," he rasped softly, a plea, a prayer, as her fingers tenderly caressed him, blurring the shadowy features of Samuel Brewster, and easing away the taint of his touch. Keir stared into her face, absorbing every detail in the moonlight, as if etching her image on his memory forever.

When his lips sought hers, one hand tentatively raised the hem of her tunic to caress the satin-soft flesh beneath. He traced her ribs and an unexpected tinkle of laughter escaped her.

"So, we're ticklish, are we?" he whispered in wonder as the sound of her merriment pushed further into nothingness the features of his would-be nemesis.

"You didn't know that after all these past weeks?" she asked, lingering traces of her laughter making her voice breathy.

His hand coming up to caress one breast was his answer, and instantly her amusement subsided as she gave herself up to the languor seeping through her, making her blood sing, her heart race. She relaxed within his embrace, and a tugging sensation shot through her lower body as his mouth replaced his hand and his teeth nipped the crest of the pale globe of her breast.

A sigh of rapture escaped her lips, and she twisted her body slightly to give him access to the other breast. "Equal time," she murmured from deep in her throat.

Keir complied, reveling in her willingness to relinquish her role as aggressor after her earlier initiative. His desire, reaching a pitch to rival the roar of the falls, temporarily erased his demons, his disappointment in his interview with Father Tomas. He only knew that he needed this young woman whom he'd introduced to the rite of love, and who'd been so apt a pupil that she could now use his own methods on himself in her efforts to love him.

Love, he thought as he pushed her tunic over her head with rising urgency, then shimmied out of his breeches. She'd said she loved him. No one had said such a thing to him in twenty years, and those simple, sincere words made up for years of deprivation of that very emotion.

He moved over her, fusing their bodies from thigh to mouth, yet holding back the ultimate bonding. He wouldn't think about what he must eventually do to her, or perhaps not if Father Tomas remained adamant. He only concentrated on the miracle of her love, of the colliding emotions rampaging through him like opposing cannon fire. She asked no questions, loved him unconditionally, in spite of the manner in which she'd been brought aboard the *Odyssey*. That sweet innocence of spirit still remained, even if he'd taught her the pleasures of the flesh, and if he could have absorbed her very essence, he would have as he prepared to enter her.

Their mouths melded, warm and wet, as their bodies did the same. The hard pulsing turgidity of his staff unerringly homed into the sliding satin of her, and Keir unconsciously committed himself to her, as he'd done so many times before without acknowledgment.

Brandy groaned against his lips, caught in the throes of

exquisite pleasure as they began their rhythmical rite to the accompaniment of nature around them. The spray from the cascading water close by beaded their straining bodies, but the natural heat of passion rendered Keir and Brandy oblivious to the chill. The brisk mountain breeze sighed over them, but could not cool the ardor that came from within.

Samuel Brewster and the memories of his defilement were swept away on a tide of pure passion, shared emotion, unadulterated bliss. They hung, suspended, for one bright, shining moment, the world a rainbow of emotions; then peaked, their souls soaring to splendored heights and uniting as shimmering sensations cascaded over them, then broke into a shower of glowing fragments of pleasure.

Keir buried his face in the sweet hollow below her throat, where her pulse thundered with the fires of still-stoked intensity, his own heart pumping fiercely in his breast as it pressed against hers. They lay in perfect harmony, warmed and sated.

After a while Keir rose to his knees and stared down at her, his gaze taking in her body gilded by the glow of the moon. Brandy opened her eyes and returned his look, her eyes huge and dark in the play of moonlight and shadows. She stretched lazily, barely stifling a yawn, her modesty unnecessary before the man she adored.

"So my lovemaking bores you, does it?" he queried, his eyebrows tenting in feigned disapproval.

"Nay," she answered with a contented smile, her lids drooping drowsily as she reached for her cast-off tunic. "But it makes me sleepy."

Keir slid one arm around her shoulders and the other beneath her knees. He lifted her, sweeping her up into his embrace. Brandy draped her arms about his neck and trustingly pillowed her head against his chest. "Don't forget my tunic," she murmured, "and 'twould never do to return to the mission without your breeches." She emitted a soft giggle, reminiscent of Abra.

269

In three long strides, Keir moved to stand beneath a chute of the waterfall, instantly soaking them both.

Brandy sputtered to life, clutching him in reaction before she tried to push away from his embrace. This time it was Keir's turn to laugh. "You don't think I want you to fall asleep on me, do you, wench?" he asked. "I have plans for us when we return to our beds . . . that don't include sleep."

He stepped from beneath the water and set her down to don his breeches.

"You are indecent," she protested with a shiver, hurriedly slipping into her tunic, scant protection against the very real chill she felt now.

Keir pulled her into his arms again and then high against his chest, before moving back in the direction of the mission. "I am most decently clad now, Mistress Dalton, if you would but open your eyes."

"And I shall catch my death," she said through chattering teeth. " 'Tisn't nearly as warm up here as down the mountain."

Keir pressed his lips to her forehead before he assured her in a low voice freighted with meaning, "I'll personally see to it that you are warmed and dried—every inch of you—by morn."

A muffled objection reached his ears, but Keir was thinking that, indeed, he would dry her well . . . every part of her, including her hair, before making passionate love to her again. And again. Until morning chased away the night shadows . . . and the bleak specter of renewing his attempts to persuade Father Tomas to see things his way.


When the sun rose, Keir felt a stab of guilt at the circles beneath Brandy's eyes, for indeed, he'd kept her awake until the darkest hours before the dawn, for purely selfish reasons. If she'd reacted to his lovemaking with an ardor to match his own, it was more than likely because of his expertise in arousing her sexually than her professed love for him, for the trek up the mountain had tired her.

He pushed aside his guilt and kissed her on the mouth before he tucked the disheveled blanket around her more securely, saying only, "Sleep, brandy-eyes, while I attend to business." He exited the hut, emerging into the brisk mountain air, glad that he'd not worn his shirt the night before, as it was now the only completely dry article of clothing on his body. A small fire had taken most of the moisture from his breeches, but their slight dampness was only accented as Keir left the warmth of the shelter he shared with Brandy.

Dionisio materialized before him in the clearing mists, startling him. The Cimaroon grinned broadly, and Keir instantly knew that the African had observed their love play at the waterfall. Of course. Just because Keir hadn't seen a guard, that didn't mean there hadn't been one.

A flush rose to his cheeks and he looked about him, willing the telltale color away. "Padre Tomas?" he asked brusquely, his gaze returning to the Cimaroon's when he'd regained his composure. Dionisio had once again donned breeches and shirt. He looked slightly less intimidating fully clothed, although Keir calculated that the warrior stood at least two hands higher than himself . . . an unusual and imposing height. His tightly curling ebony hair was close-cropped, his ears small and slightly protuberant. His nose was broad, as those of his brothers, with full lips. Taken altogether, he could put the fear of God into most men when all six-foot-eight of him or so was clad only in loincloth and mantle . . . and ax. But Keir had caught a spark of deviltry in the large, dark eyes when the Cimaroon had grinned at him—a humor completely at odds with the snarling savage they'd first encountered on the mountain path.

Keir's eyes narrowed reflectively as he openly studied the African for a moment.

As if sensing his thoughts, Dionisio grinned again, and pointed toward the mission church. Keir nodded, and ignoring the increasing activity about him, he pulled his gaze from the Cimaroon's face and began walking toward the church. Dionisio strode along beside him. *"¿Tenéis hambre?"* he asked Keir.

Keir shook his head. *"Más tarde, gracias."* He hoped the Cimaroon would leave him alone as he sought to renew his assault on Father Tomas's will. But the warrior only trotted on ahead of Keir, his long, slender legs eating up the short distance to the church with the fluid grace of a prancing Arabian stallion.

Dionisio entered the church first, to Keir's dismay. He didn't need this man present to remind Father Tomas of his commitment here. *Go away!* Keir ordered silently, frowning at Dionisio's back. But Father Tomas was already looking up from his prayers before the simple altar.

"I see you'll give me no peace, Keir St. Andrews," he said as he made the sign of the cross and rose to his feet with a heavy sigh. He pointed to the closest hand-hewn bench, but Keir remained standing, feeling the tension begin to coil through him. He noted with some relief that after the Jesuit spoke softly to Dionisio, the latter left. At least Keir would be spared an audience, albeit one who didn't understand English.

"Perhaps I've only come to give you my confession, Father," Keir said in a low voice.

Father Tomas met his gaze head-on. "I would not believe it for one moment now that I've seen what you have become." His face looked drawn, as if he, too, had not slept well.

"And what have I become? Is being a pirate so very bad in this wicked world? At least I don't kill for the sport of it. Nor do I have any traffic with slavers. I only sought these past years to fatten my own purse until I could eventually buy my way into the King of England's antechamber."

Father Tomas opened his mouth as if to speak, but Keir wasn't finished. "Aye, I plead guilty to filling my own coffers from those treasure ships of your countrymen . . .

272

your own fellow Spaniards who wiped out whole civilizations in the name of Spain and Catholicism. If it weren't for Spain, Father, you would not be needed here in quite the capacity you find yourself . . . missionary, aye, but not protector, with your flock armed to the teeth."

"And I think you find it *muy* convenient to turn the tables on me when your sole purpose in life these past twenty years has been revenge." Father Tomas shook a finger in Keir's face. "Do you not know by now that the blade of revenge is two-sided? That even if you—" He trailed off, a frown creasing his brow beneath his narrow fringe of brown and silver hair. "Just who are you, Keir St. Andrews?" He put a hand to his forehead, massaging his temples with thumb and fingers.

"Can you not remember what you heard that night?" Keir asked in a strained voice. *For if not, you can be of no help to me before the king.* But he would not dare voice this last, inconceivable thought.

The priest sank onto a nearby bench, his face twisted in concentration, his eyes closed. "There were three of them. One called . . ." he looked up at Keir, ". . . Giles, I think. Another called him—this 'Giles'—Father . . . and a third . . ." He closed his eyes again, frowning in concentration and muttering, "¿Qué dijo . . . qué dijo? ¡Piensa!"

Keir stood silently over him, afraid to breathe lest he interrupt the older man's memory process. ". . . a third man who said something like, 'He did not see who struck him . . . better to—to take the small chance that he will live—rather than to commit outright murder.' "

Keir let out a long breath as the Jesuit uttered the words that would implicate Giles St. Andrews in Keir's attempted murder . . . and restore to him his birthright. The words he'd heard recited time and again in his finest dreams, and also thought, in his worst nightmares, never to hear uttered by anyone again . . .

His gaze met Father Tomas's then, as the older man opened his eyes. A ferocious determination was drawn across Keir's features as he said, "I am the sixth Earl of

273

Somerset, priest . . . not just some petty aristocrat." He leaned forward, his eyes delving into Father Tomas's as he sensed the latter's hesitation. "My father was killed during the English Civil Wars, and then his half-brother, Giles, tried to do away with me to gain control of the earldom. One step below a duke, I am the rightful Earl of Somerset, and 'tis your Christian duty to tell Charles Stuart what you know."

Father Tomas's shoulders sagged suddenly, as if with the weight of the burden he'd just been given. He stared at his hands resting in his dark-robed lap for long moments, and then glanced around the stark walls of his humble church. The morning sunlight filtered through the unglazed windows on the east side, and a pair of butterflies flitted about one of the open apertures in courtship. Voices came to them from outside, and the smell of cooking fires and food.

"You are a *pirata*," the clergyman muttered.

"If I am, 'tis because of you."

The words seemed to bear down oppressively upon the Jesuit in the meaning-fraught silence that followed. His shoulders sloped even further. "Why can I not write a letter to your king?" he asked softly. He looked at Keir. "I can have the Governor put his seal on it and—"

"His Majesty commanded me 'Find the priest and bring him to me.' A letter could easily be forged . . . 'twould be about as valid as Henry Morgan's privateers' commissions."

The faint light of hope in the older man's dark eyes extinguished then, and Keir felt an alien twinge of regret, of guilt. With an impatient sound, he shook his head and walked toward one of the windows. He scanned the mission grounds from where he stood while he fought to suppress the unwelcome feelings that had sprouted in his breast.

"I can have you safely returned to Jamaica by March . . . April at the latest. I will see to it that your mission wants for naught . . . I can even finance the building of a new church—more weapons, food supplies—whatever you wish, in return for your testimony." He continued to stare unseeingly into the morning sunlight. "There is no other way, you see," he added with quiet emphasis, then fell silent, waiting a short eternity for Father Tomas's answer. The few moments it took the priest to answer, indeed, seemed longer than all the time it had taken Keir to meet him again.

"A hundred things could go wrong," Father Tomas told him finally, his voice dull with defeat. You can never—guarantee my safe return to Jamaica. Only God can do that."

"Life doesn't come with any guarantees, Padre, surely you know that after all these years on the Main. I would have given you more credit than that." He looked over his shoulder at the clergyman. "I can give you my promise in writing that I would find another Jesuit to take your place here in the event that anything should befall you."

"And if we are all lost at sea? You as well?"

Impatience sifted through Keir. His green eyes mirrored his thoughts, for Father Tomas unexpectedly added, "*Sí,* you have guessed. I am a *cobarde* at heart. Had it been otherwise, I would never have left that slaver without you."

Keir shrugged. "What could you have done against Brewster and his crew? I came to see it as common sense as time passed and I learned the way of things."

Father Tomas stood in agitation. His robes rustled as they fell to the dirt floor, sending a small puff of dust into the air. "I have always been a *cobarde,* but not this time! I will not desert my people for—"

"I'm not asking you to desert your people!" Keir interrupted angrily. "I'm asking you to make a small sacrifice . . . for their own good as well as mine. No matter the outcome of your journey to England, I pledge that these Cimaroons and the others will be given another 'father' to guide them through life, to protect them from anyone who would enslave them. The quality of their lives will be

275

vastly improved . . . with or without you."

Father Tomas glared at Keir, his dilemma written clearly across his face.

"Did you not ever think that perhaps God wanted it this way?" Keir asked him. "Why else would He have led me to you? Mayhap I take this meeting—the very fact that you are alive and here before me—as a sign from Him that I deserve to regain my title and holdings. That He wishes to restore to me all that He once took away."

As his words died away, the fight seemed to drain from Keir. He suddenly felt emotionally exhausted. And like a religious fool. What was the matter with him . . . purporting to know of God's plans (and since when had he ever admitted to the existence of a divine being?), and then using this newly-discovered 'knowledge' to deliver a Catholic priest a sermon like some fiery missionary chastising the buccaneers of Port Royal for their dissolute ways?

Keir gazed about the rough stone walls of the little church, feeling that if there was a God, surely He was up here in the mountains with Father Tomas and his followers. Up here in the pristine air, just below the mist-wreathed peaks that seemed to reach up to Him in supplication. For here in this settlement was harmony and trust among all but intruders. Here in this place was peace, even permanence. And, yes, he felt it, as well . . . love.

And who wouldn't seek to abide here in this peaceful, beautiful place rather than in a world of thieves and cutthroats, whether clad in riches or rags?

He felt Father Tomas's eyes on him as he pondered these things, and Keir withdrew himself from his contemplations and met the priest's regard.

"Perhaps you are right, Keir St. Andrews. Perhaps God sent you to me to right the unspeakable wrong done to you." He was silent a moment, then shook his head slowly, a doubtful look passing through his eyes. "And what if your king remains unmoved? What if you gain nothing from my speaking on your behalf?"

Keir's entire face hardened. A muscle jumped in his cheek as he fought to quash myriad emotions yearning for release. "Naught will change," he said in a voice as icy as the winds of the North Atlantic. I give you my word that I will do everything as agreed upon as far as you and this mission are concerned."

"As a *pirata* or an earl?" Father Tomas's eyes narrowed skeptically at Keir.

"As a St. Andrews."

The priest went to stand before a lovingly if crudely carved representation of the Virgin Mary that hung from one wall, tinted in the exact delicate shades one would find in the finest European cathedral, and bowed his head. "Then I will do as you wish . . . on one—condition."

Keir forced his voice to sound normal, for it wouldn't do for the stern Captain of the *Odyssey* to sound excited. Or delighted. Or ecstatic. Or wild with joy. And even if it would have been nothing out of the ordinary, Keir, just now, wasn't certain he knew how to express himself so uninhibitedly.

And, of course, he hadn't heard the condition.

"Anything," he heard himself answer, and in that moment he meant it.

Father Tomas swung toward him, his fists clenched within his robe, his expression determined. "You will remain here for three days, teaching the men how to shoot with accuracy. And you will bring us more arms and ammunition."

Keir nodded. "Easily done."

"And I do not wish anyone to know that I have left the island. Can we accomplish that, Keir St. Andrews?"

Keir couldn't find the words to tell him how simple his requests would be to grant. "We can make certain you are seen at the closest plantation—I believe the one at the base of the mountain and to westward?—once more before we leave. Then I'll send several of my men back to

Port Royal to buy muskets, powder and shot, and anything else you want, before the *Odyssey* sets sail. She'll only come around to the east, however, dropping anchor just this side of the Yallahs River. No one in Port Royal need be any the wiser."

Father Tomas regarded Keir with sudden suspicion. "You knew I would give in, did you not? You knew!"

Keir shook his head consideringly. "I couldn't ever know for certain, Father. But I had years to think and plan . . . for *any* eventuality."

Keir held a long meeting with his men after breaking the fast. Brandy was not included, but occupied herself with getting acquainted with some of the people of the mission. The women wouldn't let her lift a finger, for when she allowed them to unbind her hair, the morning sun burnished it to such an unusual brilliance that they stepped back in unison at the sight, obviously forgetting for a moment that Father Tomas had taught them that humans were not gods.

Brandy laughed, catching Dionisio's attention and bringing him over to the group with his long-legged stride. He set down his armload of firewood, and his wife, who Brandy learned was called Maria, was the first to stretch out her hand and touch the glorious fall of curls. Then Dionisio, obviously equally curious, hunkered down and took a thick lock of it in his fist with unexpected gentleness. He looked at it wonderingly before his eyes caught Brandy's and he murmured, *"mujer."*

Brandy smiled in remembrance and nodded. *"Sí. Mujer."*

Dionisio grinned shyly and Brandy could have sworn his mahogany cheeks had darkened beneath the heat of a flush.

"Is Dionisio teasing you, my child?" Father Tomas asked as he approached the small group.

"Nay, Father. Only reminding me that women shouldn't

278

dress as men."

His hands behind his back, the Jesuit nodded sagely. "Ah, yes. Dionisio would be the one to tell you that. Although he is our most ferocious warrior—and is also *muy* shy—he prides himself on his ability to appreciate beauty, be it animate or inanimate." He nodded again as he studied her. "And yours is definitely animate . . . very much so."

Brandy laughed aloud. "Why, Father, surely you cannot exercise your talent properly here. You belong in a huge cathedral, intoning to the masses with your silver tongue."

Father Tomas cleared his throat. *"Pues bien,* perhaps that is exactly why I am where I am . . . so I do not become, ah, puffed up with what you so prettily name my 'talent.' "

Dionisio relinquished his hold on Brandy's hair and stood. "Will you tell Dionisio something for me?" Brandy asked Father Tomas.

*"Sí.*

Brandy watched as the tall Cimaroon bent to retrieve his firewood and then straightened. "Tell him that I think he is a beautiful man. *Bello.* I have never seen anyone with such long, slender legs . . . and such remarkable grace. Watching him move is like listening to wonderful music."

Father Tomas looked at Brandy for a moment, and then at Dionisio. "Why, I believe you are right, child. I had never thought to put it into words."

*"¿Qué dijo?"* asked Maria.

"May I tell her what you said?"

Brandy nodded. "If you don't think 'twill offend either of them."

Father Tomas threw back his head and laughed heartily, making the others around them smile, even though Brandy knew they didn't understand the exchange. "My proud *cimarrones* like nothing more than a compliment, even though I tell them constantly that pride is a sin." He said something to Dionisio and the women tittered. Dioni-

279

sio's warm dark eyes met Brandy's briefly, before he nodded with a bashful smile and moved off with his burden.

"Well I'll be da—" Peter Stubbs cut himself off just in time from behind Brandy. "Never thought I'd see yer fierce Cimaroon blush, Padre."

Brandy rose to her feet and swung to face the men behind her. The sight of Keir made her face light up, her pulses chase after one another, as it never failed to do.

"Dionisio will get a chance to show just how he can put his nimbleness to work in the next few days," Keir said from behind Brandy. "We are to leave for England with Father Tomas in three days. Before we leave, we'll teach these men everything we know about protecting their home."

Brandy touched his arm, her eyes bright with joy for him. "Oh, Keir . . . you'll be able to regain your inheritance!"

For some reason, his gaze suddenly skittered away from hers, but her happiness was too intense to be immediately dulled by something so minor.

"What kind o' inheritance, Cap'n?" Jackie asked with boyish eagerness, echoing Brandy's thoughts.

Keir opened his mouth to speak, and then closed it, unable to say the words. The words he knew would cut Brandy Dalton from his life forever.

"Why, he is Keir St. Andrews," Father Tomas informed them all in a voice that sounded thunderous in the brief void, "lawful sixth Earl of Somerset."

# Chapter Nineteen

The words registered slowly, their deeper significance evading Brandy for long moments . . . until Jackie added, "A real *earl?* The cap'n's a blueblood?"

It was the awe in his voice as it cracked with the unpredictability of adolescence, rather than the words themselves, that penetrated her jubilation.

Sudden, crippling bewilderment crept through her, her smile wavering, then waning as her eyes sought Keir's. But he was looking at Father Tomas, his features unexpectedly bleak in the face of his triumph.

"I'm sending Foucher and Gonzalez back to Port Royal. They have instructions to avoid the plantation directly east of the sandspit. Foucher will see that appropriate supplies are procured and loaded onto the *Odyssey,* and then she'll set sail for England . . . or so 'twill appear."

Father Tomas nodded. "And she will, in truth, drop anchor as we discussed, which will only be a stop on the way to England." He blew out his breath, his reluctance apparent. "So much less a, er, fabrication. The fewer lies, the more acceptable this entire plan to me."

Keir spoke again, but Brandy didn't catch what he said, for the world was roaring around her. She may have been many things, but she was not slow-witted. In the center of the vortex of confusion and disillusionment, the words "Earl of Somerset" beat at her brain with stunning force and crystal clarity, until one final bitter conclusion surfaced in the chaos of her thoughts: Keir St. Andrews had deceived her.

It was as simple as that. Keir St. Andrews, brilliant tactician, master manipulator, had completely gulled Brandy Dalton.

Humiliation rose within her then, threatening to annihilate reason and send her either into blessed oblivion, or a tearing temper. Color streaked across her cheekbones.

*No!* something within her cried, her better side refusing to believe such a thing.

*Yes! He deliberately kept you a captive, stole your virtue and your heart, all the while knowing that he could never do the honorable thing and marry you, no matter how much he softened toward you . . . no matter how much he may have even come to love you. An earl doesn't wed a tavern wench.*

She focused her gaze on Peter Stubbs, who was watching her. Suddenly it was as if they were the only two people present as Brandy returned his look. If ever she needed affirmation, it was there, scrawled across his face . . . the regret, the pity, the repressed anger. He knew, Brandy read in his expression . . . had known all along, and now he felt responsible for having brought her aboard the *Odyssey* all those weeks ago. He had known all along that Keir had sought more than a mere piddling inheritance. Keir and his quartermaster were unusually close, she'd come to realize. Now, as she stared into Peter's eyes, she surmised that he'd always known that Keir was titled.

And had she used her own common sense, she would have guessed the truth as well . . . the truth that she had so blithely ignored as she'd basked in Keir St. Andrews' affection, euphoric with the love she felt for him. Hadn't she acknowledged to herself on more than one occasion that he was so much more than a common seaman?

Yet her own natural concern for others, the empathy and unfailing consideration that were so much a part of her makeup, paled before her own pain, her own sense of betrayal—searing emotions that were so strong as to all but blot out the silent suffering she read in Peter Stubbs's gaze. What was his guilt and remorse compared to what had just been revealed to her? After all, *she* had been the one wronged, by not only his captain, but also by Peter himself . . .

"Señorita Brandy?" Father Tomas was saying, his brows drawn together in a frown of concern.

Brandy dragged her gaze from Peter's, deliberately passed over Keir, and looked at the clergyman. "Aye, Father," she managed in a low voice, willing her wits not to desert her now. But the tincture of shock still infused her features, and her mouth would not move to a smile.

"What is it, *niña?*"

Background noises intruded now; the low hum of voices, the birds in the trees, the whisper of the breeze, the activity around the mission itself. And in the middle of her distress, she finally felt Keir's piercing perusal, the last thing she wanted — or needed — now.

" 'Tis nothing, Father," she lied. " 'Tis nothing, truly." She forced her lips into a stiff sketch of a smile, Keir's attention only adding to her burden. She wanted, in the worst way, to disappear. To disappear and allow her feelings free rein in privacy. She needed to think things over, to recover from the reeling shock of this newest revelation.

The priest said something in Spanish to Maria, Dionisio's wife, and the woman walked over to Brandy. As she gently took the latter's arm, Brandy briefly dared allow her eyes to meet Keir's. What she saw, however, was reminiscent of the expression he'd worn when she'd first met him at the Hawk and Hound. *A man back from the fiery reaches of hell,* she remembered thinking, *for his eyes were bereft of emotion.*

She could read nothing in his empty expression, nothing of guilt, nothing of remorse, nothing of regret. But then again, Brandy thought miserably as she allowed Maria to lead her away, how presumptuous of her to think that she could have ever made an indelible mark on a man like Keir St. Andrews.

As they approached the hut she'd shared with him, Brandy halted her steps. The thought of returning to their pallet was not only extremely unsettling to her, but completely unacceptable as well.

She turned to Maria. "Let me go to the falls," she said, pointing in that direction.

Maria frowned uncomprehendingly.

Brandy mimed falling water and made a whooshing sound to go with it.

Maria smiled and they swung around and proceeded toward the perimeter of the mission. The Cimaroon woman seemed to understand Brandy's desire to be alone, and left her after they reached the waterfall.

She stood looking around for a time, for although the area had a special kind of beauty at night beneath a clear, moon-and-starlit sky, the sun shining on the glassy chutes of water gave them a crystalline sheen, their sparkling waters foaming and churning in the sunlight as they were dashed into the rocky pool below. Glimpses of the cobalt Jamaican sky could be seen overhead, with plumes of pale mist spiraling about the mountain tops. So far, Brandy hadn't seen one part of Jamaica that didn't appeal to her . . . white sandy beaches, gorgeously floraled bush and marsh at the base of the mountains, the lush rain forest, and the rugged upper part of the mountains with its own stark beauty.

She stood at the pool's edge, allowing the cool spray to mist her, and thought what a fool she'd been. Her eyes closed in anguish as Keir's deliberate secrecy with her came back to tear at the open wound that was her heart. And, of course, her own gullibility. She allowed the tears that had been burning the back of her throat to spill over, cascading over her cheeks in unison with the water plummeting over the edge of the precipice above.

*Serves you right, Brandy Dalton,* her sensible side told her, *for allowing yourself to fall in love with a stranger . . . a ruthless pirate, no matter that he sailed for England. Had he ever mentioned love to you? Or marriage? Or anything that a woman might to expect from the man she loves? Just because you discovered a soft side to him, a compassionate side, you gave him your heart as eagerly as a half-grown girl with her first infatuation, expecting nothing in return.*

"And I got nothing," she whispered. "I shall be forced to sail across an entire ocean with him again, and then return to the Hawk and Hound a sullied woman. His actions this morn have revealed that he will have naught to do with me once we reach England and he regains his earldom. How can I face any of my family? How can I face myself?"

She stood there, she knew not how long, allowing the tears to flow and cleanse, her arms hugging her waist, her head bowed, her entire posture one of misery and anguish.

*If he didn't care for you, why did he bring you up here with him?* whispered a voice.

*Because he needed someone to warm his bed, even here.*

*Nay.* soothed the voice, *'twas because he feared for your safety if left on the* Odyssey *in wild Port Royal. If he feared that much, he has feelings for you.*

"Aye," Brandy stuttered between sobs, "l-like he has for D-Dudley, nothing more."

*Self-pity doesn't become you, Brandy Dalton.*

"Aye," she mumbled, wiping her silken-clad forearm across her eyes like a child.

*"Mujer con pelo como la puesta del sol,"* said someone from behind her.

Brandy swung toward the familiar deep voice. It was Dionisio, with Father Tomas not far behind him.

Brandy turned back to the water, embarrassment tinting her pale, tear-tracked cheeks.

"He called you 'woman with hair like the setting sun,' " Father Tomas said gently when he'd come near enough to speak to her without shouting.

"He — is most — kind," she answered through broken breaths. "Although I'm certain my face is the same hue, as well." She was surprised at how easily the quip rose to her lips. Was she already accepting the fact that she would soon

285

have no part in Keir St. Andrews' life?

"I wished to be alone," she said over her shoulder, her eyes downcast before the two men. "And Dionisio should be with Keir and his men, should he not?"

The Jesuit placed a comforting hand upon her shoulder. "He was concerned about you, child. Maria was to take you back to—"

"I know! But I couldn't abide the thought of returning there. And I certainly don't wish to sleep." At this rate, the entire population of the mission would appear at any moment.

She watched as Dionisio wordlessly squatted down on his haunches and stared off into the distance. "Why did you come?" she asked, dullness marring the natural lilt of her voice.

Father Tomas lifted her chin so that her eyes were forced to meet his. "I was put here to work for God . . . to provide comfort when it is needed, among other things." He glanced over at Dionisio. "And he fancies himself your protector since he saw immediately through your guise."

Dionisio spoke then.

"What did he say?" Brandy asked, curious in spite of her woes.

"That he would have you for his wife, were you willing, woman with the beautiful hair. He says that you are not only lovely, but courageous, as well. He saw not the slightest hint of fear back on the mountain path when he would have had you shed your clothing to prove you were not a man." Father Tomas flushed then and cleared his throat. "Nor would Dionisio ever cause you such unhappiness, he says."

Brandy was simultaneously appalled and flattered. "But he already has a wife!"

Father Tomas laughed softly. "He said it only as a compliment, for he knows the Christian God frowns upon such practices. But Dionisio's father was a powerful Asante chieftain in Africa, and had several wives. Traditions die hard, even in a Catholic mission."

286

Now her curiosity was thoroughly piqued, her own woes pushed, for the moment, to the back of her mind. "Dionisio's first wife was killed by the Spaniards. Maria chose him, rather than the other way around." He smiled again. "You see, *niña,* we are very limited here in population and, therefore in choices for *esposos."*

Brandy bent down, cupped cool clear water from the pool in her hands, and rinsed her warm face. "You aren't angry at his request?"

"As I said, he meant it as a compliment, not an offer. I am slowly winning these people completely over to the true religion. I would be a fool to think it could be accomplished in only a few years. I believe I further my cause by allowing him — and others — to wear their amulets to ward off harm, or to hunt and forage in the mountains clad only in the loincloths and mantles worn by their fathers before them in their homeland. 'Twould be most, er, obtuse of me to expect rapid change . . . although Mother Church might not agree." He smiled a little. "But he pays you the highest tribute, child."

Brandy mustered an answering smile, becoming color brushing her cheeks again. "Tell him I am honored that he would even suggest such a thing, but I wish to return to my home and family across the sea."

Father Tomas complied and Dionisio nodded in seeming understanding. His answer was, again, in a mixture of his African dialect and Spanish. "He says he understands that reason, but as for your loyalty to the tall stern one who hurts you, well . . ." He dropped his gaze, obviously unwilling to reveal everything the Cimaroon had said.

"Even your Dionisio recognizes a man about to discard his . . . mistress." Brandy sat back on her heels and stared blindly at the falls before her, the cool spray misting her face and relieving some of the heat in her cheeks.

"Recognizes, perhaps, but does not agree. In Dionisio's society, a man took several wives rather than commit adultery. In some cultures, adultery was punishable by death."

"His unfortunate involvement with the Spanish explains, I think," Brandy observed as she rose to her feet once more, "his hostility toward us before he knew who we were yesterday."

"Oh, do not doubt that Dionisio can be a ferocious defender, a capable leader if given the chance. I am certain that your meeting upon the path in the rain forest was frightening to you if Dionisio thought you were enemies."

"Then you needn't worry about leaving the mission if you can depend upon him, need you?"

"No. But I will, all the same." He turned thoughtful for a moment.

"Don't allow Keir to manipulate you for his own ends, Father," she advised him, an uncharactistic bitterness creeping into her words. "He is most adept at making others do what he wishes, whether by persuasion . . . or by force."

Father Tomas took her arm. "Walk with us," he said, and Brandy willingly moved around the pool below the waterfall with him. Dionisio unfolded himself with uncanny grace and followed.

"I found a small boy left for dead on an English beach twenty years ago. That was, of course, during the English civil wars. I had persuaded one of the sailors aboard the slave ship to row me ashore to see if we could find a man who had been thrown overboard by the drunken *capitán*. The sailor, Arthur Biggs, was reluctant, but I told him he would go straight to hell if he refused me." The clergyman smiled slightly in remembrance. "I was very idealistic, back then, you see, and acknowledged only what I perceived to be right and wrong . . . nothing in between. I was also filled with self-righteousness, which was to be shortly dashed against the iron will and . . . innate evil of Capitán Samuel Brewster."

"So you found Keir as a young boy and saved his life?"

Father Tomas's expression turned grave. "Keir does not seem to think I did him any favor . . . any charitable deed, for I had not the courage to insist that he be allowed to leave

288

the slaver with me when we reached Maracaibo. *El capitán* had taken a fancy to him . . . he said he would keep the boy as payment for the ship's surgeon nursing him back to health." His dark eyes turned angry, twin flames of fire igniting within them. "I nursed the boy, not that *carnicero*—that butcher—they called a surgeon! *I* shared my rations with him when they would give him little more than what passed for food among their human cargo. But for all my professed piety, I had not the courage to fight for Keir as I should have had—even had it meant my own life. And it has haunted me ever since. How can I refuse his request now? And how can I, in good conscience, refuse to help, ah, rectify something that only I have the power to do? I sentenced Keir to a childhood of the worst horrors, and then to a life of pain and violence and revenge. How can I ignore his king's summons to put all to rights? *Madre de Dios,* Keir is an earl!"

Brandy's mouth twisted. "Keir St. Andrews is wealthier than any man ought to be. He can do anything he wishes . . . buy a new title, buy a new estate, new lands. He has no right to work on your conscience when, by his own admission, he has none of his own. Nor has he any right to ask you to leave your work, your people here."

They paused in their walk down the mountainside, the heavy humidity and increasing abundance of verdant foliage and flowers indicating they were nearing the perimeter of the rain forest. Father Tomas turned to Brandy, his eyes infinitely sad. "I came from a proud, noble family, child. I was the youngest son, the son any Spanish family would have been proud to send into the bosom of Mother Church. I know that acquiring a title and holdings could never be the same as regaining that which has already been in the family for generations. It is not the same."

Brandy spotted an orchid and stooped to pick it. From seemingly out of nowhere, Dionisio's brown fingers closed over her wrist with a firm grip. Brandy glanced up into his face questioningly as he drew her to her feet and pointed to something directly beside the orchid. It was a constrictor, half-hidden among the leaves. Brandy shuddered as the snake slithered away through the foliage.

*He fancies himself your protector* . . .

She suddenly felt foolish. She laughed softly at herself, and Dionisio released her wrist, giving her his shy but good-natured grin. *"Gracias,"* she said. "Please tell him that he has a devilish but handsome smile, Father. And 'tis certainly more appealing than his furious hissing."

Father Tomas complied, and Dionisio laughed aloud, the deep strains reverberating through the forest about them. When he'd sobered, he spoke to the priest, but his eyes were on Brandy. He finished with a heavily accented version of "Señorita Brandy."

"He says you'll turn his head, telling him he is a beautiful man . . . a man who moves like music . . . a man with a handsome smile. What will the tall stern one think?"

Brandy's smile slipped from her features, only to be replaced by distress as reality intruded. "I am not his woman now. I am only a tavern-keeper's daughter, while he is an earl. There can be nothing between us again."

Father Tomas translated.

His laughter fading away with Brandy's, his great dark eyes somber, Dionisio answered her through the priest.

"He says that I taught him we are all equal before God."

Brandy raised tear-misted eyes to the Jesuit. "You taught him well, Father, but God's teachings don't apply where Keir St. Andrews is concerned. He makes his own laws."

Father Tomas nodded. "Perhaps, but as far as you are concerned, he will never be truly happy until he puts aside the barriers he envisions between the two of you now. He will not easily admit it, this much I've learned since he appeared on our mountain yesterday, but I suspect he loves you, my child, although one must look closely behind those hardened green eyes and unrelenting, ah, demeanor to see it. Hardship and suffering are etched upon his heart, it saddens me to say. Yet one day he will come to realize that all the restored material things in the world will not replace love should he cast it aside."

Brandy couldn't hold his gaze. Those tiresome tears blurred her vision once again, and the wild flowers all about them were suddenly only shimmering flecks and streaks of vibrant color, formless and unrecognizable.

"Here, here," Father Tomas said gently, and gathered her to him, holding her like a father would his daughter. "Let them out, *niña*, and you will feel better."

Brandy was unexpectedly transported back in time and place, back to the Hawk and Hound weeks ago . . . and Abra. "There, there," Brandy had consoled her little sister. "Let out those tears and Brandy will make everything all right . . ."

But there was only Father Tomas and a runaway African warrior with her in this beautiful and exotic but foreign land. And well-intentioned as they were, no one but Keir St. Andrews could take away the hurt.

*And you yourself, Brandy Dalton,* whispered reason. *One day you will heal yourself.*

"—if you wish," Father Tomas was saying, "I will insist upon separate quarters for you during the voyage. I doubt that he would, ah, jeopardize my willingness to testify by going against my wishes in any way. I could even demand he allow you to travel on another ship entirely, although finding a dependable *capitán* and crew in Port Royal would not be easy. Would that help you?"

Fresh misery rose up within Brandy, but she realized that she did have some pride where Keir St. Andrews was concerned. Why should she make herself available to him, knowing that each day would bring them closer to the final separation? Why should she act the tavern jade, as at one time they all had thought her? And especially after Keir had deceived her. That hurt more than anything. And the humiliation. After she'd assured him that she'd never let anyone hurt him again . . . Her heart shriveled within her breast at a promise so blatantly prompted by love, a love that had obviously been only one-sided. What must he think of the gullible, stupid Brandy Dalton, so deeply in love that she would do anything for him, including protect him? Take on the world for him? Or so she'd pledged.

But there was one thing she could do, no matter that it tore her apart inside to contemplate it, and here was Father Tomas offering her a chance to do it.

Brandy pulled back to look into the older man's eyes. "I am so grateful to you for not condemning me. I would be a harlot in the eyes of many," she admitted with difficulty, "yet I loved him so very much, and had somehow harbored the foolish notion that he might one day commit himself to me."

Father Tomas shrugged, and a corner of his mouth lifted. "Who am I to condemn anyone after the sins I've committed in my life? The abbot under whose tutelage I studied thought me much too vain and pompous to ever become a priest. Only the money of my family persuaded him to accept me as a student. And I lost none of that vanity or pomposity or, ah, condescension until I stepped aboard Brewster's slaver twenty years ago." He paused, glanced over at the silent Dionisio, then back at Brandy. "Nor can I condemn anyone for the 'sin' of loving someone, of giving physically to the object of that love. 'Tis the only emotion that elevates man from the savage beast, child. Love."

Brandy let out her breath at his words. "You are a remarkable man, Father Tomas."

He held up one hand in a gentle denial. "I am not remarkable, *niña*, rather 'tis God's creatures who are so, who never fail to reveal some new strength or nobility of spirit." Dionisio said something to Father Tomas then, who answered with a nod of his head before telling Brandy, "He wants to know if you would care to watch him feed Moses."

Uncertainty skipped across her face. "But shouldn't he be working with Keir and Peter?"

Father Tomas glanced at the Cimaroon, a father's pride in his eyes. "My Dionisio is a crack shot, whatever the men from the *Odyssey* might think. He watched the Spaniards on the plantation he worked every chance he got, and managed to steal one of their muskets before fleeing. He was determined never to be at their mercy again — or at the mercy of any other man bent upon enslaving others. I believe he would enjoy showing off his talents with *el cocodrilo* before *la mujer con pelo como la puesta del sol.*" Amusement curved the corners of his mouth.

At a nod from the clergyman, the Cimaroon beckoned to Brandy. "It will not take long, and you are perfectly safe with him." As he started back up toward the mission, Father Tomas threw over his shoulder, "And it is early yet. Dionisio will have time enough to hear what Keir might teach him this afternoon."

And so it was that Brandy trustingly followed the towering African warrior down towards the thick of the rain forest. The surroundings were just as beautiful as the first time, only her state of mind was vastly different. If this Cimaroon could help hold at bay her pain over Keir St. Andrews' betrayal for an hour or so, she would gladly allow him to do it. Even if it meant watching him feed a monsterlike crocodile.

When they reached the stream where the party from the *Odyssey* had met not only the crocodile but Dionisio himself, they slowed their pace and turned downstream for a stone's throw. By this time, Dionisio had fashioned a garland of the wildflowers that abounded on Jamaica and slipped it over Brandy's head. He smiled broadly at her *"gracias"* before turning, taking a few springing steps, and leaping effortlessly to a boulder almost as high as Brandy was tall.

*"Venga,"* he said to her, and reached down one hand to pull her up beside him. The view of the stream and the area around it was breathtaking from their perch. That is, until Brandy spotted Moses. The smile of exhilaration left her face then, as she took in not only his great length, but the size of his gaping jaws as he opened them when he saw Dionisio.

Dionisio roared with laughter as he pointed to Moses and then his own belly, rubbing it. *"Tiene hambre,"* he told her in Spanish.

She looked from Dionisio to the crocodile, not at all certain she saw anything amusing about a twelve-foot long, ravenous reptile. Dionisio motioned for her to stay where she was, which she was only too glad to do, and he dropped to the ground without a sound. How such a tall man could be so light on his feet still amazed her. She sat down herself, concentrating on the Cimaroon's smooth movements rather than on the creature almost directly below them. Dionisio skimmed across the stones leading to the far side of the stream and disappeared into the forest. Brandy lay her cheek on her knees, her eyes focused on the spot where she'd seen him last. She willed away the whirling emotions that would have invaded her temporary peace of mind in these lush, strange surroundings, with her unlikely but fascinating companion. One chink in the armor of her resolve, and all the hurt and humiliation, all the fury and frustration, would have levered open the door of her vulnerability as easily as Dudley had the door of Keir's cabin during the storm off the Canaries.

For one of the rare times in her life, Brandy Dalton purposefully ignored the voices in her head.

Dionisio soon appeared with a dead bird in one hand, its limp form a sad contrast to its bright plumage. He tossed it toward Moses, who came to life in a flash. Slithering off the muddy bank, his short but powerful legs and webbed feet launched him like a sleek arrow into the widened portion of the stream. Only his eyes and nostrils were at first visible as the crocodile glided swiftly and smoothly across the water with exactly the right timing to catch bird with his great jaws. The dead parrot never even hit the water. A few colorful feathers, drifting downward through the air, were the only evidence of its fate.

Brandy waved hesitantly at the Cimaroon across the tributary before realizing that he had performed the deed solely for her benefit. She swallowed the queasiness working up her throat in the wake of the frightening ease with which the croc had dashed into the water and expertly caught his prey in his pale, tooth-lined maw. Thankful that the African hadn't made her witness the crocodile devouring his meal while it was still alive, she applauded Dionisio, her smile brightening with relief.

But Dionisio suddenly stiffened where he stood, his grin turning to a frightening scowl as his eyes moved from Brandy to a point beyond her.

"Is it the crocodile you applaud, wench, or the savage?" asked an achingly familiar—and very angry—voice from immediately behind her.

# Chapter Twenty

Brandy slowly rose to her knees. She was in no hurry to confront Keir St. Andrews. A slow anger ignited and began to smolder within her. How dare he come searching for her as if she were an irresponsible child . . . and especially after what had been revealed? How dare he spoil her precious time away from him and the soul-shaking memories that accompanied thoughts of him?

And how dare he speak in such an accusatory, condemning tone . . . as if she had just been caught in the act of some wrongdoing?

He may have been the captain of the *Odyssey*, he may have been the sixth Earl of Somerset, but he had no right to be rude or highhanded. Nor, Brandy acknowledged, was she quite the meek and unworldly chit he'd dealt with those first few weeks at sea.

And he had called Dionisio a savage. That was insupportable. Especially in light of the fact that the Cimaroon had not been the one to accept her as an unwilling 'gift' from his shipmates before deciding to take her against her will halfway across the world as his prisoner.

"I believe *you* are the savage, Captain, or Lord Somerset, or whatever you are now, and not Dionisio," she said over her shoulder.

She stood then, and slowly faced him, forgetting about Moses and Dionisio for a few tense moments, ignoring the shameful effect the mere sight of Keir St. Andrews had on her senses. "And pray be so kind as to inform me, since you are not my master, what right you have to tell me how to spend my time or what activities I must choose to fill my empty hours? I am not one of your crew, *Captain,* nor am I one of your underlings, *Lord Somerset.*"

He stood atop the great boulder across from her, his eyes boring into hers as they met. He ignored her words, his stance taut for a moment as he assessed a Brandy he had not seen before. Then he wordlessly advanced a step toward her.

Brandy backed up in unthinking reaction, despite her resolve not to give way before him.

Dionisio called out something in Spanish, his voice full of menace, even from across the splashing stream, but neither Brandy nor Keir heeded.

"I turn my back for a moment and the next thing I know you are halfway down the mountain cavorting about with a dangerous runaway slave . . . to say naught of the other less obvious dangers surrounding an untried woman in a wild rain forest." He took another step toward her, but this time she stood her ground. What could he do to her?

"And I say that you are not my guardian—or whatever else you fancy yourself. You relinquished any claim to me when Father Tomas told us who you really were . . . when you were revealed an earl, a peer of the realm who should have been setting examples for others less fortunate to live by, not giving lessons in the art of deception!"

Her anger was kindling apace with his, Keir saw, as he sought the words that would bring her down from their precarious perch and make her understand what he'd just managed to do after having his identity—his life—literally stolen out from under him as a lad. But now was one hell of a time for her to show her temper . . . the temper he never knew existed. The temper dragged from dormancy by his refusal to be honest with her from the beginning.

"Come back to the mission with me."

It was a command, not a request. An alien perverseness rose in Brandy. "When cows fly, I'll go with you!"

The movement of Dionisio crossing over the stones at the ford dimly registered in her mind, but she had to make Keir leave before she either broke down before him or hit him right across his coldly handsome face. Wouldn't that be out of character for the sweet, mild-natured Brandy Dalton? And especially with Dionisio present.

"I can't talk to you in the middle of a rain forest, with a—"

"You have naught to say that would interest me now, Keir St. Andrews," she cut across his words. "The time for talking is long past. Now, if you have any decency left in you, you'll go make good your promise to Father Tomas and leave me be!"

His concern for her safety and the force of his frustration made Keir do an unwise thing. He unthinkingly reached for her, trying to snatch her away from the edge of the boulder that faced the stream. But as fast as he was, Brandy had the advantage of being just out of arm's reach. Forgetting how close she was to the edge, she skipped backward, only to suddenly find herself free falling . . . She dimly heard Keir cry out her name, but then she was hitting the chilly mountain stream waters, stunned by the unexpected turn in events . . . and the impact.

The water wasn't deep, barely up to her chest, nor was the current overly strong here directly below the ford. As she came up sputtering, however, a sobering thought struck her. This was Moses' territory.

And Moses had just had his appetite whetted with a freshly-killed parrot.

She stared up in horror at Keir as he pulled a dagger from his belt, his eyes on something behind her. "Don't move," he commanded softly, and drew back his arm for the throw.

Dionisio's voice boomed, *"No!"* just then, and Brandy half-turned to see him dive cleanly from the nearby bank into the water.

"Stop, Keir!" Brandy cried, rooted to the riverbed with fear for the Cimaroon.

But it was too late. The dagger went whizzing over her head and buried itself in the crocodile's side. His bellow of rage reverberated through the forest and a jet of blood began to dye the water around him.

Dionisio continued to swim toward the wounded animal.

"Get away from him, you fool!" Keir called, and dropped to the ground. Brandy watched, paralyzed, as the African ignored Keir's warning and approached the thrashing crocodile.

Keir slid off the bank and into the stream behind her, fear for Brandy giving him added impetus to push his sodden limbs in what seemed like slow motion through the now-churning waters.

He grabbed her by the arm and pulled her toward the bank. "Nay!" she cried, her eyes on the man and beast struggling a stone's throw from them.

"Don't be heroic, Brandy, you can't help him from here. Get to the bank . . . now!"

Realizing that he was right, Brandy did as she was bid, her heart thrumming in her chest. She pulled her gaze away from the frenzied struggle and allowed Keir to help her from the water.

"Can't you do something?" she asked, her eyes wild as they beseeched him. " 'Twas my fault . . ."

"You're damned right it was your fault, for ever having come here with him," he agreed, releasing her arm and searching the bank with his eyes. He bent and took hold of a wrist-thick branch and made to return to the water.

*But you followed us, and you wounded Moses,* she thought fiercely. *Now Dionisio may die.*

Or Keir, right along with him, she realized as he entered the water once more.

Then, suddenly, the world returned to relative quiet.

Brandy cast a quick look at the place where Dionisio had encountered the angered Moses. The crocodile was on his back, and Dionisio was stroking the beast's pale belly. As he stroked, he moved toward the near bank, pulling the now unmoving reptile with him.

"What—what happened?" Brandy murmured, the weakness of relief seeping through her limbs. "Is he dead?"

"I think not. Only asleep."

She looked at Keir questioningly, but he was watching the African as Dionisio dragged the crocodile out of the water and onto the bank. When the upper part of the twelve foot length of Moses was sprawled, relaxed and belly-up before them, Dionisio carefully removed Keir's dagger from its side, tossed it to Keir, and quickly packed the wound with mud. He straightened then and looked up.

Brandy moved toward him and Keir made to stop her. "Take your hand off me," she told him, the blood of a long line of hot-tempered Spensers finally making its presence known. "Haven't you done enough?"

Keir opened his mouth to retort, but the look on her face was so outraged that he thought better of it and held his silence. He remained still as he watched her walk toward the dripping, panting Cimaroon standing proudly erect beside the still body of the crocodile. As Brandy looked up into Dionisio's dark face for a long moment, Keir felt jealousy claw through him for the second time since he'd met Brandy Dalton. Only with Jackie Greaves, it had been mild compared to this.

Brandy took the warrior's hand then, and raised it up to her cheek. *"Gracias,"* she whispered. *"Gracias, mi bravo Dionisio."*

When at last she turned back to where Keir had been standing, he was gone.

\* \* \*

300

By the time Dionisio led her back to the mission, Brandy was exhausted, physically and emotionally. Every time the Cimaroon had indicated that they return, Brandy had allowed her unwillingness to show, and even though she knew Dionisio might have benefitted from what he could be shown by Keir and his men, she stubbornly told herself that if the Cimaroon had really wanted to return earlier, he would have insisted and she would have gone along.

At the evening meal, Brandy sat between Father Tomas and Dionisio, the latter having been invited by the priest to dine with them and learn through dialogue what he had missed earlier in the day.

Brandy suspected Father Tomas had deliberately seated her between himself and the Cimaroon, away from Keir. "Dionisio is the ablest warrior in the mission," the priest was telling Keir. "He is easily worth three men of average ability."

"So I've heard," Keir said, an edge to his words as he speared another piece of roasted beef and brought it up to his mouth without looking at either the priest or Brandy.

"Many of *los cimarrones* come from Africa's Gold Coast, home of the Asante and Fante tribes, who are particularly brave and warlike."

"On the morrow," Keir said, not bothering to comment on Father Tomas's information, "I want to examine his musket for rust or other defects that could cost him his life. In fact, tomorrow is when you shall make your presence known at the plantation west of the mountain base. You will make up some reason for going, and act as if nothing is amiss. You might even hint that your men picked off several of the, ah, visitors from Port Royal because *los ingleses* wouldn't lay down their arms before entering the mission." Keir bit into the meat, then washed it down with a draught of golden Jamaican rum, or killdevil. "And you must act every bit as deranged as the rumors say you are."

Father Tomas nodded. "And your men will leave for Port Royal?"

"Aye. Foucher and Gonzalez will leave with you, but, as I told you earlier, I want them to skirt that plantation. If the Spanish see only two of our original six returning to Port Royal, rather than being frightened into silence the Spaniards might be alarmed enough to go straight to Governor Modyford with the tale. Who knows what might happen then? What if Morgan or Mansfield, who happen to be acquaintances of mine, take it into their heads to avenge my death? It matters not whether they are sincere—and we all know they'd just as soon do it for their own gain. Men like them don't need much reason to cause trouble, and Morgan knows I was looking for you." He shook his head. "You can tell them on the plantation yourself that the remaining intruders left sometime in the night."

Brandy wondered just how she was going to fend off Keir if he chose to continue their heated words, not only that night, but on the morrow while Father Tomas was absent from the mission. The conversation became a low drone around her as she pondered her problem.

Dionisio leaned forward to help himself to the strange, deliciously sweet yams, his knee touched Brandy's, and she realized that he would remain at the mission the next day. She raised her eyes to look at him, sitting so tall and proud beside her, but Keir's penetrating gaze alighted on her just then, and she lowered her lashes, refusing to acknowledge him.

"Would you like Maria or one of the other women to fetch your things from the hut you share with Keir?" Father Tomas suddenly whispered into her ear while Keir's attention was engaged by something Foucher was saying. "You can sleep elsewhere for the next two nights if you wish."

Brandy automatically gave him a half-smile of gratitude, then allowed her regard to go to Keir. Ire lit her eyes afresh at the thought of his deliberate betrayal, and unexpected determination rose within her like a physical presence. "Nay, thank you, Father," she said softly, her tone steely beneath the naturally sweet strains. "I think I can handle Keir St. Andrews, now that I know exactly what kind of man he is."

As Keir entered the tiny dwelling they temporarily shared, Brandy was still wide awake. She couldn't help but notice that he reeked of rum, something uncharacteristic for a man who'd admitted he rarely got sotted, and when he did, usually did it in private. Her softer side went out to him immediately, for to her knowledge, Keir St. Andrews only drank heavily when he was deeply troubled or extremely agitated.

But the woman she'd become after weeks at sea with this very man—a man whose expertise at lovemaking and deception had won and then cruelly discarded her—warned her that he had probably lied about his drinking habits too, and that she was every kind of a fool to feel anything for him but outrage. She'd placed her heart in his care, as trustingly as a child, and he'd trampled over it as easily as a piece of refuse in a London alleyway.

She buried her face in the crook of her arm, essaying to erase his image . . . and the evidence that he was somehow hurting. *She* was hurting now, and for the second time in the same day she put her own pain before another's . . . especially before the pain of the one who had caused her such anguish.

"Look at me, Brandy," he ordered her, an odd timbre to his words.

"Leave me be," she answered in a muffled voice from the cushion of her arm, refusing to face him. "I have naught to say to you. The time for words is past."

He remained standing just inside the doorway, leaning against its crude frame, the tattered fabric curtain swept aside and draped over one arm as it spanned the narrow opening. She could just picture him, with the rushlight playing over his splendid features, his hair falling across his forehead like a youth's. And the lure of his body through his fine linen shirt—if he hadn't already discarded it; his long, finely turned legs that drew a female's gaze as he strode purposefully along or merely stood still. And his face . . .

No, she didn't dare look at him.

"I made you no promises."

"Aye," came her bitter answer. "Only to return me to England. I live for that moment now—to be reunited with my family—and nothing else."

Suddenly, he was stretched out beside her, pulling her off her side and into his arms. "What has this to do with us?" His breath was sweet with Jamaican rum, his eyes as soft as she'd ever seen them, shaded with desire . . . and other things that she dared not name or she would melt in his embrace, for love did not just disappear in the course of a day.

"What has any of this to do with us?"

A trembling sigh left her lips, and Brandy despised her weakness where he was concerned. "It has everything to do with us!" She finally met his gaze. "First you make me yours in every sense of the word, when you should have returned me to the Hawk and Hound immediately—especially knowing that you were no mere low-bred, conscienceless pirate! Then you take me halfway across the world, allowing me to dare hope that you felt something more than just lust. That is, until Father Tomas revealed exactly what he would do to help you regain your birthright!" She pushed herself away from him and rose to her knees, breathing raggedly with the force of her feelings. "I may be a coward, unable to stick you in the belly with a razor to obtain my freedom, but I'm done with playing the gullible fool. I've learned much from you, Captain Keir St. Andrews. You've taught me that the lot of the weak is to be tossed the way of a feather in the wind, unwilling victims in this uncaring world. And I don't choose to be numbered among the weak anymore."

"Brandy-eyes," he murmured, his eyes on her mouth, his hand moving to stroke her unbound hair. "This changes naught. You'll be mine forever . . ."

She shoved his hand away and pushed herself into a sitting position against the side of the hut, fighting her love, her confusion, her fury, with her grandfather's unwitting legacy boiling through her blood. "While you marry your countess? Nay, I think not! If you had told me in the very beginning, I would have known what to expect, but your unforgivable sin was to lead me to believe I could mean something to you."

"You do . . . you can . . . always," came his dulcet answer, his spirit-scented breath sighing over her face.

"I *cannot* after we set foot in England and you know it." A sudden thought struck her. "Or are you, the sixth Earl of Somerset, asking me to wed you?"

She knew the answer even before he opened his mouth, but she felt a contradictory need to twist the blade skewering her own heart, to sustain the anguish of betrayal as a barrier between them.

He stilled, then, at her brutally frank question. No, he never intended to marry her. But what tavern wench would not welcome the chance to be an earl's mistress?

*Brandy Dalton.*

"We have the next two nights . . . and the return voyage . . ."

Brandy rose to her knees and he quickly moved to follow suit. In a swift, unexpected movement, she drew back her hand and slapped him full in the face. An uncharacteristic fury mottled her own countenance as she hissed at him, "I may be less than nothing in your eyes, Keir St. Andrews, but I am decent! I am no whore!" She drew in a shaking breath to finish. "I am more decent and honest as a tavern wench than you will ever be as an earl!"

He knelt staring at her, his eyes narrowing and turning glacial, not so much from the physical blow she had dealt him, but rather from the verbal one. Deep down there had always been a glimmer of doubt as to whether he could ever live up to the image of his father and the St. Andrews before him. Keir had been raised among conditions that hardly befitted an earl—conditions that created criminals, not paragons of English peerage.

He sank back on his heels, his fingers touching the livid marks across his cheek. His gaze went from her face to the floor as the rum he'd consumed seemed to make his ears ring . . . or was it the effect of her angry blow? His shoulders slumped slightly as he leaned his hands on his knees and closed his eyes against the condemning echoes of her words.

She was probably right.

Brandy fought the love and pity that swept through her suddenly as she watched defeat momentarily hover over him like the quivering crest of a wave about to break. "Why did you not tell me?" she asked him in a pained voice as some of her anger ebbed away. "And why did you not at least follow me to the waterfall? Why, you couldn't even look me in the eye when Father Tomas revealed who you really were." Her voice began to break and she savagely bit her lower lip, splitting it and drawing blood in her refusal to act the part that she had determined she had outgrown.

"Would it have mattered?" His eyes were still on the dirt floor.

She ignored his question, burning with another of her own that took on even more importance in that moment. "Just what did you plan to do with me? Make me your mistress when we returned to England as you indicated earlier?" Her words could have been carved from wood, so toneless, so hollow, did they sound to her own ears, but she had to know. "And tell me the truth this time."

He slowly raised his head until his eyes met hers. There

was a drawn-out silence before he spoke, but when he did, all the physical and emotional pain, the long-denied feelings and extreme frustration of twenty years of harsh living, with an endless future of more of the same looming as a very real possibility, were evident in four whispered words. "No . . . not even that."

"You mean to tell me that my granddaughter is *alive?* Is here in London, beneath my very nose?"

Margaret Hill Dalton glanced at her husband beside her before she spoke. They were in Aimery Spenser's London town house, where desperation had driven them after weeks of debating just what to do in the wake of failing to gain the king's ear without months of endless waiting.

"You told me, Sir Aimery—"

"Lord Spenser, now," Aimery corrected with impatience.

"Lord Spenser," Margaret continued, the hue of embarrassment searing her cheeks, "that you never wanted to see me or the babe again. I feared for my life . . . an' hers as well."

"We've cared for Brandy like a daughter . . . she's wanted for naught—" Jonathon began in his wife's defense, only to be cut off.

The earl's white eyebrows raised, his eyes narrowing with contempt. *"Brandy?* Damme! What kind of name is that for a female . . . and a Spenser?"

"With all due respect, your lordship," answered Jonathon, "we thought it a pretty name—a fittin' name. You gave up your rights to your granddaughter when ye tossed her out with my Margaret here." He put a protective arm about Margaret's shoulders. "Brandy's a Dalton now, at least in name . . . not a Spenser."

But Aimery was studying the silver buckle on his shoe, an intense frown of bemusement upon his features. "And you raised her in an *alehouse?*" He brought his eyes up to meet Margaret's. "Like a common bawd?"

For the second time in his life, Aimery Spenser wanted to throttle Margaret Hill—or Dalton—or whoever the hell she was. He'd regretted his dismissal of her within weeks of his grandchild's birth, and had combed the countryside in hopes of finding the babe. The only reward for his efforts was the disappearance of his daughter Catherine to add to his burden of guilt and shame. Even his eventual remarriage and the subsequent children he had fathered had done nothing to ease his conscience. He'd eventually assumed both Catherine and the infant dead.

"Brandy's no bawd, I can assure you, your lordship. Now enough is enough!" Jonathon answered for Margaret, who had begun to cry. "We only came here to ask your help in gettin' Brandy back from the blackguard who—"

"What does she look like?" Aimery interrupted, motioning to his wife, who stood unobtrusively in the background, to bring some refreshment.

"Her eyes are the exact color of brandywyne . . ." (Spenser rolled his eyes at this) ". . . and her hair is like the settin' sun," Jonathon said, waxing poetic at the vivid memories of his beautiful adopted daughter. His eyes misted with emotion as he added, "And she's as sweet a lass as ye'd ever want to meet—with nary a harsh word for anyone."

Juliana. Just like her mother and grandmother before her, Spenser thought, and blinked away the unwelcome moisture gathering in the corners of his eyes. By the Mass! but he'd be sniveling like Margaret if he didn't get hold of himself . . .

"—kidnapped her an' sailed away. End of August," Jonathon was saying angrily.

"Kidnapped?" Aimery Spenser's attention was snagged immediately as the word registered. Fire lit his eyes. He was not about to discover that his long-lost granddaughter was still alive, only to learn in the next breath that someone had abducted her. *"Who* kidnapped Juliana?"

Margaret began to weep anew in the wake of his words, just as Lady Anne Spenser reentered the room with a tray of beverages and goblets. She wordlessly placed the tray upon a nearby table and retreated from the saloon.

"Captain Keir St. Andrews of the *Odyssey,* that's who. His men knocked my son Simon out cold an' dragged her away. I tried to get her back, but that pricklouse St. Andrews wouldn't even let us aboard to search for her." Jonathon's whole body visibly tensed with outrage, his huge hands opening and clenching at his sides. "Then they sneaked off in the dead o' night—black as the devil, 'twas!—an' took our Brandy with 'em, I'd wager the Hawk and Hound on it!"

It was a preposterous story, Aimery Spenser thought. So preposterous that it had to be true, because here was Margaret, whom he'd dismissed out of hand eighteen years ago, reappearing on his doorstep as if by magic. Surely in the face of the genuine agitation exhibited by both Daltons, the story couldn't have been fabricated.

*And you're just soft enough in your dotage to want to believe them. If you can't have your beloved Juliana's daughter back, then you'll gratefully settle for her bastard issue, soiled and sullied as she might be now.*

"St. Andrews, eh?" Aimery mumbled, distractedly waving toward the tray of Madeira and ale, too agitated to do anything but lower himself onto a settee. "St. Andrews of Somerset?"

"I know not, yer lordship," Jonathon said. "Only that his ship was called the *Odyssey,* and he said they'd just returned from the New World. Probably pirates, from the look of some of 'em," he added darkly.

Pirates? The tale was growing more unbelievable by the moment. "Well, man, what flag did this ship fly?"

"English. But that don't mean they weren't above takin' a prisoner—especially a comely female."

"The navy impresses men all the time, but taking a lone

309

female out to sea is considered ill luck. What makes you think they took Bran—er, Juliana with 'em?"

"Because we've not seen 'er since."

In the wake of Dalton's declaration, Spenser roused himself from the settee and reached for the Madeira.


For Brandy, leaving Jamaica as a free agent was worse than leaving London as a captive. Where she had been frustrated and afraid on her first leavetaking, she now felt crushed in spirit so badly that she wanted to reach out to the receding Blue Mountains, as the *Odyssey* nosed its way eastward around the end of the island, and cling for strength and support . . . for her very sanity.

Where formerly she had slowly been wooed and won by the sea and the men who roamed it while aboard the *Odyssey*—and especially its captain—Brandy now envisioned weeks of endless sailing between her and London . . . weeks on the same ship with Keir St. Andrews, the man she now knew it was futile to love. The man who had knowingly betrayed her.

Her anger had subsided, leaving in its place a deep, raw wound, and nothing in her relatively simple and sheltered life had prepared her for such anguish. Everywhere she looked she would see Keir, whether in reality or in memory's images. And if her own emotions betrayed her, if her heart would send her to his cabin, Father Tomas was there to see that she ignored the call of her love. She had his solemn promise to be her guardian until they reached England.

Her favorite passage from the Bible came to her as Jamaica grew smaller and more insignificant in the late morning sun. The words comforted her as they whispered across her soul:

Love is patient and kind, not jealous or boastful; it is not arrogant or rude. Love does not insist on its

310

own way; it is not irritable or resentful; it does not rejoice at wrong, but rejoices in the right. Love bears all things, believes all things, hopes all things, endures all things. Love never ends.

Well, little of it applied in this case, for her love had not been returned. She had given her all to Keir St. Andrews, and he had thrown it back in her face. Perhaps not with the intent to hurt her, for his values, his sense of right and wrong, his very way of thinking, had been forged from a life as different from her own as night from day. She still loved him, and she would try to rejoice in the restoration of all that was rightfully his, even at her own expense. But as for the rest . . .

The moisture from her tears mingled with the salt spray caught and flung into her face as she stood at the rail amidships, halfway across the *Odyssey* from the quarterdeck where she knew Keir stood at the helm, his back to her. Her head began to ache from trying to hold back her tears and from the blinding reflection of the sunlight scintillating on the water.

Her hand went to the tiny carved mahogany lioness that hung from a slender cord against her chest, deriving strength from the contact. Dionisio had given it to her before they left that morning. Father Tomas had told her, "Dionisio says that for all your outward fragility . . . for all your sweetness, you have the heart of a lioness. He would have you wear this to remember us."

"Some would say 'tis a pagan amulet," she had answered the priest after thanking Dionisio in halting Spanish. With a wavering smile she had fingered the smooth, miniature carving just as she did now.

Father Tomas had responded, "And so they would. But I have learned that all the lesser gods in whom the Cimaroons, the Arawak, and the fierce Carib believed at one time, are really only different manifestations of the Father. God is everywhere, in everything. Even in the ma-

311

jestic lion. The same Father watches over us all, whether in a lowly hut or a magnificent cathedral . . . whether a loincloth-clad African warrior or a vestmented European clergyman."

His words echoed over and over in her mind now. Although some might consider Father Tomas a heretic, Brandy thought him, even more so than before, really a remarkable man. "Dionisio's gift is a momento of Jamaica and our mission here. If it will offer you comfort and fond memories, if it will even help you heal in some small way, I would be the last to condemn his parting gift," he'd added.

Now, as Father Tomas's warm hand closed over hers on the rail, Brandy glanced up at him, her gaze going briefly to Keir, and then following the priest's gaze out to sea again. But not before she noticed that his eyes were wet with tears.

Suddenly Brandy knew that if this kind and tolerant man could face leaving his mission and the possibility of never returning, she could face a life without Keir St. Andrews. That did not mean that she would ever cease to love him, but life went on despite loss of every kind. One only had to draw on ones inner strength and resilience. If one could not do that, there lay only a long road of emptiness ahead before the inevitablity of death.

Brandy squeezed the Jesuit's hand as they watched Jamaica become a dot on the horizon before it disappeared. "Courage, Father," she told him. "And faith."

# Part Three

## Home

*'That which we call a rose, by any other name would smell as sweet.'*

William Shakespeare
*Romeo and Juliet*

# Chapter Twenty-one

*Somerset, England — Spring, 1666*

Keir St. Andrews, sixth Earl of Somerset, sat his great
bay stallion and surveyed the seat of five previous generations of Somersets.

*Somerset Chase, Somerset Chase* . . . The words sang
through his mind, bringing the blur of tears to his eyes for
a moment, before he willed them away . . . tears that had
been disconcertingly near the surface altogether too fre-
quently for his liking. Sometimes it seemed to Keir that he
would never overcome this new weakness, even though, he
was loath to admit, he felt as if some piece of the unwanted burden he'd long carried upon his shoulders
melted away whenever he allowed free rein in private to
what he considered his emotional outbursts.

He deliberately concentrated on the low, sprawling gray
stone building before him. Its front facade and gardens
had been designed by Charles I's architect, Indigo Jones,
in collaboration with Isaac de Caux in the '30's, a fact
that Keir's father had proudly told his young son on more
than one occasion . . . almost as if James St. Andrews
had suspected that his heir might one day be separated
from their beloved and beautiful estate.

"Look at those pavilions, boy," his father had pointed
out.

"The towers, my lord father?" Keir had asked with childish curiosity.

"Aye, but now they call 'em 'pavilions' . . . *al Italiano*. The King's architect, Master Jones, brought back from Italy the ideas for Somerset Chase's renovation . . ."

Originally a Tudor home, Somerset Chase had been renamed when acquired by the Somerset family in the mid-1500's and then refurbished in the 1630's. Jones and de Caux had added a new garden and grotto to this side of the building and changed the old, existing Tudor towers with gabled windows at the adjoining entrance front. The true innovation, Keir now realized, was Jones and de Caux's facade of calmly classical character. It hardly seemed to belong to the same century as the other houses whose robust naivete Keir had noted since his return. Its composition had a restraint and nobility hard to account for in a period of such unrest and upheaval.

The impressive *piano nobile,* or first floor, was set above a low basement. Small attic windows above those of the first floor were crowned by a carved overhang and, finally, a decorative stone balustrade. A momumental Venetian window in the center balanced the weights of the stately, pedimented pavilions at each end, and the crisply carved stone window-surrounds threw knife-edged shadows on the warm, gray local stone. The house's corinthian portico on the central axis pulled the whole design together.

Thank God the faded memory of acrid smoke while Keir had lain there upon the beach, barely conscious all those years ago, had come from a burning outbuilding, and not Somerset Chase itself. He loved his home with a fierceness greater than he'd ever thought possible over the years. The obtaining of his heart's desire had not lessened it in his eyes, as was often the case. Somerset Chase only increased in value to him because it was rightfully his; it had lost none of its remembered beauty.

An errant scrap of sea breeze teased his nostrils, beckoning, threatening to scatter his thoughts, but Keir resisted the urge to turn his mount toward the ocean just yet. He wanted to sit where he was and savor the realization of years of wishing and planning. The few changes that Keir had effected, mostly inside the house, had been made; the workmen were gone now, most of the original paintings and furniture he'd remembered from his childhood had been miraculously recovered from their dustcovers in the attic and replaced in their rightful positions. Any trace of his uncle and his family had been routed out and destroyed without a qualm on Keir's part. In fact, each time a torch was put to some object belonging to his uncle, Keir derived a savage satisfaction from its demolition.

Giles St. Andrews had fallen from grace, his family scattered, he in exile for life. Keir had had no wish to disgrace any further Giles's wife, who had come from a good and old noble family. Giles's only son, Ralph, had gone with his mother to their family home in the north of England, bitter and hateful—much as Keir had been as a youth. Only in Keir's mind, Ralph St. Andrews deserved his banishment from court and his disgrace for not coming forward and revealing his father's crime. Father Tomas had distinctly told Keir and the King that Giles's son had been present, according to what the Jesuit had overheard, that night on the beach.

*I want nothing to stand in the way of my rightful title of Earl of Somerset. And my son after me . . .* Father Tomas's testimony splintered through Keir's mind, still possessing the power to fire his fury . . . to sear his soul.

But what could the boy have done? asked his softer side for the hundredth time. How could a lad little more than Keir's age at the time have gone against his father? Even believed his father wrong?

"A true St. Andrews would have done so, would have known right from wrong," Keir mumbled to the wind as

317

he watched Jackie and Dudley come toward him at a run from a side entrance to the estate.

Dudley's ungainly body worked to keep up with the long-legged Jackie . . . and failed, falling behind fast as the tall youth gained Keir's side.

Even Jackie Greaves, the offspring of parents who had literally sold him into service on an unsavory ship for a few extra quid, knew the difference between honor and dishonor.

"You left your *amigo* in your wake," Keir said into the boy's flushed face as Jackie squinted up at him, a letter bearing the royal seal clutched in his hand.

Jackie glanced over at the laboring basset, then back at Keir. One corner of his mouth lifted slightly. "He'll catch up, Cap'n. But Master Stubbs told me te give you this right away, an' tell you the *Odyssey*'s just docked in London." He pulled in and expelled a deep breath as he waited for Keir to take the missive.

Dudley came lumbering up to them, his long tongue lolling, and plopped his backside down behind Jackie, away from the bay's hooves.

"You aren't afraid of Corsair, are you, Duds?" Keir asked the dog, an eyebrow raising.

Dudley's tail slapped the grassy ground a time or two when Keir said his name. "Duds still ain't used te horses, Cap'n," Jackie answered for his friend with a shrug of nicely filled-out shoulders. He shaded his eyes from the bright spring sun with one hand. "And it ain't as though Corsair here's exactly a docile mare." As if in acknowledgment of his own words, the youth retreated a step from the huge stallion as the bay stomped a hoof and tossed his great dark head restlessly. "I think Duds misses the storms an' the battles . . . and the sea."

"Mayhap," Keir answered before looking back at Jackie. "And do you?"

The boy colored, but he didn't stammer. "Oh, nay, Cap'n. I love it here at Somerset Chase. Why, the sea is just over yon rise," he jerked his chin over his shoulder.

Keir studied Jackie's face for a moment before he looked down and scanned the contents of the letter, a frown forming over his eyes. It was an invitation to a reception at Whitehall the following week. Court was definitely not his favorite place; he felt like a misfit. But he still needed a wife . . . The thought soured even as it formed. And, of course, the timing was perfect if the *Odyssey* was in port.

". . . that be all, Cap'n—I mean, yer lordship?" Jackie was asking.

Keir looked up, dragged from his musings. "Aye." He took in the youth's heat-flushed features and the limp-looking Dudley beside him. "Why don't you two take a walk along the beach?"

When Jackie brightened, Keir clarified, "As long as you don't drown, lad. Duds can swim naturally, but you—"

"Oh, I been practicin' in the creek, Cap'n—I mean, yer—"

"Captain is fine, Jackie. But practicing in a shallow, sluggish stream and the unpredictable bay are two different things entirely. Promise me you won't go in farther than your kneecaps and I'll let you go."

"Promise, Cap'n. An' ol' Duds here can keep one eye on me." He laughed aloud, a sound that Keir was only just becoming accustomed to hearing. He had sworn to make Jackie's years immediately before manhood better than his own had been. He knew little of fathering, but Jackie would find his place in the world with Keir's help. If necessary, Keir would create a place for an abandoned boy exposed to more years at sea than any uninitiated youth ought to have been.

"Was there any news of—?" Keir cut off his sentence before he said her name. It was habit that prompted him to ask about Brandy Dalton. Habit and a fledging flare of hope that he couldn't quite squelch.

Jackie's face fell, his mouth sobering into a tight line,

319

desolation darkening his hazel eyes. "I—I d-d-didn't ask him," he stammered.

In the momentary silence that held sway, the wind soughed gently through the trees and grass about the manor grounds, birds carolled sweetly, distinctly, and the distant crash of the surf grew more pronounced.

Jackie stared down at his feet, his obvious misery reflected in the green eyes of the man before him. It had been well over a year since the *Odyssey* had docked in London—a London caught in the throes of a bitter winter. And the plague.

Brandy Dalton had returned to the Hawk and Hound at not only her own insistence, but under Father Tomas's aegis as well. Keir, however, had been totally caught up in his anxiety over the King's acceptance of the priest's testimony, the bringing to justice of Giles St. Andrews, and the restoration of all that was his by birth. Between those concerns and his deliberations as to who would continue to sail the *Odyssey* as a privateer for England and who would go on to Somerset Chase with him, Keir was able to ruthlessly repress thoughts of Brandy Dalton. He'd supposed she was safe—as safe as one could be with the dreaded plague spreading through the city—at the Hawk and Hound.

" 'Tis all right, lad," Keir said, momentarily retrieving his thoughts. "Go on to the beach. Just have a care."

Jackie nodded, his gaze passing briefly over Keir's features before he began to move toward the bay. With a grunt, Dudley heaved himself to all fours and trotted after him.

Keir guided Corsair to the left and gave the stallion his head. They moved toward the woods that bordered Somerset Chase to the north. Then, just before they reached the trees, Keir nudged the bay to the left again, and toward the sea.

He dismounted behind one of the grassy dunes and left the horse to graze where he would. The stallion was Keir's favorite, with its burnished red-brown coloring and midnight mane and tail. He had bought it as a two-year-old and immediately changed its name to Corsair . . . a name that flayed him with the whip of guilt and regret every time he uttered it, for it had been the worst insult Brandy Dalton could think to throw at him months ago.

Keir picked a spot that suited his purpose and sat down, half-hidden from the boy and dog romping along the smooth clean sand of the far stretch of beach, and allowed his thoughts free rein.

Naturally, the sight of the water, the sounds and smells borne on the breeze, brought back a host of memories, some pleasant, others punishing. These latter he pushed aside, as he had learned to do as a defense mechanism. The others he allowed to invade his senses. Screeching gulls and roaring breakers blended their songs; sunlight shimmered on the blue-green waters, dotted here and there with the flash of a surfacing fish; salt stung his nostrils, as did an occasional whiff of driftwood and rotted fish carried on the seabreeze. Yet Keir had learned to love the sea, even though he was done with sailing as a way of life forever. He was where he wanted to be, and that was enough.

Or so he had thought until only a few months after his arrival at Somerset Chase, the lawful sixth Earl of Somerset.

He had immersed himself in the redecorating of the manor house interior with all that had belonged to his parents, and their parents before them. He'd reversed any changes that his nefarious uncle had made during the last two decades, unless they were for the better. He had wiped all trace of Giles St. Andrews from the seat of the St. Andrews, even down to the dismissal of the servants Giles had hired to replace the original staff who had been in Keir's family's employ, in some cases, for generations.

He had introduced himself to tenant farmers on his lands, taken charge of things he remembered his father overseeing, and sought answers to the question of the fate

321

of his mother and sister. But, glad as most were to see the rightful heir of the old earl returned to his home, they could shed no light on the fate of the rest of his family. Giles St. Andrews himself had denied any knowledge of their fate, even as he continued to deny any part in Keir's attempted murder.

One old servant, Rob Stevens, who had been one of two gardeners, had told Keir that no one, to his knowledge, ever learned what happened to Elizabeth St. Andrews and her daughter. Many of the nobility of England had perished in the civil wars, or simply gone into exile, never to return. "Some say they were killed by Roundheads. Some say they fled to 'er ladyship's family in Ireland."

Even the question of Keir's death had remained unsolved until he had shown up one spring day the year before, king's writ in hand, proclaiming his identity. Somerset Chase had already been vacated by Giles and his family.

"And we would've knowed ye, even without that paper," the elderly Stevens had declared, his faded eyes lighting with his conviction. "No mistakin' ye're the very image of 'is lordship." He'd squinted up at Keir then. " 'Cept fer them eyes. Milady 'Lisabeth had the greenest eyes in all England."

"Aye," Keir had answered with a hint of a smile, for he knew the man had probably never been farther than the borders of the St. Andrews lands. "And you, no doubt, have traveled all over this fair land."

Rob Stevens had given Keir his good-natured, gap-toothed grin, which reminded Keir of a broken bottle. "Aye. And ye got 'is lordship's sense o' humor, as well, by the Mass! A kind man 'e was, an' with a thigh-slappin' good humor . . . a jest always abrewin' on his tongue." The old man's eyes had grown watery then, and Keir had tactfully changed the subject. There would be other times to talk of his late father.

"You'll have to tell me more another time, Rob Stevens,

for I've vague memories of you, and also would have you refresh them further about any number of things. I've been away too long."

A fresh feeling of loss filtered through Keir now at the remembrance of his immediate family, and he scooped a handful of cool sand from beneath the top layer, and with emotion-blurred vision watched it sift slowly through his fingers. Yet as devastating a loss as that had been, he had suspected it, been prepared for it, for years.

But he had not been prepared for the loss of the woman he loved.

Keir glanced up and toward the beach. Dudley had just tramped through the beginnings of a sand castle Jackie had been building. Jackie shouted something that was lost in the wind, and he chased the wily basset into the water, splashing through the surf with high-raised knees as he playfully flung sand at Dudley's flank. True to his promise to Keir, however, he veered back toward the shoreline when the waves reached his knees. Dudley, obviously seeing the game was over for the moment, paddled around and followed in the youth's wake, his short legs visibly working against the clear water as he swam to catch up with Jackie.

But this time Jackie sat down upon the sand and stared out to sea, the set of his chin, the droop of his shoulders, anything but playful. As Dudley wedged his nose beneath the youth's elbow, there was no enthusiastic response, and Keir sensed it had nothing to do with the smashed sand castle.

Keir sighed and lay his head down upon arms crossed over his knees. He closed his eyes and relived his efforts to find Brandy. At first he had sent hired messengers, for he had known the sight of him or any of his men who were known to the Daltons would do nothing to further his cause. But to no avail. According to Hodges, "They're gettin' ready te close up the inn and move out to the country 'cause o' the plague."

323

"Did you see Brandy?" Keir had asked, his voice low-pitched, urgent.

"Nay. Dalton said she'd jest disappeared a few weeks before."

Keir had gone absolutely still. "Disappeared?"

"Aye." Hodges had shook his head and raised his hands palm up as he shrugged his shoulders. "We even had a bite te eat and stayed until the evenin' crowd came, but 'twas a thin trickle of patrons what with the alarm about the plague. An' we caught nary a glimpse o' the girl."

Keir looked at the other man, Wells. "And you?"

"I even went upstairs, pretendin' I was lookin' over the rooms, and never saw Mistress Brandy. Only came up against the little one with the dark hair a-cryin' 'er eyes out." He scowled. "An' by then, the son came up to me and threatened to turn me out fer snoopin' an' oglin' 'is little sister."

And so the same story came back twice. Brandy Dalton had disappeared without a trace. Even if there had been some knowledge as to her whereabouts, Keir strongly suspected that all the wealth he'd amassed would have done nothing to help him obtain any information from the Daltons. And he couldn't really blame them.

But all he could picture was his Brandy lying dead somewhere of the plague, away from her family and loved ones. And all because of him.

After even hiring a solicitor to make inquiries about London, Keir had finally gone himself. He had to make one last attempt before he gave up on Brandy Dalton.

As he had suspected, Jonathon Dalton gave him an icy reception. Hatred honed the features of his face, and tensed his entire body. It had been midmorning, with few customers about. And Simon had been busily boarding up the windows and securing the shutters. He had put aside his tools when he saw Keir, and the two of them, father and son, had faced him with a virulence that might have taken a lesser man back.

"So ye're an *earl* now, are ye?" Dalton had sneered with no more respect than for a street beggar. "Now ye can take whoever ye fancy and steal her virtue afore sending her on her way, eh?" His great hands had fisted at his sides, revealing not only his fury, but his willingness to tangle physically with Keir, earl or no.

"Brandy ain't here," Simon Dalton had added from behind Keir. "More'n likely she's dead of the plague somewhere 'cause of *you*."

"Why did she leave?" Keir managed to ask, his insides not nearly as calm as his outward demeanor.

"Some'd call it shame, St. Andrews," Jonathon Dalton had answered. "But then again, you wouldn't be acquainted with anythin' to do with honor, now, would you?"

A nerve twitched in Keir's cheek, his own hands closing into fists as he fought a murderous urge to smash Dalton's face. Yet he knew the man had every right to be furious with him. For apparently, after all that had preceded, his daughter had recently run away in the wake of her return as the kept woman of a privateer captain . . . a man with little credibility and stature among many, in spite of his newly gained status.

"You don't understand, Dalton," Keir had continued, mastering his urge to take on the innkeeper. "No matter what went on before, I am prepared to put things to rights . . . to wed Brandy and make her my countess."

Dalton stuck out his chin stubbornly, the gleam in his eyes brightening with his ire. "Nay, *you're* the one who doesn't understand, St. Andrews. Brandy's gone . . . d'ye ken? Gone! And even if she weren't, there's no way in hell she'd ever have aught more to do with you . . . that much was clear as rainwater." He half turned away. "Now be so kind—if ye're capable of such a thing—and leave us. You're not welcome here, and we've business to attend to—like closin' up and leavin' for the country afore they paint a red cross upon the door an' seal us in here."

325

There was something not quite right about the entire episode, Keir had decided. He had spent hours reliving over and over the scene with the two Daltons, and also reviewing what his men and solicitor had reported to him. Something did not sit well with Keir. Oh, the grief seemed genuine enough . . . or did it really? Margaret had been seen nowhere about the premises by anyone, but that could mean anything. Nor was there any proof that the child, Abra, had been grieving over the loss of her sister. Neither Keir nor his informants had seen the family spaniel, either. The child could have been crying over a lost Archie . . . or any number of things children cry about.

That the Daltons had reason enough to banish Brandy to safety until they decided Keir's ardor had cooled, he acknowledged. He also knew, however, that it wasn't like her to pick up and leave all she had known and loved. He had discovered long ago that deep down Brandy Dalton was no coward. Shamed she'd been. Betrayed she'd been. Furious she'd been. But she was no fool, no deserter, and she loved her family. The dowry he'd tried to give Jonathon Dalton had been a king's ransom . . . more than enough to make any man, noble or otherwise, turn his head to her lost virtue. Yet it had been unequivocally refused.

And Brandy Dalton, it seemed, had vanished into thin air.

Keir raised his head and directed his narrowed gaze to the beach. Jackie was trudging toward the rolling lawns of the manor with Dudley in his wake. If anything, he looked unhappier than before. Of course. He'd loved her too. No one who came in contact with Brandy could help but be positively affected by her sweetness and sincerity. Her beauty, the gently rounded curves of her feminine form, the mellifluous timbre of her voice, of course, added to her appeal. But deep down, Brandy Dalton was beautiful inside. She was good and kind and chose to see those same qualities in others. And he had abused those very qualities.

Yet, Keir St. Andrews, sixth Earl of Somerset, had numbered, he was certain, among those strongest smitten. From the beginning, he was drawn to her so powerfully that once given the opportunity, however unexpected, he had kept her at his side like any of the unprincipled pirates among whom he had grown to manhood.

*Will you never be satisfied? You have back all that you'd vowed to win.*

"Aye," he murmured into the breeze, his gaze going to Somerset Chase. "But what good all this without her?"


"If ye don't stand still I'll end up throttlin' ye," Peter Stubbs threatened as he fought in increasing frustration with the third clean cravat Keir had donned. "Damned fancy bits o' fluff. Why don't ye wear yer shirt open at the neck . . . 'tis cooler anyway."

Keir's gaze sought the carved plaster ceiling and he blew out his breath in resignation. "I wonder who's the bigger fraud, Peter . . . you or me."

Peter paused in his mangling of Keir's lace-trimmed cravat and met his friend's gaze. "At least *I* ain't complainin' about my lot. Ye're the one mopin' about like Dudley when 'e's been kicked in the backside, when ye should be combin' the countryside looking fer *her*. Instead, ye're preparin' to go to Court an' pick yerself a wife from them mincin' bluebloods."

Keir knocked Peter's hands away in anger. He began arranging his stock himself with agitated, impatient movements. "And when will you face the truth, friend? I was born one of those 'mincing bluebloods.' And *she's* gone. G-O-N-E. Gone." He swung away and walked toward a priceless Venetian mirror to face his dark-miened reflection. "By the Mass, man, this is the third cravat you've mutilated! How do you do it?"

" 'Tis easier te secure a flappin' sail in a blow than one of *them*." Peter crossed his arms over his chest and watched as Keir whipped the wrinkled cravat from his neck and flung it away. Without a word, Peter handed him a fourth.

"The *Odyssey* has docked. 'Tis reason enough for me to go to London," Keir said after a few moments of silence save for the whisper of silk and lace as he arranged the cravat at his throat.

"And no doubt ye'll remain with Tremaine an' Foucher the entire time."

Keir put the finishing touches on the cravat, smoothed several imaginary wrinkles from his fine lawn shirt, and faced Stubbs abruptly. "What I do with my time is naught of your concern. If you're so dissatisfied here with me, I can easily arrange for you to return to the *Odyssey.* Or wherever else you wish to go," he finished, an icy edge to his voice. "I grow weary of your shrewlike harping."

Keir bent to slip on his silver-buckled shoes, waving Peter away when he stepped forward to help. "Even an idiot can master a shoe," he muttered.

Peter moved toward a window overlooking the grounds. The silence gathering in the room became uncomfortable. "Will 'at be all?" Peter asked stiffly.

Keir straightened and glanced at Peter's stony profile. "Would you like to come with me?" he asked unexpectedly, his tone softening. "You can lift a mug or two with your former cronies . . ." He paused. "You can even make inquiries about Brandy yourself, if 'twill ease your conscience. To that end, I will put anything you wish at your disposal."

Peter looked at him. "But not yerself."

"I have obligations to the King."

"Which're more than paid in gold an' silver each time the *Odyssey* docks."

"I need an heir," Keir said stubbornly. "I can't spend the rest of my life searching for someone who is more than likely—" He couldn't say the word. It caught in his throat and cut him off.

Peter didn't acknowledge his words. He merely took Keir's waist-length brocade jacket from the bed and held it for him.

"And even if she could be found—even were she alive, she'd have no part of me and you know it."

Peter's gaze collided with his. "You know if that was the attitude ye'd taken when ye were lookin' fer Padre Tomas, when ye were settin' yer sights on Somerset Chase years ago, ye wouldn't be where y'are now."

Keir's movements stilled, his expression and tone softening further. "Then come with me, Peter. I've already been dubbed the Renegade Earl. Not that I give a tinker's damn about what the rest of them say, but I'd not have His Majesty thinking me ungrateful for his help."

Peter nodded. "O' course I'll come. But I'd like te do a bit o' scoutin' on my own. My father had heavy dealin's with the dregs of Alsatia . . . ended up swingin' at Tyburn fer it. Mayhap I can find somethin' o' value, mayhap not."

Keir put a hand on his friend's shoulder. "As you wish. But promise me you'll have a care."

Peter snorted. "If I survived brawlin' buccaneers an' slimy Spanish on the Main, I can take care o' myself in Alsatia, Keir St. Andrews . . . ye can count on it."

# Chapter Twenty-two

"La! 'Tis the mysterious Juliana Spenser—long-lost granddaughter of the Earl of Spenser." Lady Rosalyn's words were low and conspiratorial, her lips close to Keir's ear. "I cannot believe he has the gall to introduce her at court at all—let alone in such grand style. 'Tis rumored that her dull-witted mother got herself with child by some stableboy or the like, and the chit's a bastard born."

As she purred on, her fingers tightening over Keir's forearm, he raised his head with only token interest to look over at the newcomers. The name Spenser was only vaguely familiar, and he did not recognize the older man and his wife who'd just entered the Banqueting Hall. The mysterious Juliana Spenser stood with her back to Keir and Lady Rosalyn, although the unusual hue of her beautifully coiffed hair renewed the familiar ache in his chest that had been an almost constant companion for the last year.

"Spenser thinks to gain her respectability . . . hummph! After having sent her away as a newborn babe in the arms of her mother's maidservant years ago . . . surely you've heard?"

Keir shook his head. "You know that I don't care to involve myself in court intrigue and innuendo, Rosalyn. I've been too occupied with refurbishing Somerset Chase this past year." It was true. His rare appearances at court were only to please the king, but then, too, the plague had sent

330

everyone in the entire court fleeing last June. Only this past December had the king returned to London and Whitehall.

"Far too much for my liking," Rosalyn pouted, pulling her gaze away and looking up at him with her huge china-blue eyes. If ever Keir had seen an open invitation in a woman's expression, bawd or blueblood, here it was.

But he wasn't interested in Rosalyn Downing. Or any other woman he'd seen thus far. As she chattered on, he paid scant attention to what she was saying, wondering how long he'd be obliged to remain until he could gracefully make an exit.

"Her grandfather says that she's a widow, although he won't say exactly *whom* she was wed to. Some even say she has a babe, as well. If 'tis true, I'd wager every gown I own that the Earl's story was cococted only to legitimize her child. No doubt some lowborn lout's issue just like *she* is . . ."

He idly lifted his gaze to the Spenser party and watched as a young lordling was introduced to this Juliana. The musicians struck up a branle and the young man, having obviously obtained her grandfather's approval, led her to the dance floor.

"But with the hefty dowry the earl has endowed her, even the most finicky of men would overlook her past sins . . ."

It was in that moment that Keir recognized her.

". . . gossip has made short shrift of Spenser's story, for the newest rumor is that she spent months on a *pirate* ship against her will. Hummph."

He caught only her profile, but he knew every sweet line of that profile . . . and oh so much more. His heart stumbled in its steady cadence before it began ramming against his ribs. Everything and everyone else in the hall faded into insignificance as Keir's attention became riveted to Brandy Dalton.

He watched her smile animatedly up at her partner, not

with the typical courtly coyness employed by every other woman present, but with the open genuineness that was so much a part of her.

The world began to buzz around him. He was only vaguely aware of Rosalyn's hand upon his arm, shaking it. "Faith, Keir! *Will* you look at me?"

But he couldn't seem to function. Brandy Dalton was here in the same room with him, after he'd been told by Margaret and Jonathon Dalton that she was gone . . . had disappeared. After he had even entertained the thought that she might be dead . . .

Brandy Dalton was very much alive and, evidently, through some whimsical twist of fate, the granddaughter of an earl, bastard or not. And he didn't believe for a moment that she was wed and widowed in the year or so since he had last seen her. He knew her better than that, and it was inconceivable . . .

He couldn't recall what else Rosalyn had told him, but it didn't matter now . . .

Keir unthinkingly stepped toward the dance floor, then checked. What was he about? He looked down at Lady Rosalyn, a voiceless puppet in the face of the emotions roaring through him. Her lips moved rapidly, the growing irritation in her face only half-hidden by the shield of her swiftly plied fan. "Wine or punch?" she was bleating into his ear as she rose up on tiptoe in an obvious attempt to regain his attention.

Keir nodded. "Aye," he managed to reply, naming the woman who came to mind as naturally as breath to his body. "Brandy . . ." His answer sounded idiotic, a rational part of him warned, but his thoughts were disconnected. He allowed Rosalyn to lead him, like Dudley on a leash, to a refreshment table at the side of the hall. He automatically poured himself a goblet of brandy-wyne with suddenly shaking hands and downed it immediately. Then he poured himself another, drinking like a man downing the antidote to some poison he'd inadvertently ingested.

"Keir," Rosalyn insisted through her teeth. "What ails you?" She smiled in acknowledgment at a couple nearby, and Keir had the presence of mind to incline his head in greeting. He was, however, already in the act of pouring his third goblet.

Help came from an unexpected source. The Earl of Ashcroft, Rosalyn's father, approached them and asked Keir if he would excuse Rosalyn for a while. Keir nodded again and mumbled a few words, barely managing to control his voice. As father and daughter moved away, Keir downed his third brandy and replaced his glass. He moved through the crowd like a sleepwalker, drawn by one woman alone out of scores. One woman who was dancing with another as if he, Keir, had never existed. One woman who had the power to render his reward for years of planning and hard work, worthless. One woman who, he'd come to realize, was the only one who could fill the void in which he'd been living for the past year, in spite of his triumphant return to England.

Keir stopped at the edge of the dancers, his gaze quartering the floor. When he found her, he watched her hungrily, devouring her with his eyes—every movement, every nuance of her expression. From the feminine fall of sunset-gold ringlets to the tips of fine leather slippers, he imbibed her image—and her essence, something that nothing could change.

Her gown was of apricot satin, its hue accenting the peach-toned flesh of her face, neck, and the tops of her bare shoulders. The silk underskirt was cream-colored, and peeked from between several small bows at her bodice before flaring downward from her waist. Apricot silk bows held back the sides of her overskirt, while lace-trimmed flounces trailed from her three-quarter-length sleeves. Slender filaments of apricot ribbon wended through her hair.

The grace and carriage Keir had always been hard put

333

to equate with a common tavern wench was even more pronounced as Brandy drifted across the floor in a silken swirl of skirts. Her elegance and bearing matched that of any woman present. That she had had little need of tutoring, he would have wagered anything. As he watched her, however, Keir sensed that beneath the surface she still possessed that open guilessness that made her emotions so heartrendingly transparent — at least to him. He suspected that the sweet nature and appealing naivete of the Brandy Dalton he'd known, even though she had undoubtedly been recently instructed in the ways of the nobility, would still be no match for the acidic wits and tongues of women like Lady Rosalyn.

There was no place in the Restoration Court for an innocent like his Brandy without him at her side. A powerful longing moved through Keir in the wake of his thought, and he suddenly wanted to kill the young buck who partnered her. He wanted to wrap his hands around the man's neck and squeeze the life from him for daring to dance and flirt with *his* Brandy. For daring to glance down at her neckline where were revealed the pale, delicate mounds of the tops of her breasts. God help him, he preferred the modesty of her humble tavern wench's garb — even that of a sailor — so no other could glimpse, however briefly, what treasures lay beneath her clothing.

She was *his*. She had been from the moment he'd first seen her at the Hawk and Hound. Would always be. If someone had told him that getting Brandy Dalton back would be like trying to steal the sun from the sky, he would have been undaunted, for Keir St. Andrews had managed to retrieve his birthright. Now he'd found the woman he loved, and he would never let her go again.

The dance was coming to an end, but Keir was not about to be forced to meet the Earl of Spenser and his wife before he had a chance to speak to Brandy alone . . . no easy thing in a hall packed with people. Keir stepped toward them, his legs feeling suddenly weighted, sluggish, as though he were in a dream and going nowhere. A hundred different greetings trailed through his mind, none of them appropriate. He'd been the one who'd hurt her terribly, he knew. He'd been the one who had used her, who had literally abducted her body and then her heart before tossing her aside, stubbornly refusing to acknowledge his feelings for her.

Sweet Christ in heaven, what were the right words? What could he say to her in the few brief, precious moments they might be allowed together if she didn't turn on her heel and walk away from him?

Keir deliberately transferred his gaze to her partner, feeling Brandy's eyes upon him suddenly as the music died away. But he was intent on getting rid of this young popinjay who unexpectedly reached out to touch the necklet Brandy wore.

For one desperate moment, reason deserted Keir. If he'd had a cutlass, he'd have lopped off the hand that dared to touch her, however innocently.

"The lady granted me this next dance," Keir lied to the other man, his green eyes hard with accustomed authority and irrational jealousy. He forced himself to smile, but it was out of a habit he'd been forced to acquire at the court of Louis XIV, and now that of Charles Stuart, and had nothing to do with humor.

Brandy's partner bowed politely, obviously recognizing the Earl of Somerset's determination, then gave Brandy a half-smile that was full of reluctance, and retreated.

Only then did Keir allow his eyes to meet Brandy's startled gaze. "Hello, brandy-eyes," he greeted softly.


The dancers began to scatter, along with Brandy's wits. Her worst nightmare had come to pass: an inevitable face-to-face meeting with Keir St. Andrews. And not only did he have the audacity to confront her after what he'd done to her, but *here* . . . in the middle of a reception at Whitehall. After months of prompting and lessons, she had finally consented to appear at court, a place where one definitely did not make a scene.

The very sight of him after so long a separation set her back months in her quest to rout him from her heart. Like a blind woman stumbling about in unfamiliar surroundings, she bumbled through her brain for some defense against his nearness, his male beauty and virility, even in the elaborate garb of a peer of the realm.

She'd fooled herself into thinking she was ready to emerge from her grandfather's aegis and carry on with her life, to find a father for her child and a husband for herself.

She was dead wrong.

With a desperation which, she acknowledged dimly, surely was apparent to the man before her, Juliana Spenser snatched at the only defense she could muster in that moment . . . something she continued to consider a bane rather than a boon after eighteen years in the Dalton family. Now it had a definite use, ineffective as it might ultimately prove: "My name is Juliana." The words were hollow, stilted, the shock of seeing him stamped across her vivid features. "And I—I must return to my grandfather."

Keir smiled gently and quoted, " 'What's in a name? That which we call a rose, by any other name would smell as sweet.' "

Pain and anger rose in her eyes at the wrenchingly familiar lines from *Romeo and Juliet,* and a second, much more potent defense came to her rescue. "Am I good enough for you now, my lord earl? Now that you have seen me at court with the Earl of Spenser for my grandfather?"

Her acrid words went against court protocol, standing as they were in the middle of a fair crowd, but Keir St. Andrews, as always, she thought, followed no ones rules but his own, even if it meant confronting her

336

and goading her into outrage.

"I am less now than I was as Brandy Dalton," she continued with soft derision, "for although the Earl of Spenser would claim me as his granddaughter, no one knows who sired me . . ."

*And my mother was mad.*

"I knew naught about your change in . . . status. I sent for word of you to the Hawk and Hound, even went myself to see you, but they told me you had disappeared." He leaned closer, his gaze lancing into hers. "And it matters not who who you are or are not . . . nor your antecedents."

The musicians struck up a lively courante, and Keir put his hand on her elbow. "Will you let me speak to you alone . . . away from all this?" He motioned with his head to indicate the people around them.

Juliana stared down at his hand upon her satin sleeve, memories assaulting her like stinging needles of rain. Keir took advantage of her momentary hesitation and steered her toward a windowed alcove to one side of the spacious hall.

Her feet moved her along with him, cooperated completely, as if in collusion with Keir St. Andrews, even as her instincts cried out in warning. If she didn't stop him now, heaven knew what further damage he could wreak upon her hurtling emotions. She was still in the process of adjusting to the shock of discovering her real identity, of leaving the Hawk and Hound and the only family she had ever known. And she had not wanted to go to Whitehall, for she had seen enough of the nobility who frequented the Restoration Court in her three years at the Hawk and Hound to last her a lifetime. Had she not met Keir St. Andrews, she would have been content to marry Tim Taylor and continue on with her simple life, as a part of the common people among whom she had been raised. Even when she had returned from Jamaica, the young woman who was told she was really Juliana Spenser would have preferred to remain Brandy Dalton, vanished virtue and all.

And here she was, her worst fear realized . . . coming face to face with the Earl of Somerset, on his ground, among his equals socially. And in a world for which she had no liking.

Juliana Spenser would have given anything she had to give to be back at the Hawk and Hound, her home and her refuge. Instead, she was being led away from the relative safety of throngs of people by the man who still had the power to heat her blood. And singe her soul.

By the man who was the father of her child.

Her hand automatically went to the minuscule mahogany charm that rested against the flesh above her breasts, suspended now from a fine gold chain. As her fingers closed around it she sent a silent prayer heavenward: *Please God, grant me the strength and courage of the lioness . . .*

The tapers in the huge chandeliers overhead threw dancing light over the ballroom, the chubby, cherubic figures in Reubens' painted ceiling a blur as Juliana briefly glanced up in her plea for divine intervention.

Keir backed her into an empty alcove, taking advantage of their relative isolation as other couples, totally absorbed in one another, ignored them. He took one of her hands in his, his eyes going briefly to the other, which clutched the carved token Dionisio had given her.

"I cannot believe I've found you," he said after a few quiet moments.

Strength flowed into Juliana at the mere thought of the man who had given her the lioness. And ire . . . ire at the memory of what had prompted the Cimaroon's offer of marriage, if only as a compliment. "You held my heart once," she said, her eyes narrowing. "Yet because of your deception, I was never truly yours to lose."

"You were mine before we ever met." The words came of their own accord, from a wellspring of emotion deep

338

within him. He felt his hand tighten on her arm with emphasis, and watched several emotions flit across her features as she sought to hold together her crumbling composure.

"I was wrong to have kept the truth from you . . . to have spirited you away against your will for my own selfish purposes." The pitch of his voice dropped with urgency. "Surely you can find it in your heart to forgive me . . . to believe that I love you and want to make you my wife."

Disbelief flashed in her eyes. She tried to dislodge her arm from his grip, but he held her firmly.

"Good God, Brandy, hear me out! Don't condemn me now for my past sins . . ."

"Just like that," she interrupted angrily. "Forgive you for ruining my life? Forgive you for hurtling into my world, making your mark with careless and irresponsible ease, then discarding me like some worthless piece of flesh?" She cast a glance at the people closest to them before prying his fingers from her arm and pulling it away. "I could—I *did*—forgive you everything . . . everything but so deliberate and brutal a betrayal of my love." She drew herself up, preparing to sidestep him. "You admitted yourself that you had no intention of even making me your mistress. You severed any bonds that existed between us, and in the process of removing me from the only world I knew, you were ultimately responsible for . . . *this*." She indicated the entire gathering in its glittering, artificial opulence with an inclination of her head, the last word uttered with such vehemence that only an imbecile would have failed to understand her meaning. "Stay away from me, Keir," she warned in a low, shaky voice, "for my grandfather will go to any lengths to keep our past association buried."

Keir ignored her last words, her obvious unhappiness with her new world wrenchingly apparent to him. "Do you dislike your new life so much?"

The answer was in her eyes, a sudden desolation he had never seen there before. "I don't belong here . . . with these fraudulent courtiers." Her lashes lowered briefly, screening her tear-sheened eyes from him for a moment. "My parents—adoptive parents—went to my grandfather . . . revealed to him that I was alive. If it hadn't been for you and your meddling men, I would have happily remained Brandy Dalton, living my simple life. I knew naught else, and was content as such."

Keir smiled at her, lifting her chin with his fingertips. "You would have been happy reciting your Shakespeare at the Hawk and Hound for the neighborhood urchins?"

Her eyes met his. "Aye."

"Then be my countess, brandy-eyes, and you need never do aught you don't wish to again. You can run about Somerset Chase barefooted, your hair unbound, with no one to tell you to do otherwise. You can remain exactly who you wish to be."

She shook her head and looked away, her eyes blindly on the crowd beyond. "I can be no one else, now, but Juliana Spenser." She looked back at him, misery shading her eyes. "And I can never wed you, my lord earl, even had you not deceived me." Her gaze went beyond him again, and she suddenly dropped him a quick curtsy. "My grandfather approaches," she said in agitation. "Now we're a fine kettle of stew."

Before Keir could react, Aimery Spenser's voice came to them. "Odsfish, m'girl, what do you here?" he asked abruptly, drawing a few stares from those close by. He stopped just as Keir swung to face him. "And who, pray tell, is this?" His narrowed gaze took in Keir from head to toe, suspicion weighting his words. Keir, however, got the distinct impression that the earl knew exactly who he was.

Juliana looked at Keir, her face paling beneath her rouge, her eyes beseeching. Keir fought a swift, savage battle with his conscience . . . and lost. He owed her the courtesy of extricating her from a situation that would undoubtedly cause her embarrassment. Yet his ruthless side stubbornly refused to deny the truth to this older man, pushing him, rather, to declare his intentions where Juliana Spenser was concerned. If she was, in fact, without a legal father, if she was not Spenser's heir, then the earl would be a fool to deny her the chance to step up in the social hierarchy through marriage to another peer. Hadn't Rosalyn said that the earl was seeking a husband for her?

"My lord grandfather, this is—"

"Keir St. Andrews, sixth Earl of Somerset, your lordship." Keir bowed elegantly to Aimery. When he straightened, he was the recipient of Aimery Spenser's most virulent look.

Juliana immediately placed her hand on her grandfather's arm. "Please, my lord, not here," she exhorted softly.

*"You!"* Aimery said with quiet contempt, ignoring Juliana's plea.

The word sounded like the snarl of a trumpet.

"I assure you," Keir said into the angry man's face, "that I have only the noblest intentions where your granddaughter is concerned."

"Noble?" Aimery's lips twisted with disdain. "And what would the likes of you know of aught to do with *noble?*" He reached out a hand for Juliana and drew her to him. "You will stay away from Juliana, you bloody pirate, or you'll rue the day you ever dared show your face at Whitehall."

Spots of angry color dotted Keir's cheeks. "It seems to me, Spenser, that if you were truly concerned about your granddaughter's reputation, you would be more civil in your treatment of me. After all," his expression turned ugly, "I cannot lose something I never had . . . my good name. Whereas Brandy here could, through the slightest hint on my part, have her name besmirched through her past association with me."

"Are you threatening blackmail?" Aimery snarled

softly, his fingers tightening around Juliana's wrist.

Keir shook his head, his eyes hard as enamel. "I believe 'twas you who stooped to that tactic first, not I."

Aimery Spenser's face was livid. "Don't talk of tactics to *me,* St. Andrews. You are a disgrace to the family name. If your father knew what his son and heir had become, he would turn over in his grave. Now, I'm warning you, stay away from—"

"La, milord! Do tell who would turn over in his grave?" came Rosalyn Downing's voice. "And why?"

All three heads turned at the sound. "Have you heard any new gossip, perhaps?" she said hopefully, her eyes going from Juliana to Keir and back again to Juliana. When she looked at Aimery, whom she had addressed, if she had harbored any doubts as to the agitated tone of the conversation that had just taken place, it was obvious they were dismissed in the face of Spenser's expression.

"Good even, milady," Aimery had the presence of mind to say. "Allow me to introduce my granddaughter, Juliana. Juliana, this is Lady Rosalyn Downing, daughter of the Earl of Ashcroft."

Juliana silently applauded her grandfather his swift recovery as his vivid coloring receded and he smoothly made the introduction, thus sidestepping this Rosalyn's query. Juliana smiled at Rosalyn and inclined her head slightly, not trusting her voice.

"Keir and I are old friends," Rosalyn continued, gazing up at Keir as though he were the king himself.

"Well, you will excuse us, pray," Aimery said, "for there are many other introductions to be made before the night is over."

Rosalyn's eyes cut to Juliana with a suddenness that was at odds with her obviously affected ease. "La, but don't leave on my account!" she said with a moue. "I've heard such exciting things about Juliana here, that I simply must ask you where you've kept her hidden all these years, Lord Spenser." She gave him a guileless smile that did not fool

342

anyone. "I've heard such . . . romantic stories about her."

Juliana could not believe the woman's audacity. But then, what had her grandfather expected? One did not simply produce a heretofore unknown granddaughter at court without the inevitable inquiries the action would produce.

"I can well imagine," Aimery said with a tight-lipped smile. "But our Juliana here lived quietly in the country with a blacksmith and his wife for most of her life. I can only thank God I discovered her hale and hearty after thinking her dead these past years. There is naught more to tell." His eyes narrowed at Rosalyn in a mute but distinct warning, effectively halting her prying for the time being.

Juliana was acutely aware of Keir's silent scrutiny, the probing perusal of Lady Rosalyn. Fingers of color crept into her cheeks as she glanced at Aimery, who, for the moment at least, was holding both Keir and Rosalyn Downing at bay with his eyes. Suddenly the blended fragrance of many perfumes, the sweat of moving bodies in the increasingly stuffy hall, seemed suffocating to Juliana. Sounds and images swam around her. She felt faint in the wake of these physical entities as well as the newly kindled emotions in the midst of the hustle and bustle that was Whitehall. Suddenly the tension coiled about them like a living serpent, squeezing, tightening, cutting off her breath.

She was so out of her element, so confused. so mortifyingly unable to carry on as either Juliana Spenser *or* Brandy Dalton in those endless-seeming, numbing moments.

Keir stepped in then, unable to bear her distress, distress that he had caused. He wanted to sweep her into his arms and carry her off into the night, the whole world be damned. But even he did not dare. Instead, he took Lady Rosalyn by the elbow and sketched a shallow bow to both Juliana and Lord Spenser. "The courante calls," he said with a lightness he was far from feeling, a smile that went no farther than his lips. "Come, Rosalyn," he said. "Fie on your curiosity. Dance with me."

Her mouth a rounded O, Rosalyn allowed Keir to lead her briskly away and into the annonymity of the surging crowd beyond.

*Roger Smythe dared to glance down at the seaswept deck of the* Marie Louise. *It looked as small as a piece of driftwood from his position high up in the rigging. Of course it did . . . the ship was smaller and considerably less sturdy than the* Odyssey.

*Damn Keir St. Andrews! Roger swore silently as he struggled to gather in and secure one section of the square sail. Even as he fought the vicious wind and driving rain, Smythe could hear the curses of the other men aloft with him as they attempted to perform the same task, with the* Marie Louise *pitching and tumbling through a boiling sea.*

*Lightning sizzled across the sky, a phosphorescent flash in the dark, angry clouds. One foot slipped, and Smythe clung to the yardarm for his life, fighting to regain a toe-hold on the footropes.*

*And damn the wench! She was the reason he'd been dismissed from the* Odyssey, *and she was the reason he'd had to settle for a job aboard this second-rate French privateer so he could return to England.*

*His anger grew apace with the intenisty of the storm around him as he clung to the spar like a drenched spider in a downpour, a fragile, insignificant scrap of life. He secured the gasket, then realized that the man who stood between him and the ratlines was having trouble.*

*Was there no end to this bout of ill luck? he thought savagely, as he made to sidle over to help the sailor. What had begun aboard the* Odyssey *continued to shadow him on to the* Marie Louise *and now up into the shrouds.*

*Smythe was within arm's reach of the French seaman, tantalizingly close to the ratlines beyond. He reached his right hand toward the uncooperative canvas. Lightning pitchforked from above, one of its shimmering silver tines shooting down to strike the yardarm. Electricity buzzed along the length of it, sending a shock wave through Roger Smythe's body. His left hand reflexively tightened then released the spar, and he felt himself free-falling through the air.*

*Over the roar of the elements, he was peripherally aware of men crying out from above and around him, and horror at the realization of what was happening registered.*

*"Noooooo," he screamed. . . .*

He bolted up in bed, his body bathed in sweat and trembling like a leaf in a high wind. It was dark, except for one lone candle across the room, and cold. His drawers were soaked. So was the bed beneath him . . . but not from sweat, he realized, as the odor of urine invaded his nostrils.

He ran the fingers of his hands through his hair, disgusted with himself and frustrated, then realized with a ferocious expletive that he didn't *have* two hands any more; only the right one. And now a gleaming metal hook, which rested for the night on the table, served as his left.

He swung out of bed, grabbed the sturdy wooden crutch beside the bed, and stood up on his right leg. Pain shot through his left leg and hip and up his spine, as it never failed to do when he moved quickly. He let out a low moan, halting his movements until the hurt subsided to a bearable level, then hobbled toward the table holding the candle, the hook, and two bottles of brandy-wyne. He struggled to uncork one bottle, then downed several gulps and felt the familiar fire streak through his gullet to his belly.

But that was as far as it went. Ever since he'd fallen from the mast aboard the French privateer he'd been numb on his right side from the waist down. His left arm and leg retained their feeling, but the leg was useless. He was unable to have a woman, unable even to relieve himself like a grown man, for he had no control over his bodily functions.

*Quelle mal chance, le pauvre diable . . . he's the only one te survive . . .* Roger could still hear their voices swimming in and out of his mind over a year ago as he'd lain half-conscious in a hammock belowdecks, excruciating pain enfolding his body like a spiked glove.

*Unlucky, if ye ask me . . . he'd be better off dead . . . Il ne marchera jamais. He'll never walk again . . .*

Oh, how he'd determined then, even through the haze of his pain and shock, that he *would* walk again, if for no other reason than to make Keir St. Andrews pay for dismissing him. And, even more, Brandy Dalton, for bringing such ill luck to him. Since she first set foot aboard the *Odyssey,* every man in the crew had panted over her, witless fools that they were. She'd not only held the captain in her thrall, but his men, as well. Every last one of them, himself included.

And now he'd become what he was, less than a man, with no means to earn a livelihood, because of *her.* Because of *them* . . . the wench and Keir St. Andrews. His face became contorted with hatred, the side that was scarred and smashed from the fall taking on an unnatural, hideous expression.

Roger shivered. He'd have to change his drawers and the linens on the bed now. But he remained where he was for a few moments longer, his good eye narrowed thoughtfully. Feldon. Nicholas Feldon, that was his name . . . the fellow who, rumor had it, had formerly worked for St. Andrews's uncle, Giles.

Roger took another swig of spirits and sat down heavily

in the chair beside the table. He picked up the hook and straps that he now used as his left hand, and scored a single word in the tabletop with the razor sharp, steel tip. *Brandy.*

He stared at the word, picturing Brandy Dalton aboard the *Odyssey* all those months ago, like a ray of sunlight in the monotonous and demanding routine of life at sea. And, even more, like the dark side of Dame Fortune, alluring but deadly.

But he would have his day, all right. This Nicholas Feldon wouldn't be averse to trading information for a few doubloons or pieces of eight. What man was? And then, if necessary, Roger would dispose of him, an easy enough task in this part of town, where too many questions to the wrong person could be fatal.

And Brandy Dalton would pay. She would restore his ability to function like a man, something, Roger's twisted reasoning told him, only she could do. Then she would lure Keir St. Andrews to him, so Roger could exact his vengeance. It didn't matter how difficult it might be, or how long it might take.

What did he have to lose now?

# Chapter Twenty-three

"You should have been prepared for this," Aimery Spenser declared to his granddaughter. "I'll not allow you to go scurrying off to the country because of *him*." His frown deepened. "Surely you don't really care for this rogue? His behavior was abominable! He abducted you and forced himself on you and—"

Juliana gave Aimery a level look. "He didn't force himself on me, milord." She blushed lightly, the color accenting her pale cheeks, and looked away. "He neither abducted me, nor ravished me, if the truth be known."

" 'Tis one and the same, whether his men took you by force from the Hawk and Hound or he did. He refused to give you your freedom. He got you with child and then deserted you as soon as he touched English shores. Nay . . . *before* that!"

Juliana rose from the settee upon which she'd been sitting and walked to the fall-front escritoire. Her fingers lightly brushed its polished surface. It was exactly like the one in the captain's cabin on the *Odyssey*.

"As soon as he realized he would regain his title, he flung you aside as easily as some seaport doxy."

Brandy stared unseeingly at the bureau before her. "I *was* a seaport wench, Grandfather, if not a doxy."

Aimery studied her pallid countenance, the shadows beneath her eyes that suddenly stood out and bespoke sleepless nights. He did not like her tone of resignation. It was totally unlike his Juliana, the Juliana he'd come to know and love as if she were his own daughter. She'd been melancholy at times, yes, but that was natural after the shock of learning who she really was and then leaving her adopted family. It was also, he admitted reluctantly, to be expected after learning of the treachery of the man to whom she'd given her heart. And then bearing that man's child, a constant reminder of her love and his betrayal.

Aimery Spenser was no fool. He'd been deeply in love with his first wife, and intelligent enough to recognize that same emotion in his granddaughter, no matter how he might have wished it otherwise. The fact that she'd named the little girl after her natural father was more than proof enough.

Before tonight, he'd caught glimpses of James St. Andrews's son at court, and silently acknowledged that the Renegade Earl could turn the head of the dullest-witted female, to say nothing of Aimery's bright and beautiful granddaughter. He'd also noted that Keir's face was always set in bleak, determined lines, a harshness about him that Aimery would have expected from a man raised among cutthroats and savages. And the Earl of Spenser had determined from the outset that he would keep Juliana from St. Andrews—earl or not—at any cost.

That meant finding her a suitable husband. And continuing to deceive her.

"You are a Spenser, Juliana."

She swung towards him and met his eyes. "Aye . . . a bastard Spenser. With an unknown father and a mother who was mad."

"A Spenser all the same," he persisted. "With a queenly dowry. Your child needs a father and you need a husband."

Her eyebrows raised slightly. "You would saddle some unsuspecting man with the legacy of my mother?" Her voice quavered at the thought of the madness she'd possibly inherited. That her child had possibly inherited.

Dear God, but it wasn't fair!

As if in answer, Keir's long ago words came back to her: *Life isn't fair* . . .

Over the months her anger at him had dissipated to a dull ache, and every moment she spent with their baby daughter made the ache worse. Her life had become so turned around that sometimes she withdrew to the haven of the memory of those weeks she'd spent aboard the *Odyssey* with Keir as they sailed toward the West Indies. She had treasured the time with him after first realizing that she loved him. The brief interlude in Jamaica was, up until the discovery of Keir's duplicity, also a beautiful memory.

Now, for the first time in her life, she was alternately confused, wistful, and unhappy much of the time. Only the sight of Kerra could rouse her from her misery, even though the same sight painfully brought Keir to mind. Ambivalent as it was, part of her yearning was not only for her former life and love, but also for the new dimensions Keir St. Andrews had added to her world. The life of an aristocrat did not impress her; whereas she had acquired a genuine love for the sea (God help her!) and life aboard the ships that sailed it . . . at least aboard the *Odyssey*. Simple, unaffected. And she loved what she had seen of the West Indies. Especially Jamaica . . .

". . . don't know if you—inherited aught of your mother's illness," Aimery was saying. "There is no history of madness in the Spenser family—"

"Mother was a Spenser through marriage," Juliana broke in. "What of *her* family history?"

Aimery couldn't hold her gaze. "Not that I know of."

He glanced past her to the window that overlooked the narrow, dark street, hating himself for lying to her, deceiving her not even so much to honor the vow he'd made to his first wife as to keep her and little Kerra with him as long as possible. There was never any madness in either family, but he had promised the late Juliana Claiborne

Spenser that he would never reveal the fact that she had been careless; that she had turned her back on the infant Catherine for a few, unthinking moments and the child had rolled off the bed, striking her tiny, tender head on the floor.

And, of course, Aimery guessed that a man like Keir St. Andrews would never even consider for his countess a woman with a hint of madness in her background, even had he discovered that he'd sired her daughter. Aimery prided himself on his judgment of men. He believed he had taken St. Andrews's measure, and a man such as the Earl of Somerset might have the most unsavory past imaginable, yet would never sully the family name further by wedding a woman with tainted bloodlines or a questionable background herself. Oftentimes a ruthless outcast such as St. Andrews would embrace family name and respectablity with an unexpected fanaticism.

Aimery also refused to acknowledge the possibilty that James St. Andrews's son might harbor some shred of decency.

*You would make up for casting off your granddaughter and causing Catherine's disappearance . . . even her death?* demanded an inner voice. *If so, deception has naught to do with honor . . . or restitution! Another wrong will not right the first, you old fool.*

"I'm not prepared for marriage yet, my lord grandfather." Juliana's sweet voice scattered his bitter musings. His eyes met hers and she bit her lip. "Forgive me, milord, for what might seem like ingratitude, but may I have a little more time before . . ." She faltered and glanced down at her fidgeting fingers. "Just until autumn . . . I would spend the summer at Spenser House with Kerra, if I may." She raised confusion-clouded eyes to his. "Please?"

Aimery's conscience would not let him refuse the request. He'd begun to notice a brightening of her spirits in the last few months, and he'd dare to believe she was accepting her new life and child . . . without Keir St. Andrews. Now he realized that he was rushing things. Perhaps she did need more time to heal her heart against Keir St. Andrews. Hadn't her reaction to him this night proved as much? And who knew? Perhaps the Earl of Somerset would wed soon himself. No doubt he wanted an heir to ensure the proper succession now that his earldom had been restored.

*And you'll have her beneath your roof just that much longer, which is what you really want, isn't it? And if you push her too hard she might return to the Daltons, and you would lose your link to your first love . . .*

His mien remained stern, but his words were spoken with more gentleness than before. "Very well, Juliana. You may return to Spenser House if you wish. There's no point in rushing this, and not only is it customary to remain in the country during the summer months, but 'tis probably still safer away from London, even though the plague is on the wane."

Anne Spenser came into the room just then, followed by their oldest son and heir, fourteen-year-old Stewart.

"Country?" the youth repeated over his mother's shoulder, dismay written across his features. "Did you say that we are returning to the country, Father?"

Aimery turned to face his son. "Nay, lad," he answered. "I have some business to attend to here, and if your lady mother has no objections, you can remain with us." He frowned. "Why aren't you abed?"

Stewart's hazel eyes grew bright with enthusiasm as, obviously disregarding his father's query, he jumped at the idea of remaining in London. "Aye. I can go to the 'Change with you to learn more about your business dealings, and—"

Aimery held up one hand. "Just a moment, m'boy. What has your mother to say about this, eh?" He looked at Anne, who was standing near the door watching their exchange. She smiled at their son, kindness written in

352

every crease of her plain but pleasant face.

"If your father grants you permission, Stewart, 'tis fine with me." She looked at Juliana. "And I would be happy to accompany you back to Spenser House, my dear. Don't tell His Majesty, but court lost much of its appeal for me long ago." Her dark eyes shone with amusement. "And, no doubt, Beth and Laura will be driving Adeline to the wine celler already—hopefully for hiding rather than taking refuge in spirits."

Juliana returned her smile at the thought of Anne's two younger daughters and their martyrlike governess. Anne Spenser was one of the most generous people Juliana had ever met. A plump, middleaged woman with a wonderful sense of humor, she had graciously taken Juliana—and later her child—under her wing, and with three children of her own to care for, as well. She was also the perfect foil for the older and often acidic Aimery. Her first marriage had left her widowed and childless. and also reluctant to wed again. She'd gone to live with her older brother's family and take care of the children, whom she adored. Until Aimery, who had finally admitted that he needed a wife and an heir, had met and persuaded her to become his wife.

If she harbored any resentment toward Aimery's deep affection for either his first wife or his illegitimate granddaughter, it was not apparent. They seemed to live contentedly as husband and wife, with a quiet committment to Aimery, utter devotion to their children from Anne, and a healthy respect and affection, if not a deep and abiding love, from Aimery.

"Then 'tis settled," Aimery said. "You may leave two days hence . . . or even the morrow, if you wish. There are enough staff at Spenser House to see to your needs." His eyes narrowed, and Juliana guessed that he was also thinking about her safety. Now that Keir St. Andrews had discovered who she was, no doubt he was already making inquiries as to the location of Spenser House. From what

Keir had said to her earlier this evening, he was determined to see her again.

The thought elicited very mixed reactions.

"I thought to visit with the Daltons in the morn," Juliana said, trying to ignore the clashing thoughts threatening to play havoc with her emotions.

Aimery's snow-white brows drew together with disappoval. "The Hawk and Hound?"

"Aye. I love the Daltons, Grandfather, and naught will ever change that," she reminded him quietly.

Aimery waved his hand in dismissal. "I know that. But 'tis your safety that concerns me now that St. Andrews has seen you."

Juliana gave him a shadow of a smile that she didn't feel. "I can take care of myself, milord." At his continued, frowning silence, she added, "I'm not the untried girl I was two years ago."

"Surely you can ask Matthew to go inside with her, Aimery, if you would feel better," Anne interjected.

"*I* can go with her, Father," Stewart announced with a toss of his light brown hair as he picked up his third or fourth sweetmeat and made to pop it into his mouth.

Juliana glanced at the lad, the corners of her mouth bowing upward in genuine humor this time. He reminded her very much of Jackie. "I have no doubt that you would be the perfect escort, Stewart, but truly, I need no other chaperone than the driver. The Hawk and Hound will be quiet that time of day . . . quite dull and not at all a place that would interest a young gentleman."

At the disappointment that registered on his youthful features, however, Juliana regretted her unthinking reply. Stewart was incredibly curious about everything, possessing his father's keen intelligence if not his temper. Quite the opposite, she acknowledged belatedly. He would probably enjoy accompanying her to the inn, with Simon and Abra and Archie to keep him occupied. Why discourage him if her grandfather had no objections?

Before Aimery could answer his son, Juliana reassured the boy with an apologetic smile, "On second thought, I would be happy to have so fine an escort, Stewart, if Grandfather will permit it."

Aimery glanced at his son, then at Juliana, his lips pursed briefly in consideration. "Well, I suppose 'tis safe enough in broad daylight."

"I spent three years of my life at the inn, milord," Juliana said in defense of her former home. "Nothing untoward ever happened until—"

Aimery would not let her finish the sentence with Stewart in the room. "Aye," he interrupted with a scowl, then said to his son, "Then you may go, m'boy, provided you get to bed this instant. And don't tarry overlong and impose upon the Daltons on the morrow."

The driver, Matthew, was talking in low tones to Jonathon Dalton and Stewart was admiring the ancient weapons upon the whitewashed walls as Simon explained the origins of many of them. Twice the latter glanced askance at Juliana, mischief shining in his dark eyes, obviously interested in her reaction to some of the exaggerated stories he was telling the younger lad. Margaret and Abra sat at an oak trestle table with Juliana, plying her with questions about Spenser House and Kerra.

"Brandy, when will ye bring—"

"*Juliana,*" Margaret corrected her young daughter for the fourth time with a sigh.

"But we know 'er as Brandy, Mamma. An' she knows who I mean, don'tcha Brandy?"

Juliana laughed softly and ruffled her stepsister's dark hair. "I was Brandy for almost a score of years, sweeting. You may call me that if you like."

"You c'n be Brandy Juliana, then," the little girl asserted, her expression brightening.

"That sounds wonderful to me."

"Everyone misses ye, Brandy," Abra continued, an unexpected shadow crossing her face and her eyes filling with tears. "Nobody can read half as good as you, 'n our plays ain't much fun anymore. "Ian 'n Tommy are more interested in wenches than Shakespeare," she lamented. "But 'twould be fun again if you were back here."

Juliana felt her throat clog with emotion. "Maybe not, Abra," she said quietly. "People change . . . the lads are growing into young men and 'tis natural that they would be more interested in young girls than playacting, don't you think?"

Abra stubbornly shook her head, her chestnut curls bouncing. "Nay. *I'll* never change, Brandy. Me 'n Archie still like to sit on the stoop 'n pretend."

Invisible fingers curled around Juliana's heart and squeezed. In an effort to collect herself, she glanced away from Abra, only to find her gaze upon the table by the mullioned window where she had first met Keir St. Andrews and his men. Memories assaulted her, threatening her brief reprieve from her new role as Aimery Spenser's granddaughter.

Then Jonathon Dalton's large form came into her line of vision, pulling her back from the brink of familiar emptiness.

"Where's Kerra?" he asked, planting a kiss atop Juliana's bright head.

"Still at Spenser House, Papa," Juliana said, mustering a wavering smile for the man she would always consider her father. "I thought to wait a few more months before bringing her to London."

" 'Tis the wiser thing, Jon," Margaret said, "what with the plague still poppin' up here and there about the city." She looked at Juliana. "I was still hesitant about reopening the inn in March."

"Aye, that she was," Jonathon agreed. "But business is slowly pickin' up, with His Majesty havin' returned from Oxford this Christmas past." Juliana felt his narrowed gaze on her. "You're thin as a twig, Brandy. Doesn't Spenser feed ye?"

"Aye, he does," Juliana answered with a laugh. "And I'm not any thinner than I was before. I think, rather, 'tis that you've forgotten what I looked like before Kerra was born." Laughter sparkled in her eyes, lighting up her fine features.

"When are ye goin' to bring Kerra here, Brandy?" Abra asked, tugging at Juliana's pale blue silken sleeve to get her attention.

Juliana lifted Abra to her lap, heedless of her gown. "In September, poppet," she answered, squeezing the child to her and bussing her rosy cheek. "Or maybe you can come to Spenser House and visit us. Would you like that?"

Abra's mouth fell open, her eyes widening. "Oh, Brandy . . . can I truly visit ye there in yer grand house?"

The door to the inn swung open just then, admitting a breath of air tinctured by the Thames, and a man in the garb of a petty aristocrat. He entered the taproom with the aid of crutch, his cavalier's hat pulled low over his eyes, and moved awkwardly toward a table in the corner shadows, looking neither right or left. Juliana barely spared him a glance as Jonathon went over to wait on him, except to catch the impression of shabbiness about his slightly outdated clothing—something of which she would not have been so conscious had she not been living at Spenser House for the past year. Or seen the rich garb of Keir St. Andrews when the occasion merited.

The thump-step, thump-step rhythm of his progress, combined with the shuffle of his dragging left foot, sounded unnerving in the brief silence that settled over the taproom before conversation continued.

An alien chill feathered down Juliana's back.

"Of course you can, sweet," she answered before she glanced over her shoulder once again at the stranger. Something was vaguely, elusively, familiar about him . . . She shrugged. He'd probably frequented the inn any number of times while she had lived with the Daltons. "If Mamma can spare you for a sennight or so, I know Lady Anne would be delighted to have you. You can romp with Beth and Laura, and help me watch Kerra, too."

Abra jumped off Juliana's lap, clapping her hands with glee. She skipped about the room, wheeling around tables and skirting benches with the reckless abandon of an excited, active eight-year-old, and chanted, "To Spenser House we go! To Spenser House we go!"

"Abracadabra," Simon reproved her and scooped her up into his arms. "What d'ye think you're doing raisin' such a ruckus when we have a customer, huh?" He tossed her into the air, causing her to shriek with laughter.

"And you're not much better," Margaret said, but her smile softened her words.

"Is Abra going to Spenser House with you and Mamma?" Stewart asked over Abra's squeals, admiration in his eyes as he watched the strapping Simon effortlessly toss his sister about.

"If Mam . . . if Master and Mistress Dalton don't object."

"Father and I will return sometime soon," Stewart said, "for Father prefers the country to London."

"I don't blame Spenser," Jonathon added as he returned from serving the stranger a half loaf of Margaret's fresh bread, a wheel of cheese, and a frothy mug of ale. "I was a country man, myself." He motioned to his son, and Simon set down a breathless and disheveled but happy Abra. "Content as I am to run the inn, now and then I miss the open freedom and simplicity of life away from the city."

Abra threw Margaret an imploring look while her father spoke. She moved over to Margaret and took one work-roughened hand between her own small ones. "Please, Mamma?"

"She won't be any trouble, Mamma," Juliana added. "Beth and Laura are close to her age and can . . . teach her a thing or two," a smile tugged at the corners of her mouth, "don't you think, Stewart?"

Stewart looked at Abra, obviously trying to take her measure from the prodigious advantage of being six years older. Archie put his head on Margaret's knee and stared up at her as if pleading Abra's case. "Aye," Stewart answered. But there was nothing subtle about his grin as he caught on.

"But not you, you pesky hound," Margaret gave in. " 'Twas Abra who was invited and not you." The spaniel's long ears drooped as if in dejection, and he switched his muzzle to Juliana's knee as if seeking to solicit her support.

She looked down at him and stroked his silky head, then stopped in midmotion as the stranger pulled the pewter mug across the table. The sound was one common in a tavern, but it had a particularly ominous ring to it — which was absurd, Juliana acknowledged. Yet almost against her will she found herself stealing a glance at the man while the conversation buzzed around her.

Hunched as he was over his meal, his cloak drawn about him tightly as if to ward off a winter chill, Juliana could nonetheless see that he was not a big man. Perhaps solid, but certainly not tall or large-boned. He'd doffed his hat, and she noted that his head was covered with a poor-quality wig. From behind the screen of its dark, unkempt locks, he buried his face in the top of the tankard. Other than the scrape of the mug, he made little noise and few movements, yet Juliana had the distinct impression that in spite of his seemingly unobtrusive presence, he was alert to everything taking place in the room.

And in spite of his obvious intent not to attract undue attention, Juliana couldn't help but notice something strange about his spare movements . . .

Inexplicable unease moved through her again.

"Brandy?"

She started, then shifted her attention to Jonathon.

359

". . . sure she'll be no trouble, she can go with you to Spenser House."

"Oh, Papa! Thank you!" Abra moved from her mother to Jonathon and flung her arms about his waist. She squeezed him with her short, slender arms, then threw back her head to look up at him. "A fortnight?" she wheedled, bright hope in her eyes.

"A sennight is enough, ungrateful minx. How'll we get along without you, huh?"

"Why, Archie'll be lost without you, Abracadabra," Simon told her. "And what if we forget te feed 'im while you're gone? Especially for a fortnight?" He shook his head as he looked down at the object of his pity. "Poor Arch'll be nothin' but skin an' bones."

Abra dropped to her knees, stricken. "Oh, I'd never do that to Archie!" She clutched the spaniel about the neck and hugged his head to her chest. Juliana thought Archie's eyes looked slightly bulged, but he patiently submitted to Abra's exuberant attentions.

"Simon just wanted to remind you of your responsibilites, child," Margaret said. "A sennight should be—"

Archie coughed from the depths of Abra's embrace, evidently refusing to be put off by such an irrelevant thing as a life-threatening choke-hold in the face of his mistress's enthusiastic affection.

"Ease up on 'im, Abracadabra," Simon advised her. "Ye'll choke 'im before you even leave the inn."

Amid everyone's laughter, Abra released the dog and sat back on her heels to observe, with a repentent look, if any damage had been done. Archie stretched open his jaws and emitted a sharp, choking cough, then shook his head and returned Abra's regard, nearly nose to nose, obviously unruffled. "Good boy," she praised him, and his tongue swiped the side of her face as if to affirm he held no grudge.

"We'll leave in the morn, day after tomorrow," Juliana said when the merriment subsided. "We'll come by for

360

Abra at nine o'clock, so you needn't bring her to Grandfather's town house."

Before she could say another word, Abra had transferred her excitement to her stepsister and launched herself into her arms. "Oh, Brandy! Spenser House . . . *Spenser House!*"

No one noticed the expression that crossed the half-hidden features of the guest across the room. No one heard his soft, deep sound of satisfaction as he sat in the shadows and nursed his drink . . . and his grudge against the young woman he knew as Brandy Dalton.

# Chapter Twenty-four

It was a miracle.

Brandy Dalton was alive and well.

The thought sang through Keir's mind, leaving in its wake once again a breath of exhilaration; a euphoria that his acid-honed instincts told him was dangerous.

But he couldn't seem to quite shake the feeling that it was truly a miracle . . . nor suppress this inner jubilation that was affecting him in a manner to which he was not accustomed. It had all begun at court the night before, and continued still. First he'd been literally stunned into immobility . . . a state he had not encountered since he was a green youth. And then this newfound and utter alien joy that continued to suffuse his body like some powerful opiate.

He was standing on the deck of the *Odyssey* watching the birth of the dawn in the eastern sky. It brightened by slow degrees, limning the London skyline. Keir marveled at the way fate or destiny or God had rewarded him with not only the restoration of his title and earldom, but had also gifted him, or so it seemed, with Brandy Dalton.

In the wake of his decision to spend the night aboard the *Odyssey* — after all, it was where he had spent so much time with her — he'd slept very little. He'd lived for more than a year at Somerset Chase, deliberately avoiding his cabin — sometimes even the ship itself — when the *Odyssey* was in port, yet he'd finally elected the night before to remain overnight and allow all his thoughts and emotions free rein. And in their tumultuous wake, he'd been awake most of the night.

Everything aboard the ship reminded him of Brandy. Yet now there was no pain involved, only the sweet stimulation of excitement and a brazen hope of happiness. And he certainly wasn't tired or sluggish from his insomnia; rather, he felt as if he could do anything.

The second miracle was that she'd been living practically in his own backyard. Sir Aimery Spenser's granddaughter . . . no, the Earl of Spenser's granddaughter, now. Although the families had had little contact until the civil wars, Keir was dimly familiar with the name. But he'd been too busy at Somerset Chase this past year to bother with his neighbors. Even if someone had told him that Spenser had a beautiful and eligible granddaughter, Keir wouldn't have paid much heed. His days were taken up with learning his new role. And his nights with dreams of Brandy.

Still, it was obvious that Spenser and his household had been close-mouthed about the return of the granddaughter. Surely there was more to the story than he had heard, and he'd already vowed to waste no time trying to learn everything that he could regarding Brandy and her real family.

Keir lifted his head to the fading stars, closing his eyes and conjuring up her image. Brandy . . . Sweet, sweet Brandy . . .

*My name is Juliana.*

His lips curved. "You'll never be aught but Brandy to me, my love, no matter what they call you. Always Brandy. Forever Brandy . . ." he whispered to the stars.


"I've found her, Peter."

As Peter Stubbs stepped from the connecting plank to the deck of the *Odyssey,* he caught Keir's words. The older man looked tired, sporting a day's worth of beard, and smelling like the bottom of a rum keg, but the words instantly riveted his attention to the ship's owner.

He looked up questioningly at Keir in the early morning light as he drew even, and remained silent another moment, obviously absorbing the meaning of what he had just heard. Then he moved even closer to Keir, until they were shoulder to shoulder.

Keir's eyes met his. "Last eve . . . at court." His voice was just loud enough for Peter to hear above the bustle and noise of the docks around them, but not so loud as to be heard by anyone else close by.

"So the lass is alive . . . thank God!"

"Aye." Keir was thoughtfully silent a moment. "By the grace of God—or the luck of the Cimaroon's amulet—" a corner of his mouth quirked with irony, "she is unharmed." His lips pursed slightly, his forehead furrowing in remembrance. "And, evidently, she is the long-lost, illegitimate granddaughter of the Earl of Spenser."

Peter's eyes narrowed in thought. "Spenser? Earl of Spenser?" He spat into the river. "How in the—"

"Margaret Dalton, if court gossip can be credited, was ordered from the Spenser estate after Spenser's only daughter gave birth to a bastard babe. She took the child with her." He shrugged. "Put the rest together yourself, Peter. Margaret wed Jonathon Dalton and they kept Brandy as their own, with none the wiser. Not even Aimery Spenser."

"But you saw her in the flesh? *Our* Brandy?"

Keir permitted himself a smile. "Aye. *Our* Brandy. Only now she is known as Mistress Juliana Spenser . . . and you should have seen her, Peter. She put all the other women to shame . . ." His voice died away at the memory, his features softening.

"Hummph. Always did, in my mind."

Keir glanced at his friend, catching the shadow of disapproval in his eyes, as well as his words. "Aye, *amigo*. In

364

mine, as well, though I was loath to admit it." He stared down at his fingers closed firmly about the smooth deck rail, flailing his soul with thoughts of all the injustices he'd ever done her.

"Then we gotta get 'er back. Ain't a moment te lose."

Peter's statement roused Keir from his reflections, and his gaze met Peter's once again, a sudden urgency in his voice. "Why? What did you learn in Alsatia?"

"A plenty . . . and none of it good." Peter scowled as he turned his back to the docks and, crossing his arms, leaned against the rail.

Keir swung around. "Such as?" The tethered tension in those two words was reminiscent of the stern, bleak Captain St. Andrews who'd sailed the seas for so many years. He had shed his court attire and once again appeared every bit the privateer captain. "Smythe is livin' in Alsatia. And stokin' a real hatred fer you."

"He's not the first."

Peter shook his head. "Seems like this bloke named Nick Feldon used te work fer yer uncle." Keir's chin jerked sharply. "Been down 'n out 'n easin' his pain with the bottle since Giles's hasty leavetakin' . . . and then the death of his wife and little ones from the plague." Peter scratched his bristly chin. "Smythe struck up a friendship with Feldon . . . keeps him in spirits in exchange fer information, or so I've heard."

"But what can he possibly tell Smythe that would put any of us in real jeopardy?" He waved one hand in contemptuous dismissal. "Smythe and his kind are no serious threat. They're the dregs of society. Scum."

Peter laid his hand across Keir's forearm and lowered his voice. "Seems he's been a-searchin' fer Brandy Dalton, too, Cap'n."

Keir went absolutely still for a moment. "Brandy?" His lips hardly moved as he uttered the name, alarm skittering through him.

"Aye. 'Twouldn't surprise me if he somehow tries te get

te you through her." His fingers tightened, then fell away.

The sounds around them momentarily melted into a singing silence as Keir absorbed Peter's observation. "Don't you think that's rather farfetched? I had him dismissed, aye, but it happens all the time." He shook his head, willing away the chilling premonition that overtook him in spite of his calmly voiced rationalizations to Peter. "Why would he cling with such tenacity to the idea of revenge? For so common a thing as dismissal? And over such a period of time?"

Peter opened his mouth to speak, but Keir continued, half to himself, "This makes little sense . . . If he hasn't found her in all this time, why wouldn't he aim his anger directly at me? I've been at Somerset Chase for over a year . . . for all the world to see." His brows drew closer together in an ever-darkening expression as, out of habit, his eyes caught and followed one of the winches hauling a dock-bound load of mahogany. "And what man wouldn't want her?" he mused aloud. "She's sterling through and through—"

"Cap'n," Peter interrupted him. " 'Tis more than lust—more than jest gettin' even fer a dismissal . . ."

He halted as Keir's gaze shifted slowly from the lumber to him. The ship listed ever so slightly in response to the heavy cargo moving toward the wharf amid the creaking of the machinery and the shouts of the men, which now seemed to grow in volume to a strident pitch. Peter wet his lips, a rare sign of edginess.

"Well?"

"He fell from the riggin' on the ship he took back to England. He was badly maimed . . . lost a hand an' the use of one leg."

"His sailing days are over," Keir finished softly. "Sweet Christ," he whispered as Roger Smythe's grinning countenance superimposed itself over Brandy's in his mind. A seaman feared loss of limb more than anything, for it would render him all but useless.

366

Keir muttered an imprecation. Would there never be an end to the obstacles that stood between him and happiness? He'd thought to leave be the woman he loved, giving her time to accept the fact that he wanted her to become his wife; giving the irascible Earl of Spenser time, as well, to accept the fact that he, Keir, would have her, no matter what.

Now what he'd considered his immense good fortune was turning to bitter, unwelcome reality as Roger Smythe came catapulting back into his life, representing a threat so dire as to leave Keir feeling weak at the thought: danger to Brandy Dalton. And, he was certain, warning Spenser would be of little avail, save to further turn the earl against Keir in the face of what surely would look like a privateer's ploy . . . a trick utilizing one of his own blackhearted cronies as a villain to insinuate himself into Spenser's good graces.

A familiar bleakness enfolded him, renewing the feeling of suffocating desperation he had carried with him for years; nay, *multiplying* it tenfold.

"This could be merely a bitter man's empty dreams . . . wishful thinking in the face of what he considers his bout of bad luck," he heard himself saying.

"Bad luck generated by his dismissal from yer ship," Peter pressed softly. "Ye can't jest leave it at that. And, Cap'n," he added, "Nick Feldon was found dead last eve—murdered in his bed with a hook through 'is neck." His voice was almost a whisper.

Keir dragged in a deep breath of moist morning air, a habit he'd acquired long ago at sea. Only now the air was not fresh or bracing, but ripe with decay. It stank of decomposing fish and garbage, of sodden, rotted piles and planks. And the picture of this Nick Feldon lying in his own blood, hooked like human bait, flashed in his mind's eye . . .

The inhalation, combined with the guesome mental image, had an unexpected negative reaction. He coughed, turning aside his head while, as if in accord with his churning emotions, his lungs and stomach rejected the stale offering. Peter reached up and smacked him between the shoulders, forcing him to clear his throat and capture another deep swallow of river-rancid air. It wasn't stinging sea air, but it served the purpose of steadying his spastic lungs and heaving stomach.

"Wait here," he ordered in a rough, terse voice, and swung away towards the second mate, Will Jackson, who was giving orders to another crewman.

Within moments, Keir moved back to Peter. "Let's go," he told his former quartermaster. "We'll get Gonzalez to feed you, and then we've work to do."

He turned then, and strode toward the quarterdeck without waiting for an answer.


Too late.

Keir realized as he lifted the knocker on the door to the town house that he should have changed his clothes. He glanced sideways at Peter. Bleary-eyed, sporting the beginnings of a beard, and smelling of stale smoke and spirits, he looked even more disreputable than Keir.

Well, he thought grimly as the servant who answered the door looked them over with telltale suspicion in his superciliously arched brows, there was nothing to be done about it now.

He discreetly nudged Peter, who was up until now, silent. Peter cleared his throat loudly. "The Earl o' Somerset," he announced, "requests an audience with 'is lordship, the Earl o' Spenser."

Just as the servant opened his mouth to speak, a voice with the distinct ring of annoyance called out, "Who is it this early in the morn, Oliver? Send them away!"

The sound made Keir's heart beat faster, not at the thought of sparring with Aimery Spenser, but of seeing Brandy . . . of being in the same house with her after months of separation.

*Concentrate on the matter at hand.*

"Good God, not *you*," Spenser growled softly, then stepped forward, nudging the servant aside none too gently in his agitation. "I'll have none of you or yours in my home," he continued through set teeth, "or near my granddaughter, do you hear, Somerset?"

Keir stepped through the door, deliberately brushing past the blustering older man. He hoped Peter was following in his wake.

"I am a belted earl, Spenser—"

"An accident of birth, and most unfortunate."

Keir took the insult in stride. "Nevertheless, I would remind you that you cannot shut the door in my face with impunity—"

"What do you want?"

"I've come to warn you of a very real danger to Brandy—" Keir began, briefly wondering from whom Brandy inherited her sweet disposition.

"There is no Brandy here," Aimery interrupted curtly.

Keir ignored the correction. "I won't mince with words, Spenser, but Peter here," he indicated Peter, who was indeed right beside him, with a tilt of his head, "was witness to collusion against me—"

"I've no doubt there are any number of men plotting against you, but you'll not drag Juliana into any of your dirty dealings." His scowl deepened and the flush of anger rose to the roots of his snow-white hair. "Are you finished?"

Keir's jaw tightened visibly, reciprocal anger roughening his voice. "You are twice a fool, Spenser, if you think either my man or I speak idly. The man to whom I refer has been inquiring as to your granddaughter's whereabouts. He already knows what he needs to about my circumstances, and is determined to wreak his own havoc against me through Brandy."

"*Juliana,*" Aimery snapped, as if it were of tantamount

369

importance. He pointed an accusing finger at Keir. "Will you not stoop to anything? If Juliana is the object of enmity from any of your cohorts, 'tis solely your doing, and you alone can deal with it. Do you hear me, Somerset? You keep away from my granddaughter—"

"For the love of God, Spenser, be sensible! There's a very real danger!" Keir felt his anger and frustration gaining the upper hand.

Now, damn it all, was hardly the time or place to do battle with his disobedient emotions . . .

He looked at Peter. "Tell him what you heard," he said.

But Aimery broke in, "And I suppose *you* are volunteering as her guardian? Her protector?" His narrowed eyes skimmed over Keir with contempt as the Earl of Somerset stood ramrod-straight in his carelessly donned cape, black boots and breeches and open-necked linen shirt. "All you need is a cutlass and a patch over one eye to complete a most accurate picture of your nature and character."

Peter drew in his breath sharply, a sound that was especially ominous in the seething silence that pressed down on the three men. The servant had long since disappeared.

Keir's low-spoken words cut the air like a razor with the force of his conviction. "I am a St. Andrews, and rightfully so. What would you know of me or my circumstances during the past twenty years? You know naught of me, Spenser, save my name and the fact that I held your granddaughter aboard my ship against her will . . . until I fell in love with her, and she with me."

"And then you deserted her like some clap-ridden doxy when you discovered that you could claim an earldom. I know of the kind of love you speak, you cutthroat, and it means less than *nothing.*"

The two men stood almost nose to nose, Keir a hand taller than Aimery, but the fierceness of Aimery's temper making up for the slight height deficit.

"If I weren't so convinced of the danger to Brandy, I'd

gladly leave here and never cross paths again." Keir's fists were clenched at his sides, tightly restrained, lest he throttle Aimery Spenser in his own household in a manner befitting the cutthroat the older man had named him. "But, like the reprehensible sort you think me to be, I *will* stoop to pointing out *your* less than admirable behavior almost twenty years ago, if rumors are to be given any credence, when you banished an innocent, newborn babe from your home in a fit of rage. Look into your own heart before you cast the first stone."

Keir had the satisfaction of seeing the high color drain from Spenser's face, albeit an empty sense of triumph. But he was up against a man unfairly prejudiced against him, with Brandy the ultimate victim should he fail to convince the Earl of Spenser of her vulnerability before a man like Roger Smythe.

Peter cleared his throat awkwardly. "Yer lordship," he said, "this man we're speakin' of is livin' in Alsatia . . ."

He broke off at the virulent look Aimery turned on him. "Alsatia?"

"Aye." Peter licked his lips and glanced at Keir before continuing. "The Cap'n here—I mean 'is lordship—dismissed this man from the *Odyssey* in Jamaica. This man—Smythe—then seems to've returned te London on another ship an' was badly crippled from a fall during the voyage. He's bitter against his lordship, blamin' him fer 'is misfortune."

"I assure you I am quite capable of ensuring Juliana's safety, whether from overzealous court bucks, or unsavory—"

"Grandfather?"

All three heads turned at the sound behind Aimery.

Keir's heart jumped to this throat at the sight that met his eyes. His Brandy. Her shimmering hair was tumbled about her shoulders in splendid disarray, a sleepy look of puzzlement in her lovely eyes that Keir knew so well from their time spent in the same bed aboard the *Odyssey,* as

371

she leaned over the side of the balustrade of the stairs leading to the second floor.

One hand went reflexively to the loosely laced edges of the neckline of her dressing gown, her other immediately to her mouth in surprise when she saw Keir and Peter standing before the door with Aimery.

"Go back to your room, Juliana," Spenser said. "These intruders were just leaving." He swung back to Keir and said through stiff lips, "Weren't you?"

Keir seized the golden opportunity before him. "Nay. I must speak to you," he said over Aimery's head as his gaze remained locked with Juliana's. "Please."

Aimery sucked in his breath with a hiss, but Keir was more aware of the play of emotions across Juliana Spenser's face. In spite of her obvious surprise, she looked — at least to Keir — happy to see him, not stricken like the night before. And, not for the first time, he was aware of the need to enfold her in his love, to shield and shelter her from the everyday ugliness of life. She was — and would always be — an innocent.

And she was his.

He stepped toward the stairway. "I *must* speak to you, if only for a few moments," he said again.

"And *I* say get out, or I'll have you removed!" Aimery threatened, his flush deepening. "Oliver! Bring my pistol!"

"No!" Juliana said, advancing down a step. "I will speak to him, Grandfather."

"Stay out of this, girl," Aimery warned her.

Peter mumbled something and slipped out the door, but Keir hardly noticed as he watched Juliana Spenser move down the stairs, her vivid face bathed in becoming color.

"What harm can it do, Grandfather, to speak with him as a . . . friend for a few moments?" She reached the two men standing tensely, their eyes on her. With a tremulous smile, she put one hand on Aimery's arm. "The Earl of Somerset will do nothing untoward, I promise you."

"Don't ever give assurances as to my behavior where

372

you are concerned, brandy-eyes," Keir said softly. " 'Tis risky business."

"There! You see?" Aimery said as he flung out his right hand for emphasis. "Even *he* admits he is capable of anything."

Juliana turned to Aimery and looked into his eyes. "He but goads you, Grandfather, don't you see?"

Keir watched the interplay with interest, and realized suddenly: *Why the old man loves her! In spite of everything, he is genuinely concerned about her.*

"Hasn't he done enough? Now you would have me leave you alone with him?"

"I took her all the way to the West Indies, then brought her back safely, Spenser," Keir said. "Surely you can grant me a few moments with her under your own roof?"

"Your definition of 'safely' differs vastly from mine!"

But there followed a long silence. Aimery openly studied Keir, obviously weighing his words and his granddaughter's wishes, against his own inclinations. Then he looked at Juliana, his gaze, Keir observed, softening ever so slightly. When he glanced back at Keir, his eyes were narrowed. "If I hear one raised word between you, or Juliana asks for intervention, you'll rue the day you ever returned to England, Somerset. Is that clear?"

Keir nodded. "Perfectly."

"And Somerset?"

"Aye."

"After this meeting, you will leave Juliana alone. Find yourself a wench as befits a renegade like yourself, or I'll hunt you down like the vermin you are and put an end to it."


With shaking hands, Juliana closed the door behind Keir and watched him as he walked into the center of the saloon. He turned to face her, the material of his cloak rustling softly as it swirled about his long, booted legs and then settled. His hair was still sun-streaked, like the mane of a lion . . . that beautiful, sun-kissed gold layered over the darker hair beneath. They could have been aboard the *Odyssey,* so vividly was Juliana reminded of the man she had met all those months ago.

In those few moments before he spoke, she could have forgiven him everything. Could have told him of their child. Could have told him she would gladly wed him and live with him until the end of time. For, stripped of his courtly clothing and formal mannerisms, she could see now that he had somehow changed. Softened. If she had wondered at it the night before, in the bright light of day she was certain.

Or was it wishful thinking?

Well, it didn't matter. Tomorrow she would be safely ensconced at Spenser House.

"I am appalled by my grandfather's behavior, Lord Somerset," she told him. "No matter what he thinks of you, he has no right to speak to you so."

He didn't seem to hear her. "Brandy," he whispered, and held out his hand. "Come here."

It was more of an entreaty than a command, and she obeyed, knowing she was walking into flames, yet helpless to heed the call of common sense. With the desperation of a sailor marooned at sea without drinking water for days, her fingers touched his and eagerly succumbed to the sensation of him—skin, bone, muscle. His hand closed over hers and he drew her toward him with aching slowness, his eyes plumbing the depths of hers, questioning, welcoming, and yes, something more. Something infinitely more tender than she had ever seen.

Bittersweet joy flooded through her.

"Brandy," he murmured, and pressed her to him with a controlled need, his lips brushing hers once, twice, as if tasting of her very essence.

The feel of him, the scent of him, reawakened all the pent-up desire of the past months, the controlled and suppressed yearning. Anger, bitterness, the pain of betrayal . . . all faded into forgetfulness for the moment as Juliana pressed herself to him with an urgency that threatened to overwhelm her.

"Brandy," he whispered between sweet, sweet kisses, "I love you, my Brandy . . . so very much." His fingers found their way up and into her hair, caressing her scalp, and imprisoning her in a maelstrom of delightful sensations as she met and matched his eagerness with her lips, her arms circling his neck, her body cleaving to his.

If he had moved to take her on the carpeted floor, she would have willingly, joyfully obliged him, in spite of the fact that her family was just on the other side of the door.

"I care not what your grandfather says or thinks, love," he said against her lips. "I am an earl. He cannot tell me what to do or not to do." He pressed her to him with renewed fervor, resting his head against the top of hers. "I want you for my wife, if you'll have me. If you'll forgive me." His voice was strained with emotion, and Brandy felt the benevolence of forgiveness flow through her in a cleansing rush.

"I know I'm a hard man, a rough man, but I need you more than you can know." He gazed down into her eyes, his own brimming with emotion. "I sailed the seas, a poor benighted fool, yearning for revenge . . . to retrieve all that was mine. Then I met you, and you taught me more of life in weeks, than I ever learned in years." His thumb traced the tilt of her nose, her petal-soft lips, and he smiled. "You taught me to laugh . . . and cry." His smile deepened. "Can you not tell? I want you to bear my children, to be mistress of not only my home, but of my heart, forever . . ."

At the words "bear my children," reason raised its head. Her euphoria was extinguished like a snuffed candle, bringing her thought processes to a jolting halt. What was she about? What did it matter if she forgave him? There was no way she could ever marry him with her terrible secret . . . the secret of madness passed on from her mother, and even now could be working in some insidious way to twist her mind, and the mind of the child she adored.

Perhaps she could deceive another man, a man she didn't love, in a marriage of convenience. Perhaps even a widower with his own children already established as his heirs . . .

But never Keir St. Andrews. She would cut out her heart before saddling him with such an onerous burden, in spite of his sins against her. Even though Kerra was his child, Juliana Spenser could never bring herself to wed a healthy, intelligent, and vital man like the Earl of Somerset and then face the prospect of bearing him children possibly tainted by insanity. She loved him too much.

She struggled to push away from him, from an embrace that seemed like a snare now, rather than a haven. "I cannot marry you," she told him, her happiness draining from her like blood from a wound.

His arms tightened about her. "Why? Will you not forgive me? Can you not see I am no longer the bitter and ruthless man whom you first met almost two years ago? I've learned so much . . . see things so differently now . . . Please believe me." His mouth descended toward hers with agonizing slowness, his beautiful green eyes pulling her soul to his. On a whisper of breath, his lips formed the words, "Trust me."

# Chapter Twenty-five

At his words, a dull ache rose within Juliana. What she once would have given to hear those very words! But now they offered little comfort in light of her decision. She couldn't waver now, for there were more important issues here than her own happiness.

With a monumental effort, she collected the shreds of her reason and self-control, deliberately stifling her natural inclinations. "Why did you come here?" she asked abruptly, turning aside her head against his kiss.

His arms held her fast when again she attempted to pull away. She steeled herself against him . . . against her weaker side . . . against the love that refused to die.

"Brandy, I pray you, forgive me. You *must*."

It went contrary to everything in her nature, ignoring an apology. Yet the fact that she'd melted in his arms at the sound of his voice, his touch, only caused her shame and frustration. She'd always been a poor liar, and this was no way to convince him that she didn't love him, even if only for his own good.

As his breath misted her cheek, she deliberately concentrated on the negative aspect of his words and actions, lest she heed her heart.

"No, you haven't changed," she said in a low, agitated voice, her gaze going to a painting on the wall across the room. "You are still trying to impose your will on me, exactly like that first night aboard the *Odyssey*. You

377

just grab what you want, and the devil take the consequences." Her mouth settled into a grim line as Juliana struggled to stand her ground against him. "Well, you can't have your way this time, Keir St. Andrews."

"Why? Have you forgotten what you said to me in Jamaica?" he asked, bringing a keen, bladelike pain to her breast at the memory. His embrace loosened, but Juliana's relief was short-lived as his fingers wrapped around her upper arms, holding her firmly in place. She avoided his direct gaze, however. "Tell me you don't love me, Brandy . . . Look at me and tell me!"

The sheen of tears liquefied her golden-brown eyes as Juliana at last allowed her gaze to meet his. "What has love to do with marriage among your kind? You are a fool, Keir St. Andrews, if you think to marry an illegitimate woman." She tried to inject scorn into her words. "I am not titled. I cannot add to your prestige as a peer of the realm in any way, only detract from it." Her voice changed, lowered with the force of the anguish cascading through her.

"You discarded me once," she continued, and his fingers tightened about her arm, his lips thinning at the damning reminder, "and you did the wisest thing then. My anger and pain were caused by your deliberate dishonesty, not by the fact that I could never be anything more to you. Now you want me because you can't have me. There's no other reason." She pulled away and distanced herself a few paces from him to stand before the cold ashes in the hearth. "Go and live your life, Keir," she said over her shoulder. "Find a good woman to love you and give you . . . children. Please, if you care for me in any way, you will forget your designs on me and go live your life."

Keir stood frozen, trying to absorb her denial through the layers of defenses that struggled to erect themselves and shield him as they had for years. "Designs? You

378

think me so low as to want you merely because you are forbidden to me? And by whom? Your grandfather? The Daltons?"

She whirled around, the flush of anger creeping up her cheeks. "*I* don't want to have aught to do with you, don't you understand? There's no more to be said!"

He advanced toward her, looking to Juliana very much like the old, determined, ruthless Keir St. Andrews in demeanor now, as well as garb. "Listen to me—"

"Nay, *you* listen to *me*. You haven't changed," she lied, "since first I met you. You are still trying to take what you want, no matter how indecent or unjust the act."

Keir halted his steps, a royal battle engaging between his love for her and his conscience. The last thing he wanted was to cause her to think him the same ruthless privateer she'd first met.

*What does it matter?* asked a voice. *You will have her one way or another.*

No!

He felt like he was walking on the edge of a crumbling cliff, afraid to step in either direction for fear of the ground giving way beneath him and sending him toppling into the chasm below . . . in this case, the chasm of a dark, dreary life without the sun. Without laughter. Without love.

Juliana read his indecision, sensed the struggle waging inside of him, proof positive that he had, indeed, gone through changes. This was a softer, mellower Keir St. Andrews, as she'd not had the wits to perceive the night before at Whitehall. And from the moment she'd seen him from the top of the stairs, she was drawn to this aspect of him with undeniable potency . . . drawn to him so powerfully that she had forgiven him everything in moments.

And almost forgotten the insidious secret that would

always keep her from him.

In the wake of his silence, Juliana dredged the words up from deep inside her, knowing that she had to somehow convince him of the futility of his quest. "I cannot add to your life in any way, Lord Somerset," she said softly, each word a lance through her core. "Nor can you add to mine. And even were it otherwise, my grandfather would never hear of it."

"Brandy—"

"Please," she beseeched him, holding her hands up, palms forward, as if to ward him off. "Don't make me call my grandfather." Her eyes went to the door beyond him.

But instead of protesting, he merely asked her, "Will you kiss me goodbye then, brandy-eyes?"

Capitulation she hadn't expected. Not that quickly or easily. Her eyes met his, suspicion shadowing hers. But he stepped toward her and pulled her into his arms before she could muster a convincing reply.

Once again, Juliana was caught up in the enchantment that materialized between them as swiftly and surely as the first time he'd kissed her in his cabin after sending her senses reeling with brandywyne . . . the lean, solid strength that lay just beneath his clothing, the warm, sweet taste of his lips, his masculine scent . . . His mouth against hers drew the distant echoes of resistance out of her, like a poultice pulling the poison from a wound. Her body began to tremble for want of him, while at the same time, desperation rose in her as she acknowledged again just how great was his hold over her senses, her heart, her mind.

His hands skimmed up and down her spine through the silk of her dressing gown and he pressed her hips to his, his lips worshipping her mouth, her eyes, her temples, the sensitive area just below one ear. His tongue delved into that delicate aperture, sending molten heat spearing through her midsection, to settle deep within her lower body. The familiar and welcome languor filtered through her limbs in answer to the aphrodisiac of his love. *Fool, you are lost . . . lost . . .*

Even as he seduced her physically and emotionally, the taunting tones of what was left of her reason teased the edges of her mind. Juliana felt the press of tears grow behind her eyes as her ability to resist him melted beneath his gentle yet persistant assault. Moisture tumbled down her cheeks, wetting Keir's face, as well. And it was then that he suddenly drew away and looked down at her, a frown between his eyes.

"Have I hurt you?"

Juliana found her voice, a husk of sound. "Aye . . . beyond the telling."

Taking advantage of his loosened hold, she swung away unsteadily, one fist pressed to her mouth, and moved toward the door.


The morning mists blanketed the countryside, a far cry from the sunny spring day before. Only an errant tree branch here and there bravely reached out as if in search of the sun. London receded slowly behind them as the travelers made their way west: a coach and four, and three mounted escorts.

"Brandy, *when* will the fog be gone?" Abra fretted. "We can't see aught but mist!" She raised the leather curtain that covered the open coach window higher and squinted into the swirling whiteness. The swaying, bouncing conveyance was enough to bring on motion sickness in the most strong-stomached, but one particularly nasty lurch pitched the little girl forward into Juliana's lap.

"Are you all right, poppet?" Juliana asked as she pulled Abra up beside her, catching sight of blood

381

threading from the child's upper lip. "What's this?" she asked with a frown as the coach lunged into another muddy rut and threatened their balance again.

Abra's face was pale, her manner suddenly subdued. "I think I bumped yer knee, Brandy." Her pink tongue darted out in brief exploration and swiped at the blood before Juliana could dab it with her handkerchief.

Juliana hugged her stepsister to her side and put her lips to her forehead. "Spring is my favorite season, but not for traveling the rutted roads in a coach." She looked down at Abra. "Stay beside me where you'll be safer. Are you better now?"

Abra's dark curls bounced with her nod, her good humor quickly returning. "I had tickles in my belly." She frowned briefly. "But they weren't fun 'cause they made my throat burn." She made a face.

"I know, sweeting. Let's think about something else."

Abra's eyes lit. "Is there a dog at Spenser House?"

Juliana's smile dimmed. "Nay. Not any more." At Abra's obvious disappointment, however, she gleaned her mind for something to keep the little girl's attention off the jolting coach beneath them, and her own thoughts from the Earl of Somerset and his kisses. She thought of Archie, and then inspiration struck. "But would you like me to tell you about Peg-Leg Dudley the dog?"

"Dudley? A *pirate* dog?"

Juliana's smile was renewed. "Well, he was more of a privateer, which isn't quite as wicked as a pirate." The familiar sense of emptiness once more began to settle over her, in spite of the cheerful front she put on for Abra.

"Did 'e really sail on a ship?" Against the dark cushion behind her head, the frame of her chestnut hair, Abra's hazel eyes were suddenly enormous.

"He did."

"The same ship *you* were on?"

382

"Aye. But they called him Duds for short."

Abra digested this silently for a moment. Then, "Why was he called Peg-Leg Dudley?" She snuggled closer to Juliana.

Juliana gathered her into her arms and rested her chin atop the child's head, staring at the curtained opening that served as a window. She was suddenly caught up in memories. "He loved storms and battles, and always managed to gain the deck unless he was locked in."

*You know how Duds can streak like lightnin' through an opening when 'e wants out in a gale.* Jackie's long-ago words had penetrated her semi-awareness after the storm near the Canaries. Now they came rushing back unexpectedly to remind her of what once was, and could never be again.

Rain began to dance on the coach roof. It was a soothing sound to Juliana in the midst of her roiling feelings.

"What kind of dog was he?"

"A basset hound. The strangest dog I'd ever seen, with a long, low body—like a great sausage—and short stubby legs covered with many folds of skin." She chuckled softly, her pain pushed aside for the moment. "And he always looked so forlorn—"

"What's ferlorn, Brandy?"

"Unhappy."

"Why? Were th'other pirates mean to 'im?"

Juliana laughed again. "Nay, sweeting. 'Twas only that his eyes were shaped so—the skin on his face hung downward—and his long, droopy ears fell almost to the floor."

Abra pushed herself away from the haven of Juliana's lap. Color had returned to her cheeks. "I never seen a hound like that. I think 'e shoulda been called Droopy if his coat drooped so, don't you?"

Juliana nodded. "One day, during a storm—"

The sound of rain on the roof increased to a steady tattoo, almost drowning out the sound of Juliana's voice.

"—he wiggled through the cabin door when I opened it for a breath of—"

The report of a shot thundered through the air. Another followed in quick succession, and a man screamed. The coach was hauled to a stop, slamming Juliana and Abra forward into the opposite cushioned seat.

"Brandy!" Abra cried.

Juliana pushed herself back onto the squabs, pulling Abra with her. "Hush," she said in a low voice, and groped for the cord on the shade with an unsteady hand. As the leather rolled upward, a third shot rang out. Another man screamed. The sound of cursing men and clanging weapons came to Juliana then, muted by the sound of the drumming rain. She could see nothing.

Highwaymen?

She was torn between a need to see what was happening and the instinct that urged her to quit the coach and flee to safety with Abra.

Another man cried out in pain and a horse whinnied loudly. Juliana could feel the four coach horses stirring with frenetic movements in the traces, causing the coach to pitch and jerk. Another shot pierced the heavy air, and Juliana heard a heavy thump from the driver's seat.

Horror washed over her at the thought of what was happening outside.

"Brandy!" Abra whispered, clinging in terror to Juliana. "What's happening?"

Brandy put her mouth to the child's ear. "Be still, Abra. You must be still!" Some instinct made Juliana force Abra to the floor. "Don't move, Abra," she said, "and be as quiet as a mouse." She quickly lifted and settled her full skirts over the little girl until Abra was completely concealed.

384

"But, Brandy—" Abra protested in an a frightened, muffled whisper.

Before Brandy could reassure her, the door was yanked open and the barrel of a smoking pistol was thrust into the coach. Juliana drew back at the sight, and Abra whimpered softly. The acrid smell of gunpowder filled the interior as a man's face appeared from out of the mist immediately behind the gun.

He grinned at Juliana, ignoring the sounds of chaos behind him. "We've waited a long, long time fer this," he crooned.

Juliana drew back, feeling Abra clinging to her leg. "Get out!" she demanded, her fear for the little girl overriding her caution. "Get out, I say," she repeated as recognition nagged at her memory. Where had she seen this man?

"Nay, Brandy girl, *you* git out," he taunted, his eyes narrowing nastily.

She leaned back and quickly thrust one foot out from beneath her skirts in defense, intending to kick the pistol from his hand.

"Ah, ah, ah, missy," he warned. "I'll blow that dainty foot right off if ye think te use it."

"Smythe!" a voice bellowed from somewhere beyond the intruder. "Over here . . . help me!"

"Don't move," he growled and withdrew from the coach immediately, just as Brandy realized who he was.

"Brandy," Abra sobbed from the floor of the coach, "they're g-g-gonna hurt us." She emerged in a panic, fighting her way out from beneath the concealing material. "I'm afeared, Brandy," she added, and threw her arms about Juliana's waist, burying her head against Juliana's breast.

The sound of that broken little voice, the small body shaking against Juliana, summoned every protective instinct within her. "Nay, Abra. Not if I can help it."

Reaching across the little girl, Juliana turned the handle on the opposite door, relief seeping through her as it gave easily and the panel began to ease open.

*Damned fog,* Keir thought angrily as his second and last shot went wide of the man across the way. He pulled his sword free, hastily tucking the useless pistol into the waist of his breeches with his left hand.

He heard Peter cursing behind him as he engaged one of the miscreants with his cutlass. Keir slid off Corsair, landing lithely on the ground. He sprinted toward the man whom he'd missed with his pistol and who was still atop his skittish horse.

"Come down," Keir challenged harshly, "and match your sword with mine!"

He could barely see the man's face as the highwayman struggled to reload his own pistol. Obviously not the best horseman, the miscreant swore violently as Keir neared him and his madly dancing mount.

"Smythe!" the man roared in panicked anger as the pistol dropped to the ground. "Over here . . . help me, damn it!" He hastily dismounted, reaching for his cutlass, and slipped in the treacherous mud. The drawn weapon looked strangely disembodied as he disappeared for a split second in the swirling mists and dwindling drizzle. He reappeared just as Keir approached, squinting through the foggy veil as he struggled to gain purchase, his sword wildly flaying the air.

"Cap'n! Guard yer back!" Peter shouted, and launched himself toward a figure driving from behind the coach directly toward Keir.

Keir whirled about and thrust out his sword blindly. Too late. He heard the roar of a pistol an instant before the ball took him in the chest.

*Brandy!* His lips formed the name as the breath was

driven from his body and he began to crumple. *Brandy,* he screamed silently.

The shouting and confusion increased around him, but as he descended into layers of soft, still blackness, Keir was unaware of anything but the crushing realization that he had failed the woman he loved . . . again.

As the spring sun began to burn through the fog, the Earl of Spenser's misgivings increased. He couldn't quite shake off echoes of the Earl of Somerset's warning: *He already knows what he needs to about my circumstances, and is determined to wreak his own havoc against me through Brandy . . . There's a very real danger . . .*

As much as Aimery Spenser disapproved of Keir St. Andrews, he'd perceived a real depth of emotion on the latter's part for Juliana. His nobler side kept reminding him that Somerset's father, James St. Andrews, had been a fine man . . . and staunchly loyal to King Charles I, and later his son, Charles II, all through the Civil War, until his own untimely and mysterious demise. Aimery hadn't known him well, yet his sensible side, the side that wasn't tangled in the emotional issues concerning Catherine, Juliana, and Keir St. Andrews the privateer, was naggingly persistent, in spite of Aimery's earnest attempts to ignore it, in its warning of judging a man prematurely . . . and on the basis of the perceived injury he'd done to Juliana.

"He's a black-hearted renegade," Aimery muttered to himself as the sun broke through the mists at last and began to penetrate his aching bones. "And more the fool I for heeding anything he says."

Now, here he was, plowing through this quagmire of calf-deep mud and ruts that passed for a road, not in a comfortable coach, as a man his age ought, but rather

387

on a spirited roan with George and James beside him, armed like two sentries guarding the royal vault. All they needed was a cannon or two to convince anyone they met that they were going to war with the damned Dutch . . . or had escaped from Bedlam, he thought in real irritation. He had better things to do than go chasing through the countryside simply on the word of a prick-louse like Somerset.

He glanced surreptitiously at James, on his right, two pistols bulging at his sides, and a grim look to his features. George, unable to hit the broad side of a barn with any firearm, was armed with a sword and hidden dagger beneath his jacket.

Aimery returned his attention to the road, a scowl on his face. Another mile or so and he would turn back. And swear his two men to silence about this entire farce. Just one more mile . . .


The sound of babbling voices came to Aimery from around the bend, rousing him from his very uncomplimentary thoughts of the Earl of Somerset and his prophetic warning.

"Someone up ahead, m'lord," James said, his right hand going to the butt of one of his pistols.

"Highwaymen well-schooled in stealth, no doubt," Aimery replied with heavy sarcasm, feeling more and more foolish. He wondered briefly if the Earl of Somerset had seen him and his men leave the city this morn, and laughed at how easily they had fallen for the ruse.

He also wondered if Somerset himself would attempt to snatch Juliana and whisk her away. In fact the more he thought about it—and the closer they came to rounding the bend in the road—the more likely it seemed. Or was he, Aimery, merely grabbing at the absurd to counter the real alarm Somerset had roused in him?

Upon rounding the jog, Aimery's deepest, darkest fears were comfirmed.

The Spenser coach and four was standing at right angles to the road, driverless, its team nervously tossing their heads and stomping their hooves. The lines hung to the ground. Several farmers, whose goods-laden carts were pulled up across from the coach, were bent over two men lying in the middle of the morass that was the road. Several other bodies lay helter-skelter and unmoving, as well.

There was no sign of Juliana or the little Dalton girl.

Aimery heeled the roan into a quicker gait, impeded greatly by the soft, sucking muck. It seemed to take an eternity to reach the group.

"What happened here?" he demanded, dismounting quickly and unaided in his alarm.

Peter Stubbs looked up from where he was kneeling beside Keir in the road. His eyes slitted when he recognized Aimery. "Is this," he inclined his head toward the bodies lying in the mud, "what ye call an escort, Spenser?" he asked trenchantly, his voice harsh as gravel.

Aimery moved toward him, unable to believe his eyes. "Where's my granddaughter? And what are *you* doing here?" he demanded, transferring his growing fear for Juliana and his anger with himself to the man kneeling in the mud with Keir St. Andrews's head in his lap.

"Ain't ye concerned 'bout yer men, either? Two out o' three, dead. The coach is empty. And the Cap'n here's lookin' mighty bad te me."

At a curt order from Aimery, George and James moved through the milling bystanders, one of whom was ministering to one of the fallen Spenser retainers. James dropped down beside the latter, while George briefly examined the inside of the coach.

"No one in here, yer lordship," George called to Aimery. "Neither Mistress Juliana nor the little girl." He

389

jumped down and bent to examine what appeared to be a discarded wool cape beneath the coach. Tiny fingers stretching from beneath the garment clung to a spoke of the great front wheel. George picked up one muddied edge of the cape and slowly raised it. "I won't harm ye, child," he said gently, and continued to uncover what proved to be . . . Abra.

From the tensely coiled position she held, Abra lifted her tear-streaked face to his and said through trembling lips, "They *hit* Brandy! I *seen* 'em . . . then they took 'er away!"

"Your lordship, look here," George threw over his shoulder, and helped a very muddy and distraught Abra from her hiding place.

Upon seeing Aimery, she ran toward him and grabbed his hand, looking up at him with a child's candor and utter disregard for protocol. "They took Brandy, Master Lord," she said, "and we gotta *find* 'er!"

Aimery stooped down to her level. "They took our Jul—er, Brandy?"

She nodded her head vigorously. "Aye. But you'll get 'er back, won't you, for ye're a great man."

Aimery straightened and accepted Abra's hand as it slipped trustingly into his. "Aye, little one. We'll get her back."

George turned away from them and proceded to move from body to body in the road, shaking his head.

"Ain't no one else alive," said one heavyset, bushy-bearded bystander to no one in particular. He stroked his beard absently. "A reg'lar rout, this one be. Must've met up with some nasty ones."

Aimery walked the few steps to where Peter held Keir. He stared down at the wax-faced Earl of Somerset, essaying to organize his whirling thoughts, and calm his thundering heart. "It seems he was telling the truth . . ." His eyes suddenly knifed into Peter's. "Or was he to have been a part of this sordid little scheme?"

Peter scowled. "Cap'n don't lie. Ever. He's losin' a lot o' blood. He'll die if he ain't attended to properly . . . and soon." He looked down at Keir, and pressed with the palm of one hand on the folded, gore-soaked cloak being used to stem the flow of blood.

"We've got to get him to a physician," Aimery said, quite unexpectedly feeling that if anyone could find and rescue his Juliana, it was this man lying statue-still upon the ground. That is, if she were yet alive. And if Somerset himself survived what appeared to be a ghastly wound in his chest.

Peter appeared preoccupied with Keir's comfort, and didn't answer Aimery.

"Did you hear me, man? We must take him back to the city."

Peter squinted up at him, a savage light in his eyes. "He ain't exactly fit te mount and ride a horse now, is 'e?"

"Don't be absurd. We'll put him in the coach . . . and my other man over there, as well, if he's still alive." He turned to George. "Help him get the earl into the coach."

As George bent toward Keir, Peter said to Aimery, "What? An' dirty yer coach? You wouldn't want te be seen rescuin' a . . . *cutthroat* like Keir St. Andrews, would ye now? An' who's te decide *where* I take 'im anyway?"

Aimery nodded toward George and then James, his look full of meaning. *"I* do."

Just then Corsair, who'd been standing restively at the side of the rode, neighed shrilly, an eerie, unnerving sound in the quiet, and walked toward where Keir lay. He nudged aside one of the gawking bystanders with his great head, and then lowered it further to nuzzle Keir's leg.

"Get this beast away from him," Aimery said, "and get him into the coach. Quickly!"

A raggedly dressed young boy stepped forward and tentatively reached for the bay's reins. "There, there, big fella. Easy now . . ." He stroked Corsair's sleek dark neck, calming him.

As the horse was led aside, Peter and George carefully lifted Keir between them. He groaned softly, his lips ashen, his closed eyelids as still as in death. The sun, now shining with a vengeance, failed to animate his pallid features.

"Bring along the bay, and any other animals you find," Aimery told the youth who was still speaking softly to Corsair. "You'll be well-rewarded." To another bystander who looked sympathetic, he added, "And if you'll be so kind as to see that my two men," he pointed to two other bodies, "are taken to the city, as well." He grimaced in distaste. "The others can rot and feed the crows, for all I care."

"Cap'n'll have my hide if aught happens te Corsair," Peter mumbled, a seeming afterthought.

Aimery caught the horse's name. "Corsair?" he asked as he held the door open. The irony in his voice was heavy, but Peter appeared preoccupied with his task and didn't reply.

Abra pulled on Aimery's hand. "What about me, Master Lord?" she asked, a frown chasing across her small features as she looked up at him. "Do I have te go back in . . . there?" Aimery felt the shiver that swept over her body. "I'm afeared."

"Nay, child. You can ride with me if you aren't afraid of Dancer there."

Abra took in the stallion Aimery indicated, and nodded her head, evidently preferring to ride the imposing Dancer than inside the Spenser coach.

When Peter was settled with Keir inside the coach, the

other wounded man was brought in. James remained with him on the opposite seat, staring at Peter with grim suspicion.

Just before closing the door, Aimery said to Peter, "If he survives, if he helps me recover Juliana safely . . ." He shook his head. "Well, we'll see . . . We'll see."

# Chapter Twenty-six

Juliana awoke to a pounding headache. She was disoriented at first, and shivering from cold and shock. She concentrated on her sore and constricted limbs, her aching head. The odor of stale sweat and urine, the sharp smell of mildew invaded her nostrils, and she tried to bite her lip as her gorge rose, but a rag was tightly bound about her head, pressing her lips against her teeth. Her wrists were tied, as were her ankles.

She slowly opened her eyes, fearing to increase the pain with even the slightest movement.

She lay on her right side on a pallet, in a small, dimly lit room. A rickety, rough-hewn wooden table leaned drunkenly on its uneven legs against the far wall. A battered lantern, giving off a fluttering, feeble light, sat atop its stained and pitted surface. Several empty bottles lay in one dim corner, along with a mound of what appeared to be discarded clothing.

On another wall was an ash-filled hearth, cold and absolutely useless to Juliana in the damp chill of the room. Scratching, shuffling sounds came from another shadowed corner. A shudder of revulsion rippled through her at the thought of the creatures causing the noises.

She struggled to sit up, in spite of the acute discomfort her movements caused her. Using her arms for leverage, Juliana pushed into a sitting position, trying to will away the wave of nausea that threatened to swamp her. Once upright, she dug her heels into the filthy lump of mattress and awkwardly eased herself back toward the wall. The ancient wood stud behind her was welcomely solid, in spite of the shabbiness of the room, and Juliana let her head fall back, trying to draw in more air.

She would not allow herself to dwell on the suffocating size of the room . . . the way the walls would begin to close in on her if she allowed it. There were more urgent matters at hand, and she would need a clear head to deal with them.

From somewhere above her came the muffled sounds of raucus laughter and rough, loud voices. Feminine shrieks combined with thumping and scraping sounds, and Juliana guessed that she was below a tavern of some kind. A wild and bawdy place with, evidently, little regard for any type of order.

She could only surmise that she had been brought to the infamous section of London known as Alsatia . . . the old Whitefriars District. She hoped she was wrong, but Alsatia was the breeding ground of and home to thieves, prostitutes, highwaymen, murderers . . . and worse. Where else would men who had accosted a coach on a road near London take her? The authorities avoided this section of the city, and even the most notorious of criminals could find sanctuary here.

Juliana closed her eyes against the throbbing in her head, trying to relive the events leading up to her imprisonment. She had opened the coach door and Abra—

Abra!

Dear God! Had Abra stayed safely hidden beneath the coach, as Juliana had bidden her? And where was she now?

A groan of remorse and frustration escaped the rag over her mouth as memories came rushing back . . . shoving Abra beneath the coach . . . a familiar voice shouting, *Cap'n, guard yer back!* . . . a pistol shot hard on its heels.

Then, as she groped her way to the back of the coach, a sharp pain lanced through her head, sending her spinning into mindlessness.

The face of the man who'd burst into the coach appeared before her suddenly . . . Roger Smythe, the sailor from the *Odyssey*.

Or someone who looked just like him.

Her eyes flew open. He had been the one to spoil the sport that afternoon aboard Keir's ship. What had Foucher called him? *Cochon* . . . pig. In a way that was anything but playful, this Smythe had slapped the mop on Jackie's head and shoved him into the midst of the dancing sailors. Oh, how well she remembered! Keir's grim words . . . the way Smythe had stared at her from across the deck . . . And then, of course, the sweet interlude afterward . . .

Keir. She was almost certain it was Peter Stubbs's voice she'd heard shouting a warning to someone—to Keir, she was almost certain, as well. She didn't know why Smythe and his henchmen had attacked their coach, nor could she guess why Keir and Peter would have been present, unless they knew of the plan.

But if Keir had wanted to prevent the attack, or rescue Abra and herself, it hadn't worked. And she'd heard a shot immediately after Peter's warning. Was it Keir's shot or another's?

Lightheadedness assailed her in the wake of such unsettling thoughts. Not only was she trussed and helpless, but she had the added burden of not knowing whether Abra was safe or not, nor what had happened to Keir, if, indeed, he'd been involved. Her empty stomach was knotted with apprehension, and the walls seemed to ripple and sway before her, animated adversaries threatening to close in on her and crush her.

Juliana shut her eyes tightly against the images undulating before her and fought against the nausea and fright that threatened to rise up her throat and choke her behind the constricting gag. Frustration pushed her further into the abyss of despondency . . .

Thump-step, thump-step, thump-step . . . a pause. Then the door burst open on squealing hinges, startling Juliana out of her acute misery. A man stood across from her, a bottle of spirits in one hand, his other arm over a crudely fashioned crutch to support his left side.

Something odd caught one corner of her attention, and it wasn't until the man moved the crutch forward again that Juliana realized what it was. As her eyes followed the line of his left arm from his shoulder down to his wrist, she saw that instead of a normal human hand, a wicked-looking hook curved over the horizontal support. It glinted dully in the meager lantern light.

Unconsciously, she pushed into the unyielding wall behind her.

"Ye like me new hand, eh?" he asked, moving through the doorway and into the room. With his staff, he pushed the door closed behind him, producing an ominous sound of finality.

In the face of her stunned silence, he continued, "Thought ye might, seein' that *you* were te blame."

Juliana shook her head, her eyes widening before moving to his face, then, with a terrible fascination, back to the metal hook.

"Ye deny it?" he said moving toward her. Slowly the implement on the end of his arm came closer to her, but Juliana was frozen in horrible fascination, watching his useless left leg scrape along the floor. As he halted beside the bed, he bent his left elbow and raised the hook to within inches of her cheek. Juliana shuddered, averting her face, hot panic surging through her.

He chuckled without humor. "So we turn t'other cheek, do we? How very *Christian* of ye."

The cold metal tip touched her tender flesh and Juliana

397

closed her eyes, paralyzed.

"Wouldn't want te mar this fair cheek, would we, now? Cap'n wouldn't like that."

Instead of the pain of tearing flesh, Juliana felt pressure, and then a jerk on the rag around her head. The sound of rending cloth split the air. The gag fell away, and she instinctively pulled in a ragged breath, afraid to look up at her tormentor.

The rounded portion of the hook stroked her cheek with a bizarre gentleness, then, with the precision of a striking snake, dug into her cheekbone with swift, savage intent, and sent her head slamming back against the wall.

Brights spots of light exploded in her head . . . and brought anger to her blood. Purging anger, born of reckless desperation, that swept away her sick fear. Her eyes darkened as her head snapped up and she met the stranger's gaze head-on. "Who are you?" she asked through set teeth.

Smythe sank slowly to the bed, his eyes never leaving her face. "Who am I?" he repeated, leaning toward her. Holding the hook up in the air before her, he examined it slowly, deliberately, turning it this way and that. "Why, don't ye remember Roger Smythe, Brandy-girl?" His wine-rancid breath seared across her face.

"Smythe?" she whispered, taking in his scarred face with its flattened left cheekbone. It made his left eye look larger than the right. "But, in the coach . . ."

" 'Twas me brother, sweetheart." He grinned at her, a misshapen movement of mirth. "I imagine 'twas easy enough te mistake 'im fer me, seein' as how you and I ne'er quite met up close."

"What — what have I to do with your hand?" Her voice dropped to a hushed murmur, her tongue feeling like sandpaper in her dry mouth. She acknowledged that he had been a fair-looking man when last she'd seen him, no matter what she'd thought of him at the time.

"Oh, but ye did, me fine lady . . . ye most certainly

398

did." He leaned even closer, until Juliana could see the fine network of veins in the whites of his eyes. "A female's bad luck at sea. Didn't St. Andrews ever tell ye that?"

Juliana looked away from his probing gaze without answering, her flesh crawling at what she suspected he was going to tell her.

"B'cause o' you, we met up with that bad blow off the Canaries . . . 'n a few other problems." His look turned ugly, his lips drawing back, his eyes lighting with a maniacal hatred. "Then yer precious Cap'n gave the word te dismiss me from the *Odyssey.* An' aboard the *Marie Louise,* in the service of 'is Majesty, Louie o' France, yers truly had a mishap up in the riggin' during rough weather."

Juliana shook her head, still refusing to look at him . . . at what he'd become, or so he believed, because of her. She suspected that nothing she could ever say to him would show him the folly of his reasoning.

"You 'n me're gonna get te know each other real good, Brandy-girl," he said, tilting the bottle and sliding its lip from the side of her chin down to the hollow between her breasts.

"Where's Abra?" she whispered, hoping not only to learn what had happened to her stepsister, but also to divert his attention, however briefly.

"Abra?" he repeated slowly. "Ye mean Abracadabra?"

He chortled as Juliana's head jerked around to meet his gaze. How did he know of . . .

Realization struck. " 'Twas *you* the other morn!"

"None other." He leaned over slightly to set down the bottle, then with surprising swiftness positioned the hook at her neckline and rent her gown from neck to below her breasts. The fragile satin gave way, but the fine lawn of her lowcut chemise escaped damage. The damp, chill air kissed her exposed skin, causing gooseflesh to rise. A stain crept up her cheeks, but she refused to cower like a beaten dog, and kept her bound hands in her lap. She clung to the hope that Roger Smythe couldn't function

399

sexually if he had suffered such serious injury below the waist.

But there were other horrors equally abhorrent as rape.

"Me 'n you're gonna get te be good, ah, *friends* afore this is over with, Brandy-girl. First we're gonna get te know each other real intimate, ye know what I mean?" He chuckled softly. "I figure ye can do more fer me if yer hands're free, but ye have te promise te behave yerself, or I'll have te call Sam an' his friends in here . . . te teach ye yer place."

"What are you going to do to me?" she asked, deciding that no one had seen Abra, and bringing it up again might put the child—or anyone from the Hawk and Hound—in danger. Relief seeped through her. Thank God for that, at least.

"What do you want with me?" she asked again, feeling some of her anger ebb away as tremors of chill and fear seized her once more.

"Jest yer company, fer now." He produced a knife and cut the ties that bound her hands. As the blood rushed through her wrists, causing them to tingle painfully, he added, "We're jest gonna wait a while . . . until Cap'n St. Andrews recovers from his wound. *If* 'e does."

"Keir?" Juliana said before she was aware she was speaking.

He stood with an ungainly push from the pallet and a shifting of weight to the crutch. "Aye. 'E must've been fixin' te take ye from the coach, jest like Sam, but me older brother beat 'im to it. Put a pistol ball in 'is chest, too."

Juliana's breath caught, her heart lurching beneath her ribs as her worst fear was realized. Shot? Keir?

"Sam said someone comin' along the road te London would find 'im maybe afore 'twas too late." He shrugged. "Mayhap 'e's tough enough te survive a pistol ball, our cap'n is." He stared at the peach-tinted swell of her breasts as he said the next words. "So we'll jest wait fer 'im te get better 'n come lookin' fer ye, Brandy-girl. Me 'n Sam got plans for 'im." His eyes lanced into hers. " 'Tis gonna be a long, hot summer, sweetheart, no matter *what* happens."


"He ain't gonna like this one bit," Peter Stubbs muttered to himself. "Of all the places . . ."

"I beg your pardon?" the physician asked as he straightened from examining Keir and looked at Peter.

Peter shook his head. "Jest thinkin' aloud, 'tis all." His gaze slid from the questioning physician's face to Keir's. Creases of concern seamed his forehead. "Is the cap'n gonna pull through?"

Sir Nigel Sisk, a small mite of a man with sharp blue eyes behind his spectacles, looked assessingly at Peter. "If the wound doesn't fester. He appears young and hardy enough to heal. Surely, if he survived the wounds indicated by the scars spread over his back, he will come through this." His eyes narrowed a fraction. "If he gets proper care until he's out of danger, the earl should be fit again in several months."

Peter slanted a surprised look at him. "Months?"

"Aye. 'Tis no mere scratch, Master . . ."

"Stubbs. Peter Stubbs."

"Ah. Master Stubbs, then. A hair's breadth to one side or the other and 'twould have penetrated either of his lungs. Perhaps even his heart. As it is, aside from a fractured rib or two, 'twas a clean entry and exit as far as I can tell. Most unusual. Luck was certainly on his side."

" 'Tis about time," Peter muttered, then cleared his throat and said, "I won't leave 'is side. I stood in fer ship's surgeon when I was needed aboard the *Odyssey*. I know a few tricks o' the trade."

"I see." But Sir Nigel didn't look as if he saw anything beyond Peter Stubbs but a rough and ignorant seaman.

"How many months?"

Sisk gave Peter a small bottle of liquid, then began

401

gathering his instruments. "I would guess two or three at least."

"But then he'll need te regain 'is strength an' movement."

"Exactly. I will be back periodically to mark his progress. Meanwhile, if he worsens beyond a mild fever, send for me immediately." He closed his physician's bag and stepped back from the bed. "Is that clear, Master Stubbs?"

Peter nodded.

"You may give him the laudanum as needed for pain, but sparingly, I warn you . . . 'tis opium-based. And I still say he would benefit from a phlebotomy."

Peter shook his head vigorously. "Cap'n don't believe in bloodlettin'. Says a man needs all his blood."

Sir Nigel cast Peter a look that conveyed several things, among them annoyance. He lifted his eyebrows above his spectacles, looking just like an owl. "And exactly where did the earl perform his doctoral studies?"

Peter scowled. "In the university o' life," he answered with his own brand of irritation. "Cap'n 'n me've pulled more men from death's jaws than any fancy-taught physician, I warrant."

Sisk's expression changed to one of amused patronage. "No need to take offense, Master Stubbs. I suspect you are quite capable of caring for Somerset, with or without a phlebotomy." He nodded his head, cast one more look at Keir, then swung toward the door.

"What's this about a phlebotomy?" Aimery Spenser asked as he came into the room.

Peter remained stubbornly silent after a glance at Aimery. "Master Stubbs suggests that the Earl of Somerset would not agree to the procedure were he in any condition to make the decision."

Aimery opened his mouth to speak. As his gaze alighted on Peter's face, however, he changed his mind. "Mayhap he's lost enough blood for now," he said, not wishing to offend Peter Stubbs and therefore send him packing with the incapacitated Earl of Somerset. That would surely be a death sentence for the latter. "Perhaps on the morrow," he said, and ushered Sir Nigel out the bedroom door.

Peter could hear the low hum of their voices from down the hall. He looked at Keir. "Should've taken ye back te the *Odyssey.* at least," he muttered. "A doctor could o'seen te ye there jest as easily . . . Now we're stuck *here,* of all places!"

Keir moaned softly, and Peter put a wet cloth to his lips. "Ye gotta mend fast, Cap'n," he told the unconscious man. "Brandy's in the hands o' Smythe, God help us all."

"Let me sit with him for awhile," Lady Anne said to Peter.

He started from a doze, almost tilting over the chair on which he'd been slumped.

He saw her concerned face above his, all kindness, and he shook his head. "Much obliged, milady, but—"

"No buts, Master Stubbs," she insisted with a hint of a smile. "You cannot help him if you're not rested yourself."

Before Peter could answer, Keir mumbled something in his sleep, then groaned. "Why, he looks fevered," Lady Anne said, biting her lower lip. She rinsed a cloth in the basin of water beside the bed and laid it against Keir's forehead.

For a moment, the pained expression on Keir's features eased, then he moaned again, his lips flattening against his teeth.

Peter reached for the bottle of laudanum. "Guess 'tis time fer this," he said. He handed her the spoon and bent to ease Keir's head and shoulders up from the pillow, his grip gentle but firm. As soon as he settled Keir again in a prone position, the latter began to thrash. Bright new blood blotted the clean wrappings over the wound.

403

"Jesus, Cap'n," Peter muttered. "Lay still, fer God's sake!"

But the ruby stain continued to spread.

"As soon as the laudanum takes hold, he'll calm down," Lady Anne said, replacing the cloth that fell from Keir's forehead with a fresh one.

"Maybe we should change his dressing," Peter said with a worried frown.

Lady Anne shook her head. "Not until he stops moving about. Why don't you go downstairs and get something to eat? You look like you could use some sustenance yourself, Master Stubbs. And Aimery has some good French brandywyne," she added, with a suggestive lift of one eyebrow.

Peter stood, his eyes still on Keir. "Don't want none o' his hospitality, but I could use a stretch." *And a privy,* he added silently.

"Don't you think 'tis a bit late to refuse my hospitality?" Aimery asked from just inside the door.

Peter looked up. "The only reason we're here—where we're not wanted—is because Somerset Chase is too far fer the Cap'n te travel." Hostility curdled his words. "And because you made no bones about having it any other way. Jest as soon as 'e can be moved, we'll be on our way." He moved toward the door, glancing over his shoulder at Keir one last time as he exited, as if uncertain of Keir's safety in the presence of the Earl of Spenser.

"Ungrateful lout," Aimery said when Peter was gone.

"What did Sir Nigel say?" Anne asked him.

Aimery rubbed his face wearily before he answered. "He's never seen a man's back so badly scarred . . . among the gentry, that is. But, in spite of the fresh wound, he thinks Somerset will live." His mouth turned down at the corners. "He'd better! 'Tis his fault that Juliana's been taken . . . again. If she'd never met him, she would be here with us now." His eyes misted at the thought. He lowered himself to the chair, his gaze on the floor so Anne wouldn't see his emotion.

She put her hand on his shoulder. "You're wrong, Aimery. You wouldn't have ever known that she was alive."

The truth in the statement gave him pause. As much as he would have liked to deny it, it was true. "So now he's gravely wounded, and Juliana's in the hands of felons . . . denizens of Alsatia, no less." He stood in agitation. "I will talk to the Lord Mayor himself and have men sent to search the city. I'll even go myself—"

"You're mad as a March hare if you think to do such a thing," Peter said from the door. "You'll sign her death warrant."

Aimery's angry gaze met his. "And by the look of you, you *would* know such things, wouldn't you?"

Peter bristled as he stalked into the room. "A man's past is not always to his liking . . . or his fault. The important thing is te do the best ye can with what ye've got te make yer life better. The Cap'n here ne'er asked fer what happened to 'im when he was but a lad. An' he's a good man . . . harsh but fair. And loyal to a fault. He'd come out smellin' like a rose, I'd wager, when compared te most o' yer so-called bluebloods and their shameless ways."

"He's quiet now," Anne said to Peter. "Let's change his dressing."

As Peter complied, Aimery watched the two of them work in tandem to unwrap the blood-soaked linen around Keir's upper torso. Odsfish, Aimery thought, the man's bronzer than a heathen savage. How could he be anything more?

. . . *so-called bluebloods and their shameless ways.* Peter's words echoed through the passages of his mind. The sight of Keir's exposed back, however, as Peter held him so they could proceed to wrap the fresh linen around his torso, made Aimery's former judgment seem petty and superficial. He doubted if any courtier would have survived

405

the kind of punishment Keir St. Andrews had obviously suffered.

"He kidnapped her, like any common criminal," Aimery countered in obstinate tones.

"*I* took 'er from the Hawk and Hound that night," Peter said, his eyes and voice full of defiance . . . and remorse, "and not Cap'n St. Andrews."

" 'Loyal to a fault,' I believe you said," Aimery pressed. "He was no such thing to Juliana."

"I never said 'e was perfect. We all make mistakes. But the cap'n admitted his 'n sought te make amends. How many o' yer precious bluebloods woulda done such a thing?" Peter gazed down at Keir as Anne adjusted the covers beneath him once more. "Can't ye tell by the way he looks at her? He's in love with her. Ye don't think he jest decided te pursue 'er fer the fun of it because he saw 'er at Whitehall. He's been miserable ever since he realized how much she meant to 'im and that she was gone . . . even dead. Cap'n ain't exactly an expert on love—'n how te handle it—since 'e ain't received much himself."

Aimery fell silent in the wake of this unexpected—and unusual, he guessed—revelation, pretending to watch the other two work over Keir. His mind, however, was sifting and sorting through old prejudices and new evidence—cut and dried decisions of the past, and more open-minded understanding gained through the years, as experience revealed that so much of life fell into that shadowed area between right and wrong.

"And now . . . what of Juliana?" he asked in a low voice.

Peter slanted him a look. "Dalton's quietly makin' inquiries among his patrons who might have connections in Fleet Street an' Whitefriars. I—"

"Peter?" Keir said in soft, rasping voice, gaining everyone's attention as his eyes opened.

Peter moved even closer to the bed, and placed his hand on one of Keir's that lay alongside him. "Don't talk,

Cap'n. Save yer strength fer healin'."

Keir's eyes were a dull hazel, sunken against his drawn face.

"Brandy . . . got to find Brandy and . . . Smythe."

"All the more reason fer ye to keep quiet an' get stronger. Can't do it without ye, ye know." His expression turned bleak, the pressure of his hand over Keir's visibly increasing. "Don't think he'd dare harm 'er . . . 'specially if he wants te use 'er to get te you."

Keir sighed and closed his eyes, his expression full of defeat. "How long . . . how long until I—"

"Doc says 'bout two months."

Keir sighed again, his head lolling to one side. "Do what you . . . can, meanwhile . . . Peter . . ." He fell silent.

"Aye, Cap'n. I will. You jest mend quick, so we c'n pay Smythe a visit when I learn exactly where he's hidin'. A visit he'll never ferget."

A long silence prevailed. Then, with a soft bitterness, Aimery said, "There are other ways, every bit as damaging as physical, that he can hurt her, you know."

Peter met his sober look. "Aye. I know it. Cap'n knows it, too."

Keir muttered something unintelligible, his face contorting, whether in rage or pain wasn't clear, but his eyes remained closed. Soon, his features relaxed, and he slipped into laudanum-induced slumber.

Lady Anne persuaded Peter to go downstairs with her to eat, but Aimery remained with Keir. He studied him as he lay sleeping, as if Aimery could glean information from just being in his presence, from just studying his unmoving form.

*The Cap'n here n'er asked fer what happened to 'im as a lad . . .*

It was probably true . . . that much Aimery was willing to believe. He determined there and then to find out from Peter Stubbs exactly what had happened to Keir St. Andrews when he was a lad.

He stared off into the middle distance, deep in thought. He was not an unfair man. He would just have to speak privately to Peter, and then at length to Somerset.

"Brandy . . ." Keir mumbled. His head moved from side to side, in obvious anguish. ". . . taught me so much of life, my Brandy . . . please forgive me . . ."

Aimery leaned closer to catch his words.

". . . my countess . . . bear my children . . . brandy-eyes . . ."

And then Aimery noticed a glistening drop of moisture nestled beneath the Earl of Somerset's thick, dark lashes, hovering on the lower rim of one eye. At first Aimery had missed it, the tear easily blending with the sprinkling of gold at the tips of the eyelashes. But he saw it now, and watched it spill over and meander down Keir's cheek, leaving a telltale path of pain in its wake.

"Brandy . . ." Keir whispered once more.

"Aye, Brandy," Aimery said softly, and, quite unexpectedly, found his own eyes wet with tears.

# Chapter Twenty-seven

*July, 1666*

"Me brother's got the plague, ye devil's daughter!"

Juliana instinctively shrank from Roger Smythe's fury until her back came up hard against the crude slatted tub he'd procured for her. She still wore her chemise and drawers, a precaution taken against an intrusion just like this.

It was the first bath she'd had since being brought to Alsatia, and in spite of the low level of water and its tepid temperature, it was an undreamed of luxury. So much so, however, that Juliana, lost in thoughts of Keir and Kerra, her grandfather and the Daltons, and even her friends in Jamaica, had failed to hear Smythe's awkward approach.

"Sam?" she asked, as she tried to collect her wits in the face of this newest turn of events.

"*Sam,*" he hissed. "And 'tis because o' *you!* Big, strappin' tar like Sam don't get the plague . . . 'less 'e's been cursed." He brought his face even closer to hers, transferring his hook from his crutch to the fragile flesh on the back of one hand crossed protectively over her breasts. He didn't draw blood, but Juliana knew that if she moved her hand the slightest bit, the tip would break the skin. "I heard ye hummin' in here . . . like ye was mighty satisfied with what ye've wrought." A crude charm against the plague hung from a piece of cord about his neck.

At the same time, the children's song about the plague danced through her mind:

> *Ring a-ring a-Roses*
> *A pocketful of posies,*
> *'Tishoo, 'tishoo,*
> *We all fall down!*

The odor of old urine and sour spirits came to her, wrenching her thoughts back to the man before her, and she worked at her lower lip to keep from gagging.

She feigned fear, even though Roger Smythe did not inspire much fear in her anymore. Rather, she felt pity for him, and a bone-deep weariness with the situation. She'd discovered, however, that her anger or defiance only fueled his temper and determination to brand her as his now . . . something, thank God, he'd been unable to do thus far. As much as she hated acting the frightened female, it was better than chancing his physical ability to rape her, remote as the possibility was. Perhaps Roger would contract the plague from his brother and die . . .

For once Juliana Spenser did not pull back from the thought of another's death.

"I had naught to do with your brother's illness," she said, her eyes downcast. "How could I?"

"Then why are ye turnin' red, eh? 'Tis a lie, that's why, ye witch!" He bent to retrieve his fallen crutch and pushed himself away from the tub. While his back was turned, Juliana carefully drew her knees to her chest more tightly and hugged them. She lay her cheek against them, which was cooling to her warm skin. The warmth in her face was from embarrassment, and not guilt, but Roger Smythe would never believe that.

With a soft sigh, she closed her eyes, willing him to go away. Trying to recapture her scattered remembrances . . .

"Ye're gettin' scrawnier than a plucked hen," he said suddenly, jerking around toward the tub. "Ye ain't got nothin' te hide no more. Ye ain't woman enough now te

410

make any man wanna rut, let alone me." He rubbed at his crotch with his right hand, as he'd done so many times before in his pitiful attempts to become aroused physically. But Juliana was no longer disgusted by the motion, for it was one of empty frustration.

"Manhood comes from the heart and mind, the soul," she said slowly, distinctly, finding herself comparing what Roger Smythe had become to Keir St. Andrews. She lifted her head from her knees and met his gaze levelly. " 'Tis something a man is born with. It can never be taken away."

His eyes slitted, his mouth turning down with growing rage. Juliana was reminded of a caricature puppet at a village fair, one side of its face flattened from storage during the winter months. A *frisson* of purest distaste moved through her. This man was no mere puppet. He was flesh and blood, and wanted to kill Keir St. Andrews. And herself. And heaven knew how many others he'd set his tormented mind to.

Realizing she had perhaps gone too far, she sought to reason with him. "Perhaps I can tend to your brother," she offered. "I had the plague when I was a child, and so I cannot contract it." At least it would be something to do, and perhaps would offer some sort of opportunity for escape. Or maybe she could even maneuver it so that in exchange for her release, she could offer to nurse and cure his brother. Although the plague was fatal more often than not, Roger believed her to possess some sort of power. Could she somehow use it to her advantage?

The thought was like a beacon in the darkness of her despair.

"I wouldn't let ye *touch* 'im!" he snarled. "I'm payin' fer good care fer him—no pest house fer Sam!—and ye'd better pray he survives, Brandy-girl, or yer life ain't worth a privy pot." He dragged himself over to the pallet where Juliana slept and sat down, obviously waiting for her to stand and step from the tub. "Ye better cooperate, wench, or I'll tell all the customers o' the *establishment* upstairs

411

about ye. Even though ye're Keir St. Andrews's used goods, the gents above," he jerked his head toward the ceiling, "always welcome a new face."

"And what establishment is that?" she asked, trying to catch him off guard.

"Never ye mind. Ye'll get no information from me, Brandy-girl. No one's likely te find ye here 'less I tell 'em." He barked out a laugh. "An' then, they'll trip over each other tryin' te get te ye first."

"Roger," she began in one more half-hearted attempt to reason with him, "let me tend Sam . . . I'm familiar with the treatments for the Black Death—"

"Don't ye call it that!" he warned harshly. "Sam ain't a-gonna die! An' if he does, there'll be naught left of ye to *find* when Keir St. Andrews comes a-snoopin' round."

"Let me go, Roger," she said, weariness dulling her voice. "I'll do aught that you wish—"

"Make me a man, then!" His eyes fired with the desperate intensity of a man ready to give anything for one last precious chance.

Juliana looked away, dry-eyed, her answer emphasized by the silence.

"If ye can't return te me what ye robbed me of, ye'll *never* leave here," he said, heaving to his feet. He shuffled toward the tub, the expression on his skewed face a blend of ferocity and frustration. "Not until ye're put in a pine box . . . with Keir St. Andrews."

He slammed the side of the tub with his heavy crutch. "Ye hear, wench? Not until ye're both dead." He leaned forward, trembling with a terrible, unnatural anger. "Enjoy yer bath, Brandy-girl."

When the last echoes of his awkward passage faded, Juliana allowed herself to relax. At least as much as she could or dared. Her constant fear was that some ruffian, possibly worse than Roger Smythe—such as his healthy older brother Sam—would come bursting through the

412

padlocked door. Roger had warned her to keep quiet and place the bar across the inside of the door whenever he left, or she could suffer stiff consequences. Whatever those might be, he evidently considered them worse than anything he might do to her, if anything he said or implied could be believed.

One thing she did know, however, was that if she were actually in Ram Alley, or some other location in Alsatia, there was nary a decent man about. If she were somewhere in Fleet Street, she wouldn't fare much better. Who would hear with the unrelenting racket coming from above? Roger had unbound her wrists and ankles, and permanently removed the gag—indication enough that she would be jumping from the embers into the flames were she foolish enough to attract the attention of any who might be around her.

Sam Smythe, however, had the plague. One less obstacle. And, in spite of all her dire reasoning, in the back of her mind she continued to nurse a tiny tendril of hope that perhaps if someone *did* discover her, a woman, perhaps, or a man with a thimbleful of common decency, she might yet gain her freedom.

She'd even seriously contemplated escaping through the chimney. Her examination of it only ended up with her choking on soot and bitterly acknowledging it was an all-but-impossible feat. But after almost two months of imprisonment, Juliana found the temptation increasing by degrees, with every day that passed, to take her chances. The worst thing that could happen was rape.

*Or murder* . . .

She pushed aside the very thought. Juliana Spenser was too full of life and the love of it to even consider death as an alternative. But a profound sense of frustration with the situation was wearing on her, especially now that she was almost certain Roger Smythe was no more than a pathetic shell of a man, one who could inflict more easily mental than physical abuse.

"I'll bide my time, until I sense my chance," she vowed

softly. "He cannot keep me here forever."

*Or mayhap Keir will come for me . . .*

That thought was welcomely uplifting, and she felt her spirits lighten again. After all, hadn't Roger said, ". . . when Keir St Andrews comes a-snoopin' round"? Surely he would know by now whether Keir had survived the injury?

Suddenly the bath held no comfort for Juliana. She watched the scum gather around the water's edge, and wondered just *where* Roger Smythe had obtained it. She stood abruptly. The water cascaded from her skin, and she stepped out of the tub. Stripping her chemise and drawers, she drew her tattered and soiled dress over her head with a grimace and began to scrub her underthings in the bathwater.

She would build a small coal fire, in spite of the season, to dry out her undergarments, then she would launder her dress and do the same. She couldn't stand the filth, especially over her clean body. Then she would wash what she could of the bedding . . . anything to pass the hours.

The tiny lioness on the chain about her neck tapped against the lip of the tub and caught her attention. The thought of the one who had given the amulet to her what now seemed a century ago brought a rare smile to her lips . . . and another rush of determination to bide her time just a little longer. Just until she could effect her escape.


"I'm fit as I've ever been," Keir said to Peter, fire in his green eyes. " 'Tis ludicrous to coddle me so when God knows what's happened to Brandy!"

"And ye'll be more the fool if ye hie yerself te Fleet Street or Whitefriars lookin' fer her afore ye're ready."

Sweat glazed Keir's forehead. "I've been abed almost two months, man. I'm *ready!*" He flung the covers aside and made to swing his feet over the side of the bed. Dizziness assailed him and he stilled for a moment, trying to gain his equilibrium.

414

"That's a good lad," a voice said to him from the door of the bedchamber.

Keir raised his gaze and met Aimery Spenser's. Behind him stood James, pistol pointed at the floor.

"Sir Nigel said a few weeks more. September, to be exact."

"And since when are you so concerned about my health?" Keir gritted against the dull ache in his chest as he pushed himself back against the pillows.

"You promised you would retrieve my granddaughter, remember?"

"Aye. But I can't do it from this bed."

"Nor can you meet with any success while you're weak as a pup."

"I can't build my strength, *your lordship*, while lying abed."

Aimery walked into the room, and James disappeared.

"My thanks for calling off your man," Keir said, heavy irony infusing his words. "I wouldn't think it necessary to threaten a weak pup with a pistol."

"One never knows what to expect when dealing with a reformed pirate."

Keir opened his mouth to retort, then decided not to take the bait.

Aimery continued, "After a light repast you may take a walk through the townhouse—even into the garden—if you like, so you can prove your prowess to all and sundry. And if you behave, perhaps I'll even take you to the king on a litter to collect some sweetmeats for your valiant efforts."

Keir's temper was raw from inactivity as well as an all-consuming concern about Brandy Dalton. He was angry, impatient, frustrated—and weak. The prospect of walking about the house, going up and down the stairs, even outside, was like a bright light at the end of a tunnel. He knew that once he was up and about his strength would return quickly. So he bit his tongue in the face of Aimery Spenser's sarcasm and took a bowl of soup from the tray

Peter offered him.

But Keir had never sustained such a serious wound from pistol ball or sword, and he was bitterly disappointed in what he considered his paltry progress about the Spenser town house. The walk down the stairs was the worst. His limbs felt like rubber, and he began perspiring profusely.

As he clung to the newel post at the bottom of the steps, Peter offered placatingly, " 'Tis a damned hot day, Cap'n. We're all a-sweatin' like—" He trailed off at the withering look Keir threw him.

"Take me to the garden," he said through clenched teeth, gripping Peter's arm.

Peter obliged him, but Keir realized that if he walked about the small garden he would never have the strength to return to the bedchamber upstairs with only Peter helping him. With an expletive under his breath, he swung back toward the stairway. Rivulets of sweat trickled from his brow, and the back of his linen shirt was slowly being soaked. His legs began to tremble in earnest as he ascended the stairs, but he refused to crumble into a quivering heap under Aimery Spenser's roof.

"I'll do it," he huffed, as Peter helped him into bed. "By God, I'll be fit by August's end, or die in the attempt." He looked at his friend. "But I'll need your help."

Peter nodded.

"And, Peter? Bring me something more substantial than soup—some of Gonzalez's fricassee of bacon and eggs . . . and some brandywyne."


It was early September—the second or third day, if Juliana's calculations were accurate. The dingy room where she'd been staying for three months was unbearably stuffy. She sat on the pallet, staring dully into space. Rows of tally marks on the wall behind her indicated the passing of days, weeks, months. She had lost weight from the erratic meals she was given. Sometimes she chose to eat nothing, so melancholy had she become, and sometimes the food brought to her wasn't fit for consumption.

Much of the time she lived in a world of sunshine and warmth and love . . . a world of the past, a world made up of memories. Keir's face flashed before her countless times, warming her briefly from within and giving her fleeting hope. Kerra's, as well, came to her, and stoked the ache within her breast for her child.

She hadn't seen Smythe for a week now, and she didn't know whether to be relieved or concerned. She sensed that now might be the time to find a way to free herself from her prison, but she lacked the physical and mental energy such a task would require.

A faint voice warned her, *Don't lose hope. You must do something before you are not able . . . before you sink any deeper . . .*

She bowed her head wearily. What could it hurt? Why not try to attract someone's attention? Anything was better than this.

A sound outside the door roused her. She caught the unmistakable sound of Roger Smythe's approach: *thump-step, thump-step*. Only something was different about it today . . .

She waited, her eyes riveted to the door. She would incapacitate him in some way . . . he'd never expect it of her now. Or she would kill him. She had to, for he had never left her alone for more than a day or so before. He was losing interest in his plan of revenge, perhaps, and would eventually desert her . . . leave her to rot in this place below some ramshackle tenement. Or just kill her outright.

He rapped at the door, which she'd obediently kept barred from within. She was half-tempted to refuse to answer, but seven long days and nights of isolation propelled her up from the pallet and toward the door.

She put one hand on the solid bar, her ear to the door. She heard the murmur of voices and felt a stab of fear move through her. Was it Roger or someone else pretending to be Roger? Someone even worse?

"Lemme in," he demanded, thumping at the door.

"Brandy-girl . . . open the door."

She lifted the bar and stood back. The door opened slowly, until Roger Smythe stood before her . . . and his hulking, apparently healthy brother, Sam.

He was a replica of Roger—or what Roger used to be. A bit larger in stature, a few more lines in his face, but definitely his look-alike brother.

Instinct made Juliana move quickly to close the door, but Sam shoved his foot between the panel and the jamb before she could slam it shut. The force of the door against his foot registered in a flash of surprise in his eyes, which quickly turned to irritation.

"Still got some fight in 'er, little brother," Sam said, placing his hand on the door and pushing it open as easily as if Juliana were not even there. The power of the motion induced pure panic in her. This was a far cry from the crippled Roger; and while the threat of Roger had been mitigated over the weeks, she was totally unprepared for this new, unexpected threat.

After all, Sam Smythe supposedly had the plague only weeks ago . . .

Sam held out a brawny forearm to Juliana, as she backed away from the door. "Here, Brandy-girl," he offered. "Pinch me te make sure I ain't a ghost." He grinned. "Not everyone dies o' the pestilence, ye know."

"If 'twere up te her, ye'd be pushin' up daisies," Roger said sourly, and pushed clumsily past his brother and into the room.

Sam closed the door and dropped the bar in place. When he turned his attention to Juliana, she was almost face to face with Roger. "Lookin' a bit pale, she is," Sam said. "Lost some o' them curves, too, as I remember." He scratched his head thoughtfully. "Wonder if St. Andrews'd want 'er if 'e could see 'er now?"

The mention of Keir's name gave her renewed purpose.

"Have you come to release me?" Juliana asked Sam warily, trying to take the initiative. "If not, you'll fare no better than your brother." She didn't know where the

418

courage and defiance came from, but the words tumbled out.

Sam slowly circled around her while Roger eased himself down on the pallet. "Roger tells me ye been uncooperative, Brandy-girl," he said in a cajoling voice. "So I thought te help 'im convince ye that ye *owe* 'im . . ."

"I owe him nothing! Please . . . please," she said, "listen to me . . . I'm sorry about Roger's accident, but surely *you* understand that I couldn't possibly have had anything to do with it . . . or his dismissal from the *Odyssey*. Or your illness." She glanced over at Roger. "If I had some kind of mystical power, as he seems to think, why would you have survived the plague? Why wouldn't I have let myself out of here by now? Tell me!"

"Your pretty words won't work on Sam, neither," Roger said. "Now that we know St. Andrews is mendin', things are fallin' into place."

"I won't be a party to any schemes you hatch," she answered, "and especially involving Keir St. Andrews."

"Well now," Sam said. He grabbed her wrist and pulled her against him. "And I wonder jest how sassy ye'd be if we told ye yer cap'n was dead of a pistol ball through the chest?"

Uncertainty flickered in her eyes as she stared up at him.

"That's better," he said into her face with a meaningful grin as she stilled in mid-motion. He put one hand on her hip and pulled her even closer, jolting Juliana out of her momentary hesitation.

She began to struggle, moved to action by sheer terror, but he held her tightly, as if she were no more than a doll. When she finally realized she was only arousing him with her efforts to escape his embrace, she stilled. She glanced over at Roger, and an idea suddenly pierced the frantic jumble of her thoughts.

"That's enough!" Roger snarled at his brother. "She's mine, remember?"

Sam released Juliana and swung toward his Roger. He

stared at him for a moment, then threw back his head and shouted with laughter.

Juliana backed away, looking around for a weapon she knew didn't exist in the bleak room that was her prison. Her only option, at the moment, was Roger Smythe. She went over to him and knelt at his feet. "I'll do anything that you ask," she offered in a low voice. *"Anything.* Do you understand?"

He glanced down at her bowed head, and then back to Sam.

Juliana raised her gaze to his. "If you let him touch me, I swear by all that is holy, I'll take my own life. Do you hear me, Roger? You'll have no means to get even with Keir St. Andrews . . . all your work and planning will have been for naught."

"No secrets!" Sam said from behind her, and Juliana felt herself being hauled to her feet by the back of her dress.

Roger pushed himself to his feet, his face livid. "We came te get 'er te write a message! Ye promised ye wouldn't do nothin' else—"

*"Fire . . . fire!"*

A distant but distinct voice came to them, cutting across Roger's words. The two men looked at the door, then at each other.

" 'Twas nothin', I warrant," Sam said. "Some fool tryin' te—"

The sound of heavy footsteps above them caught his attention . . . footsteps of many, moving toward the door of the tavern upstairs. The noise level increased tenfold, and Juliana sensed panic and chaos in the thunderous movement over them.

A woman screamed from somewhere on the other side of the door, a sound of genuine terror. It raised the hackles on Juliana's neck. She moved toward the door instinctively until Sam's heavy hand on her shoulder stopped her cold. "An' where d'ye think *ye're* goin'?" he demanded.

"Fire! There must be a fire nearby," Juliana answered,

feeling her claustrophobia rise up in hot waves at the thought of being locked in the room with a fire burning nearby.

Sam shrugged it off. "Always fires a-burnin' in London. Ain't no need te' panic."

Roger stood and leaned on his crutch, a crooked frown between his eyes. "We'd better go an' see." He began to make his way to the door. "We c'n come back fer her if we have to."

"Don't fret, Brandy-girl," Sam said with a lascivious wink and a pat on the bottom before he shoved her away from the door. "We'll be back te fetch ye . . . 'cause we got somethin' more special in mind fer ye than fire." He chuckled as he lifted the bar from the door and pulled it open for Roger, then followed him out.

Dawn pearled the eastern sky over the smoke-shrouded city of London. Already the air was close and still; the sign of another stifling, late summer day. The hot morning air sat like an unwelcome blanket upon the wooden hodgepodge of houses that was London; they leaned drunkenly towards each another over the narrow, twisting, cobblestoned streets.

Keir spun from the looking glass before him to face the others in the room. He wore a black patch over one eye, and his nasty grin revealed that several of his teeth appeared to be missing. He sported a moustache and short beard, and his dark periwig was long and unkempt, with only a stained kerchief tied about his forehead to keep the hair out of his face. His waistcoat and breeches were out of date and ill-kept, and his boots scraped and worn. A bulge beneath his waistcoat hinted at the weapon he carried, while a cutlass and sheathed dagger brazenly hugged his hips.

"You're a credible highwayman," Aimery observed with acerbity. "In fact, you were made for the part."

Keir accepted the comment with a slight inclination of his head.

"And, of course, you're less likely to be taken for aught but a criminal than I."

"Surely that's a credit to you, Spenser, as you continue to so vociferously malign the privateer."

Aimery cleared his throat and looked studiously at the colorful Aubusson rug at his feet, for once holding his tongue.

"Ye sure ye're ready, Cap'n?" Peter asked him. He, too, resembled a miscreant with his walnut-stained hands and face and cheap, shaggy periwig hiding his thinning hair. "Strong enough?"

Keir drew his sword and slashed the air a few times; the blade whirred menacingly in the quiet of the room. He tested the balance of the hilt on his palm, tossed it to his left hand, and repeated the procedure before smoothly sheathing it with a metallic *clink*. "I'd better be."

"Have you enough men?" Aimery asked, standing and pacing the room with agitated movements. "How can you find Juliana with just the two of you? Why, she could be *anywhere!*"

Keir adjusted his belt, then met Aimery's eyes. "Jonathon Dalton has access to all kinds of information through his clientele. And Peter, here, has been doing his work, as well. We already know with fair certainty that Roger Smythe and his brother have been seen with fair regularity in the vicinity of Fish Street Hill and Thames Street, near St. Magnus's. 'Twould seem as if they're avoiding Alsatia deliberately. If 'tis true, our work has already been cut considerably."

Keir was anxious to leave. They'd waited as long as they'd dared, making certain that he had reached close to his former state of health and strength. He could have used a week or two more, he acknowledged to himself, but some sixth sense told him to move at once. He glanced in the mirror once again, over his shoulder. Satisfied with what he saw, he turned back to the other two men.

"Can you trust Dalton?" Aimery asked.

"He raised your granddaughter as his own, Spenser. He came to you for help in rescuing her from me, for God's sake. How can you doubt his sincerity?" He raised his eyebrows sardonically. "Or is it that the higher you move up the social ladder, the less you trust those not so fortunate as yourself?"

That stung, Keir could tell by Aimery's face. It was meant to. He had no doubts about the Daltons, and he also had no wish to have Spenser throw a wrench in their plans out of misguided caution or concern.

Aimery looked out the window facing southeast. He closed his eyes, shook his head, then squinted into the distance. "Good God!"

"What is it?" Keir asked, stepping up beside him. Peter was at his heels like a shadow.

"Smoke. Looks like near the Bridge. Can you tell?"

London Bridge. From what Keir could see, the older man was right, but it was difficult to tell from this distance, and with so many buildings standing between the Strand and the area about the Bridge.

Of one thing Keir was certain: it was much too close to where the Smythe brothers had been purported to be living. St. Magnus's Church was near the Bridge. So was the southern end of Fish Street Hill where it intersected with Thames Street, which ran along the river.

"Let's go," Keir said sharply, and turned away from the window. He offered a silent prayer for, just one more time in his miserable life, a little simple luck.

# Chapter Twenty-eight

*Fire . . . fire . . . fire . . .*

The word beat at her brain, spewing terror through her at the thought of being trapped in a cellar with no way out while catastrophe inched closer.

For the first time since her incarceration, Juliana pulled the bar from the door and beat at the panel, screaming, "Help me! Please, let me out!"

The noise overhead and all around her only seemed to increase, drowning out her cries. The heels of her hands became bruised, and splinters from the rough wood scored her skin, but she continued to pound until her arms ached and then fell to her sides, leaden.

She leaned her head against the door to catch her breath, exhausted and dry-eyed. How could she ever get out? If she hadn't achieved her freedom in three months of careful examination of every aspect of the small room, how could she manage now if no one came to her aid?

She whirled and put her back to the door. The stick she'd used to make hash marks on the wall was under the pallet. She reached beneath and pulled it out, noting with keen disappointment how dull the tip actually was. Frantically, she scraped it against the rough stone floor, slowly turning the tip as she did so, sharpening the point to more resemble a weapon. In a surprisingly short time, Juliana sat up with a soft cry of triumph.

Her crude lance might not get her out, but would certainly help ensure her getting past anyone who dared to open the door.

*Dear Lord,* she prayed, *please make one of them come back for me* . . .

She stood and tucked the short, makeshift pike down the gaping front of her dress, scraping tender skin in her hurry and feeling her chemise snag in the process. For several more minutes she returned to her pounding on the door, then spun away in frustration.

With shaking, sore hands, Juliana moved her fingers over the crude wooden walls of the room, searching for something she might have missed in her earlier inspections. She earned more splinters for her efforts, and nothing that would help her gain her freedom.

Was it her imagination or was it getting warmer? And wasn't that a hint of smoke in the air? The building was quieter now, too, the noise coming from outside and more toward the side of the room that Juliana had decided fronted the street.

*Keep your wits . . . keep your wits,* reason told her, even as panic loomed over her.

Suddenly she heard her name. Someone thumped on the door. "Brandy-girl? Sam? You in there?"

"Aye! Here!" she cried, and without hesitation lifted the bar and flung it aside.

Roger Smythe blundered through the doorway, heaving past her in awkward haste. "Where's . . . Sam?" he rasped, his breathing heavy. He smelled of sweat . . . and smoke.

"Sam?"

"Aye, you stupid bawd! I thought 'e came back fer ye. Did ye—"

"He's not here. Please, let me out of here—" She took a step forward, and was stopped by the rounded side of the hook slamming against her breastbone. It took her breath away.

She looked at him in bemusement. An ugly look of suspicion crossed his soot-smeared, skewed features. "Ye did somethin' to 'im, didn't ye? He said 'e was goin' te fetch ye . . . so why ain't 'e here?"

Juliana shook her head in denial. "Sam never came here, I swear. Take me with you and we can look for him together . . ."

"Ye think I've bats in me belfry? Te let you outta here jest like that, when I think ye done somethin' te Sam?" He pushed her back toward the pallet, limping along before her, looming over her like some wild-eyed escapee from Bedlam. "Ye don't confess te me and ye'll bake in here like a Christmas goose! Now where *is* 'e?"

Months of pent-up anger and frustration suddenly blew sky high the lid of fear and caution that had tamped down her outrage, and once again, as long ago on a faraway island, Juliana Spenser's legacy from her grandfather stirred to life. It roared through her blood . . .

Without warning, she knocked away the frightening hook that acted as Roger Smythe's left hand . . . knocked it so forcefully that the crutch skidded out from under him and went clattering to the floor. Taking instant advantage of the situation, Juliana placed both hands on his chest and shoved him backward with a soft grunt of exertion.

Taken completely by surprise, Roger windmilled his arms and stumbled backward on his good leg. He landed hard on his backside against the stone floor. His look turned from a pained grimace to a menacing scowl as his eyes met Juliana's.

But she wasn't about to wait for what he might have to say.

She scrambled past him, heading straight for the door, sweet freedom beckoning from a few feet away.

Without warning, she felt the cold kiss of steel about her ankle, jerking her left foot from beneath her. She went sprawling to the floor beside Roger, her out-stretched hands inches away from the unlocked, unbarred door. She hit her chin, knocking her teeth together and sending white lights exploding through her head. She lay still a moment, stunned . . .

Until Roger's voice came to her from a distance, ". . . ain't a-goin' nowhere, wench. Ye're gonna burn in here jest like ye was in hell itself—"

No!

She kicked at his wrist, feeling the tip of the hook slice down her foot, through the thin leather of her shoes. Pain zigzagged up her leg.

*Don't quit now . . . move!*

With a colossal effort, Juliana heaved herself to her feet and, after one glance over her shoulder at Roger Smythe, bolted through the door and into the alleyway—

And pandemonium.


The orange glow on the eastern skyline was not the early morning sun. It was fire. Billowing smoke cast snaking shadows over the eastern end of London, on the north bank of the Thames.

By the time Keir and Peter reached Cannon Street, people were streaming toward the west side of the city. Keir stood in the midst of the surging throng, trying to block the blind panic that threatened to deprive him of all common sense, the cool reason he'd always taken for granted.

*"Baker's house . . . Pudding Lane . . ."*

Keir caught scattered snatches of hysterical babble as he and Peter made their way south and east against the tide of fleeing Londoners.

*"The Bridge is burning . . . Fish Hill Street and Thames Street . . ."*

Fish Hill Street! Thames Street! The words shrieked

through his mind, conjuring images of the timber stalls and sheds along Fish Hill Street, the littered alleys that ran from Thames Street to the river . . . stacks of wood and coal on the wharves, bales of goods in the warehouses, barrels of oil, tallow, spirits. Spirits . . . wine . . . brandywyne . . .

Brandy.

*"Hundreds of houses destroyed already . . ."*

The area along the river was crammed with poor wooden houses covered with pitch and tar, fodder for the flames. August had been hot and dry, and the pitch was peeling from many of the houses in flakes.

*Oh God, Brandy . . . Brandy,* his heart whispered in growing anguish, *where are you? Where are you?"*

Men and women manned wooden carts laden with household goods, children herded pets and younger brothers and sisters before them. Others hefted their pitiful belongings in their arms and on their backs. The sick and feeble were carried away in their beds.

"Can't get through this way," Peter shouted to Keir as they came within throwing distance of Fish Hill Street.

Firefighters in leather helmets formed chains here and there, passing along leather buckets full of water. But the latter merely made hissing sounds in the crackling, consuming tongues of flame billowing out the windows and doors, along the rows of buildings . . . droplets of water spitting ineffectively at towering sheets of flame.

Keir and Peter passed several of London's primitive fire engines, but the stacks of household goods in the streets and the frightened, shouting people gave the vehicles no room to maneuver.

"Here!" Keir called back, and veered left, plunging northward in an attempt to evade the leaping flames and searing heat. "Gracechurch," he shouted, "then south to Fish Hill . . ."

They passed the Lord Mayor, obviously overwhelmed by the crisis. He looked exhausted, a soiled and limp handkerchief around his neck. He was directing the pulling down of houses in an attempt to halt the spread of the fire. "Lord, what can I do?" he cried to a man near him. "I am spent: people will not obey me. I have been pulling down houses, but the fire overtakes us faster than we can do it."

The wind was high, from the northeast, fanning the fire like a colossal blacksmith his bellows. Fire drops flew into Kier's face, singeing his flesh. The roar of the rampaging flames dogged their steps and muffled into insignificance the voices of those straggling behind the growing crush.

An ache in his chest sprouted and blossomed through his torso. He broke out into a sweat, as much from a lingering weakness, he knew, as from the heat and exertion.

*Help me . . . help me!* he appealed a silent diety in his struggle for the former strength and stamina that had never deserted him until Roger Smythe put a pistol ball through his chest.

Roger Smythe. The very thought of the man gave him renewed vigor, strengthened his resolve. When he caught up with Smythe, he would kill him, and take immense pleasure in doing so.

Keir channeled his fury into energy and drive. He had to find Brandy. He *would* find her.

And then he would find Roger Smythe, the conniving bastard, and make him wish he hadn't survived the fall from the rigging.


The light of day was blinding after the dark room that had been her prison. The noise and confusion were mind-numbing.

Juliana stood still for an instant to marshall her wits, but she quickly found herself swept along in the tide of blind panic roiling all around her. The

429

taste of fear coated her mouth.

She was forced to move along the alleyway, stumbling on her injured foot, the light stinging her eyes, the smoke searing her lungs. And with every other step, pain went shooting up the outside of her left leg, making it difficult to hold her own in the surging throng. The thoroughfare was littered with abandoned household goods and personal belongings, which only added to the confusion and difficulty.

She kept hearing Roger Smythe's cries for help in her ears. Reason told her Roger would never bother her again. Guilt told her he would be with her forever.

She realized, however, that she had no time, nor the stomach, to worry about either of the Smythe brothers now . . .

The fleeing tide of humanity soon forced Juliana into a main street . . . she could only guess that it was Tower Street or Fish Hill Street. She was also unsure of her location, and therefore had no solid sense of direction.

Unused to activity for weeks, weak from a diet which had been skimpy at best, her body began to fail her. Her legs grew rubbery and uncooperative as she limped along, her breathing labored, and her head ached from the light and noise.

Juliana deliberately began to press toward the edge of the crowd, where the pace was less frenzied. She glanced around before dropping to the front stoop of a deserted house. She crossed her arms over her knees and lay her forehead upon them, laboring to draw in air. She saw the outline of the tally rod beneath the bodice of the rent remains of her dress. It had rubbed raw the fragile flesh between her breasts.

She eased it out, causing fresh pain to bubble through her. She clutched it in one hand, memories of her captors cautioning her to hold onto it, but fatigue loosening her grip.

Where am I? she wondered briefly, deciding that she'd

better move on as the urgency of the situation prodded her to push herself to her feet. She swayed, then caught herself against the rough wood door, fighting against dizziness.

"Move on, you little fool!"

Juliana clenched the stick and forced her eyes open, her body suddenly tense with expectation. It had to be Sam Smythe, come to avenge Roger's death. Well, he wouldn't find her quite so meek now. She was free and had only to follow the fleeing Londoners to safety . . .

A highwayman—he couldn't have been anything more respectable—loomed before her. His hair—or wig—was unnaturally dark and unkempt, and kept from his face with a ragged cloth strip about his forehead. His beard and moustache hid a good part of his features, and a sinister-looking black patch covered one eye. His lips were drawn back in what could have been a grin, revealing a handful of missing teeth. Except that the man looked a buccaneer, fresh from the Spanish Main, and buccaneers smiled when about to commit mayhem . . .

Marry come up! she thought in horror. Was this to be the story of her life? Assailed at every turn by pirates and highwaymen?

The pirate's dusky-skinned companion grinned at her like the fox approaching the unguarded henhouse, and Juliana railed against the fate that had been so punishing to her.

"Nay!" she cried, and, clutching the tally stick like a dagger, launched herself toward the taller of the two, striking him with the clumsy point of her crude weapon.

She hit him square in the chest. His visible green eye registered surprise and pain, and one hand went to his ribs protectively as he bent over in reaction.

"Mistress Brandy, are ye *addled?*" his companion yelled.

*Green* eye?

"Get away!" she ordered through clenched teeth,

431

"or I'll skewer you where you stand!"

"Sweet Jesus," Peter said as he watched fire flare in her amber eyes. " 'Tis the *cap'n*—"

*Green eye?*

The taller highwayman was jostled by a youth sprinting past, a squalling infant clutched to his chest. The assailant was forced to take a stumbling step toward Juliana before he regained his balance and attempted to straighten. He wore a signet ring of onyx and gold on the hand that rested against his ribcage . . .

*Mistress Brandy, are ye addled?*

In a split-second of revelation, Juliana recognized Peter Stubbs . . . and Keir.

Tears gathered at the back of her eyes. "Keir?" her lips moved soundlessly to form the name.

"At your service, milady," he answered, his face taut with pain, but his green eye twinkling. "Such a greeting for the dragon-slayer," he murmured as he gathered her to him briefly, his lips at her ear. "Are you unharmed? Can you keep up with the crowd?" he asked.

"Aye, Captain," she answered through waves of tears. "I think I can do anything now."

"Brandy, ye look like a scarecrow," Abra said. "Didn't them pirates feed you?"

"Abra!" Margaret Dalton reprimanded her daughter.

Jonathon and Simon, however, laughed at the little girl's words. And Juliana, tucked into bed at the Spenser town house, joined in.

"Not enough, I see," she answered. She pulled Abra down beside her, holding her hand. "Will you come home to Spenser House and help me?"

"Oh, Brandy! Can I truly this time? No more bad men?"

"No more bad men, I promise," Juliana said with a misty smile. "We'll ask my lord earl to escort us home.

Will that set your mind at ease, sweeting?"

Abra looked over at Keir, who was standing quietly to the side, observing the scene without being a part of it. Then she looked at Aimery Spenser, considering. Turning back to Juliana, she asked, "The old earl or the young one?"

Margaret flushed to the roots of her flaming hair, and Jonathon Dalton cleared his throat. Aimery coughed loudly, and replaced his half glass of Rhenish on the desk with more force than was necessary. He shot Keir a sidelong glance and muttered something under his breath.

Juliana looked down at the light blanket covering her, a corner of her mouth curling upward against her will. "I think, perhaps, if either earl would so honor us, we would be safer than anyone else in England."

Abra bounced excitedly on the bed, jarring Juliana's injured foot. As the latter tried to hide a wince, Anne Spenser said, "Easy, my dear. Juliana's foot will never heal if we don't keep it still, will it?" She smiled at Abra.

"Oh, nay!" Abra said, her small features sobering instantly. "I'm sorry, Brandy."

" 'Tis all right, sweet—"

A loud boom shook the very floor beneath them. The objects on the bedside table danced and clinked, then stilled. Juliana looked at Jonathon Dalton, a question in her eyes.

"They're blowin' up houses in the path o' the fire. 'Tis the only way to stop it."

Juliana nodded thoughtfully, then asked him, "The Hawk and Hound? Did it . . . ?"

"Nay, child. 'Twas spared, by the grace of the Almighty."

"The fire's under control? We're in no danger here?"

"The Strand was spared," Aimery told her. "But not so Fleet Street."

"And you should've seen the Duke of York and the King himself!" Stewart said in an awe-tinged tone. "Both fightin' the fire . . . why they supervised the blowing up of some of the buildings themselves, mixing right in with the people and—"

"And even dismounted their horses te lend a hand and set an example for the common people," Simon added.

"Did my heart good, child," Jonathon told Juliana, "after we had such a devil of a time tryin' to gain an audience with the king." He nodded his head approvingly. "Two brave men they are, the king and his brother, and showed their concern fer the people while riskin' their very lives."

Abra pulled at one corner of the coverlet to get Juliana's attention. "And ye shoulda seen all the lighters on the river, Brandy," she told her, her eyes wide with excitement. "Everywhere ye looked . . . people even threw their things into the river *without* lighters. We saw lots o' things floatin' along in the water!" She put the tip of one forefinger in her mouth and contemplated Juliana solemnly. "Brandy, when're ye gonna come te the inn and see Archie? He's a papa now . . . four babes."

"Puppies, Abracadabra," Simon corrected.

"Puppies," she repeated. "But they're still baby dogs. Brandy, when're you comin'? On the morrow?"

Anne Spenser smiled at Abra again, smoothing her dark hair back from her face. "Sir Nigel—the doctor—said that Juliana can be up and about in a week or two. Do you think the puppies will wait until then?"

"Oh, aye, m'lady. They can't even *see* yet. How could they go anywhere?"

"In a fortnight they'll be roamin' all over the inn," Stewart answered her. He looked at Jonathon. "Can I go with Juliana when she visits?"

"Of course," Margaret said immediately. "You're welcome any time, lad."

Stewart's face lit up.

Jonathon looked over at Keir. "Ye're welcome, too, milord. We all appreciate what ye did for Bran—er, Juliana."

Juliana felt the heat of a blush in her cheeks and couldn't meet Keir's gaze.

"Thank you, Master Dalton. 'Twas my pleasure." His eyes were on Juliana, she could feel him watching her.

"What of Sam Smythe?" she asked with a frown.

"If he values life and limb, he'll have the good sense to stay out of sight for a long, long while," Keir answered. "Roger deserved to die for what he did, but as far as Sam is concerned, I'd as soon kill him as catch sight of him in London."

Juliana sighed, suddenly feeling tired. Good, secure, relatively happy . . . but physically drained.

"Let's let Juliana rest for a time, shall we?" Anne suggested.

Abra climbed toward the pillow and kissed Juliana on the cheek. "I'll come an' visit ye before the fortnight's over, Brandy. A fortnight's forever, ye know."

Everyone laughed. "It won't be so long when you've four pups to keep you busy," Juliana told her, "as well as your everyday things to do at the inn."

As they filed out, Juliana felt a sense of relief, for not only was she tired, but she felt like a haggard crone . . . a scarecrow, just as Abra had described her. And beneath Keir's unwavering regard, it was difficult to completely at ease, even with the Daltons.

Relieved and happy to see him, to be with him, she was also mired in indecision. How could she ever tell him why she wouldn't wed him . . . watch his face turn stony when she told him of the insidious blight she carried, and probably had passed on to their daughter?

He came forward from the shadows. The sunlight from the window hit his hair, highlighting the sun-bleached strands that contrasted so unusually with its naturally dark hue. It tipped his lashes and shone in his

435

eyes. Or was it an unspoken emotion that lit him from within?

Or was she being a lovesick romantic, with echoes of *Romeo and Juliet* lingering in her mind?

Well, no matter if he loved her or not. He wouldn't feel the same after she revealed her secret. And she couldn't bear to watch his affection shrivel into indifference. No, not that.

"You look lovely," he said.

Juliana looked up into his eyes. There, again, was that new warmth there, something she had noted for the first time when he'd come to see her after the ball.

This was what she'd prayed for aboard the *Odyssey* and in Jamaica. This was one of the crowning achievements of her life thus far. First, winning this man's love. Then, of course, giving birth to his child.

He didn't touch her, but rather stood gazing down at her. He seemed to be searching for something . . . waiting for something . . . What?

Juliana wanted to reach out to him, but uncertainty held her back.

"Keir," she blurted, feeling suddenly the need deep down in her soul to tell him the awful truth, "that morn after we met again at Whitehall . . . there was something I was afraid to tell you."

His dark eyebrows drew together, his expression very grave. "I know, brandy-eyes. You're a bloodthirsty wench who has skewered many a man before you threatened me. Peter is still wondering about that, you know."

He was trying to disarm her, she realized; to make light of something that was very serious to her . . . and, ultimately, important to them both.

"Nay. This is — well, it concerns me — us . . . 'tis the reason I told you I couldn't wed you."

"Because you cannot add to my life in any way, or so you believe. Because you are illegitimate. Because — "

"Because my mother was mad. And her madness was

436

passed on to me."

He stared at her long and hard, but the warmth in his splendid green eyes never changed. "You'll have to think of a better excuse than that."

She adjusted herself against the pillows, her mouth tightening with determination. He had to be made to realize the risk.

"I don't speak idly, Keir."

"I see nothing of madness in you. Only the woman who taught me of love and laughter. The woman who brought the sun into my cold and shadowed life. The woman who taught me of feelings I'd crushed beneath ruthless determination. None of that will ever change."

"Our children could be affected . . . why, I could become a mindless lunatic—"

"I'll take my chances."

Juliana stared down at her tightly fisted hands in her lap. "I won't let you take any chances! You mean too much to me, Keir, for me to saddle you—your heirs— with such an affliction."

She heard him sigh. Moments ticked by . . . several explosions sounded in the distance, children shouted in the street, the murmur of voices came to them from downstairs. A hint of acrid smoke tainted the breeze drifting in through the partially opened window.

She finally looked up at him, her eyes sheened with tears. "Please, Keir. Go on with your life. Surely there are other, more important considerations, than love . . ."

He shook his head slowly, deliberately. "Not to me."

A sense of futility rose in her. Why was he making it more difficult? He was still stubborn . . . accustomed to having his way . . . taking what he wanted, no matter the consequences.

"Go then, and talk to my grandfather!" she told him, irritability edging her words. "If anyone can convince you of the gravity of the situation, *he* can."

"Nothing he can say will make any difference to me,

brandy-eyes. But if it will make you happy, I'll speak to him."

*Nothing will ever make me happy, without you,* she thought, a profound sense of loss pressing down upon her.

"And Keir . . . thank you for . . . yesterday."

"I owed you that. And so much more." He bent and touched his lips to her brow gently, lingeringly. "I'll see you after you've had a chance to come to your senses, Brandy Dalton," he murmured.

And he left the room before she could think of an appropriate retort.

# Chapter Twenty-nine

She was a charming picture of contradictions.

A warm September sun shone brightly upon her as she sat on the stoop of the inn. Her shimmering copper-gold hair hung loose down her back, like that of a simple, peasant girl; dainty pink toes peeked from beneath the ruffle of her fashionable green silk gown, and only the edge of the white binding about the outside of one foot was visible to remind Keir that life had not been kind to Brandy Dalton of late.

Abra sat beside her, dark head bent beside that of brilliant auburn, wearing Brandy's discarded kid slippers. As Brandy pointed to something in the book in her lap, Abra clapped her hand over her mouth and giggled. Brandy threw back her head and laughed with her, a captivating sound that sang around the yard and made Keir's breath catch in his throat.

He noted that she was still thin, her cheeks a trifle pale, her face a bit drawn, but that would slowly be corrected. He sensed that she needed nurturing and healing in heart and mind, just as she had once done for him. He would be only too happy to reciprocate.

*Perhaps she will not want you, even now.*

Keir willed away the unwelcome thought, refusing to acknowledge such a thing.

Corsair snorted and flung back his head, catching

Brandy's attention. The smile froze on her face for an instant, then began to fade.

Abra could only stare agog at the huge dark stallion beneath Keir. "Gemini!" she exclaimed in awe. "He won't hurt Archie, will 'e, m'lord?"

At Abra's other side, the heretofore sleeping spaniel raised her head drowsily, and Keir laughed aloud. Four pups were dozing in the sun in the slight shadow of her body.

Archie, it seemed, was a female.

Keir shook his head in answer, dismounted and led Corsair toward them. The stableboy appeared from behind the stable. "Take yer horse, milord?" he asked Keir.

"His name's Corsair, and I won't be staying."

At the lad's look of disappointment, Keir added, "But lead him to water and give him some grain."

Rob brightened and bobbed his head. "Aye, milord. I'll see that 'e's taken care of."

Brandy watched as Keir approached them, a sinking feeling within her. He'd spoken to her grandfather, she was certain. And now he'd come to say goodbye.

*Wasn't that what you wanted?*

Archie growled softly, but at a word from Abra, quieted.

"Hello, brandy-eyes," he said softly.

"Hello, Keir."

"Brandy, c'n I go an' see m'lord's fine horse?" Abra asked.

Brandy glanced back at Keir. "Is he gentle?" she asked him, feeling the question sounded ridiculous in light of the size and gender of the animal.

Keir smiled and squatted down before Abra. "Corsair's about as gentle as his master once was, but he's improving . . . as am I." He ruffled Abra's hair at her puzzled look. "Go, child, and give me some time to speak to Brandy." He stood and reached into a small

440

pouch beneath his waistcoat. "Here. Corsair has a sweet tooth."

Abra took the offering and asked, "What's a Corsair?"

Keir looked at Brandy, his expression full of meaning, and answered, " 'Tis a pirate who sails the Mediterranean Sea. The name has special meaning for me."

He glanced back at Abra, but, having accepted his answer with a child's uncomplicated trust, she was already skipping toward the rear of the stable where Rob had taken the stallion.

"Careful with him now," Keir called after her.

She stopped suddenly and turned back. "Mayhap Brandy'll tell you 'bout the pirate dog, Peg-Leg Dudley. And since ye're lettin' me feed Corsair, maybe Brandy'll show you baby Kerra. But ye must be gentle, m'lord . . . just like with the puppies." With that she swung away and disappeared around the corner of the stable.

"Kerra." Spenser hadn't mentioned the child's name, and Keir savored the sound of it. "Kerra." He looked at Brandy. "Why didn't you tell me, Brandy?"

Several emotions crossed her face before she could speak.

"Nay," he amended suddenly. "Don't answer that. You had good reason after the way I treated you."

Brandy reached out to touch his arm, a natural reaction meant to comfort him, to ease the pain and self-reproach in his voice.

He took her hand in his, instead. "May I see our daughter?" His voice was not quite steady.

Brandy nodded. "But this changes naught. You must know that." She pulled away and led him into the kitchen of the inn. Past the cook, and Margaret, and Jonathon, who'd just come in from the taproom. Up the stairs, her slight limp more pronounced now, through a hallway that was dim compared to the brilliant day outside, and into a room that Keir knew immediately had been Brandy's when she'd lived here.

Brandy stood aside and watched him walk over to the hand-carved oaken cradle, clinging to her resolve like a dying woman clinging to her last breath.

As he stood looking down at the sleeping child, a feeling of wonder, of infinite tenderness . . . and immense gratitude flowed through him like a benediction. For here was the product of their love, proof of that love. And he'd almost thrown it all away.

For what? For pride? For an inheritance?

Emotion blocked his throat, and the child's tiny, fragile features undulated before his tear-filled eyes. Here, contained in this humble room, was his entire world. Everything else faded in importance.

"Grandfather told you."

"Aye. It seems that I rise higher in his esteem every day. He said that I had potential, and that one day I might make a fair husband. For the right woman."

Brandy glanced down at the floor, then remembered that she had given her shoes and stockings to Abra to play dress-up. Her face flamed. Here, after all, was a peer of the realm. An earl descended from five earls before him. The son of a proper earl, not a newly made earl like her grandfather. And she was still, after all, a bastard. The adopted daughter of a tavern-keeper and his wife, borne of a mother who's mind had ceased to grow apace with her body, who'd unwittingly shamed Aimery Spenser into banishing her bastard issue.

*Stop feeling sorry for yourself. You were content enough before Keir St. Andrews came hurtling into your life.*

Silence gathered in the room as Keir gazed upon his little daughter. With infinite gentleness he reached out to touch the shining auburn curls that proclaimed her a Spenser. After what seemed a very long time, he said softly, "And so you think this child all the more reason to cut my losses and flee from you both?" He turned to

Brandy, his composure genuinely shaken. "What manner of a man do you think me to be?"

"This changes nothing, Keir. I said it earlier. 'Tis merely a reminder of what could happen if—"

"I told you once that life wasn't fair, brandy-eyes, and now I tell you that it's also full of uncertainties and risks." He backed away from the sleeping child and came to stand before her. He put his hands on her shoulders and looked into her eyes. "I love you. I will always love you. And I'll not rest until you are my countess. I'll dog your every step until you give in, for you belong at my side, as does our child."

She gazed up at him, balanced precariously over heaven and hell, hope and despair. In the end, she could do nothing but move into his arms, seeking his love and comfort. He was a fool. And she a bigger one.

"Brandy," he murmured into her hair, his arms tightening about her. "Say you'll be mine. Say you'll come to Somerset Chase with me. Say we'll raise our children together, greet each day together, meet each challenge together . . . Please."

She began to cry against his shoulder, for so great a love was no match for her feeble reasoning, her feeble resistance.

He rocked her back and forth in a slight but soothing motion. "Say yes, Brandy. Say yes."

She managed to nod her head. "But what if—"

"Hush, now." His lips descended to meet hers, and he tasted the salt of her tears.

The kiss was gentle, loving, sealing the vow, and Brandy felt like a tremendous burden had been lifted from her shoulders. She wrapped her arms about his neck and clung to him as she'd ached to do for months.

"I miss—Dudley," she confessed in a low, shaking whisper. "And Jackie . . . and Peter."

Keir smiled, resting his cheek against her head. "They're all at Somerset Chase, love."

Brandy looked up at him, her smile tremulous but genuine. "Truly?"

"Truly. And if you've a mind to sail the seas again, we can do so whenever you like . . . But there is one more thing I must tell you now."

A frown chased across her forehead and then was gone.

"I had a long talk with your grandfather, and learned something that I'm certain will be very important to you. I didn't tell you earlier, because I wanted you to agree to become my wife, in spite of your fears."

Brandy pulled away from him, afraid of what he was going to say.

"Come now, give me a bit of sunshine, my love, and smile, for 'tis not so dire as you obviously think."

Brandy obliged, out of love and trust, and the pure brilliance and beauty of her animated smile renewed Keir's faith in the world just the smallest bit.

"It seems," he toyed with the carved lioness that hung from its slim chain about her neck, "that your grandfather is a romantic at heart, in spite of everything that would indicate otherwise." One corner of his mouth pulled up at the thought.

"Grandfather?" Brandy shook her head. "I've never suspected such a thing."

"Well, there's much about Aimery Spenser that would surprise everyone, I suspect, but Lady Anne. You see, he made a solemn vow to your grandmother, the first Juliana Spenser, that he would never reveal what happened when your mother Catherine was an infant."

Suspicion shaded her·eyes as Brandy gazed up at him expectantly.

"According to Aimery, his first wife was inadvertently careless while Catherine was still a babe. She—Juliana—turned her back on the child as she lay upon the great bed. Before she even realized the danger, Catherine had rolled over the edge, striking her head upon the floor."

444

"An accident?"

He nodded. "No one was in the room to witness what happened, and Juliana, in a complete panic, made Aimery promise to say nothing about the incident."

Brandy shook her head slowly in disbelief. "She feared to be named careless more than to have Catherine bear the stigma of insanity?"

"Juliana was young and naive. She died before too many years had passed and the true extent of the damage could be determined." Keir shrugged. "Aimery loved her deeply, and could not bring himself to break the promise, even after she died."

"Oh, but how could he?" Brandy said, bewilderment creeping into her voice. "Grandfather lied to me?"

"He will tell you his reasons himself, I believe, but I suspect that once he'd found you again, he wanted to keep you at his side for as long as he possibly could. And, I don't doubt but that he wanted to keep you away from me. In the process, however, he underestimated me, and my feelings for you."

"And you wanted me to agree to wed you while I still believed that—"

"I wanted you to know that it changed nothing. And I wanted you to consent to marry me by your own choice, in spite of what you believed."

Brandy pursed her lips with rue. "You certainly made it difficult to deny you, Keir St. Andrews."

"As I said before, I wouldn't take no for an answer, no matter how long I had to wait."

"So you have your way again, as always." But the tone of her words was more teasing than censorious.

He grinned, gently stroking the sweet slope of her jaw with the back of his fingers. "Some things are more difficult to change than others, brandy-eyes."

She lifted her face to receive his kiss, delicious anticipitory sensations wending through her before their lips even touched.

"Brandy!" Abra's voice came to them from the yard. "Look, Brandy!"

They moved to the open window, while Kerra, contentedly sucking on one tiny finger, slept peacefully on. There, immediately below, sat Abra upon Corsair. She looked like a toy atop the huge bay's broad back. Rob was holding the stallion's reins, his face a study in frustration. "Now *I'm* gonna get thrashed, pesky brat, 'cause ye popped up on 'is back afore I could stop ye . . . C'mon. Get down." He glanced up at the window, saw Keir, and blanched.

Keir waved one hand. "Just keep him quiet until I get down there, lad." He looked at Brandy, amusement shining in his eyes. "She reminds me of a young woman I knew who wouldn't obey orders, either. I suppose we'll have to take her out on the *Odyssey* and teach her some proper discipline."

Simon's voice drifted up to them. "Abracadabra, what the devil—"

"Abra!" cried Margaret. "Get down from there *this instant!*"

Brandy laughed, feeling the euphoria of pure joy for the first time in months. "I suppose we shall," she said as they made their way to the hallway. "We could always introduce her to Lug . . ."

Keir laughed softly. "Or we could take her to Jamaica. A meeting with Moses might be enough to put the fear of God in her."

Keir swept Brandy high up into his arms. "To spare your foot, love." He smiled into her eyes, love and tenderness softening his features. "I really have turned into quite the gentleman, in spite of your declaration back in Jamaica."

Brandy blushed at the memory of her heated words, but Keir brushed her lips with his and descended the stairway. "I may never be quite as good an earl as you were a tavern wench," he murmured in

446

her ear, "but I shall devote the rest of my life to trying."

He set her on her feet and took her hand in his. They walked out into the sunlit yard, to meet the challenge — and promise — of the rest of their lives together.

## SURRENDER TO THE PASSION

**LOVE'S SWEET BOUNTY** (3313, $4.50)
by Colleen Faulkner

Jessica Landon swore revenge of the masked bandits who robbed the train and stole all the money she had in the world. She set out after the thieves without consulting the handsome railroad detective, Adam Stern. When he finally caught up with her, she admitted she needed his assistance. She never imagined that she would also begin to need his scorching kisses and tender caresses.

**WILD WESTERN BRIDE** (3140, $4.50)
by Rosalyn Alsobrook

Anna Thomas loved riding the Orphan Train and finding loving homes for her young charges. But when a judge tried to separate two brothers, the dedicated beauty went beyond the call of duty. She proposed to the handsome, blue-eyed Mark Gates, planning to adopt the boys herself! Of course the marriage would be in name only, but yet as time went on, Anna found herself dreaming of being a loving wife in every sense of the word . . .

**QUICKSILVER PASSION** (3117, $4.50)
by Georgina Gentry

Beautiful Silver Jones had been called every name in the book, and now that she owned her own tavern in Buckskin Joe, Colorado, the independent didn't care what the townsfolk thought of her. She never let a man touch her and she earned her money fair and square. Then one night handsome Cherokee Evans swaggered up to her bar and destroyed the peace she'd made with herself. For the irresistible miner made her yearn for the melting kisses and satin caresses she had sworn she could live without!

**MISSISSIPPI MISTRESS** (3118, $4.50)
by Gina Robins

Cori Pierce was outraged at her father's murder and the loss of her inheritance. She swore revenge and vowed to get her independence back, even if it meant singing as an entertainer on a Mississippi steamboat. But she hadn't reckoned on the swarthy giant in tight buckskins who turned out to be her boss. Jacob Wolf was, after all, the giant of the man Cori vowed to destroy. Though she swore not to forget her mission for even a moment, she was powerfully tempted to submit to Jake's fiery caresses and have one night of passion in his irresistible embrace.

*Available wherever paperbacks are sold, or order direct from the Publisher. Send cover price plus 50¢ per copy for mailing and handling to Zebra Books, Dept. 3627, 475 Park Avenue South, New York, N.Y. 10016. Residents of New York, New Jersey and Pennsylvania must include sales tax. DO NOT SEND CASH.*